LETTING
LOOSE

Novels by
Christopher T. Leland

———————————

Mean Time

Mrs. Randall

The Book of Marvels

The Professor of
Aesthetics

LETTING
LOOSE

❖ ❖ ❖

Christopher T. Leland

Z

ZOLAND BOOKS
Cambridge, Massachusetts

First edition published in 1996 by
Zoland Books, Inc.
384 Huron Avenue
Cambridge, Massachusetts 02138

PUBLISHER'S NOTE
This book is a work of fiction. Names, characters, places,
and incidents are either the product of the author's
imagination or are used fictitiously. Any resemblance to
actual events or persons, living or dead,
is entirely coincidental.

FIRST EDITION

Cover illustration by Wendell B. Minor. Copyright
© 1996 by Wendell B. Minor
Book design by Boskydell Studio
James Baldwin quote from *Giovanni's Room*, courtesy
Bantam Doubleday Dell Publishing

Printed in the United States of America

02 01 00 99 98 97 96   8 7 6 5 4 3 2 1

This book is printed on acid-free paper, and its binding
materials have been chosen for strength and durability.

Library of Congress Cataloging-in-Publication Data

Leland, Christopher T.
Letting loose / Christopher T. Leland—1st ed.
p.   cm.
ISBN 0-944072-69-0 (acid-free paper)
1. Vietnamese Conflict, 1961–1975—Veterans—United States—
Fiction.   2. United States—Social conditions—1960–1980—Fiction.
3. United States—Social conditions—1980– —Fiction.   I. Title.
PS3562.E4637L48   1996
813'.54—dc20   96-16396
CIP

FOR ANNETTE AND JONATHAN,
SUZY AND JOHN,
FOR HARRY SMITH,
FOR BUDDY AND RICHARD, FOR PIETR,
FOR ANDREA AND WALTER

FOR JO, FOR BROOKE, FOR WEGS,
FOR 60,000 NAMES ON A WALL,
FOR 315,000 DEAD, AND COUNTING . . .

It takes strength to remember, it takes another kind of strength to forget, it takes a hero to do both.

James Baldwin
Giovanni's Room

WEDNESDAY

✧   ✧   ✧

1

There was a flag on the casket.

Fred stared for a moment, standing there next to Marco Di-Giovanni. He cleared his throat and brushed a hand across his nose, then looked away.

The room was hung with soft blue velvet, with a couple of cream-color pedestals on either side capped with vases of white and yellow roses. There were pale pink cushions on the pews and, above the coffin, a cross of bleached oak.

In the distance, a phone was ringing.

Marco shifted next to him. "I'll have to catch that," he said. "Rhonda's gone home early."

"Go ahead." Fred shrugged. "I'm just going to sit here is all."

Marco had not wanted to let him in. It was late, and with that and the ice storm, he probably hadn't expected anybody to come this afternoon. No wonder. Driving down glazed streets with his foot barely on the pedal, the pickup skittish on the slick, Fred had felt his ass clench when the truck turned suddenly weightless, threatening to fishtail or simply skate into the oncoming lane. The first time, he smiled: the old pucker factor.

And as soon as he thought it, he cursed.

There were three more days of viewing before the services on Saturday. That was better, Fred thought sourly, than even President Kennedy got if he remembered right. Time for a lot of shuffling through and paying respects there beside the roses. And most of those sniffling and saying a prayer would have no more connection with this corpse — what was left of it, anyway — than they had with the ones in the Tomb of the Unknown Soldier. A lot had changed, a lot of people had come and gone, since this body — fine and alive — walked the streets of Rhymers Creek. He had heard that all the service clubs were sending delegations to the funeral and that, next day, the entire Legion post intended to put in an appearance around lunchtime.

He slumped into the first pew. Well, that was just dandy, wasn't it? The whole goddamn American Legion. He reached into the pocket of his Army drab greatcoat — bought secondhand at the St. Vincent de Paul up in Mockdon — and pulled out a pint of Wild Turkey. He took a jolt, then raised his eyes to the coffin.

"Well, Bobbo, you glory-hounding peckerhead," he said aloud. "Couldn't leave us all in peace, could you?"

Twenty years. Twenty-five? It had been that long since he'd last seen Bobbo; that long he'd assumed he was dead. He was, of course. Here was the proof, whatever there was of it, right there under the Star-Spangled Banner. Fred shook his head and took another swig. It was all fugazi, a word that had not crossed his mind in ages. Why now? Why now, after all this time?

He smirked. Because Bobbo Starwick wouldn't come back, even in an aluminum box, until it was right, until his return could be a damn good excuse for speeches and a band. It hadn't been like that for Fred, or for Waldo Henderson or Ricky Graves or any of the rest of them. Fred slunk home with his tail between his legs, more or less like the vet groups always complained. He wouldn't have wanted much celebration anyway after what he had been through, which wasn't much compared with many others. But it had been enough. Enough for the nightmares that, once in a while, still sneaked up on him sly as a Charlie sapper to blow all his careful forgetfulness to kingdom come; enough that a backfire or the whir of a bicycle or a certain song could suddenly, before he realized it, bathe him in sweat and race his heart like an idling engine when you ram the pedal to the floor.

He took another hit of Wild Turkey.

He had never really liked Bobbo Starwick — Starprick, as they, the defensive line, had called him almost from the day he appeared at junior varsity practice, fresh out of West Virginia and ready to show Rhymers Creek a thing or two. It was not peculiar they should hate him in a clean, inchoate way, the way they always hated the offensive squad. On the line, all you could finally hope for was that magical mistake, that Grace of God that somehow delivered a fumble into hands unaccustomed to the feel of pigskin. That could make you a star, for a week anyway, especially if you managed to stay on your feet and lumber, amazed and unobstructed, to the goal line.

But after the next game, it would all be forgotten, as once again the quarterback and halfbacks and tight ends resumed their rightful place in the heaven of public acclaim. And though you knew that you could lift more and press more and bear-crawl with more conviction, it was no good, because Grace did not devolve on them but was theirs by birth: that scampering, sparkling speed of pass and fake out and run that destined them to be heroes while you slogged and sagged in the mud.

But even from that first late August afternoon, as they plunged through the summer's dust and gulped salt pills, Bobbo was different, deserving of a hatred darker and more pure, for even then — at fifteen, sixteen — Fred and his aching comrades could see this stranger had a special gift, one that would make him, by the time they were seniors, fall's chosen boy: recipient of the biggest trophies and most triumphant headlines and the unchaste desires of their own girlfriends. Bobbo never flaunted it, which made it worse, as if he simply knew he had been made for this glory, and there was no need to draw attention to what was obvious for all the world to see.

Fred let the Wild Turkey swirl down his throat, warm into his body, which, despite it all, had braved an ice storm and accidents to come this first afternoon. For, if Fred knew he hated Bobbo (had hated him virtually as long as he had known him), he realized too he loved him. It was more than nostalgia — the dim shimmer of shared exhilaration and despair those autumn Friday nights — that made all the old hatred juvenile and beside the point. It was the War. And, more especially, it was that last moment he had seen him, when Fred realized that what would (he understood even then) haunt him for the rest of his days had taken the boy who had been both his hero and his secret enemy and transformed him into a madman.

It was at a bar in Quang Tri, crowded and hot despite the air-conditioning. He was there by accident, up from the base thanks to misdirected matériel: mortar rounds and flak jackets and body bags that should have gone to Quang Tin instead. Minor oversight. Slight misreading. Somebody stoned, most likely. He had wanted to chopper up, but after two hours, he got word that he could hitch a ride with a newby lieutenant and a couple of APC drivers back from R & R.

He had misgivings. Fred did not like leaving the base, and, if he had to, he did not like staying on the ground. A road trip could take hours, and, all along the way, there was the chance of ambush, the fear some old man or pretty girl might, just might, have a satchel charge hidden in that basket, have planted a mine in that pothole.

But it was a dull trip, with gripes about the price of beer in Hong Kong and luxurious descriptions of fucks imperfectly remembered:

"I swear, two hours, man. Pronged her two fuckin' hours!"

"You're full of shit."

"Two hours!"

"Did not."

"Did, too."

"Did not!"

"Did, too!"

It went on for what seemed like forever. And Fred thought that it had been since he was eight or nine years old that he had heard voices pushing back and forth like that. Until he got to Nam — "Remember that gook I greased . . ." "Mama-san I fucked . . ." "Sniper I blew away." Did not! Did, too! Did not! Did, too! Like bragging boys, now making not trouble but babies and mayhem.

The jungle rolled away, green on green, more greens than there had been in the sixty-four-color Crayola box his little sister, Lila Mae, had coveted for her last birthday. More trees, Fred thought, than God could ever have intended — more creepers, crawlers, flowering vines; bugs, leeches, tigers, and snakes. It gave him the willies. He wanted to be back at the base, where he could see the sea, knowing that home, though infinitely far in both distance and mind, was at his back. He had imagined sometimes — in the unimaginable nightmare that even they were somehow overrun, charged by Chinese hoards smuggled down the Ho Chi Minh Trail and crashing in Kamikaze waves through mines and razor wire — that he would simply run and plunge into the ocean, swimming powerfully, hopefully toward the sun rising, ultimately, over Rhymers Creek.

He would drown, of course, exhausted in the Pacific vastness, or be picked off by sharks, lazily circling as in a cartoon, striking sudden, again and again, shaking him like dogs with a toy as hunks of his flesh disappeared into those frowning mouths.

But then, these were what he expected here, weird, silly fantasies that came easy as breathing, in this place whose very names seemed taken — half and half — from fairy tales and dirty jokes. Sometimes, at his desk, Fred would simply stare at the old map big as a door on the opposite wall, heavy Magic Marker lines delineating "I Corps," "II Corps," and so on, the black, American scrawls, hard and new, obliterating the mysterious places underneath: "The Mouths of the Mekong," Bong Son, Faifo, My Tho,

Dong Hoi, Ban Me Thuot, the Perfume River, flowing through the city Sergeant Michelsen called "Hoo-ey," one of those places they had destroyed in order to save just before Fred had arrived.

He dozed on and off as those swaggering twenty-year-olds recalled and embellished days that, in a few hours, would seem something from another life. After they tired, in a vague, surreptitious, but deeply mean way, they ragged the lieutenant, nipping at his confidence like ratters, as it should be, Fred thought tiredly as they wandered up Highway One, because whatever the man — fresh faced and ROTC trained — had been taught back home would have absolutely nothing to do with what he found when he got in the bush.

Fred came in for some ragging, too. He was a pogue, after all: safe behind the lines, sending this and that all over the theater from the C-130s that disgorged beer and bullets and rubber ponchos onto the tarmac. Not for him the jungle rot and heatstroke and Charlie bullets, but rather clean sheets and hot showers and checklists, requisition forms and sweet, marijuana-fumed nights with the newest boom-boom girl at the Club Los Angeles just beyond the gates. It made him feel guilty sometimes, but barely. It was not the idea he had had the September after graduation as he stood in the Army recruiter's office. Signing the papers, he, like most boys in the same offices all over the country, had wanted to be a hero.

He had his reasons. Any boy from the defensive line, perhaps, would have reason enough. But more than that, Fred was going to show Daddy after all the whippings and lectures and favoring of Lonnie, only two years younger, that he was the man good as those ghosts his father remembered from Normandy. That was the sense he took with him to boot camp, knowing his brother was already looking at college catalogs and would take a deferment while he, Fred, was on the front lines defending freedom and America and all the cowards like Lonnie who would not do their part.

Only when he was in training — shaved and shorn and shouted

at, stunned and angry and scared like he had never been in his life — did he comprehend in a single, bright bolt while rolling through a drill with live ammunition that being a hero had no more to do with will than the serendipitous fumble that transformed forgotten, overweight boys into the momentary objects of adulation of South Mockdon High. All those overgrown children by his side — anonymous in the same haircut and uniform and yes, sirs/no, sirs as they might have been in jerseys that identified them only with a number — had the same chance as he did of finding themselves in a moment when catastrophe struck and a man did the right or wrong thing, lived or didn't, was remembered as a giant or a fool. He had kept that knowledge to himself, but, unbeknownst to him, it shone through. Shone through for those who had been at it long enough to recognize the healthy suspicion of the doubter. That was when the lifer took him under his wing and guided him toward the Quartermaster Corps, so as to spare him combat, so as to put him in line for not Purple Hearts and Silver Stars but survival. He owed Vernon, grizzled and alcoholic. He had owed Sergeant Vernon ever since, though he was dead of cirrhosis before Fred ever got back.

The snafu at Quang Tri had not been hard to take care of, and as the sun settled on the infinite greenness of Nam, Fred settled behind a beer, with no other notion particularly than drinking himself to a stupor and heading back to the bunk they provided, so he could return to base next day. As the evening wore on and there were more and more men from the bush and from Saigon and Hue and the networks and he sank deeper and deeper into bottles of Bud, he found himself with some grunt fresh from the field, black as night, a spade from Kansas City: Rogers.

They talked about girls and people they knew who had lost it, about what it would be like once they were back in the World, and Rogers, unlike so many Fred had known who loathed those who had not shared combat, seemed sympathetic to his being so close to war and seeing only its results, being too near Graves Registration at the base. Day after day, the planes and helicopters landed, spewing forth the bags anonymous as TV dinners for ID and registration and embalming and delivery in lightweight aluminum boxes to next of kin.

"I don't know, man," Rogers said, "maybe I got it better than you pogues — and I can tell you I never thought that before — 'cause at least I got flesh and blood around me and ain't lookin' over some fence all the time at the guys who bought the farm." He leaned across the table. "Why don't you get yourself transferred, huh?"

And Fred was actually thinking about it — putting in to see if he could get to Saigon, Dong Ha, or even here at Quang Tri — when there was the fight on the other side of the bar. Suddenly. Without voices rising gradually to signal some anger, probably not entirely clear, that words would not assuage. This one burst unexpected as heat lightning, which still should not have drawn Fred's attention. Fights in bars were not to be made issue of, among men too young and too drunk and too far from home. But what arrested him was the face he saw as he looked, bleary and unconcerned, across the room.

"I know that guy," he said matter-of-factly, as a fist flashed quickly, viciously into the jaw of somebody else he had never seen.

"You know him?" Rogers said.

"Sure." Fred shook his head as the stranger went down and the lean, blond outline of the tight end of the South Mockdon Leopards loomed above him. "Sure," he said. "Bobbo Starprick, class of 'sixty-six!"

Had the bar been quiet, his voice would have carried, but in the din of conversations and rooting and the high, gloating squeal of triumph that escaped Bobbo's lips, it was lost.

Rogers touched his arm. "You know him?"

He turned to the flat, black face, smiling. "Sure. Old Bobbo."

But Rogers did not smile back.

Through the beer, Fred felt a funny disquiet.

Rogers shook his head. "Old Point Man. That's him. He always a crazy motherfucker?"

Fred raised his eyebrows.

Rogers sighed a tired laugh. "I got a brother in his company. That buddy of yours is one sick asshole," he said.

And in that instant Fred could see it, a kind of evil smirk on Bobbo's face that he couldn't remember from any time before, not even those moments when, thanks to an official's inattention or the stupidity of the other team, things had gone unexpectedly his way on the field. Bobbo stood over the other grunt on the floor, leering, then brought his foot back and kicked the downed man full in the face.

Rogers hissed audibly. Two other grunts grabbed Bobbo — still with that strange grin — and pulled him toward the door.

Rogers took a sip of his beer. "Always walks point," he whispered. "That's what my buddy says. Ain't no John Wayne, get it? Just fucked up." He whistled. "That's what this place does to pretty white boys. Bet he loved his momma and all that shit, and when you knew him he was sweet as pie. They's the worst. They get to Nam and they get crazy real fast. He be greased even now when he's still walkin' on two legs. You ain't gonna see him back home."

And even though he wanted to object, there before that face he knew — old loved, hated Bobbo Starwick — Fred could feel in the pit of his stomach that Rogers was right. That squealing wicked laugh that was not drunk echoed from the doorway over the rumble of talking recommenced and other, lesser disagreements there at Quang Tri. Fred turned back to Rogers, suddenly thankful that he was there and, too, that he, Fred, was a pogue after all. Because he understood, in a way he had never imagined, that the birthright Grace that had shone from the very body of Bobbo Starwick from the first time Fred had seen him had flown and that, from the instant it had left him, he was as good as dead.

Late, late in the evening, as Rogers — in accord with the old code of the drunken — staggered him off to bed, Fred's arm slack over that black shoulder, Fred sang to him the "Pogue Song" they had made up one night, stoned and dazzled by the tracers, all of them atop one of the watchtowers hard by the airfield. It was something, he thought woozily, maybe Rogers would like for its Motown beat, and remember, and repeat sometime at one of the firebases:

> Take my stool at the bar like a he-man,
> I'll be porking your girl by the weekend.
> Drink your beer, warm as piss, by the mortar,
> Hunker down or you'll be two foot shorter.
> Back at base, I'll be sucking a cold brew,
> While my boom-boom is giving me chew-chew.
> Once I'm home, I will tell them the story:
> How you just got your ass blown to glory.
> > My sergeant told me,
> > You better be a pogue.

The Wild Turkey was gone.

"My sergeant told me," Fred sang under his breath as he stared at the casket, "you better be a pogue."

And then he began to cry.

✧

Marco DiGiovanni was beside him, his hand on his back, then under his armpit, lifting him up, like Rogers at Quang Tri so many years before.

"You okay, Fred?" Marco said, and it did not sound like a mortician's practiced kindness. "Can you get home on your own?"

"Sure," Fred said. "Sure I can."

Marco saw him out of the viewing room, down the corridor to the refinished, bronze-handled doors that led outside. The cold hit Fred pure and white as a phosphorus flare. It was snowing now.

He pawed for something right to say, having embarrassed himself, recalling Bobbo there at Quang Tri for the first time in a long time, the last time he ever saw Bobbo alive.

"You done good by him, Marco," he blubbered meaninglessly.

Marco smiled, shrugging. "I don't know, Fred. A body's a body when it comes down to it, no matter how little's left of it or how many years it takes to find it . . ."

Fred's stomach jumped, and his head ached. As he teetered down the steps, unsteady for the whiskey and the ice, past Marco and toward his truck, it was all he could do not to turn around and slug him.

2

Belva rolled over. It took her an instant to remember where she was. "What time is it?" She yawned.

Basil stuck his head out of the bathroom. "A shade past three, pet. But I've got that four o'clock, and there's no telling how long it can take me to get to school in this weather."

Belva moaned and snuggled against the pillow. She should probably call Melva, though if there were some emergency at the store, her sister knew where to find her. She wished she could simply sleep the afternoon away. The weather put her in a foul mood, and besides, with all the ice, not much of anyone was doing any shopping.

Basil walked out, toweling his hair. She spied on him through half-closed eyes as he rustled through his underwear drawer. She loved his furry, lean behind, and he had certainly given the last few months a little dash. If, over the summer, someone had suggested that, before Halloween, she would have an English lover — and one so much younger at that — she would have laughed out loud.

"Can you get away Friday morning?" he asked amid the squeak of hangers. "Tomorrow's shot for me."

She rolled onto her back. "I've got an appointment at the beauty shop. Wallace has us going to dinner with some people from Chicago."

"*Malhonnête!*" Basil grabbed his jacket. "I adore you, my spoiled angel." He lurched toward her and kissed her hard on the lips. "Leave me a message on the box. Ciao!"

And he was gone.

Belva stretched, saronged the sheet around her, and wandered into the front room. There was still a little coffee in the pot. She poured a cup and put it in the microwave as she dialed Melva.

"Anything up?" she asked before her sister even had time to chime: "Letting Loose. May I help you?"

"Quiet as a tomb around here," Melva said, "what with the storm and all. That boyfriend of yours gone to work?"

"He just left."

"Fine as ever?" Melva's voice had a slight cattiness to it.

"Fine as ever," Belva said smoothly. "You know, honey, it sure is nice when they can get it up more than once in an afternoon."

Melva snorted. "I didn't think Wallace had done that since your honeymoon. Speaking of which, he called a half an hour ago . . ."

The bell on the microwave pinged. Belva bobbled the cup when she touched the hot stoneware. "Ouch! Damn," she hissed.

"I said you went to the post office to raise Cain over the Christmas mailing. Which you should do one of these days."

Rubbing her fingers together, Belva settled at the dinette. "You know I will," she said soothingly, "but it's been a week since I could get away, and I hate to put Basil off."

She heard Melva cluck her tongue. "Well, be here at four. Jamie needs the station wagon to run his gang to dance class."

Belva hung up. She knew her twin's snippiness wasn't really about dancing lessons. Melva hated covering for her, though she had been doing it since they were girls. Of course, she would do the same for Melva, given the chance. The opportunity just never arose. Once, Belva had found her sister's determined fidelity a kind of accusation, but these days she thought it more an eccentricity, like a taste for Kool-Aid or an interest in Eastern religions. Where men were concerned, Belva had more in common with their little sister, though the good Lord knew she had a better eye than Tammy, with her unfailing weakness for shysters, drunks, and drug addicts.

She lit one of the Dunhills Basil had left, though English cigarettes made her cough. She had still not quite adjusted to the notion of a lover almost twenty years her junior. She had not even been alive that long when she lost her virginity. Back then, the thought she might be having sex at her age, much less outside her marriage with a man, biologically speaking, young enough to be her son, would have scandalized her.

Basil's Englishness would have been another improbability, along with his being a professor. There had been no professors in Rhymers Creek then, much less British ones — Mockdon County Community College not yet even a gleam in some local booster's eye.

She twirled the tip of the cigarette in the ashtray and shrugged. She had had enough affairs over the years not to dwell on their spontaneous origins, pleasant surprises, unexpected ends. She knew Basil was looking for a more prestigious job elsewhere, and could not be certain anyhow that, by May, all the things that made him so charming and distinctive might not have paled.

Sighing, Belva riffled through the stack of books on the breakfast bar beside her: Austen, Eliot, James. So many words in such small print on so many pages. It was a wonder Basil had any eyesight left. She turned back to the table and reached across for the *News and Gazetteer*, skipping the articles on the troubles in what was once again Russia and the financial scandal in the local schools, which was getting worse by the day and of which she was heartily sick. Since the headline was below the crease, she did not notice it at first:

HERO'S FINAL RITES
SET FOR WEEKEND

She caught her breath, coffee in her throat as if she had just pulled back the plastic of that package he had once sent her.

She swallowed, took a breath, skimmed the two brief columns. She had known about it, and wondered now why it had taken so long to get him back. It had come out in the papers before Thanksgiving. Among a collection of remains the Vietnamese had delivered to an American delegation in Hanoi for identification and repatriation were those of her old boyfriend, her boyfriend from July of 1965 to February of 1966, from Independence Day to Valentine's Day, to be exact: Robert Edinger Starwick the Fourth.

"Well, well," she said aloud. "Welcome home, Bobbo Starwick."

✧

The weekend before Fourth of July, there was a pool party at Sally and Ronnie Peltz's house. Belva had acquired a rather daring two-piece, and though she came with Sammy Gould, it was clear that their three months of going steady were at an end. She had heard from friends that Sammy thought she was a little fast, so she had no qualms about suggesting that Sammy himself was a little slow, "if you know what I mean." They were maintaining their mutual loyalty, from Belva's viewpoint, only so long as nothing more appealing came along.

That something appeared about 1:30 P.M. in the person of Bobbo Starwick.

She had always thought he was conceited, as you might expect of a football player, and his dating Monica Fitzer until the previous May indicated he didn't have much taste in women either. Monica was cute, of course, but she had no class. Belva herself had been cultivating a rather more sophisticated air, listening to the Kinks and Bob Dylan rather than the Beatles and

Gerry and the Pacemakers, and giving her entire set of rollers to Melva, so she could let her own hair go straight and natural. She had even asked Sammy if he knew anybody who could get some marijuana.

He didn't.

So it was not a football player she was particularly looking for by the pool that Saturday, but as Belva watched Bobbo frolic in the water, silly as an otter, she felt her heart beat faster. He was blond like those surfers you saw on television: shoulders aripple and hair shimmering white against the bronze of his skin. A couple of times Bobbo splashed her, and his sweet, baritone *Gee, I'm sorrys* sounded as insincere as they were seductive. When he pulled himself out of the pool, she stared from behind her sunglasses, reasonably sure nobody would notice her fascination with the triangle of golden hairs just above the cleft of his ass.

She later thought that was the first time she had really appreciated a man's body, watching it glide effortlessly — disciplined and powerful — across the deck. It was not the body itself that fascinated her (though it was nicely turned, no doubt about that), but the grace of it. Male anatomy per se had never been a mystery to her. She had a little brother, after all, and had sneaked into the boys' locker room on a dare at camp when she was thirteen. And then, of course, she'd had the chance to see a naked boy at full attention the night of last year's Football Pep Sock Hop.

The most embarrassing thing about losing her virginity to Peter Jencks was not the loss but Peter, wan and a bit flabby even at seventeen. But that had to be balanced against how tired she was of hearing so much about "it." When he presented himself that evening with both a place (his uncle's apartment out near Olinda) and a rubber, Belva simply decided to get going all the way out of the way. Later, in her world philosophy course, she encountered the perfect description of it: "nasty, brutish, and short."

But after Peter brought her home, after she tearfully confessed all to Melva and crawled beneath the canopy of her French provincial bed, she felt peculiarly at peace. When her period came ten days later, she hadn't the slightest doubt it had all been worth it.

But it would have been nice, she thought that summer afternoon, if the first time it had been not Peter but Bobbo Starwick.

For the next half hour or so, she bestowed a number of smiles, a mooning glance or two, and one wink at Bobbo, who swam some laps and then played underwater tag with Ronnie and a couple others. Finally, he stroked lazily to her side of the deep end and heaved himself out, flipping the spray from his eyes with a gesture, it occurred to Belva, not all that different from the arching spasm of Peter at climax.

"Sally said she didn't know whether you'd make it." Bobbo smiled. "I'm really glad you came."

The words touched the devil in her. Belva sat up slowly and looked directly at the crotch of his bright red trunks. "Why yes, Bobbo, it looks like you *are* glad to see me."

He really didn't have a hard-on, but she knew he would not be entirely sure if he was showing more than he intended. Bobbo's face fell, and, even through his tan, a pink flush shone on his cheeks.

She giggled and put her hand on his forearm. "I'm sorry," she said. "They told me you were cute when you blush." He seemed so shocked or embarrassed she wasn't sure she hadn't overstepped. "And it's true," she added with modulated breathiness. "It's hard to believe with somebody cute as you are anyway, but it is." He still looked wary. "I've been hoping you'd come over so I could see for myself. I figured out what I'd say to try and get a rise" — maybe that was too suggestive? — "out of you." She hedged her bets. "I didn't scare you, did I?"

"No, no." He laughed — a little falsely? "You want a Coke?"

"Sure. This sun is im-possible. Here, I'll go with you and we can sit in the shade."

By the time the afternoon was out, she was almost ashamed she had been so brazen. For all his football glory, there was still something boyish about Bobbo. She was surprised. In the end, though, Belva got what she wanted. Before he left, after he had put on his jeans, they made out briefly behind the cabana. At the gate, Bobbo kissed her good-bye and told her he would call her. When she turned around, triumphant, Sammy Gould was sulking by the barbecue, but Ronnie was smiling at her like a Cheshire cat, and Sally flipped her the peace sign.

It took longer than Belva expected to get him to bed. Part of that was her own fault, for despite Peter Jencks she did have certain standards, and, Bobbo or no, she drew the line at backseats and picnic blankets. He did not press her, though he certainly demonstrated more ardor than Sammy had. He was a fine and unexpectedly gentle petter. His big palm up her skirt would rest softly against her, as, one by one, his fingers played across her and her chest heaved while his hot breath blew over her breasts.

The opportunity came in November. They were on a half day due to a teachers' meeting. Melva had a special band rehearsal. Their mother had planned a shopping excursion with her bridge club and would not return until dinnertime. Daddy would be at work; Rhett and Tammy, at school. This fortuitous convergence had struck her only a week before, and Belva was electrified. She plotted it day to day, teasing Bobbo with information each time a little more overt: "You don't have early practice that half day, do you?" and "Don't you plan anything for that afternoon," and "You know, Mom's going shopping," and, finally, as they clutched in front of the gym in full violation of the public-displays-of-affection rule: "You better be ready because almost anything could happen tomorrow."

Bobbo was not stupid, for which she was grateful, but he was nervous. She only wondered after they had broken up if he were a virgin then. He spilled the Coke she served him, and she literally had to take his hand to guide him upstairs. He almost balked when she led him into her parents' room, but she had decided that, whatever the school psychologist might say, she wanted her debut with Bobbo Starwick to occur on the house's only double bed, thank you.

All his stalling and clumsiness made her bristly, but that passed as he grew more confident, and she allowed herself to drift softly into a sweet and lazy desire. That he had brought at three-pack of Trojans convinced her that he'd looked forward to this with the same anticipation she had. When finally he stood beside her, hard and naked, she stretched her arms up and led him to her as if they had done this a hundred times before.

When he was first inside her, she was barely past the pain before it was over. He made as if to get up and dress, but she coaxed him to hold her, and he seemed honestly surprised when, soon after, he was stiff against her again. The second time, as he slid easily inside her and ran his tongue softly across her cheek, Belva understood finally what all the commotion was about, what Peter, what not even Bobbo had shown her in his first attempt: those sweet, soft ripplings-out, as if there between her legs she had grown a second heart, beating together with the one her lover had sprouted and now pressed deep within her.

❖

There at Basil's table, gently sad, Belva recalled the talk on her parents' bed with the afternoon sun pooling pale beside them. It was past two, and, very soon, Bobbo would have to go. But she did not hurry him, listening to his wandering thoughts about football and life and the future. It was the first time she knew he was thinking about the military.

"But if college doesn't work out, there's always the service," he said. "Maybe I should do that first anyway. It would pay for college later. Besides, there's a war on."

She thought of the clips she caught when her father was watching the news, and certainly she'd heard other boys talk about signing up or worrying about the draft. It was getting ugly in Vietnam, which she had never known existed till a couple of years before.

"Bobbo, why on earth would you want to go over there?"

He propped himself on one elbow. "It's what guys do, isn't it? I mean, my real dad was a soldier, and my dad now was a soldier . . ."

She vaguely remembered her mother saying something about how Bobbo's two fathers, his real one and his present one, had been buddies. After the first one died, the second one had taken Bobbo's mother as his wife. Her mother said it was very romantic.

She turned toward the clock. "Honey," she said, "we better get dressed. The kids will be coming soon."

She did not think about the words then. It would occur to her more than twenty-five years later: how somebody overhearing might have thought that she and Bobbo were married, a couple who had stolen an afternoon's fun away from jobs and housework and raising children, and now had to return to their real and serious lives.

They made love various times after that. As she talked about it in college, in those giggling sessions in the dorm, she decided it had been good, an adolescent relation to be cherished. She did not regret breaking up with Bobbo. He deserved it for stepping out for old times' sake with Monica, and perhaps she was tired of him in any case. But that warmth she had felt allowed her, when his first letter came from overseas, to feel a pang and write back secretly, for at the time — even at a generally patriotic women's college like Siegerford — correspondence with soldiers was a questionable pursuit.

They wrote for only a few months. By the time the package came, she had not heard from him in nearly a year, knowing only that somewhere along the line he had signed up for another tour of duty.

When she started screaming, only Linda Pearson — who everybody thought was a dyke — was in the suite. But Linda held her not like a lover but like a mother, appalled but strong there before the inexplicability of men. It was Linda who bundled her off to the infirmary, where they shot her full of phenobarbital to quiet her down. It was Linda, too, the other girls told her later, who took the box and threw it, that very afternoon, into the campus incinerator — barreling past the drowsy janitor, grabbing the crowbar, opening the maw of the furnace, and casting it in.

What had it done, Belva thought, what had Vietnam done to Bobbo Starwick? And what had she done to deserve that gruesome trophy? It was only as school started the following August they got word he was MIA. In her anger, she was glad, but with time that mellowed as, with more time, it was forgotten. She married Randy Ditmars, played around, got pregnant, miscarried, divorced Randy, played around, married Wallace, played around, got pregnant a second, then a third time, played around, stayed with Wallace, and played around some more.

Which was what brought her to Basil Smyth's apartment, remembering a time when it was all new and quite untried, a sweet-tempered blond boy who would be the first not to fuck her but to show her what making love could be. One she would break up with, one who would go away to college, be disappointed, and become a Marine. One who would, in the end, send to her — purposefully, meanly, as if forever to blot out her recollection of his beauty and his kindness — one final gift.

A human ear.

3

When he dreamt of Rhymers Creek, it was always summer. Dusk.

The August heat lay on the land, heavy like the smell of bread, and the air was thick with pine and sweat and charcoal smoke. His mother and the other women swarmed around backyard tables, while they — the children — played games somewhere behind him: Tully and his brothers, the Belmon boys and Bannister girls. But he had stopped, stepped away, looking through the gloaming at the men there on the rise.

A couple sat in lawn chairs, but most stood, hands apocket, arms akimbo, wearing T-shirts, polo shirts, Bermuda shorts, or jeans. He was not sure who they all were in the half light of the dream. But he knew how they looked: confident, young, one or two of them tattooed. Men who had fought wars, killed people, come home to tell the tale. His father was there, and Mr. Coe and Mr. Renberg . . .

And right on the edge, so close to the lip of the rise it seemed at any instant he might fall, down on one knee like the football star he was, shy but assured, was Bobbo.

For all his years of childhood there, for all the years he had been away, that was the Rhymers Creek he carried in his dreams: the image of his brother, Bobbo Starwick, teetering on the brink of manhood. He was not sure that precise moment had ever occurred, or was it something his mind had invented to remind him of Bobbo long after he had had to let him go? If, since his brother (his half brother really), he had known many men far more surely and truly, still Bobbo was his first hero. Bobbo Starwick was the first man he had loved.

The propellers' drone lulled him as they approached Mockdon County Regional Airport. Barry had never imagined his return this way. When he was last in Rhymers Creek, there had been only a landing strip for private planes. But, then, he'd never really let himself imagine a return at all to that place he had left at nineteen and had never seen again.

It began with his father on the phone, a kind of caring long since forgotten singing over the line.

"Barry," he said. "Barry. Bobbo's coming home."

In the early morning black of his Twenty-eighth Street flat, he listened to that voice he usually heard only on holidays — the one he had anticipated the following week, on Thanksgiving afternoon — thin with elation and sadness, telling him something they had all wanted to hear for twenty years, though, as those years wore on, they knew those words could mean only the end of something.

"Sure. If you want me there, I'll come, Pa." He regretted it even as he said it, hoping when the moment arrived there would be a sitting he couldn't cancel, some assignment he couldn't avoid.

Mendelsohn, snuggled at the foot of the bed, stretched, then slunk up the spread to his side. Barry scratched the cat's head idly. Dreading the answer, he finally asked, "What's left?"

There was a pause. "Not much, I guess," his father said, unwilling. "But he's coming home. We have something to bury . . ." He corrected himself. "A body to bury."

Barry nodded to no one but Mendelsohn, groping for words. "I'm sorry, Pa," he murmured, though he hated to, as if it were an apology for all the mysteries that had existed between them since even before Bobbo was missing. "I wish things were different . . ."

The silence was so long Barry thought the connection had been broken.

"Barry," his father said firmly. "We want you here. Your mother, too. And China. Whatever's happened doesn't make any difference now. It's Bobbo, after all."

"I know, Pa." He had a headache. "Give Ma my love." What he had been sending for decades. "Call if you need anything."

And they hung up.

✦

Bobbo.

To this day, he always told people Bobbo was the best big brother anybody ever had. It sounded silly, especially in Manhattan, where people, continuously reinvented, did not even speak of the lovers you saw them with last week, much less the families who had made them. The glory and curse of life in New York, as opposed to someplace like Rhymers Creek, was that you were finally only who you said you were and what the people you knew (or, better yet, the papers that made you better known) made of you. In Barry's world, you were indeed only as good as your last notices, printed in the *Voice* or the *Times* or, more tellingly, exchanged over a martini at One Fifth Avenue or a Miller Lite at Boots and Saddles.

But it was true, what he said about Bobbo; true, despite how different they were; true despite the last words he had ever heard from him, and how, in many ways, Barry should have hated him, so certain and golden. Much of what he was, he suspected, he owed to his brother, first in Grafton, where Barry was born, even more after the move.

It was Bobbo who made him a photographer, Bobbo who gave him the Kodak for his thirteenth birthday and who was the subject of those black-and-white snapshots: mugging in his swim trunks or his black and orange jersey. Later, Barry picked up the Leica at a garage sale in Olinda and began taking pictures in earnest, the preferred photographer first of *The Leopard's Roar* at South Mockdon High, then of the Mockdon County *News and Gazetteer:* Barry Carraway, who had a gift, who could catch the best shot of the last football game or the election of the Valentine's queen.

The camera became the way he could distinguish himself. And, too, as time passed, he came to understand it also helped him distance himself from those around him, whom he knew were touched deep inside by things that ought to but did not touch him. And it was Bobbo — unawares, of course — who made it evident to Barry from the very first that he was somehow not the same.

That was why, though it did not fit any of the theories he knew about, Barry sometimes thought it was Bobbo who made him queer. You could not live in the light of a boy so chosen for all your childhood and not conclude that it was him you should want and his love you should seek as the best the world had to offer. And since his dying (his disappearing, better said, for only in these last weeks had his death been finally real), you had often searched for his double, his star-blessed not-crossed twin, and the consequence of that was not just endless beddings and one dazzling love but a career of shooting photographs of men who might reveal divinity in a frozen pose, the blossoming Barry's single dream of childhood made manifest: Bobbo at that instant of blooming potential.

But Bobbo's bestness was not merely the consequence of some unsated incestuous wanting — this despite their boyhood "secret game," like doctor, with curious fingers and blunted pencils, the strip poker with Cousin Richard when Barry was ten, the later gropes and probes of boys discovering their bodies or filled with the stirrings of a lust potent and polymorphous: the grappling and roughhousing and wrestling that left them both frightened and (Barry, at least) shamefully hard. The big brother Barry recalled was more than that, one who prized him, protected him, primed him for a world to which both perhaps realized he did not belong. Barry's last year in Grafton had been awful, he, a twelve-year-old who, among boys he had grown up with, felt a spreading rift as they played less and less at war and cowboys, more and more at football and softball and basketball — grown-up games conceived by men who were dead, ruled by committees that decided what traveling was and how many time-outs you got.

But Grafton's, at least, was a familiar misery. Barry did not want to move to Rhymers Creek, regardless of the opportunities it offered to his father as those in West Virginia grew poorer and fewer. Grandparents and cousins and church and school were left behind as the family made its way to an unknown place in an overloaded station wagon. Ma and Pa sat in front, and Barry and China fought in the backseat, and Bobbo rode in the wayback, shoehorned beside the suitcases, all burgeoning adolescence. Barry hated the notion of going someplace where he had to make new friends and where they would probably laugh at his name and China's name and maybe Bobbo's, though at least Robert was something other people were called, too, not a name that had been in the family for generations and so you got stuck with it despite the fact that nobody in 1963 would have answered to Barach.

But Bobbo was excited at starting afresh. In Rhymers Creek, he knew what mistakes not to make; he who, at Montgomery Ward's, wheedled two madras shirts for Barry out of their mother, who thought they were only for older boys. On the first day of school, he unbuttoned Barry's top button as soon as they were out the door because, he said, wearing the neck closed made you look like a dope. He told him not to carry his book bag anymore: guys carried their books on one hip, and never more than three at a time. He taught him to walk with a swagger, and when Barry whined that he was no good at football or baseball, taught him to dance.

"Girls like guys who are good dancers," he explained, "and if the girls think you're cool, the guys will, too."

That was not entirely true in the seventh grade, but it gave Barry the confidence to forge a new identity: bright but apologetic for his brightness, a bit of a clown, a shade of a smart aleck. He was pleased, especially when Bobbo surveyed him with smug tenth-grade pride. Deep within himself, Barry knew he was a fraud, but he grew into the part Bobbo had written for him as his big brother flowered into the beloved of South Mockdon High, easy in his athleticism and perfect blondness.

Despite their common mother, they did not look at all alike. It was their fathers they resembled — Bobbo blond and tall, the Nordic severity of his good looks softened somewhat by a Celtic boyishness; Barry shorter, darker, coarser featured, his expression possessed of a peculiar, almost Mediterranean languor it had startled him, years later, to note on the faces in an exhibition of Roman grave paintings. It was to the friendship of their fathers that they owed their half brotherhood: to Robbie Starwick and Ezra Caraway and the United States Army. Their fathers had been boys themselves then, picked up from California and West Virginia by the flood tide of the great Second War, carried through training and cast up together on the beaches of Salerno, moving like the wash of a wave up the long boot of Italy as the bond between them grew stronger. By the time the battles finished, they were joined as sure as if by blood.

Ezra went back to Grafton; Robbie to Santa Monica, the first working for the B & O Railroad, the second drifting from job to job between long stints in the surf. They sent letters across the continent, remained in touch over two years, till Robbie asked Ezra to be best man at his wedding.

He took the time off without pay, rode on his pass to St. Louis, hopped the GM & O as far as Kansas City, and then picked up the Santa Fe for points west. He spent a week in Southern California with Robbie, his best friend in all the world, and Myrna, the transplanted Iowan from Long Beach who — as he stood beside Robbie in the little Catholic chapel by the sea — Ezra felt a bit in love with himself.

Barry wondered if Robbie had told his friend that Myrna was pregnant. That was not, of course, part of the family legend. Barry had figured it out at fifteen, just as Bobbo left for college. He took Bobbo's birthday and the date on the wedding picture in an album he had found in the attic. Only seven months and five days.

But, Barry imagined, that would not have surprised his father, for it was Robbie's recklessness that perhaps first attracted a Grafton boy, steeped in a dark and rigid Protestantism, to the blond Catholicity of a child of the Pacific. His father must have viewed it all with a mix of horror and wonder refracted by love.

Ezra went back to Grafton, back to the B & O, back — so the story went — to some desultory courtings of his own. The letters from Santa Monica continued, though more and more the author was not Robbie but Myrna. She told Ezra of their house, of walks on the beach, of how Robbie had found work with a company planning an irrigation project in the Imperial Valley. They had bought a lovely Oldsmobile, and Robbie frequently drove east to talk with surveyors and try to convince some small-timers to sell out. With time, her tone grew more intimate, as her ankles swelled and she came to feel ungainly. She must have worried, Barry thought, that Robbie was looking at other girls still svelte and sweet and not so tired all the time.

Ezra would have written back to assure her (even if he weren't entirely sure himself) that Robbie would be true, confiding, perhaps, his own unsure romances, his feelings that it was time to settle down and start a family. Myrna would have told him not to rush; that he was young, and serious, and deserved the best.

The first telegram came in March:

BOBBO ARRIVED 3/16 STOP 8 LBS 4 OZS STOP ALL WELL STOP ROBBIE.

"Bobbo," Ezra often said, "what a name to tag a kid with," though, with all the Robert Starwicks in Robbie's family, surely they were running out of nicknames. Ezra went to his mother and got one of his own baby blankets, blue, and sent it, along with a new red rattle so they would not think he was cheap. Myrna mailed an ugly hospital baby picture and told him Robbie wanted Ezra as the boy's godfather when it came time for baptism.

The second telegram came in August:

ROBBIE GRAVE STOP ACCIDENT STOP PLEASE COME STOP MYRNA.

He left in the caboose of a fast freight two hours later.

By the time he hit Amarillo, Robbie was dead.

He could not have known that in Texas, speeding west. When, Barry wondered, had that been calculated backwards, just as he, years later, calculated that pregnancy? Ezra arrived in time to be a pallbearer in the very same church and for the very same man he had stood up for the previous September. His neck broken, one lung collapsed, it had been miraculous Robbie had not died instantly. There were suspicions he was drunk, though Barry had only picked those up from his mother's late-night keenings when he was in bed and Bobbo had gone to a football party. "I tell you, Ezra, if he's drunk, you give him a spanking. I don't care how big he is. I could not stand it. I couldn't stand it if he ends up like his father. You understand?"

Bobbo's mother — Barry's mother — was there in the church where only a year before her veil had been white not black, when her baby had been only a tiny secret sealed in her stomach, not a soft squirming thing that cried in her arms. Her sister was on one side of her, and Ezra on the other, between her and her parents. Apparently, they had already noted the boy from West Virginia, their son-in-law's best friend and yet so different: so much more responsible, hardworking. Perhaps that was why they made place for him.

He stayed a week, then ten days, until his foreman called long distance and told him to get his ass home soon or he could no longer save his job. He hurtled back to Grafton, arrived at 4:00 A.M., and punched the time clock at 7:30. Before he went to sleep that night, he posted a letter to Santa Monica.

It was another year before he made his proposal. They both needed time to mourn. But when he asked her, she said yes without a moment's thought, Myrna would later tell Bobbo and Barry and China, boarding the train eight weeks later with the same wedding dress she had worn only two years before. Her mother went with her, and Bobbo, and that was all. Her matron of honor was a sister-in-law she had never met. But she had never doubted that her decision was right.

And had it come into question since, Barry wondered, given how things turned out? At least there was China, married to Doug, the parents of cute babies now schoolchildren he knew only in pictures. But Barry? he thought. Barry and Bobbo?

❖

The plane was circling Mockdon County now as, below, they plowed the runways and spread salt. The ice storm that had closed the airport earlier was over, but still, the pilot announced, there were strong winds and snow showers. The stewardess came through offering drinks, and Barry, despite a desultory pledge some months before, ordered a Scotch straight up.

All day, all week, every month since November, he had tensed when he remembered that call. The coming home was bad enough, the return to that place where, he had known at nineteen, he could never be who he really was. The reason for his return was even worse: a couple of ribs, a femur and tibia, a death's-head ring, and a piece of jawbone with enough teeth to suggest that these were the mortal remains of Bobbo Starwick: 1948–1970.

The details of his dying were obscure. He was out on patrol — he and a man named Ewing from Lincoln, Nebraska, and another by the name of Louie del Río. Back at the firebase, the company heard small arms, and a platoon was ready to move out to save Bobbo and the others when the main body of the North Vietnamese Regulars fell upon them. The battle was short and bloody, and the captain finally called in air strikes on his own position. In the confusion, the Americans escaped, regrouping and returning the next day with gunships.

But when they arrived, the enemy had vanished like mist into the jungle. And Bobbo, too. And Ewing and del Río. They searched for them. And a second time. And a third. Lucklessly. There was the suspicion that they had been caught in the bombing, perhaps already dead, perhaps alive — those young bodies blown to pieces or incinerated in an instant by the napalm strike. That, for Barry, was the most horrible prospect of all: Bobbo still whole and alert and moving back toward the company, hearing the noise and looking around to see the jungle behind him blooming in flames, the wave of fire closer instant to instant, and the realization that he was about to burn to death, just before his hair and eyebrows and clothes ignited and he went down as his screams were sucked soundless from him in the roar of the firestorm.

Since there was no body, Bobbo was only MIA, and he had remained MIA ever after, until now. For a while, Barry had imagined him a prisoner in some dank cell. Other times, especially when he was stoned, he would think that Bobbo had just sickened of war, slipped into the black hole of Vietnam, a white man in a loincloth with a kidnapped wife and hard-bodied Eurasian children, quiet as leopards, whom he taught to scavenge and steal.

But even from the first, Barry knew that these were fantasies, that Bobbo was gone. And in a way, he was prepared, and even glad, for in the years since he went overseas, Bobbo had become less and less the boy Barry knew and more and more some murderous cipher on the other side of the world. It had taken only about three months for his letters to take a peculiar turn, and then, after his year was up, he had volunteered for another hitch at war. Finally, he had met their parents in Hawaii, always in uniform, with that ring he had acquired, which made his father queasy and his mother cry.

Then none of them had ever seen him again.

Even after he vanished, letters kept arriving, ghostly missives from a brother lost. The last, the definitive one, let Barry know that Bobbo had found out what had happened at the draft board.

They began their descent, and as they broke through the clouds into air sparkling with snow, Barry felt a great weight on his chest: the weight of all his childhood and all that had gone since, the weight of Bobbo loving, rejecting, finally lost, and now found again in a few scattered pieces. Further mourning after all the mournings of the last decade. He did not want to be here. Certain things were better unresolved. But there was nothing to be done.

As the icy earth rushed toward them that winter afternoon, he closed his eyes and made a wish perverse, obscene. They touched down, and the props roared, and Barry found himself praying — fleetingly, fervently — that there might be a bomb at the end of the runway.

GROWING OLD

✦   ✦   ✦

1

By eleven o'clock, she had the last load started and the first was dry. Myrna pulled the warm sheets from the clothes pole and filled the wicker basket, then made her way to the back stoop. The sun of late May felt good, warm but not yet hot. It would not be long before summer began in earnest, and she would dream of those dry California Augusts as the humidity of Rhymers Creek nearly killed her. But it would be a while, and she was willing merely to enjoy the weather for now, not fretting about the dog days to come.

She did that more and more lately — taking the good without worrying about the future. It was not like her, someone always planning for tomorrow, but, in the last couple of years, it seemed simply accepting what was given was the only way to stay sane.

All her life, Myrna had tried hard: to be good, to be strong, to be normal. Even as a tiny girl, she had had the reputation of a sweet and tractable child. After the move to California, she had adjusted, conscientiously worked to fit in. She was a nice girl — serious but not sober, affectionate but not easy. The golden mean, her mother said, was what a woman should aim for. It had paid off in a mild popularity when she was in high school. Nothing extreme. She had been sought after, but not too hard.

When the time came, she tried hard with Robbie. She was not accustomed to being courted with such insouciant zeal, an abandon her parents found unseemly. Her dizziness before his assaults of laughter, tantrums, contrition, lust lurched her again and again into lovemaking, though it violated every rule she had sworn to abide by.

He was a difficult man to be married to, probably a man who should not have been married at all, but he was sweet enough and handsome enough that she ignored what that little part of her heart told her. She was sure, in El Centro, there had been others. When he died, there was a phone number in his wallet she called months later. She heard a voice, deep and breathy, hardly a woman's voice at all: "Hello."

Myrna did not speak.

"Hello?"

She put the receiver softly back in the cradle.

But she would not have left Robbie if he had not died. She would have made do, and perhaps with time he would have settled down. Having a boy as beautiful as Bobbo would have kept him close to home, and there would have been more babies, anxious as he always seemed for her, even if he were playing around. But then there was the accident, and it was not a decision that had to be made.

And with Ezra, like the song said, the second time around it had been lovelier, and they had made it right: for Bobbo, then for Barry and China. Theirs was a kind home, a quiet home of small but certain comforts. They owned a sturdy, modern house with three bedrooms and a finished basement, in a neighborhood good enough that even people established in town had moved there. They had a two-year-old car and reliable appliances. There had been money to send Bobbo to college, even though that hadn't worked out. There would be money for Barry and China as well.

But now, in these last two years, it had all been put in play, not for anything they had done, not for silly investments or a drinking problem or her and Ezra falling out of love. It was not a job lost or those sicknesses like diphtheria and whooping cough that, when she was a girl, still capriciously carried playmates away.

It was as if the world itself had betrayed them.

Her one son was now 10,000 miles from home — her first-born, orphaned football star — and, at every moment in the back of her head, she dreaded the drab green car that might pull up with a Marine and an Episcopal priest inside, bringing her news she would forever connect with whatever silly thing she was doing in that instant: vacuuming or opening a can or talking on the phone.

And her two other children, thirteen and sixteen, who ought to have had nothing more on their minds than dates and cliques and classes, had sat at her table that very morning, arguing violently. Instead of teachers or whatever was this week's best hit, they talked about the primary election on the West Coast. Barry was for Eugene McCarthy. China, barely in bras, loved Bobby Kennedy. They were at it constantly — there at breakfast, after school. She would hear them sometimes when they were supposed to be doing their homework, haranguing each other not like children but like Democrats.

Myrna did not intervene, for she liked the fact that they were independent and was proud they were smart enough to be interested in the larger world. Still, it made her uneasy, remembering an uncle who had supported Henry Wallace and lost his job in Sacramento because of it. In any case, she had forbidden them to discuss their opposite loyalties at the dinner table, so as to spare her husband their political passions. Back in 1862, the Caraways were among the Republicans who took West Virginia away from the Old Dominion.

More than that, of course, there was Bobbo.

It was stunning and terrible for someone whose own memories were of the Second World War, when everyone had a brother or father or fiancé in harm's way: Bobbo getting shot at as his younger brother and sister fought not about what strategy would bring quick victory but about who could end the war sooner, each embracing a candidate who said what their brother was doing was not only futile but wrong.

It was not fair. It was not fair that she and Ezra had worked so hard to make their children's lives an idyll, only to have the times perversely make them mean. It was not fair that Bobbo was in Vietnam, that Barry already worried about the draft, that China watched the spectacle of bodies torn by bullets or shrapnel flickering nightly across the television. Robbie and Ezra had fought a war. That should have been enough.

"Myrna?"

She barely heard the voice at the front door, but she knew it had to be Dora.

She leaned against the screen. "I'm out back!"

A minute later, Dora Coe came around the corner of the house.

"Hi, honey," she said, and then, before Myrna could reply, continued: "Did Barry walk to school with Tully this morning?"

Tully was Dora's eldest and had been Barry's first friend when they moved to Rhymers Creek. He was a cute, half-fat kid whom everybody loved, one way or another.

"They called and he's not there." Dora plopped down on the stoop, her considerable bottom taking up most of the lowest step. "If he's playing hooky again, Del will take it out of his hide and I won't do a thing to stop it! I tell you, that boy!"

"I didn't see him this morning," Myrna said. "But then a lot of times Barry meets him up at the corner."

"Oh, I'll get the car later and run him down. He's either at the Rexall or out at the dry lake. You'd think when they ditched, they'd go someplace we wouldn't think to look for them." She reached over and plucked a sock from the basket and smoothed it across her knee. "So, what's new around here?"

"Not much. Ezra's cranky about one of the pits that keeps flooding. He thinks they've hit a spring. And the kids got into it again this morning about the California primary."

"It's the limit, isn't it?" Dora said. "Do you know the other day when Wellesley was going out to play war, Tully said, 'Get a lot of practice. You're gonna need it in Vietnam.' What a thing to say to an eleven-year-old! I could've spanked him."

"They're obsessed with it." Myrna nodded. "It's so sad."

They sat for a minute. "I don't know," Dora said. "When Tully skips school or stays out too late, I can't quite bring myself to be as mad as I should. It's like you can't be sure that this won't be the only chance he has to have fun. Del was never the same after Korea." She paused. "Have you heard from Bobbo?"

She should have known the question was coming, but it took Myrna a little by surprise. Perhaps it was because she had put his last letter so firmly out of her mind. It had been strange, not so much what it said, but how. His letters from boot camp were boyish: griping or marveling. In the first one after he arrived in the field, he had sent her a leaf from the jungle, a piastre, a pencil rubbing of his dog tags. His note had shone with a naive weariness, a dirty-job-but-somebody's-got-to-do-it patriotic flair.

But recently, his letters possessed an exhilaration that scared her. The latest one was taken up with a firefight — a luxurious, bloody description laced with ugly turns of phrase that Ezra had explained to her half shamefaced. There were a few even he was unsure of. They were unprepared for Bobbo's enthusiasm for war.

"Bad news?"

"No. No," Myrna said quickly. "We got a letter last week. But with him in the field, I worry all the time."

Dora nodded. "I remember that with Del. It's like an itch you can't scratch. You know Fred Bower's there now? Alice said they thought after his first posting he'd stay in the States, but, with the fighting this winter, they decided they needed more boys."

Myrna could not stand Alice Bower: intense and bigoted. But perhaps now, she might feel differently. "Is she all right?"

"From what Tully gets from Lonnie, Fred's got a nice desk job. But to hear Alice, you'd think that he was all alone on top of some tree. She told me that Pincher Bowdin got his draft notice. You know him, I think. He was a year behind Bobbo."

Myrna had a vague recollection of the boy — greasy and strange. Dora sighed. "Pincher Bowdin. Junior Loomis. Ricky Graves. Fred. Bobbo. The list gets longer and longer. I have to tell you, Myrna, I hate it. You went through it with Ezra and I went through it with Del. You'd think that would have been enough."

She simply nodded, a little spooked that Dora's mind was running the same way as her own. All those little children.

"I better get along" — Dora grabbed the banister and pulled herself up — "and see if I can find that damned kid!" She tossed the sock back in the laundry basket. "I don't think I'll say anything to Del. He'll just whale on him. I can't blame the boy sometimes."

"I know," Myrna said. "Don't tell him."

Alone again, Myrna sat, a light sheen of sweat on her arms and face in the noon sunlight. Everybody knew it wasn't fair. They all worried about their sons, all somehow having thought their husbands had finally finished with the dirty business of war. But it wasn't true. It just wasn't true.

She stood and picked up the basket. Was it always this way, looking around and finding you had to pity your own children, grown up with words like *holocaust* and *annihilation* as part of their daily lives? They had learned to duck and cover, talk easily about fallout and ICBMs. In elementary school, China had worn a metal tag, not unlike the one her brother wore now in those jungles far away. Myrna overheard her once explain to a playmate that these would identify them in case they were burned beyond recognition in a nuclear blast.

What kind of children knew such possibilities from the Book of Apocalypse? And this day as every day, what sort of little girl had to wonder about her brother each night as she watched the evening news?

Myrna heaved the basket onto her hip and opened the back screen.

"Poor China," she said aloud.

Poor Barry.

Poor Bobbo.

2

In nothing but panties and her Siegerford T-shirt, Belva sat at her desk and stared out the window. In the courtyard below, various dorm mates, slathered in Coppertone, lay on the grass, straps slipped beneath their armpits, backs of their two-pieces un-hooked, chasing away unsightly lines of white. She considered skipping her last Survey of Art class, but Professor Aker was such a stickler for attendance, and she could not remember exactly how many times she had cut already. She sighed. She ought to be getting dressed.

Instead, she picked up a cigarette, glancing at the piece of sta-tionery on the desk before her.

> Dear Bobbo,
>   It seems impossible it's been a month since your letter got here. Things have been so busy and . . .

She took a drag, then picked up the paper, wadded it tightly, and dropped it in the trash can by her feet.

What was she supposed to say to him: school's almost out, the Blue and Gray Ball is this weekend, nice weather we're having? Students were rioting in Paris. They were burning draft cards in Berkeley. But things at Siegerford were placid. Perhaps that was what Bobbo wanted to hear, that at home things were not that different from how he remembered them, that, in these parts, no-body but the radicals and a few outside agitators were making noise about the war.

His own letters were a little weird. She got the impression he was drinking a lot just from the way he put sentences together, though perhaps it was more than beer at work on his head. Some-times, whole paragraphs were scratched out, as if he had thought better of telling her all the details of what Vietnam was like.

What he did tell her was, frankly, more than she cared to know.

"God! It smells like the high school girls' room in here!" Roxanne, her roommate, blew through the door, waving her hand in front of her nose.

Belva snuffed her cigarette. "Appetite suppressant."

"Right." Roxy snorted. "Here's your lunch, Miss Scarlett." She spilled four packs of soda crackers and an orange onto the desk, along with a Tab from the vending machine in the basement. "If you don't start eating, you're going to end up with mono. Seriously!" she insisted, plopping on her bed. "Toast and tea. Crackers and fruit. Salad for dinner. I swear, didn't they teach you about the four major food groups back in home ec?"

Belva wolfed down a cracker. "Thin is in," she said, "and I come from a long line of the pleasingly plump."

"Bel-va." Roxy sighed. "Face it, you'll never be Twiggy. And why are you complaining? Most women would kill for your boobs."

She smiled. Her bosom — as her mother always called it — was eye-catching, even in this day and age. "Maybe so." She shrugged. "Sometimes it doesn't seem fair. Ten years ago, I wouldn't have worried. Everybody wanted to look like Marilyn."

"And now everybody wants to look like a boy."

"Don't be silly. Who wants to look like Linda Pearson?"

Linda — round faced, round bodied, with round glasses and a pageboy — bore a more than passing resemblance to a chubby ten-year-old.

"Shame on you." Roxy giggled. "I mean, at least she's no slave to fashion, and you shouldn't be either."

"Spare me!" Belva felt one of her friend's lectures coming on. "I'm not going to burn my bra for you or anybody else."

"With those tits, I wouldn't either."

They made an odd pair. They had met as freshmen — "Freshwomen" as Roxy insisted — and had ended up as sophomore roommates more or less by default. It had worked surprisingly well, though they had few interests — and increasingly fewer friends — in common. There had been some tensions, but now, in the twilight of their year together, they engaged in a lot of good-natured teasing.

"Rob Wicker's looking for a date for the Blue and Gray Ball."

"Jesus, Belva" — Roxy groaned — "will you quit trying to set me up with Randy's horny frat friends."

"Come on. Your social life's a zero. Rob's nice."

"Right. Like all the other Siggie-Piggies."

Belva rolled her eyes. Sometimes she didn't know what they were going to do with Rox, as she had taken to calling her, as in "dumb as a box of . . ." Since she had decided to major in political science, she had become more and more radical in just about every way. Regularly, Roxy rode over to the university with three or four other Siegerford girls for the antiwar teach-ins, and she bombarded congressmen, the president, the local newspapers, and *Time* magazine with letters. She hardly wore makeup anymore and talked about not shaving her legs. She hung out briefly with one boy with hair so long and shoulders so thin Belva first thought, when she saw them from a distance, that Roxy was kissing a girl. Her roommate had said outright she thought Randy Ditmars — who Belva had taken up with in March — was a Stone Age jock, and she took an even dimmer view of the other boys in his fraternity.

"Hi, Belva." Linda, in her standard sweatshirt and jeans, slumped through the open door. "Roxy, can I get that red marker of yours?"

"Sure." Roxy reached in her purse and flipped the pen to Linda.

"It should do," she said critically. "It can pass for blood."

After she left, Belva reached for her shorts. There was her art class at one. "What was that all about?"

"It's for the demonstration. Linda's making some posters."

"What demonstration?"

Roxy did not answer. When Belva turned to her, there was a slight smile on Roxy's face. "The one at the Blue and Gray Ball."

"What?"

"Look, Belva" — Roxy sat up — "it's sponsored by the university ROTCy. All the cadets will be there in their uniforms, for God's sake! And all the other guys are renting those soldier suits. It's disgusting. There's a war on!"

For an instant, Belva was speechless. The Blue and Gray was a tradition, famous for generations as the best end-of-the-year dance for miles around.

"I cannot believe you," she huffed. "What the hell does a dance have to do with that damned war! Why can't you leave it alone?"

Roxy rolled off the bed. "I'm not going to fight with you about it. You can't see it, but down the road you will." She was to the door by then. She turned and looked Belva full in the face. "There are times when you have to take sides."

✧

Maneuvering the front seat of Randy's GTO was no easy task in a hoopskirt, but Belva managed it with something approaching grace. She thought honestly that it was a silly-looking rig — the formal she had bought for her high school junior-senior recut and otherwise altered so it could pass for a gown out of *Gone With the Wind*. The concept of the Blue and Gray Ball, in which those men who were not in ROTC were expected to appear in rented uniforms of either the Union or the Confederacy, had arisen in the twenties as a way for students from the North and South to demonstrate their regional loyalties. Randy looked dashing enough dressed as a Kentucky colonel, though she had to admit, beer-bellied Rob in Federal Blue — set up with some freshman ("freshwoman") whose name she had trouble remembering (Lina? Lana?) — looked like an extra in *F Troop*.

They had dinner at the University Chop House, where little girls looked enviously at Belva and a couple of older couples stopped by their table to reminisce about their own dances years before.

"It's so nice to see you kids dressed up," one woman gushed.

"Oh, honey, they're not all hippies," her husband said.

Randy smirked, and Belva glowed appropriately. She actually hated that kind of remark. It made her feel like some kind of generational traitor, just a good and dutiful daughter of Rhymers Creek. And "dressed up" was exactly what they were, of course, costumed like kids in some primary school pageant.

In the car on the way to the student center, Randy pulled a fifth of bourbon from under the seat. He and Rob took several long drags on the bottle before offering it to the girls, who both indulged in some ladylike sips as they wound onto the campus of the state university. Signs led them to the official Blue and Gray parking, right behind the ballroom. Randy gallantly tried to help her out, but Belva finally had to find the right leverage on her own. Lanie, in back, had even more trouble. Carriages had apparently been better designed for hoops and frills. They straightened their dresses, then both escorts presented their arms, and the two couples swept with something like grandeur toward the front of the building. In that instant, Belva felt a little surge of elegance. Maybe it was not so silly after all, being part of something that went back for years, a tradition. The bourbon made her warm, and the dinner seemed to have lifted the lethargy of malnourishment she had been experiencing the last couple of weeks.

They could hear them before they could see them:

> Hey, hey, LBJ!
> How many kids
> have you killed today?
> Hey, hey, LBJ! . . .

They turned the corner. The buildings entrance was blocked by fifty or so people carrying picket signs. The two couples froze.

"Shit," Randy muttered.

In the sunset, a contingent of Campus Security looked confused, alongside them some deputy sheriffs who seemed no more sure of themselves. But in front of them all was a phalanx of a dozen men, outfitted like invaders from another planet: bright, white helmets with smoky visors and clear plastic shields, long black truncheons in their hands, and guns strapped to their hips.

"Christ," Randy whispered with an odd exhilaration. "It's the Riot Squad from the State Police."

Belva saw Linda Pearson, holding high her homemade poster bright with Magic Marker blood: AMERIKA LIES/INNOCENTS DIE. Beside her was that boy with the shoulder-length hair she had seen Roxy kiss, and Roxy herself, face contorted in anger: "Hey, hey, LBJ! . . ."

There were other people she knew from Siegerford, a few she had glimpsed at the university, along with a dozen professors she recognized, a woman with a baby, several gray-haired ladies — all of them shouting, vehement. Vulnerable.

"What bullshit," Bob whined, though it had to be a shout over the chants. "The goddamn communists!"

She turned upon him fiercely. Her roommate might be many things — feminist, stupid, inexplicable — but Roxy was no communist. But before she could open her mouth, a voice squawked over a bullhorn. "You have been asked to disperse. If you do not disperse in thirty seconds, you are subject to arrest."

She swung around. The aliens had raised their shields. They began to strike the concrete with their truncheons. *Tack!* . . . *Tack!* . . . *Tack!* . . . It was an unsettling, ominous sound. Randy reached out and put his arm around her. *Tack!* . . . *Tack!* . . . *Tack!* . . .

"Hey! Hey! LBJ! . . ."

"Shit!" Randy said again.

"Clear the area! Clear the area!" the bullhorn commanded.

"Roxy," Belva whispered aloud.

Stomp. Tack! Stomp. Tack! Stomp. Tack! Stomp.

The State Police began to move forward, advancing on the

protesters, on Roxy and Linda and the long-haired boy and the gray-haired ladies, Campus Security following timorously behind.

"Fuckin' communists!" Randy shouted.

"Bunch of queers!" Rob yelled.

Stomp. Tack! Stomp. Tack!

Belva put her face on Randy's shoulder. "I want to go," she said with as much firmness as she could muster.

Stomp. Tack!

There was a scream. Belva whirled around, and there was the long-haired boy on the ground, holding his head. She could see blood. The aliens advanced beyond him. The protesters were pressed into a tight mass, and she saw one of the old ladies fall.

Stomp. Tack!

"I want to go! Now!" she shouted.

Stomp. Tack!

Another of the old ladies fell.

She grabbed Randy's arm. "Now!"

"Stop it!"

"Fuck you!" she screamed in his face. "I want to go!"

❖

She slept with him that night. It only seemed right. He had spent a lot of money to take her to the Blue and Gray Ball.

He had wanted to stay: to see what happened, to see the truncheons connect again with something besides the ground and a couple of demonstrators. It made Belva feel oddly guilty that she had torn him away, dragging him back to the GTO as Rob stood with his arm around Lanie, who accepted what was happening with a peculiar passivity. Perhaps she saw no familiar face in the crowd that gradually fell back before those men in masks. But Belva could not watch, not merely because it was her roommate or suite mate who might be hit, but because anyone might be hit. When she saw the long-haired boy go down, she could not abide it another minute.

But Randy had spent seventy-five dollars, and Rob and Lanie

had had to find their own way home. So, in the car as she waited for him, she knew what she would say: "Let's go back to the frat house. There won't be anybody there. I want you so bad."

That was what she did, and he seemed somewhat mollified, and the sex was good, though, as she examined herself in the mirror at four o'clock in the morning in her own dorm room, she saw that she had two bad hickeys and a bruise on her shoulder from where he had grabbed her as he came. The violence had excited him, much as it had frightened her.

And, odd as it seemed, Bobbo's letters suddenly made a great deal more sense. If the crushing of a small group of students and grandmothers could drive a frat boy to ecstasy, what could happen to men immersed in a kind of bloodletting words could hardly express? There before the mirror with her little battle scars, she felt a new kinship with and sympathy for the American soldier she wrote to on the sly.

She and Roxy did not speak for three days. Her roommate, along with Linda, had avoided arrest, which would probably have meant expulsion. But that boy Roxy had kissed had ended up in the emergency room, and then, within an hour of having his head stitched up, had been taken to jail. Belva did not want to think of what had happened to him on his way to the tank.

Gradually, things in their room returned to normal, though it would take until the following fall when they had coffee together for them to really talk about what had happened. Roxy cried then, and Belva did, too. But in that first week afterward, as exams pressed and she stayed up till three cramming and drank too much Tab and coffee and gulped caffeine pills and once a Dexedrine, the one thing Belva made sure she did was sit down at 4:00 A.M. on Wednesday and in the unsteady hand of someone who is speeding, pen:

Dear Bobbo:
    I am sorry I haven't written. Everything is moving much faster than I would have ever imagined . . .

3

There was a knock on the door.

"Don't come in," Barry said. "I'm developing."

"I bet you are. Just let me know when you get there."

It was Kathy Jordan, and he smiled. In the tank, the images of last weekend's carwash were coming into view. For the seniors, graduation was only a week and a half away, and they had put on quite a show: lots of wet t-shirts, Sherry Lindsay slipping her bra down, and Bill Evans and Tom Walter mooning the camera. He would have to save those. They'd never appear in *The Leopard's Roar*.

As Bill's face took shape in the tray, Barry could see the very beginnings of a moustache and his sideburns creeping below his ear lobes. Smirking over his shoulder as he dropped his pants, his hair, too, would probably have fallen below his collar if he'd had one. The seniors were declaring their independence, ignoring the rules on what clothes and hair and whiskers should look like.

He pulled out the prints and flipped off the red light. Kathy was sitting outside the door, her legs folded ungracefully beneath her as she read her history book. She was not a pretty girl. Her nose was too big, and her horned glasses made her look like a bit of a caricature. And yet, she was Barry's greatest pal, with the exception, maybe, of Tully. With Kathy, he could talk about almost anything, and she was sympathetic and funny and unperturbed. And he would do the same for her, gladly, and often did, as she passed through boyfriends and her parents' divorce and the unfounded conviction she wasn't really much good at anything.

"What's happening?" he said as he came out of the darkroom.

"Pincher Bowdin just got drafted," Kathy said. "There's a big party out at the dry lake Friday night. Wanna go?"

He hesitated. He had never liked Pincher, who did drugs and dressed strange and treated everybody with unmitigated contempt.

Barry shrugged. "Maybe. What're you gonna tell your folks?"

"There's a sock hop that night." She grinned. "I figure I can justify things till at least one."

"Probably," he said. "You gonna pick me up?"

She nodded. "I think I can get the car. And if I can't, Tully has his."

Things had been strange with Tully lately. He and Barry were drawing apart. He had gotten a gray Mustang with what he'd saved from his summer job at the pits and a loan from his father. He spent most of his time now with Billy Peters, who had a Mustang, too.

"Okay," he said, "I'll plan on it."

"Bitchin'," Kathy said. "I'll try to get by about seven."

"Neat," Barry said, shuffling through the pictures. "I'll be out in front. If I'm not, honk for me."

"Sure thing," Kathy said, flouncing suddenly off.

Barry stood there, the photographs forgotten in his hand. It would be fine, going out to the dry lake. The fact that the party was for Pincher was a little strange, and that it was a send-off to boot camp and maybe Vietnam even stranger. Maybe if Bobbo had been drafted out of high school instead of signing up a year later, some of his old friends would have given him a party, too.

The draft was on all their minds, one way or another. Last weekend, at a party at Tom Walter's, he had had a long talk about it with Kathy and Eddie Hammersmith. Eddie was adamant that, if you were called, you had to go, but Barry was not so sure.

"What're you gonna do then? Run off to Canada?"

Barry shrugged. "People are going to jail."

"Great," Eddie snapped. "Your folks'll love that, and all the perverts in jail, too. Don't be stupid, Barry."

"It's not stupid," he insisted. "It shows you're really serious."

"Yeah, serious about screwing up your life, or getting screwed."

Barry winced, and Eddie left not long after that. A few other people drifted by. Then Kathy and Barry were alone.

"You wouldn't really go to jail, would you?" she asked.

"I don't know what I'd do, to tell you the truth."

"Eddie's right." She put her hand on his arm. "A lot of really bad things could happen to somebody like you in jail."

He looked at her, unnerved, but the concern she showed was innocent. Then she smiled.

"Look, if you get drafted and you don't want to go, I'll take you to Canada."

He laughed and pulled his arm away.

"I would! I'd get my folks' car, or borrow my sister's V-Dub. All you have to do is call," she continued, her grin growing. "I mean, we could have a password so you wouldn't even have to say what we were doing in case the line was tapped."

"Like what?"

"Oh, I don't know" — she furrowed her brow dramatically — "something mysterious, like . . . like 'The wet bird flies at night.'"

He cracked up. "Right, Kathy. 'The wet bird flies at night.'"

They leaned together on the stairs and giggled about it for a minute or two. Tom Walter wanted to know what was so funny, but they waved him off. Gradually, their laughter died.

"That was really far out, Kathy," Barry said.

She touched his chin and turned his face toward hers. She was not smiling anymore. "I'm serious, Barry Carraway. I'm as serious as I've ever been in my life."

He took another look at the pictures and shook his head, smiling — *The wet bird flies at night.* It was too bad they wouldn't let the paper print the one of Tom and Bill: "South Mockdon Moon Shot" would make a good caption. And that one of Sherry could be . . .

Against his will, he wondered if Pincher had anyone to call.

When Kathy picked him up, she told him Tully had gone on ahead.

"Figures," Barry mumbled. It was like being twelve again, except that this time, instead of losing his friends to football and basketball, it was Mustangs and Camaros.

"Did you guys have a fight?" Kathy asked.

"Naw." Barry slumped in the seat. "It's the damned car. He and Billy do everything but screw them."

Kathy laughed. "They've probably tried that, too."

Barry tried to imagine Tully with his cock up the tailpipe — the vibration would likely be nice, but the carbon monoxide would do him in before he came.

They were silent for most of the way. Kathy cranked up the radio in her mother's Nova, and, after skipping through buttons all set to Mantovani, they finally found BOSSROCK out of Henderson, and Barry played dashboard while Kathy sang along with "Somebody to Love" and then "White Rabbit," since it was a twofer.

It did not take long to get to the dry lake, where there were already a dozen six-packs laid out on the cracked earth. Tully's Mustang had the windows open with "Let's Spend the Night Together" blasting from his eight-track. Other cars were scattered in a rough circle, with Chris Eldon's 1954 Dodge pickup pulled off to one side. Rhett Beauford was dancing lewdly in Tully's headlights with Karry Piggott, who was new in Rhymers Creek and who Kathy called Swine Woman for having stolen Rhett away, though Barry was not sure he had been Kathy's to lose.

At first, they did not see Pincher, leaning against Chris's truck. Everybody knew he was stoned half the time, but unlike the few other dopers they came upon — people who lived down around Ambrosia Lane — marijuana did not make Pincher red-eyed and dreamy but even more morose and morbid than usual.

"How's it hangin', Pincher?" Barry said as they approached.

Pincher looked him and Kathy up and down, slowly, meanly, until they both stopped walking. "What's it to you, Carraway?" He laughed pointedly, Billy and Chris joining in.

Barry steeled himself. Pincher would have said it to anyone.

He shrugged. "Too dark, man. You wear them so tight that in the daytime nobody'd have to ask."

That got a laugh from Kathy, who licked her fingers and dragged them over an imaginary scoreboard in front of her: "Two points."

Billy and Chris laughed again. Pincher smiled, not willingly, took another drink, and said, "Glad you made it, fucker."

It was warm that night. Barry moved with the group around Pincher — Tully and Billy and Eddie and a couple others — there by Chris Eldon's truck. Meanwhile, Kathy was putting a quiet make on Chris himself, which, Barry reflected, she probably would not have done if she had come alone. He was good for that — a girl's good buddy, an excuse if things didn't go as planned.

Barry sighed. He ought to have a girlfriend. He was sixteen years old. Bobbo, at sixteen, had had girlfriends to spare. But he was a football hero, and besides, unwillingly, Barry suspected it would be a fraud. Then again, so much of what people knew of him was a fraud anyway, what difference would it make? Sprawled in the truck bed with his head propped on the wheel well, beer in hand, he could see himself, looking cool, distracted, paying elaborate inattention to Tully, who was talking about Elwood Pomeroy.

"Hell, go and make yourself a few extra bucks, Eddie. Elwood'll treat you nice."

"Fuck you, Coe."

"Naw" — Tully laughed — "even old Elwood Pomeroy couldn't pay me enough for that."

"What if he gave you another Mustang?" Billy Peters walked up with a six-pack dangling from his hand.

Tully paused for effect. "Well . . ."

Barry took a long draw on his beer.

Everybody knew about Elwood, Doc Pomeroy's oldest son. Long before the county had gone wet and his father's flourishing bootlegging business closed down, Elwood had moved to California, to Laguna Beach. Doc set him up with a McDonald's there, which, so the story went, had been parlayed into a fortune in real estate. As if to prove it, Elwood had come back to town in 1965 and thrown up a vacation cottage on the river near Olinda.

Elwood's good fortune and ostentatious show of it would probably have been enough to earn people's animosity. Worse, however, was the fact that he was a six-foot-three-inch man with a Corvette Sting-Ray who wore white linen pants and belted silk overblouses, along with three large diamond rings. There had been rumors ever since Elwood's first stint back that he had a stable of kept boys. It was said though never proved that he had paid five football players from Central Mockdon fifty dollars apiece to let him blow them one by one.

"Say, Pincher!" Tully was talking too loud, his hand on Pincher's shoulder and his face too close. "Why don't you head on over there? Elwood ain't half bad, and we could sneak up with a Polaroid. That'd get the draft off your ass in no time."

He chortled drunkenly, but nobody else joined in. No one had really mentioned what the party was about. Pincher turned slowly and put one hand in his pocket. His other went to Tully's collar.

There was a click, and then they could all see the knife glimmering in the vague, refracted glow of the headlights.

"Why don't you shut the fuck up," Pincher muttered.

The knife was so close that Tully's breath fogged the steel. Seconds passed.

Pincher folded the switchblade and slipped it out of sight.

"Get me another beer, asshole."

Tully did what he was told.

✧

People came and went, as did nine o'clock, then ten. After Pincher had shown the knife, Tully, Billy, and Eddie drifted away. They didn't want to look scared, Barry knew, but they didn't want to look stupid either. If he lolled his head over the side of the truck, he could see them dancing. The beer he held was warm, and for some time now he'd just been lying there, staring at the sky.

"Want a toke?"

He lowered his eyes, and there was Pincher. Barry's nose twitched at an itchy, unfamiliar scent. He squinted. In his hand, Pincher had a joint. At least it looked like the pictures Barry had seen of them in *Life*.

Though woozy, for he was not much of a drinker, Barry thought gravely that this was a momentous occasion. He had never smoked marijuana before, and here was Pincher Bowdin — a doper and a hood and about to be inducted into the U.S. Army — offering him a hit. He saw himself take the joint between his fingers and raise it to his lips. Tully's eight-track was playing "Piece of My Heart."

He inhaled.

"You hear anything from Bobbo?"

Barry was concentrating so hard on the burning in his throat and suppressing his urgent need to cough that he didn't even hear Pincher's question at first. His eyes began to tear. With supreme effort, he blew out what little smoke he'd taken in.

"Huh?" he rasped, handing the joint back to Pincher.

"You guys get much news out of Bobbo?"

"Yeah," Barry managed. "Yeah, we had a letter last week."

He watched the joint flare and light Pincher's face. He was afraid his own registered his surprise. He had never expected to find himself alone tonight with Pincher, talking about Bobbo.

"What's he say?"

"About what?"

Pincher's voice grew thin as he held in the smoke. "About Nam, asshole. What's he say about Nam?"

Barry took the joint again and this time managed a respectable toke, holding his breath for a long moment, less for the marijuana than to buy time. He understood that what Pincher wanted was reassurance, that somehow it would all not be so bad: going to the army; maybe going to Vietnam. But perhaps Pincher knew that there would be no maybes, that someone like him — who looked like him and had an attitude like him and, Barry thought, had his kind of luck — was sure to go to Vietnam.

"It's okay," he said. "He doesn't like it, you know?" But what he remembered was those latest letters, in which it seemed Bobbo had indeed begun to like it, "greasing gooks," as he wrote. "But it's not like you're fighting all the time. And it's only for a year."

Pincher blew his lungful out in a guffaw that ended in a wracking cough. "A fucking year." He gasped. "Jesus, Carraway . . ."

They were silent for a few moments as the joint moved back and forth. Barry wondered if his eyes were red and tried to decide if he felt funny. Pincher stretched out flat on the bed of the truck.

"I'm gonna die, Carraway," he said softly.

Barry stifled a moan: Pincher getting morbid like he did when he was fucked up. But then, it was not like before. Pincher might indeed die, just like Bobbo and Fred Bower and Ricky Graves and all the others over there. And there was Raymond Garcia and Pete Edwards, who were dead already, and a couple from Central Mockdon and more from St. Cyprian's. Why should Pincher's chances be any better?

"No, you won't, Pincher," he said, though he didn't believe it particularly. "Shit" — which was the word Barry said though he rarely uttered it; perhaps it was the dope — "Jocko DiGiovanni got sent to Germany. They could send you there. You know, beer and fräuleins."

He was amazed at the way he was talking — serious, sort-of-uptight Barry Carraway sounding like Bobbo used to, or Bobbo's football buddies: all bravado and broad winks.

"No chance, man. They'll send me to Nam." Pincher huffed a brief laugh at the rhyme. "And when I get there, they'll kill me." He stared for a long moment at the stub of the joint in his hand. "You want to eat the roach?"

Barry considered it, then shook his head. Pincher wet his

thumb and forefinger, and there was a soft hiss as he crushed the ember. Then he popped it in his mouth.

"My ass is grass, man," he said softly. "I'll never get outta there alive."

✧

It was after midnight. Barry's eyes were heavy and dry. He had always heard that the first time you smoked dope, nothing happened, but he was afraid that wasn't true. Tully's tape deck was still blaring, and Barry had been aware of people coming and going. Pincher did another joint by himself, then split one with someone else. They offered it to Barry, but he simply smiled — he could tell it was stupidly — and waved his hand no.

He was worried. If his parents found out he had smoked grass, he'd be grounded or worse. He raised his head. It was not too bad. He heard the opening riff of "Let Me Stand Next to Your Fire."

"Are you stoned?" He turned, and Kathy was crawling up over the tailgate. "Tully said you smoked with Pincher."

He smiled. "Yeah."

"Well," she whispered excitedly, "what's it like?"

He considered the question for a moment.

"Weird . . . ," he said.

"Nice . . . ," he added.

"I wish I'd been around. That Chris Eldon!" She grimaced. "Ramblin' fingers and rushin' hands. And he kisses like a guppy."

Barry felt giggles gurgling up from his stomach, from the beer or the dope he wasn't sure. "A . . . a guppy . . . !"

And though Kathy had probably had no more than two beers and hadn't smoked at all, she caught them, too. "Yeah," she half-choked, puffing her cheeks. "Bwop. Bwop."

Soon, the two of them were helpless on their backs, tears in their eyes and their chests sore from laughter.

"You should've told me you'd gone fishin' kissin'."

"Really he's more like a grouper . . ."

"A groper?"

There was a sudden, earsplitting roar, then a dry grinding. The music faded rapidly.

"Hey. Hey! Goddamnit!"

Barry and Kathy staggered up. He banged his knee on the wall of the bed and swore, though he could hardly feel any pain. The air was heavy with the smell of exhaust. Holding tight — he because of the dope, she because of the laughter — they leaned against each other.

In the middle of the circle of headlights, foggy through a cloud of smoke and dust, stood Tully, stomping his feet, his arms flying madly around him, shouting: "The fucker took my car! He took my goddamn car! Goddamnit! Goddamnit!"

As the others gathered around, his voice had the edge of tears.

"He took my fuckin' car!"

Pincher was gone.

✧

There in the late morning, Barry tapped on the basement window. "Tully. Tully," he said in a low, harsh voice.

He could see him inside, rocking slowly back and forth on the edge of the bed. That was probably how he had spent most of the last thirty-six hours. Rocking, Barry knew, somehow made it all seem better. That must be why they rocked babies. And that seemed about all that was left to any of them.

After Pincher had stolen the Mustang, Tully had gone with Chris Eldon, with Rhett and Eddie in the back of the truck, to see if they could find him on Route 9. Kathy and Barry and Sandy drove into town. Willie Belmon took off with Tom Walter to check out Olinda, while Billy Peters and Karry Piggott headed Billy's Mustang north toward Mockdon and the pits.

It was Willie and Tom who found him, crumpled against the abutment of the old bridge that had washed out in the forties. Except for the gash on his forehead, Willie said, there didn't seem to be a scratch on him, though there was that thin drool of blood down his chin. They tried to pull open the door and, when that didn't work, tried to coax him through the window. But Pincher didn't move. When Tom tried to drag him, Pincher wouldn't help.

That was when they got scared. Willie jumped in his car and drove into Olinda and called an ambulance, which came with the Sheriff's Department. They ripped the door off with a crowbar and strapped Pincher to a stretcher. The door didn't make much difference by then. The nose of the car was shattered, and the windshield was gone. The engine had been shoved into the front seat.

Barry couldn't figure it. He had been stoned and talking with Kathy when they all heard a car revving wildly. They had looked over to see Pincher at the wheel, and then there was the clutch and the slam of the door, and Tully's Mustang — his brushed-silver, supercharged Mustang — was gone, BB-gunning them all with dust and mud as Pincher streaked off before any of them even had time to react.

Then everything was crazy and there was a sort of powwow right where the car had been in which they argued about what to do and where to go and whether to call the cops. And Tully just stood there swearing and almost crying because he couldn't believe that Pincher Bowdin was out joyriding in his Mustang, that Pincher would do that to him after it was he himself who had made sure Pincher had a party before he went off to Vietnam.

Then again, Barry thought, what did Tully expect? Pincher *had* pulled a knife on him.

"Tully!" Barry raised his voice and smacked the glass hard.

Tully looked up. "Huh?" His eyes met Barry's through the window. He got up and snapped the lock.

"You okay?" Barry said tentatively as he dropped inside.

Tully sighed. "Yeah. Yeah. Come on in."

Barry closed the window, then sank down next to the bureau.

Tully sat on the bed and propped his chin in his hand. "Are . . . ah, you in deep shit?"

"I got about that close to getting my butt whipped" — Barry

indicated an inch with his fingers. "If they had any idea I was stoned. I'm lucky we were running all over the county till four in the morning. Kathy says everybody's in a lot of trouble." He started to draw his finger back and forth over the carpet. "She had bad news."

"What did you hear?" Tully looked sick to his stomach.

Barry's finger stopped moving. "Pincher's paralyzed."

Tully groaned.

"It's not a sure thing," Barry added quickly, "but Kathy went down this morning, and that's what they told her."

"Shit," Tully murmured. He sat straight and crossed his arms to stifle a shudder. "How paralyzed?"

"The waist down." Barry's voice was rough. "His back's broken."

Tully hunched forward slowly. "Oh, Jesus!"

"It's not your fault, Tully," Barry said softly. "Nobody asked him to steal your car."

Tully sat there breathless, as if somebody had slammed him to the ground with a shoulder toss. "The bastard," he said. "Why did the bastard get so fucked up?"

"I don't know." Barry looked at his hands. "We thought he could handle it, I guess. I mean" — his voice thinned a little — "I smoked with him."

Tully shrugged. It was his turn to offer absolution. "Look, Barry, he didn't need you to get stoned."

There was a long pause. Barry started to play again with the green shag carpet. "He was scared, Tully. He asked me a lot about Bobbo. He didn't want to go. To Vietnam. He thought he'd die."

Tully raised his eyes toward the ceiling. "Thought he'd die in Vietnam? So he takes my car and tries to kill himself?"

"I guess. I know it doesn't make much sense. But when you're afraid like that, you're not making much sense anyway." Barry shrugged, then looked up. "I mean, Tully, what are we gonna do when the time comes? You don't want to go any more than I do."

Tully sighed. "Hell if I know, Barry. I've got that blood sugar thing. If that doesn't work, I'll come up with something else. We've got another year or two. It could be over by then. Look" — Tully put on an impatient face — "you're the one who's always saying it's a bad war. So you don't go getting blown away in it, okay?"

Barry picked at the carpet some more. "Bobbo's there, Tully." He could see Tully stiffen.

"Barry," he said slowly, "I got the health stuff. You want to go back east to college. You'll have a 2-S. Bobbo tried that and he couldn't hack it. And he joined up, remember? He made a choice. We'll all make choices."

They did not speak. Barry was thinking about Bobbo. About all the upperclassmen over there. Mostly, he was thinking about Pincher, and what he'd done not to go. That was scared — to get yourself before somebody else got you. And he hadn't even gotten it right.

Tully shuddered again. "He won't be able to fuck, will he?"

Barry just shook his head.

"How's the car?" he asked after a while.

Tully put the heels of his palms to his temples and rubbed them slowly. "It's destroyed. I don't know how fast he was going when he hit the bridge. Pincher ought to be dead." He lifted his head. "I owe my dad twenty-five hundred dollars for that car. We'll get some insurance, but it won't cover it. I don't know what I'm gonna do."

"Was he cool? Your dad, I mean," Barry said.

"He's pissed as shit." Tully sighed. "My mom was just crazy, but after he yelled for a while, he let up. How 'bout yours?"

Barry pursed his lips. "Pa was okay. I thought I'd get a whipping. I was scared he'd think it was a good excuse to really get me. He's mad at me about the McCarthy thing. His people are all Republicans, and he thinks . . ." Barry's voice trailed off. He took a deep breath. "He thinks I'm screwing Bobbo over. Of course, he didn't know I was stoned. My mother was like yours, all threats and everything. But after a while, Pa just wanted an explanation.

So I had to tell him. Even though I'd lied, he didn't really blow. He came up this morning and told me things like this happen." Barry shook his head. "But I guess I still think it was my fault, smoking with him. Or maybe if I'd told Pincher different about Bobbo."

Tully sighed. "Barry, you could have told Pincher Bobbo gets laid three times a day and a fourth on Sunday and it wouldn't have done any good. Nothing was gonna change what he did."

"Maybe." Barry glanced at the clock on the nightstand. "I should get back. I'm grounded. Ma's at the drugstore. Pa sort of let me come over here to see you, but he only gave me a half an hour because officially I can't do anything until school's out."

"Hell, me too," Tully said. "I'm probably gonna be grounded the rest of my life. Won't make too much difference," he added bleakly. "Where am I gonna get a new set of wheels?"

"Where's Pincher gonna get a new set of legs?" Barry snapped. They looked at each other sharply. Then Barry said good-bye.

4

It was not like being hit in the face. That was how most people described it, but that wasn't it exactly. It reminded him most of a blanket party the year before with Stribling, the guy nobody liked at Fort McElvay. They threw the wool blanket over his head at 4:00 A.M., then punched him anonymously for the next twenty minutes. Stribling didn't resist much. He lay there and took it until they were done. Though he landed a few punches himself, it made Fred sick. Stribling asked for a transfer next day with his two black eyes and bruised gut. Nothing was said. He was gone within hours.

That was what the heat was like every day: first the blackness, then the blow.

Stepping out of the air-conditioning, Fred automatically

shifted his eyes to the left. To the right was Graves Registration. All day, they had heard the helicopters — *Fwack. Fwack. Fwack. Fwack* — landing and taking off again. No one mentioned it. But they knew. Somewhere, something was going wrong. Men were screaming. Buddies were shot, punji-sticked, Bouncing Bettied. The medics could not move fast enough. Radios buzzed with curses and the strange poetry of positions. Here at base, they were bringing in the body bags, while back in the World, the telegrams were being readied for Tulsa, San Luis, New Bedford, and Augusta. In Brownsville and Tampa and Port Townsend, the priest and the soldier were climbing into the car, on their way to tell some mother and father that little Tommy, Jerry, José, Leroy wasn't coming home.

The heat smothered him. All the humidity of Rhymers Creek put together from his whole life was nothing compared with the wet air of Nam. His body exploded in sweat. He stopped in mid-pace. He had never believed he would be here, and now that he was, though he had never set foot more than two miles off base, it was worse than he ever imagined.

He had gotten his orders right after Tet. He had experience, had dealt with major supply orders for the last two years. From his base in Alabama, six of them were chosen, but after they landed in Saigon, Fred was separated from the others. Ten days went by before he got his assignment. They had been promised they would be kept together, but what did promises mean in the U.S. Army? Now, he found himself — and he had to assume his buddies were in the same boat — just the fucking new guy, some stateside cherry who would have to learn the ropes and get into the groove before anybody treated him right.

He got his breath. He began to move. He could go back to barracks, but Eggleson would want to smoke dope and then, once they were stoned, would rag him for being a newby and make him feel stupid. He could get a pass and get drunk and then go get laid. But that still embarrassed him. Last time he was at the

EMC, a chaplain sat next to him and spoke to him about the temptations a man had to face, and Fred felt ashamed. He was not accustomed to a war zone. Not accustomed to this war zone.

As he strode down the road, never acknowledging still Graves Registration, he saw Mercer Shaw, the MP who had hassled him the previous night, who smirked at him. He already hated the black-haired, blue-eyed bastard, who seemed to take particular pleasure — when the police burst into the whorehouse, taking IDs of guys with their pants down and dicks up — in calling him "soldier": "You okay, soldier?" "You druggin' it, soldier?" "Don't let me catch you here again, soldier." As if half the base wasn't barebutt at that hour somewhere or other. But Shaw had taken a dislike to him.

Fred saw Canterwell on the steps of Hospital Unit 2. He hadn't figured Canterwell out yet. People seemed to like him, though he was determinedly, consciously different. It was not just that he was a whittler. There he sat, shaving a piece of wood he'd gotten God knew where down to nothing. But more than that, he actually knew about Vietnamese history and culture, spoke something of the language beyond *du mama* and *chu hoi:* "fuck you, I surrender." He was a skinny South Dakota farmboy, a draftee, but everybody treated him with an odd respect. He had been good to Fred from the first.

"What's happening?" Fred said as he came up the gravel walk.

Canterwell looked up from his whittling. "Hi, Bower. Buddy of mine's torn up. I'm just taking care."

It moved Fred, that Canterwell would take care, that here, 10,000 miles from home, there were at least a few people who, when they heard that somebody had gotten blown away, would take the time to come and sit the deathwatch, just like they would for some high school pal who'd cracked up a car in the Badlands.

"Sorry to hear," Fred said.

Canterwell shrugged. "It'll work out, one way or another."

They sat there side by side in the heat. Choppers rattled in and out of the base while, in the distance, the jets out on air strikes whined and farted, setting fire to areas the size of Mockdon County, destroying hamlets as big as the town of Olinda, blowing up the highways and byways of a whole country bigger than Fred's home state.

Fred watched Canterwell whittle. The rough stick smoothed and then got smaller, narrower. The far end broke off, but Canterwell's knife kept up its easy stroking, as if pacifying, soothing, letting the wood go quietly, piece by piece, into an oblivion of splinters.

"That MP, Shaw, tried to bust me for drugs with my pants down last night," Fred said.

"Don't pay attention to Shaw." Canterwell eased the blade down his whittling stick. "Shaw's a dick. Everybody knows it. Even his CO. He likes to throw his balls around, but they don't mean shit. Who the hell cares about drugs around here?" Canterwell held the knife in the air and examined its edge. "Everybody giving you a hard time, Bower?"

He was surprised that anybody in this mean, male world would ask the question. He was cautious. Even with Canterwell, he didn't want to seem to bitch.

"I guess." He sighed. "I mean, I am cherry, you know? I guess it's only right."

Canterwell went back to whittling. He didn't speak for a while, the knife whispering down the wood. "It's not right, Bower. It's the way it is though. You'll be cherry till the next cherry comes in, and then he'll be the one who gets fucked." He turned to Fred with a bitter smile. "And you'll ream him out as good as Kirkpatrick or Eggleson or anybody else does you, you know that?"

Fred started to protest. The door behind them opened.

"Mr. Canterwell?" It was a woman's voice, soft, exhausted. The name had a falling sound, a sound that said hope had passed away a while before.

Canterwell stood up. "I gotta go, Bower. I know his folks."

Fred sat there for a while, in that awful heat that, even as the sun sank, showed no signs of forgiveness. He thought about what Canterwell had said. And in that instant, looking out past the wasteland of the base toward the distant and infinite green of Nam, Fred hated that prediction, as much as he suspected it was true.

5

"Bobbo's dead."

Swimming up out of sleep. China's voice in his head.

"Bobbo's dead."

The words filtering in, getting louder.

"Bobbo's . . ."

"What? What!" Scrambling awake. His sister there before him, thirteen, tears in her eyes.

"Bobby's dead."

"What did you say?" But clearer now: *Bobby.*

"Bobby. They shot Bobby Kennedy."

He stared at her. She looked utterly bereft, not like a girl who fussed with her hair and was dying to wear more makeup than the lipstick and blush she was permitted only on special occasions. She looked about six in her baby dolls, her face scrinched and tearstained, there beside her brother's bed.

"They killed him!"

In that instant, bolt upright in bed, Barry knew he should feel something other than what he felt, for all he felt was old. He was sixteen, yet what was in his mind was the moment he had been on the phone two months before — talking about a silly high school party with Kathy Jordan — when his mother walked in and said flatly, "They've shot Martin Luther King," and how, then, he had thought of his first autumn in Rhymers Creek, listening to the intercom in the industrial arts room in 1963, and all he knew was that, in his young life, there had been too much death.

He hopped out of bed in his underpants into the sticky June morning unembarrassed before his little sister and hugged her in a clumsy attempt at what he knew from movies was comfort.

"I'm sorry, honey. I'm so sorry," he said, though he never called her that. "It'll be okay."

China cried harder. Somewhere within Barry a little flicker of anger rose, for why should he feel responsible for the way the world was? Bobbo had not felt that just three years before. He had worried about dates and championships and making sure that Barry and China were all right and that his parents were proud. But then, it had all been different, and Bobbo was a Marine now, and overseas, and his dying was, this morning, the first thing that had come to Barry's mind.

The world that Bobbo had known at sixteen was already dead.

"It'll be okay," he said again, though he knew it would not be, now that they'd shot Bobby. "It'll be okay, China." Thinking, At least it wasn't Bobbo. It was bad enough it was Bobby, but if they lost Bobbo, it would be too much to bear.

The night before, China had wanted to stay up. She was gloating, for even the first returns showed Kennedy would win, and then, unless Humphrey pulled a fast one, it would be Bobby who got the nomination. At midnight, their father pulled the plug, telling them it was over and they could talk about it in the morning. He looked resigned, bewildered he could have raised two Democrats.

Barry glanced up, and there was his Pa in the doorway. He did not know how long he had been there. And in those eyes of a man looking upon his children, Barry saw the look he expected was in his own — that helplessness, that inability to make things better.

"Come on, kids," he said softly. "You'll be late for school."

Slowly, China pulled away and, still sniffling, pushed past her father, eyes downcast, and slipped toward her room.

"She'll be all right, Pa." Barry's own voice was rough.

"Okay." His father turned to go. "I'm sorry, Barry."

Alone, he sat back. His body ached. All the killing. All of it going on and on: not only in Vietnam but in the riots in the cities, on political platforms . . .

He bit his lip. They were shooting everybody. And soon there would be no one left, because everybody — rich and poor, important and not — would have been shot, till only the shooters were left to shoot each other.

✧

When they were all gone, Myrna sat down at the kitchen table and brewed herself another cup of tea.

It had been hard to make China go to school, but she had to. It was not just for the girl, who needed to learn that, when bad things happen, you go on, do your business, shoulder the hurt. Those were the lessons of Depression and war, of a scrabbling childhood and the loss of a husband before you really got to know him.

But, too, Myrna wanted her out of the house. She wanted them all gone, so she could be alone.

Ezra had gotten up first. She lay there, waiting for him to bring her some orange juice. He had done it since they were first married, for she was cranky in the mornings, whereas he had a resigned cheerfulness from the instant his feet hit the floor. It was from the service, he told her, when you had to be alert as soon as you awoke, when you were grateful the Lord had given you another day.

She heard him in the kitchen, and the subdued hum of the radio. It stopped, and there was instead the television in the living room. She waited a minute, a minute more, then got up and put on her robe.

She found him on the sofa, hands clutched between his knees as he stared at the screen. All she had to hear was the past tense as the announcer said, "Senator Kennedy was forty-two years old . . . ," and she knew what had happened.

The last week or so, everything had turned. There had been the letter from Bobbo, reminding her that something terrible was in progress, that an awful scarring had begun and she might not recognize the man who came back as the boy she sent away.

On Friday, there was Pincher Bowdin. That hit her doubly hard. She feared for Barry, who she was sure had been drinking at the party, who had lied about where he was going. Her boys had been good boys, and now, in a few days' time, both had started becoming strangers to her.

Then there was Pincher himself. Barry had told her yesterday, when she would speak to him again, that Pincher had been afraid, had asked about Bobbo and about the war. The accident, for her, inevitably brought back Robbie from twenty years before.

But it was all so strangely backwards. Her first husband had been to a war, and then, in a mean trick of fate, had died on the highway outside El Centro. Here was a boy — a friend of her son, more or less — who, rather than going to war, had tried to escape it by killing himself and had ended up maimed sure as if he had been cut in half by a Vietcong bullet.

And now this morning: her little girl dissolving in tears as her hero was murdered right at the moment of his triumph. As she and Ezra sat in the living room, they heard China upstairs. Her clock radio would have told her. They heard her shriek, and then there were her footsteps in the hall, running to Barry. Over breakfast, Myrna looked from one face to the next to the next, Ezra to Barry to China, glazed and disbelieving as her own must have been.

It seemed like just yesterday she had sat in the sunshine with Dora Coe, and they'd agreed the world was going all wrong. And, in mere days, it had taken a fearsome turn for the worse.

Before, it had worried her.

Now, she was scared to death.

THURSDAY

❖   ❖   ❖

1

Belva punched the disarm code into the alarm keyboard hidden behind the Keith Haring poster. She was tired of Keith Haring, frankly. Perhaps she was tired of the store. As she went to the stockroom to plug in the coffeepot, she heard the front door open and knew it was Marybelle.

"Yoo-hoo. Anybody here?"

Belva stuck her head out the curtain behind the counter. Marybelle, slightly nearsighted, smiled, squinted, paused. Then her face fell. She had obviously been hoping for Melva.

"Why, howdy, Belva," she said, mustering a halfhearted grin. "I stopped by Dunkin' and picked up some doughnut holes. Wanna share?"

The ritual had been repeated for years. Marybelle ran The Phone Store next door, a business maintained only by the skill of her husband, Heck, at installing illegal equipment and otherwise helping others evade the charges of Ma Bell. Marybelle sold an occasional cord or jack, even now and then a Mickey Mouse phone, but for the most part she sat in a store bereft of customers and ate.

She had discovered early on that Letting Loose was equally empty in the mornings, and the twins provided good company over her second breakfast. Both Melva and Belva watched their figures, which for Marybelle meant a half hour or so of conversation at the cost of no more than three or four doughnut holes, plus free coffee. Melva was the more indulgent. Belva found the woman a trial. Still, the morning promised to be slow, and the alternative was arranging stock untouched by human hands in the last two days.

"Come on in." She sighed. "Hold on and I'll get us some coffee."

She brought out two cups and a metal folding chair, the little wicker seat in the corner being no match for Marybelle's girth. Marybelle sat down and set the bag of doughnut holes — assorted — on the counter.

"So what have you been up to?" Belva said, picking a raisin-crumb ball from the bag.

"Oh, honey, I had a flu! A flu you just wouldn't believe . . ."

Belva scuffed her fingers together. This alone could take twenty minutes. Marybelle loved to talk about disease — congenital or contagious, transient or terminal. She was especially graphic where her own maladies were concerned. Belva knew far more than she cared to about Marybelle's battles with gout and assorted female troubles.

"But never mind that." Marybelle leaned forward with powdered sugar all over her lips. Belva had lost the thread of the conversation. "Do you know who's over in the Ramada Remington?"

Marybelle's brother, Win, was one of the hotel security people. Belva took a sip of coffee, trying to look interested. "Who?"

"Barry Carraway," Marybelle whispered.

For an instant, Belva simply stared blankly, reviewing her limited mental files of game show hosts and college basketball coaches. Carraway? Barry Carraway . . . Then it registered, the thin echo of another moment in her life.

She shrugged. "Well. So?"

Marybelle's voice was low with scandalized glee. "So, don't you think it's amazing he'd show his face? It's bad enough he's like he is. But those pictures. They can't even print them! He was in the magazines and everything. Win couldn't believe it."

Belva looked at Marybelle coldly. "Why?" she said smoothly. "Wouldn't you come home to bury your brother?"

Marybelle hurriedly — voraciously — popped two cinnamon doughnut holes in her mouth and didn't speak again until she had swallowed. "Well, yes. Of course. I mean that's why he's here, I guess. For the funeral. For Bobbo. But really" — her voice fell again to breathy naughtiness — "he must be wondering what people think."

Belva huffed a laugh, her tone even sharper than she intended. "Anybody who lives in New York City probably doesn't give a fat damn what we think about anything."

Marybelle grabbed another doughnut hole, in her eyes a tiny spark of rage, like that of a little girl whose joke has been ruined by some upright playmate. "Well, you're probably right about that, Belva," she said with insincere conviction. She dabbed her lips with a napkin. "You dated Bobbo Starwick way back when, didn't you?"

The skin on Belva's shoulders crawled. She could hear Marybelle later in the day: *Never got over him, I guess. Defended his little brother to me today, big as you please . . .*"

She took a deep breath. "Yes, I did, as a matter of fact. And it's certainly something I've never regretted." She lowered her eyes, with the effect, she hoped, of a truly crushing superiority. "I expect Wallace and I'll go to the funeral on Saturday. Bobbo was missing for so long, after all. Will you and Heck be there?" She caught herself self-consciously. "But of course, neither of you knew much about him, really. Except for what you read in the papers." It sounded unctuous and mean, which was precisely what she intended. "Well, honey," she added, "we'd better get on with the day, don't you think?"

Marybelle looked at her with a barely disguised resentment. "I guess you're right," she said, heaving herself up and grabbing the bag with the remaining doughnut holes. "Now, when you get to that funeral," she said as she lumbered toward the door, "even though we didn't know him, you give Barry Carraway and all the rest of his family our regrets, now, won't you?"

Belva smiled weakly as the door closed. "Bitch," she hissed.

✧

She might be, Belva thought, the only person in Rhymers Creek who had actually seen a Barry Carraway photograph, one of the photographs that had made him a minor sensation, famous or infamous. Not in a book. Not badly reproduced in a magazine or some hysterical brochure. But hanging on a wall. The print he had made. The way he wanted you to see it.

It was from a time in her life she did not like to recollect, from the one affair she did not like to remember — the one that had ended badly, the one in which she might truly have been in love.

The limousine had picked her up in front of the Pierre, wound slowly down-island to Murray Hill for Eve, then swept on to Wall Street to get Edgar and Michael. With the men aboard, they all had a drink in the car. They were due for dinner in Brooklyn Heights, and it was a few minutes before Belva looked intently out the gray-glazed window and said, "Aren't we headed in the wrong direction?"

"Oh, Edgar's dragging us off to some queer art show." Michael snorted. "How do you get roped into these fag things, anyway?"

Eve smirked at him and cuddled up to Edgar, who smiled sheepishly. "Lay off. It'll be fifteen minutes. But I promised Lydia. She says it's the most scandalous thing she's done yet."

At the gallery, there was the kind of reception Belva had grown to expect in the eighties: champagne flutes and icy bowls of crudités alongside brochures and discreet price lists. Belva was introduced to Lydia, and then, as the New Yorkers chatted, she wandered off to look at the work.

All of it was photographs. All of it was men. All of them were naked. Some were shocking, she had to admit. That somebody could do that with a fist! But many were beautiful. There was an exceptionally sensual series of a blond — well defined and massively hung — that she meant to ask about.

But then they were ready to leave, and she stuffed a brochure in her bag, and they were gone.

It was only late that night, back at Michael's, that she read it. He was on the phone, talking to someplace where it was day. There were always deals to be made after hours — after dinner, after dancing, after sex, after the drowsy pillow talk. It was not so inconvenient for her, given she was married and only in New York now and then. Michael was single as far as the state or the church was concerned. But he had a wife far more demanding than any woman could have been. He was married to making money.

She unfolded the glossy brochure on the glass and marble coffee table, massaging her feet as her eyes wandered over the reproductions hardly bigger than the gummed Post-its that littered Michael's nightstand. Here was something by the photographer who liked black men and leather. Here was one by another artist who apparently chose his subjects exclusively for their tattoos. There were a couple shots of the pretty blond she had liked, a slightly larger piece from a photocollage of what she assumed were pictures taken in gay bars.

She glanced only half-attentively at the explanation of the show's purpose, hearing Michael shouting in the bedroom. Two A.M. deal making was a loud and often unpleasant business. Her eyes skimmed the brief biographies of the artists: one from Queens and one from California and a Moroccan raised in Belgium and one from Rhymers . . .

She sat suddenly straight.

Rhymers Creek. Barry Carraway?

She shook her head in wonder. This sort of thing never happened to her, certainly not in New York. Bobbo Starwick's little brother.

She smiled. She remembered him: darker than Bobbo, shorter,

and so serious, always with a camera, even in high school. There was the business, she recalled, when everyone found out he was homosexual, something to do with the draft, but she had been spending a lot of time in Memphis that summer in the first, heady days of her engagement to Randy Ditmars, and the details had been sketchy for her even then, much less a dozen years later. Thinking about it, maybe someone at the country club had said something about him being a photographer — or pornographer? — sometime over the last couple years.

"Jesus." Michael came out of the bedroom, his tie open, looking drained. "I don't think even the Nips know how the Nikkei works." He glanced at the brochure. "Getting ready with a little beefcake?"

She snuggled against him. "I don't need pictures to get myself ready for you."

"You can look at them all you want. You'll never get the time of day out of them." He smirked. "Your hands aren't big enough."

"Don't be a pig!" She giggled. "It turns out I know one of the photographers. He used to live in Rhymers Creek."

Michael stretched and pulled her closer. "Jeez. You and Edgar'll both be out now, beating the drums for the queers. Come here" — he nibbled her ear — "we've got better things to do."

And she acceded. He was the most inexhaustible lover she had ever had, at least at first. He was better than a teenager: reloaded after only the briefest pause but with all the skill and staying power of a man. Perhaps even then she should have suspected how he got by with so little rest.

She spent most of the next two days with him, then met Melva at La Guardia and flew back to Rhymers Creek. Her twin gave her the silent treatment on the flight home, resentful about the *Cats* ticket they had wasted and the buying responsibilities that had fallen to her. It was a week before Belva even remembered to mention the show and brochure to her sister. And then, she forgot all about it.

2

From his hotel window, through the gray and wintry light, Barry looked down upon the Square. The Courthouse, now some kind of shopping complex, stood squat and respectable before the gathered oaks. The Rexall had become a frozen yogurt shop. I. J. Bannister's Garage and Esso had disappeared, and Harley's Hardware had given place to two eight-story brick-and-glass apartment towers.

He could see the bench where he had sat the night before. A police car had slowed as it made a lazy circuit of the Square. They had stopped him three times — or was it four? — in 1970, in those ten days he was back. He had forgotten what it had been like then, when merely the length of his hair was enough to invite suspicion, when from the mouths of many people, *hippie* was as good as *nigger* or *faggot*, and there were vast stretches of the country that he and his college friends saw as little more than enemy territory.

In his postmidnight meanderings, he had turned down Lafayette Street, stepping off the sidewalk onto the only slightly less treacherous grass — brittle with ice and then covered with snow. He walked a few blocks, approaching a gaggle of gingerbreaded bungalows he recollected as having slipped inexorably toward blight. In those days, they were occupied by a crazy quilt of others and outsiders: young families in from the hill country, blacks escaping the Archersville section down by the river or Tincup in Mockdon, single white men and women running from the respectable neighborhoods of Rhymers Creek or Littlefield and Henderson, the first hippies he had ever met. He remembered excursions here on Saturday afternoons to take photographs with serious, adolescent pretensions founded in Jacob Riis and Walker Evans.

But the pictures he most liked even then were not of the dirty-faced children behind pickets peeling and lolling like drunkards. Rather they showed the houses themselves, painted like psychedelic rainbows with the leavings of Harley's stock: a kelly green house next to a purple one beside an orange one. There was one on Ambrosia Lane that was most spectacular of all, with a brown porch, pink walls south and east, blue ones north and west, yellow dormers, and a violent red garage.

Now, at the corner of Lafayette and Ambrosia Lane in the soft glow of gaslights, all the houses shone white and perfect as the homes in a Victorian diorama. The moldings were probably more intricate than they had been when the houses were new, and landscaping was apparent even beneath the glaze of snow. There were no cars along the street, in accordance with the No Parking signs harmonious in iron standards black as stove polish.

The last time he had been here, the summer after his senior year, the street was littered with VW bugs and vans, chromed-up Mercurys, Cadillacs with fuzzy carpeting on the dash, even a couple of monstrous choppers gleaming potent and threatening. Tully had brought him, right to that phantasmagoric house where he loudly promised they would find chicks and dope.

Standing in the living room, where two kegs of beer sat in loose ice on the hearth, Barry felt ill at ease. Most of the people there he still thought of, despite himself, as grown-ups — people not just out of high school but married or divorced already, with real jobs and obligations: twenty-three, twenty-five. There were Negroes, hippies, unwed mothers, bikers, probably queers. He felt a desperate shyness he hoped might be mistaken for cool, a terror he would be revealed as callow, foolish, and a virgin to boot.

With time, though, with effort, he relaxed, had a beer or two, and finally danced outrageously with the hostess, Mariana González: plump and loud, less Mexican than the fantasy of a Muslim queen in the alcoholed imagination of a Rhymers Creek white boy. She took his arm and pulled him to the middle of the room, and they gyrated and jiggled and rubbed suggestively to scattered whistles and applause for all seventeen minutes of "In-a-Gadda-da-Vida."

"Nice moves," Mariana said as they slumped sweaty together after the last boom of the bass. "Maybe I can see you later."

She swirled away, but he felt a jolt up his spine as he imagined what she was proposing. He was not completely inexperienced. He knew a breast's softness in his cupped hand, the wet warmth of his fingers between a girl's legs. Yet it had all been fumbling, uncertain, quick, and confined. Perhaps tonight it would be different.

Tully wanted to leave at midnight. Barry resisted, though he did not tell him why. He was careful not to drink too much, both because he did not want trouble at home and because, so he had heard, too much beer could affect a man's performance. Mariana, meanwhile, had made out with two or three of the men at the party. Then he lost track of her, and he began to feel foolish, as if everybody knew why he had not left, and that a woman like Mariana would not waste her time with a boy barely out of high school.

"Here you are!" Suddenly she was beside him, and he could smell something strong and hot on her breath. "Come here, precious."

He leaned into her. Her tongue curled lazily against his, then along the inside of his cheek. He reached and pulled her to him.

"Come upstairs," she whispered.

He looked up. No one seemed to be paying much attention except Tully, wide-eyed alongside some girl Barry didn't know.

He grinned and followed Mariana.

She guided him through the kitchen and up a flight of rickety stairs. He could see nothing but the faint glow of a stick of incense. The air was thick with the scent of strawberry. He sneezed. Mariana hugged him and gave him another long tongue kiss.

Her fingers were fumbling with the buttons of his jeans, and his own were pushing her blouse up; then his lips were fluttering anxious across her breasts to her hard nipples.

"Oh. Ohhh. Slow down." Her mouth was against his cheek, and he could feel her smile. "We've got time, sweet thing," she said.

He willed himself toward some kind of control. They kissed some more, and he stroked her softly as she took off his shirt, then her own. Music throbbed through the floorboards.

Mariana pushed him toward a narrow bed against the wall. He collapsed as if in slow motion, pulling her beside him. Methodically, he acted out passages recalled from dirty books and locker room stories, from his own unsatisfied make outs: his tongue in her ear, along her throat, his fingers busy at her nipples, then dropping down to where her slacks were gone now. He felt clumsy and unskilled, but Mariana coaxed him along: "Be gentle. That's it."

Thoughtfully, cautiously, he continued, aware as he held her, nuzzled her, that it was going to happen now, how Tully would be proud of him, how he would not be a virgin anymore and could talk with that smug and easy knowledge of men. He would not have to worry now about being different. Weird.

His pants went down below his knees. She held him stiff in her hand, and he was afraid he would spurt right then. She guided him toward her, and — with a slow, steady pressure . . . a nudge . . . then an easy, wet glide — he was inside. Once there, it was all symphonic, rhythmic as a baton shafting into the soft moistness of her. He saw himself, as if from above now, his ass rising and falling . . .

It did not last long. Suddenly, without his really preparing for it, the shudder smashed through him, and he clasped Mariana in a crushing embrace as he felt himself grabbing and grabbing as he came.

He puffed, soaked with sweat, above her.

From downstairs, he could hear "Satisfaction."

✧

Barry did not know what had become of Mariana. He hardly knew what had happened to his friends. Tully was still here. China had mentioned in a letter a few months back that he had gotten married. But Kathy Jordan? Billy Peters? Pincher Bowdin in his wheelchair? How had those faces changed with twenty years and more gone by? Who was fat? Who was pretty? Who was happy? Who was dead?

He glanced out the window. What was China driving now? Probably some van, some sport utility vehicle, something sensible and suburban. She was sensible, after all, the one who had defied the family rule, who came to see him in New York when she was twenty, there on her college urban studies field trip. She had come again with her new husband when they were on their way to London for their honeymoon.

But after that, there was a life to make, children to raise, her own jobs and Doug's career. It had been a decade since Barry had laid eyes on her. And beyond all the responsibilities that tied her to home and hearth, certainly she too carried some resentment and bereavement from when, at merely fifteen, she went from only girl to only child in the space of less than three months, from having two older brothers to having none, neither dead and buried really, merely vanished: one somewhere in the jungles of Vietnam, the other in the jungles of New York; one missed and mourned, one renegade.

There in New York, on her first trip, he took her barhopping, a thrill for her at twenty. He was becoming a bit of a clone then, with a mustache and his hair cut close. He had even begun to work out. He was anxious to show her a good time in the big city:

sophisticated and jaded and a mite dangerous (though not too dangerous — she was his little sister after all). Late in the night, with her amazed that the bars stayed open till not two but four, she had told him, told him about that summer when her whole life had changed.

"There was never a word about you. I heard the fight. It came up the heat ducts, but I was afraid to come downstairs, and then you were gone. Nobody said anything. Mom stayed quiet for a week, and I was scared to ask what had happened. I found out from Laurie Fraiser, who'd found out from her brother, that you were" — she caught herself — "that you were gay."

The word sounded odd from her mouth, as if she were just learning it.

"I don't know that even then I cared very much, Barry. Some of my best friends are gay, in the drama department." This time it came out with easy assurance. *Some of My Best Friends Are . . .* It had been the title of one of the first pornographic movies he had ever seen.

"Then it was August, and I'd gone with Laurie and Melanie Morton out of Mockdon Plaza." China looked down at her hands, there in that loud bar on Seventh, and Barry almost stopped her, told her she didn't have to go on.

"We tried on clothes at Delaney's and flirted with these boys from St. Cyprian's and walked across the street to the Dairy Queen, and I remember that on the way home — we were in Laurie's convertible, her dad's FIAT Spider — we were listening to 'Make Me Smile' and I was worried Mom would be mad because I'd spent a fortune on a pair of Foster Grants." China shook her head, smiled ruefully. "I still can't listen to Chicago.

"When we stopped in front of the house, Daddy's car was in the driveway, and I knew something was wrong. Mrs. Renberg was out in front of her house, and she was looking at me, and she had her hand over her mouth. We were all laughing, and then suddenly Laurie and Melanie got real quiet, and I knew they knew there was something wrong, too."

China glanced toward the crappy band that was playing, and Barry understood that if she didn't she wouldn't continue.

"I got out of the car, and I didn't say good-bye. Mrs. Coe was standing in the screen door. And I knew it was Bobbo."

✧

The phone jangled. Barry let it go for a full six rings. It was going to hurt to see her.

He met her in the restaurant. Across the atrium, there in the weak January sun, she stood in soft chiaroscuro.

His throat constricted.

He raised his hand and, as she approached, was moving toward her as her own pace quickened, so when they came together in an embrace, it might have hurt. But nothing would have hurt as his arms enveloped her and he heard himself rasping: "China. China."

"Oh, Barry." He felt her face pressed hard against his shoulder.

He did not know how much time passed. When they looked again, people were staring. China giggled, and wiggled out of his arms.

"Let's sit," she said, and when that was done she whispered, "Before the day's out, Doug'll hear I'm having an affair," and giggled again.

He arched his eyebrows. "Given whatever reputation I've got around here, that really would be shocking."

They ordered lunch, and China caught him up on Rachel and Seth — "You know, those old family names Daddy loves have finally come back into fashion, so the kids don't feel so weird. But I still haven't found another China, or Barach either." She talked about Doug's practice, the house, her own projects.

"How're Ma and Pa?" he asked casually.

It brought her up short, and then she smiled. He realized how odd it sounded to her. China, like he and Bobbo, had called their parents that once, but after they came to Rhymers Creek, living in a smart subdivision where "Ma" and "Pa" sounded like the sort of thing hill people used, she had started saying, "Mom," "Dad," "Daddy."

"Pretty well, under the circumstances." They still had not discussed those. "They're excited you're here, I think."

Barry sighed. "Ma, too?"

After the first, appalled rage, it was their father who had tolerated if not accepted Barry. For their mother, it had been some terrible betrayal. It was Ezra who broke down and sent the telegram to New York that August of 1970. He had taken Barry's phone call, and had been taking them ever since. Myrna had written Barry, first sporadically, then rather religiously for the last decade. But not only had she not seen his face except in magazines and photos he sent but she had not heard much more than his "hello" in all those years.

China nodded. "Mom, too."

"That's good," he said simply.

The food came. At some point, they would have to say it, admit the absence at the table, the reunion incomplete, never to be had.

China set her sandwich down and looked at her lap. "It's too bad, you know, that it took this to get us all together again."

Barry could feel the expression on his face, skeptical and sad at once. He shrugged. "Maybe it was always Bobbo that kept us together. Things were never the same after he left."

"Maybe." It sounded like she was not entirely sure she agreed. "Even if he'd been around, it might not have made any difference."

From her friendly but neutral cards, the occasional phone call, the letters with pictures of the kids and all kinds of gradually less significant information, Barry had concluded that China was the least romantic of the family, the one who had least patience with grand gestures, most inclined to live and let live. He suspected she thought that, much as Bobbo might have loved Barry, he, even more than their parents, would never have accepted what he had become.

"Well," Barry said, "at least we've got a piece of him back."

She blanched at the sarcasm, and that made him feel guilty. But it was true, after all. Accurate. A piece. Pieces of Bobbo. That's all they would ever have. All they had had really since he went to war.

"I never understood," Barry continued, "what happened to him there. I used to talk to vets . . ." He paused. "I used to sleep with vets. And I'd ask them. I'd tell them about my brother. And they all seemed to know somebody who that happened to."

China shook her head. "I try not to think about what became of him. Not the dying part. That I've accepted. But before he died, when he kept signing up for another tour."

Barry tried to control his hands as they lay there on the table, the fingers playing with the edge, as if, by caressing the bare wood, he could somehow disperse the tension that he felt across his brow, even in his shoulders. "It was the drugs, I think," he said, though the way he said it made it clear he was not convinced. "He was doing ups and downs all the time. Acid when he could get it. Dope to relax. He'd speed out in the bush. He said the stuff was so good he could see in the dark."

"Even when I was fifteen, his letters didn't make sense a lot of the time." China took a sip of wine. "He'd write me on notebook paper. Or napkins. I didn't understand what was going on till I got to college. I was doing Quaaludes one Saturday, and I remember distinctly seeing every word I thought printed in the air like it was on a computer screen. And then I knew what had happened."

Barry sat there, marveling and chagrined. China on downers.

"Sometimes, Barry," his little sister said wistfully, "I think it would have been different — with Mom and Dad, I mean — well, if what happened with you and what happened with Bobbo hadn't come so close together. They would have had trouble with it, sure, but it might have blown over a lot quicker if we hadn't lost Bobbo so soon after."

He snorted a rueful laugh. "Do you think I hadn't thought of that? I know it wasn't easy for them. It wouldn't have been even if he hadn't been killed. Even now." He touched her hand. "I made my peace with that a long time ago."

"Have you called them?" she asked.

"Not yet." He took his hand back again. "I will. But I wanted to see you first. I had to see the town, and then you, and I'll call when I go back upstairs. I've got a lot of calls to make. Tully. Eddie Hammersmith. Is Kathy Jordan still in town?"

China looked grateful the subject had changed. "She got married ages ago. They're in Houston now. She came to visit a while back. Tully's still here, though. He got married. I think I wrote you about that . . ."

"Yeah. Old Mr. Chicks and Dope. I couldn't believe it."

"You're not alone. Marilyn, his wife, she's new in town. She'd have to be to marry Tully. Remember his little brother, Wellesley? He got married too, to Lila Mae Bower, Fred and Lonnie's sister, the one who was married to Eddie Petrowsky?"

He could feel it opening up, the void of years that separated him from those things China had absorbed as naturally as she would take in air. How strange: all these people he knew once — now bank vice presidents or in the Junior League or moved to California; some parents of children old as he was when he'd last set foot here.

There were other names — "Billy Peters?" "Married. Divorced. Married again. Three kids." "Eddie Hammersmith?" "County Prosecutor." "Pincher Bowdin?" "ODed. Back in the eighties, I think."

He felt that sad smile again. "It's been a long, long time."

The rest of the talk was small: the hotel, how he got lost on the way in, an evaluation of the rental car. She stayed until nearly one-thirty, then hustled away, dodging puddles on the sidewalk on her way to the parking lot as he waved from beneath the awning.

He had not asked her if she had been to the funeral home. It would not have been fair, given he had yet to make a visit. After she left, he realized even more viscerally what he had lost: the fifteen-year-old girl now well into her thirties, all her generation torn from her in a single summer. But she had made do, gotten along, married, had kids. Of all of them, she was the one who had done what a person — especially a person in Rhymers Creek — was expected to do. And no one really, Barry thought, would have appreciated her pain, their sympathies or antipathies directed toward their parents, toward Bobbo, toward himself. China was perhaps the bravest of them all. Faced as a teenager with inexplicable fates, she had made her way regardless, and he regretted — there in the sleet and ice of the town he had grown up in — he had not told her that.

3

Melva did not arrive until after two, in the midst of a sporadic mix of precipitation Belva did not even try to guess the nature of, which meant even more tree limbs were coming down. Blessedly, the weatherman was predicting a warming trend next day.

"Much business?" Melva asked as she stripped off her gloves.

"Unless you count Marybelle, which I certainly don't," Belva said, "not a living soul."

"You're too hard on her, Belva. She's not that bad."

"Anything you say, Mother Teresa." Belva shrugged and poured her sister a cup of coffee. "Actually, she did have one piece of news. Barry Carraway's in town. Win saw him over at the Ramada."

Melva looked blank, then, blatantly, as in a cartoon, her face lit up. "Oh. Bobbo's brother. The photographer."

"Right." Belva nodded. "I guess he got in last night. Marybelle could hardly talk, she was so scandalized."

"I don't know what she expected" — Melva hung up her coat — "though I guess he never has been back."

"It's sad if you think about it." Belva handed her sister her coffee. "You kind of forget what a time that was. That whole family just went to pieces in about three months' time. In the nostalgia stuff, they never mention how scary things were."

Melva clucked in agreement. "No kidding. And these days, you never know what little country's going to get itself in trouble. Just driving over here, on the radio —"

"I don't even want to hear about it," Belva said, hugging herself. "We finally get over the Bomb and look what happens. I get so tired of all those places that can't take care of themselves."

Melva shook her head sadly. "It makes me sick, especially with Jamie . . ." She took a sip from her cup and grimaced. "Bleh!"

"I put it on when I came in," Belva said defensively.

"No. No. It's okay." Melva wrinkled her nose and drank some more. "Barry Carraway. He graduated with Rhett, didn't he? Nineteen sixty-nine? At the Ramada. How in God's name had Win ever heard of him?"

"The newspapers, I guess. *People?* The *Enquirer?* He came up in all that stuff about dirty art a few years ago, remember? Win must have seen his name in the register. I don't think any of us would recognize him after all this time."

"I hardly remember him anyway," Melva said. "You saw some of his pictures once, didn't you?"

"Yeah. It's funny, I was just thinking about that."

Melva shrugged. "What were they like? There were a lot of tattoos, right?"

"No. No. Barry was the one who did the blond guy."

Suddenly, Belva felt an odd shiver, as something occurred to her that had never struck her before. The images, stored far away and never retrieved in her memory, flitted before her eyes: that beautiful, naked, blond man with a dreamy, naughty smile.

"In fact, you know," she said tentatively, wonderingly, "the man in the pictures. He looked a little like Bobbo."

As she sailed into the den from out of the cold, the first thing she noticed was the ring on the coffee table.

"Have you been into the beer again?" she snapped at Ross, sprawled on the sofa with his Walkman.

"Wha . . . ?" He raised one of the earphones.

"The beer!" she shouted over her shoulder, her momentum unbroken, pulling her coat off as she went.

"Huh?" he mumbled. "No. I mean . . ."

There in the closet, she had to smile. It was ironic that she, of all people, had raised a son incapable of a convincing lie.

"Your father may not be able to figure it," she said as sternly as she could, pointing at him as she turned, "but I wasn't born yesterday. You could at least learn to clean up after yourself."

She took a swipe at the ring with a Kleenex she pulled from her pocket, as Ross stood there looking perplexed and miserable.

"Jamie was here, wasn't he?"

He seemed stunned she knew. Teenagers, she thought, were so incredibly dense. They were old enough to think they were smarter than grown-ups but not old enough to realize there was little they could do that grown-ups themselves had not done long before.

"Yeah. Yeah, he was here," Ross said with a defiant innocence.

She sighed. She had little use for her eldest nephew, who had a smart mouth and a crafty mind. His interest in ballet, she had long ago concluded, was merely a ruse to keep his parents off balance, so afraid their boy was gay that they let him get away with anything.

"I swear, Ross, you let him lead you by the nose. I've told you to stay out of the liquor. You're grounded this weekend. Got it?"

He slouched off to his room, and Belva headed toward the kitchen. She hated playing the heavy, but, in that department, Wallace was no help. He was a good father, but discipline was not his long suit, even with Ross. With Leisel, he was hopeless.

She pulled chicken from the freezer and popped it in the microwave to defrost, then started some water boiling for the rice mix. She picked up the remote from off the toaster and turned on the television as she reached in the cabinet for the dinner plates.

On the news, they were talking about some new crisis. Where was it now? Eastern Europe? South America? Belva stopped, listened. It was strange how, in the last couple days, the threat of any new bloodletting was getting all mixed up in her head — maybe in Rhymers Creek's in general — with that old one, the one nobody could really forget. How strange it was to be haunted these days by Bobbo Starwick, so long gone and suddenly so present. Now, you could worry that boys young enough to be the sons that Bobbo never had, old enough to be your own, might be whisked off as peacekeepers or policemen to some country you had never heard of just as you had never heard of Vietnam years and years ago.

It was like the yellow ribbons that sprouted whenever somebody was missing or in trouble or some international incident loomed. Belva found it a stupid and irrational custom, based on a song she had never liked, and yet, there were times when, seeing one of those bows, her heart would suddenly ache at the desperate silliness of it. It went on year after year, all those years of supposed peace but with a little war here, a little war there, here a war, there a war — Cambodia, Iran, Nicaragua; Lebanon, Grenada, Panama. Kuwait and Somalia. It was like not stepping on a crack or not walking under a ladder, that the proliferation of yellow ribbons might generate some potent magic and bring those boys — and girls these days — back home, safe and sound. But down at Mason's Mortuary, there was, for Rhymers Creek, the reminder that all those who left did not return, or returned in a way that would not be wished by anyone.

4

They were back. They were back. They had all come back.

Nothing would stop them. Not beer. Not bourbon. Not Scotch. Not gin.

Goddamn you, Bobbo. Goddamn you. Goddamn you.

All the times. All the faces. Grunts and pogues. LURPs and SEALs. Kowalski, O'Rourke, Michelsen, Randolph, Glickstein, D'Angelo. Gómez, Ling, Washington, Lonewolf, Beaubien, Canterwell. McNeilly.

Eggleson.

There in the trailer. Out on the driveway. Plastic bags and aluminum boxes. All the careful years of burying them one by one by one blown to hell. And sitting on top of them, lying on top of them, leaning against them: dead guys and live guys and maimed guys and guys he never knew what happened to, buddies and those he had only seen once jostling and leering and just looking pathetic and sad and lost. Nothing could stop them. They kept coming, so Fred couldn't know finally what was happening; and sleeping dreams and waking dreams were all the very same and what he had seen and what he had only heard about and what he had merely imagined were equally real and equally remembered, vivid as his own face, and for the first time in a long time Fred thought he would go mad.

It was the noises first. He was in the truck, pulling out of the parking lot at The Watering Hole with a fifth of Wild Turkey and a pint of Gordon's and three six-packs of Carling's on special, a little buzzed already from the pint at the funeral home, half-ashamed of himself for crying there in front of Marco, in front of Bobbo. It was snowing harder now. The steering was dicey. Then there was the noise as he shimmied out onto the highway.

Fwack.

Something caught in the wheel rim.

Fwack.

A fallen branch, probably, slapping the undercarriage. *Fwack. Fwack.* It would fall off, break off — *fwack, fwack, fwack, fwack* — soon, it would be silly to try to stop and pull it off — *fwack, fwack, fwack, fwack* — because if he stopped before he got home he might not get started again and — *fwackfwackfwackfwackfwack* — *the fine red grit from the backwash of the rotors stung his cheeks and eyes and he tried to turn away at the same time a voice inside kept telling him* "No the road, the road, it's icy," and he gripped the steering wheel, leaning into it, bellowing at the top of his lungs:

> Fight 'em, Leopards,
> Bite 'em, Leopards,
> Claw right through that line!

to remind himself he was not there but here, that — *fwack-fwackfwackfwack* — he was not hearing or feeling or anywhere close to the rotors of a chopper roaring into the skies to return or not but in Rhymers Creek, drunk and on his way to his trailer, where he would be safe.

He got home by dint of the miracle that seemed always to get him there when he was smashed and of the branch that finally, when he turned into the park, must have snapped off so there was momentary but blessed silence as he skied down the gravel toward the haven of home. He lurched out of the cab and staggered toward the door with the sack heavy in his arms, fumbling with the lock and slamming inside and onto the sofa, where he dug out a beer first thing and popped the cap and drank deep.

He should have thought they would be waiting for him.

Kawhoom.

It was the wind. Just a blast of wind outside.

Kawhoom.

The wind.

Kawhoom.

The claymores. The claymores around the perimeter. Somebody was setting off the mines. They're coming. They're coming.

Kawhoom. Kawhoom!

"Hey! Hey! Mines! The mines!"

"Bower, you're so full of shit it's coming out your ears." Eggleson next to him, Ronnie Eggleson from Moline across from him at the table in the trailer, in the bunk there in the barracks. "It's the fuckin' mon-soon season. Thunder, you asshole. Thunder.

That's what we call it here in Nam. Ain't no fuckin' claymore. Jeez!"

Sheepish and scared at once, Fred there in the gloom.

Rustling. Rustling. Maybe that was the wind, the wind grown softer, whispering now through the ice-clad branches . . . Or Eggleson, kicking back the sheet, his boxers over his bunk, sitting up. "Here, man. Shit, have a smoke" — the dry rattle of cigarettes in a pack — "Got me all freaky-deaky now. Jeez, Bowery Boy, at least have a smoke with me."

Fred's fingers reaching, reaching toward nothing or toward that butt offered across years and miles and death. *Nooooo*, the voice whining like the wind in his head, like Eggleson's voice, *Nooooo*, but his hand keeps moving, on and on, forward, forward and so, back, back . . .

"Oh, wow. This is good shit, man. Here." The ember toward him. "Want a toke?"

Fred inhaling the stiff, sweet smoke.

"Jesus, we gotta steamboat this stuff sometime, Bower. Get it real deep and stay stoned for a week, man. Yeah."

"Yeah." Fred's own voice hoarse and dreamy.

Eggleson giggling. "You know what I heard today? Barton from the Cav, that redheaded guy, they had to go up and bring out some jars who'd gotten into bad shit. When they get out there, there's only half a dozen of the fuckin' jars on two feet, so Barton and the other chopper guys go out beatin' the bush for the guys who bought the farm or maybe are just fucked up. Anyhow, this buddy of his gives him a shout and . . . and Barton runs over and — Jeez, it's so incredible, man — there's these jars out in the jungle, both of them stiffs, there's this two of 'em, Christ." Giggling louder and starting to cough. "Christ, they're there on the ground and . . . and they're like sixty-nine, man. They're suckin' each other's dicks, man, and they got greased! It's just so fuckin' far out! Ha Ha Ha!"

Out of control now, and the cough sputters up full of phlegm. Both of them shaking, out of breath in the darkness.

And then Fred with his head in his hands. "Eggleson, damn it. Damn it. I'm sorry. So sorry." Reaching for the lamp switch.

In the light, he was in the trailer. Alone. He shuddered all over. It was happening. He had to sleep or it would happen some more. He opened the Wild Turkey.

Kcchh.

Just a vague hiss like dripping water.

Kcchh.

An icicle melting, the muffled plunk in the snow.

Kcchh.

"Firefight."

"Huh!"

"Out in the paddies somewheres. Little probe. Ol' dink likes probin' jes fine. Old Victor Charlie goose our ass all the time."

Some scary-looking spade from Marine Recon, Kirkpatrick's buddy: Mohawked; fine, white, parallel scars, three on each cheek.

"Only double vet I know." Kirkpatrick bragging that afternoon.

Fred shuffling requisitions. "He in Korea?"

"Bower, Bower." Kirkpatrick sputtering. "You are the most unhip . . . unhip dumbfuck I ever met, you know that!"

"Jesus, Kirkpatrick." Eggleson getting into it. "All those crazy-fucks in Recon are double vets, double-double vets, double your pleasure, double your fun, double good, double good double-mint twin vets. Christ, what a cumwad."

"Yeah, well, fuck you." Kirkpatrick sulking.

"Well, well, fuck you and your mother, too."

Later: "So, what did he mean a double vet?"

"Kirkpatrick's right, Bower. You are a dumbfuck. It's no big thing. I mean, it is, but it's not like it's that special."

"What?" Fred all exasperation.

"It means . . . well, it means that you, like, go into a village and find a girl — if you're lucky, a pretty girl — and you fuck her, you know, like rape her, and then you waste her."

"Waste her?"

"Kill her. You know. Jeez. No more boom-boom for mama-san."

Fred shaking his head. "Fuckin' sick."

"Hell." Eggleson sniffy. "Sometimes they waste her first. That's the sickos."

Still later, all of them with Kirkpatrick's buddy, out in the watchtower, there in the trailer, sprawled on the rough planks, sitting at the table, Fred wanting to ask, "Are you . . . ? Did you . . . ? Which did you do first . . . ?"

And he doesn't either time.

The room is swirling, and Fred can see where the cheap paneling is warping from the walls above the dining nook, but where the kitchen ought to be is that map: I Corps, II Corps, the Mouths of the Mekong. "Hoo-ey, Hoo-ey, Hoo-ey," says Michelsen, who is standing there now with Eggleson and Kirkpatrick and his wild Zulu buddy and McNeilly and Bremer have dropped over from next door with some guy Fred doesn't know whose name tag says Mobrey. And he sucks on that bottle, he sucks on that bottle like the teat of oblivion because he knows who is coming, who will come here and who he does not want to see, not now, not ever.

"Look, Bower." Eggleson's hand on his shoulder. "Look. You stay out of trouble, hear me!" His first weekend on his own. "I taught you right. Stay clear of the MPs, and watch the Recons and the LURPs because they got piss for brains and'll waste you as soon as look at you, and, when you're on the street, don't get stuck in a crowd of grunts 'cause Charlie loves to blow away bunches. You hear me?"

Fred nods, stupidly, the bottle at his lips. Just a quick black-out, that's all. Just a fast slide into dreamless sleep.

"You hear me, numbnuts?"

"Yes," Fred says, pathetic, hopeless. "Yes, I hear you, Eggleson. I hear you! I hear you!"

McNeilly laughs. It's getting crowded now. More of them coming: Randolph and Beaubien from the EMC and Gómez, who bit the big one on a resupply mission when he didn't even have to go along but was trying to get to Saigon quick because his sister-in-law was on her way to see his brother in Bangkok. Glickstein, who used to talk about the job his uncle had waiting for him in New York, and Canterwell from South Dakota. There is a din of voices, people in the back where he sleeps where he can't see. All talking, recollecting, reenacting the moments he had known them, seen them, passed them in the streets.

Gin all gone, and the bourbon low. In the cabinet by the door there were two swallows of Scotch and some piss-poor brandy left over from card night. Fred pulled it out. Oh, Jesus, please, let me sleep. Let me sleep. What day? What day? Is it day or night? Is it snowing? Is there sun?

Eggleson jiving with Kirkpatrick like some stand-up team: "Well, all right, foxy lady, are you experienced? Don't think twice, it's all right. Here I am, pride of man and born to be wild. Let me stand next to your fire, and shotgun satisfaction in the presence of the Lord and ten thousand light-years from home will make you feel like a natural woman. My magical mystery tour cures manic depression and California dreamin'. I hear a symphony, love child. Chances are, sooner or later, love is gonna win . . ."

Everyone is laughing. Randolph and Beaubien are setting up a free round and Kirkpatrick and Eggleson are giving each other the high five and they are all there in the EMC that has the map from the office and is in Fred's trailer and he is downing that brandy and laughing louder than anyone. No matter here that half of these are dumbfucks who got greased, and of those who remain, another half may be just like Fred, in trailers or apartments, this very night entertaining the very same crowd, and he wonders, fleetingly, how many parties he's attending though he doesn't even know he's there.

He brings the bottle down from his lips and turns to offer it to Eggleson, and then his hand goes to his mouth and he chokes and a stream of brandy flames out his nose.

They are hurrying. They are hurrying because they're late, and they jostle through the crowds that spill into the streets. Eggleson pulling Fred along, his hand gripping his shoulder.

"Michelsen'll tear us both a new asshole if we miss that friggin' bus. He told me. He told me he didn't want us both out here 'cause we'd get fucked up and I'd take you for some boom-boom. So not a goddamn word, you hear me?"

Fred silly and excited. And grateful, too.

"I talked him into it 'cause in a month I'm outta here and you gotta know the score. But if we're fuckin' late, we're both in a sling, and I don't mean arms, asshole."

They're half-running, and Fred is sure, in one instant, he feels something strange, some touch too intimate for a push or shove. He sees a boy, no more than ten, slide by, quick through the crowd like a snake through creek water. They're almost to the stop: a dozen Americans who need to be back on base — two Seabees, mixed grunts, some major, and what look like a couple of civilians.

"Jesus, I think we're okay," Eggleson says, and Fred is feeling his back pocket, where his wallet ought to be, and the old familiar lump isn't there on his butt.

"Oh, fuck, that little fucker!" he sputters, pulling his arm from Eggleson's.

"What the fuck!"

"That little bastard, back there." Fred blindly moving away, searching for the kid who got too close, who bumped him wrong, in that jumble of faces that are all the same to him, men and women, old and young. "Goddamnit! Goddamnit!"

Farther and farther. Eggleson shouting after him, "Hurry up. Hurry up. It's coming. Come on. Forget it! Come on!"

Grabbing blindly at any boy around him, shaking him, shouting, "Where's my wallet, you little fucker? Where's my wallet!"

And then the explosion.

People screaming, the force enough to knock them down twenty and thirty feet away, broken glass and a couple small fires. Fred stunned and stone still in the lurching crowd. Then, unthinking, pushing wordlessly, pushing harder than he has ever pushed, pushing beyond what he had ever pushed on the line of the South Mockdon High School Leopards, throwing people left and right, plowing forward, on to Eggleson. Eggleson.

One of the Seabees is decapitated. A civilian is laid out with a bloody stump where his arm used to be. The major doesn't move. One of the grunts is screaming, "Hail Mary, full of grace, blessed art thou among women, and blessed is the fruit of thy womb . . ." while next to him another growls, "Cocksucking motherfucker cocksucking motherfucker," distinctly, rhythmically, again and again and again.

Eggleson is opened up like a gutted fish, his whole chest split. Fred thinks, kneeling beside him, he can see in that bloody mass his heart beating, his lungs filling and then voiding themselves of air. There is a terrible smell of burn and blood and shit. He reaches for Eggleson's hand.

"Ronnie," which he has never called him before. "Ronnie."

Eggleson's face shimmers with his own gore. He can barely speak. "Noooooo," whines out of his lips. "Nooooooo." Like a winter wind through ice-clad branches, like a ghost already. "Noooooo."

Fred no longer knows if he is awake or asleep, whether he drinks for real or there is only a phantom bottle in his hand. Is it Wednesday, Thursday? Night or morning? Eggleson lies a bloody mess on the table. The dead and alive crowd around and more come forth from the bedroom and Fred can hear the *Fwack-FwackFwack* of the rotors and the *Kawhoom!* of claymores and *Whomp!* of mortars and *Kcchh! Kcchh!* of single shots and the castanet rattle of automatics growing closer and closer.

Then through the windows and in the doors, up through the floor, come coffins and body bags, one after another after another, piling up in the living room and straining the walls and the ceiling. Endless, hundreds of them, thousands, like the brooms in *Fantasia*, like the cells of some creature aborning. The ceiling shatters and they rise toward heaven, shimmering aluminum and olive plastic, higher and higher, and, finally, as Fred, terrified, looks toward the peak of that mountain of corpses, there is Bobbo Starwick, Bobbo resplendent, Bobbo shattered and scorched, shape-shifting every second, leering down regnant, having dragged Fred back to the worst moments of his worst dreams, shouting triumphant across the years from the realm of the dead, from where he died in the northernmost quadrant of that mysterious map, laughing and weeping at once: "Victor Charlie. Victor! Charlie! I Corps. I. Corps."

HOMECOMINGS

✧　✧　✧

1

When he stepped off the Trailways, he was on a mission, and, though nobody knew it, his bridges had already been burnt.

Ten months before, Barry had boarded a bus headed in the opposite direction, rocking east to college — that school in New Jersey for which a picture-taking boy from Rhymers Creek represented a purebred exotic, worthy of loans and scholarships. Those first few weeks away had not been easy. Barry's roommate, Kip, and the others on the hall were prep school boys or those from eastern Catholic highs denied admittance to Dartmouth or Amherst or MIT. To them, Barry talked funny and had strange tastes in music. They did not like his photos much: sober, gritty, black and white. Their fascination with frats and football and the girls' school up the road, St. Mary of Bethany, did not attract him.

But Barry made an effort, made do, this time with no Bobbo there to help him. He put away the records Kip and his lacrosse buddies disapproved of and learned to like Procol Harum and the Moody Blues. He went to dances, dated a couple of girls from St. Mary's, helped the fellows in the dorm with Spanish homework. And so he achieved a modus vivendi with Kip and his friends, thrilled at their butt-slapping camaraderie, so like what had surrounded Bobbo three years before. There was, too, disquiet in that thrill, a quiver inside him before the foulmouthed, hard-bodied beauty of them.

It was politics, however, that proved his salvation. It was the great autumn against the war, and he, within days of his arrival, was part of and unofficial photographer for the Student Mobilization. The leaders liked him, that kid from far away, who took good pictures and had one credential none of them could boast: a brother in Vietnam, sucked into the killing machine and spat out on the other side of the world, rifle at ready and automatoned by screaming sergeants and opiated grass. They assumed Bobbo had been drafted. Barry did not disabuse them.

The lacrosse team, meanwhile, introduced him to the PATH — the trains slinking, worming through the tunnel from the marble-floored, copper-sheathed Lackawanna station in Hoboken; squealing squirming under the Hudson toward Wall Street and Christopher and Thirty-fourth. Kip and the others set off on drinking expeditions, Barry tagging along, slight and a little wary amid their square, bulked energy.

Each time he went he was more intoxicated: the vastness and noise and towers soaring; tumbling along sidewalks thronged and alive with flash and grit. The smell of electricity in the subway and his first roasted chestnuts and the sinuous, threatening geysers from the steam pipes beneath the streets. As autumn began its slow wane, again and again, after the Moratorium meetings, after hours in the darkroom, after the reading was done, the paper postponed, all alone, he would stand in the tunnel tight as a catacomb, waiting for the train like a toy that would take him from America to New York City.

Mid-October, there was a rally and a Walk for Peace around the campus and into Hoboken. The looks from those trapped on the street as the students paraded glinted with fury. There was the occasional boo or catcall, but mostly grim-lipped, angry silence. Still, for Barry and the others, it had been good, though merely a practice run. Before the day was over, Barry went to the commons room, where the Moratorium Committee was huddled, discussing what had been learned and might be of use in the Great March.

A month passed. His excursions to Manhattan slacked off as he spent more and more time with his friends in what he now called the Movement. He read Marcuse, Trotsky's *Literature and Revolution*, and met, with childish wonder, student shock troops from the Columbia uprising the previous spring. He spoke up in committees, distinguishing strategy from tactics, mastering the rhetoric of the immense and decentered general staff mobilizing for invasion.

On the twelfth, at lunch, Kip took his arm. "I've been doing some thinking," he said. "Look." He handed him a postcard, addressed to his sister at Stanford.

Dear Barb, it said, *I am going to the Moratorium March in Washington. Do not tell Mom and Dad till I get back. Love, Kip.*

Barry laughed and hugged him. "Right on!" he said, and for the first time, the words sounded genuine when they came out of his mouth.

✧

They were riding the bus to Washington through the chill November night. Others were driving, hitching, taking the train. Barry sat next to a girl from St. Mary of Bethany, Pamela from Pasadena, redheaded and clear-eyed. Her credentials were impressive: she claimed already to have been expelled from a tony girls' school for activism, though others suggested meanly it had merely been for drugs. Barry sensed she had sat next to him purposefully on this trip, a notion reinforced when he awoke about four to find her snuggled against him closer than might be accidental. But sweaty in his coat in the overheated bus, he did not give it much thought, too flush with righteousness and dread as someone in the back with a joint and a guitar softly sang "I'm a Liberal" and "Alice's Restaurant" complete.

In the bright, cold dawn, stiff from the trip and with a mouth full of cotton, he pulled out his camera and began to take pictures: the faces of friends and Kip leaning against the bus and then the masses behind and before them from Swarthmore and

UNC and Oberlin and SUNY-Buffalo. His shutter clicked, again and again, in the hope that roll on roll of film might capture his wonder as they gathered from all over the country — or was it the world? — this young army met not to make war but to end it. Thousands upon thousands shuffling serpentine down the avenue until finally they claimed they were a million strong with another half million a continent away in San Francisco, snaking past monuments and temples of governance, chanting and singing — "All we are saying, is give peace a chance"; "One, two, three, four, bring the troops home, end the war!" — for hours and hours in a parade of desperation and renunciation, of anger and mourning and defiance. There were hand-lettered signs and slick reproductions of the cover of a new paperback edition of *Johnny Got His Gun*; paint-spattered banners: WITHDRAW NOW; NOT ONE MORE AMERICAN DEAD. And flags: American flags, Vietcong flags, anarchists flying black and communists flying red, a yellow-and-white one for Another Mother for Peace. Monitors lining the avenue wore armbands, and the Progressive Labor people seemed to have been dressed by the Gestapo. And all along the route were pigs — the word that now came off Barry's lips as smooth as spittle — grim eyed and uniformed, riot batons at ready.

He was afraid. They were all afraid. Before the day was out, not far from the Capitol, Barry tasted his first tear gas, drifting over, they told him, from the showdown between Yippies and pigs at the Justice Department. But even so, he felt a growing exultation, a stunned, warm certainty that this was making a difference, that history was with them, that they really might indeed, all million of them, end the war. And, lolling by the bus in the chill, early dusk, tired from marching and cheering and chanting, he realized if only they could do that, then Bobbo would come home.

They were writing letters. Barry dealt in secret with the envelopes he had learned to pull from his mailbox and slip with a magician's sleight of hand among his notebooks: Bobbo reupping;

Bobbo's rambling evocation of another firefight; Bobbo's fury at faggot hippies stabbing him and his buddies in the back, who, when he returned, he promised to waste as easy as he wasted slants.

Barry wrote back about drugs, a subject Bobbo adored, a little about studying, a great deal about girls from St. Mary of Bethany, raiding the boasts of Kip and his lacrosse buddies to convince his insatiable brother of his prowess as cocksman while his un-easy desires — ignored, denied — shadowed him more and more. Bobbo asked him to send pictures — "Hey, big photo man" — of his girlfriends, naked, with their legs spread: "Tell them you got a hot-cocked Marine bro itching to slam it right home and keep it up till they scream!"

Barry clipped pictures from *Playboy* and sent them to Bobbo, who told him they were boring; so then, on Forty-second Street, he would buy with a mix of bravado and humiliation the randi-est magazines he could find: hard-flash beaver shots that even Kip found disgusting when he accidentally discovered the scis-sored remains of one in the trash. Barry told him that Tully Coe had asked for them, unable to admit that they were for his brother in the fields of fire.

If they could only end the war, maybe they could save him. Barry felt his brother falling away; ever worse since earlier in the year, when his parents described that trip to Hawaii, when Barry knew what was happening was far more horrible than their strained, vague comments could convey.

They rode back from Washington, exhausted and exhilarated. Pamela sat next to him again, for which he was more than happy: she was pretty, she was smart, and they had politics in common. Too, Barry had learned she had a reputation. He slipped his arm around her, and by the time they were through Philadelphia, his hand was up her blouse and hers was down his jeans. They made out passionately among the sleepers and dozers and other cou-ples similarly engaged. When he got off, she promised to get a ride down from St. Mary's as soon as she had showered and slept for an hour or so.

When Pamela arrived that afternoon, Kip smiled knowingly and said he needed to check his mail and go to the library. Barry put on James Taylor and pulled the remains of a jug of wine from the closet. They talked a few minutes — about the March, about school, about how she had been on the Pill since she was fifteen. Then, they were on the bed, jeans and shirts crumpled on the floor, nakedness stroking nakedness. It was different than with Mariana. Lazier. Less urgent. Pamela had a fine, soft kiss that made him so dreamy he could not tell if it was her lips or the wine that caused his high.

It did not take long.

"That was fun," she said, and in half an hour left.

It was not until an hour after that Kip returned. Barry was still on the bed, the blanket thrown over him, elated that he had done it a second time, that now he might have a girlfriend to flaunt in front of Kip and the lacrosse team. Yet he felt a slushy disappointment. Was it that woman's touch that had driven him to release, or was it his own vision of himself, locked in the act of love?

"So how was it?" Kip said, dropping his books on the desk.

"Great. Really great."

"I hear she's a pretty hot chick." Kip smiled. "Responsive?"

"Yeah." Barry nodded, anxious for approval at the same time he did not like the thought that Kip knew others — maybe others he himself knew — who had slept with Pamela.

Kip was changing his jacket. "Gotta go. I'm taking Madelyn O'Conner to dinner. That tall brunette? We'll see if I can get some, too." He winked and headed for the door, then stopped. "Oh, take a look at this." He reached in his pocket and handed Barry a postcard.

Dear Kip, it said, *I am going to the Moratorium March in San Francisco. Do not tell Mom and Dad till I get back. Love, Barb.*

Barry laughed.

"Just goes to show," Kip sang as he hustled out, "the times to-day are a-changin'."

✧

At Thanksgiving, Pamela flew to the West Coast. Barry was hurt. He had called her a half dozen times but only caught her once, when she claimed she was studying for a big physics test and couldn't talk. He sulked. As Kip left for vacation, he said, "Look, she's a good lay, but that's it. Now, don't you want to come with me?"

Kip had invited him to King of Prussia, and others had offered the long weekend at Paramus and Hartford. West Virginia, Barry had decided, much less Rhymers Creek, was too far and expensive to get to for the holiday. Since now he had a slightly broken heart, it seemed better to stay on the deserted campus to nurse his wounds and feel neglected. Wednesday, he tried to read his economics assignment with minimal success. The next morning, he told himself, he would go to the Macy's parade, but he drank the Scotch in Kip's underwear drawer and woke up too late. The cafeteria served processed turkey and canned cranberry sauce. He sat with a dozen other people from too far away and realized he neither knew nor cared for any of them. He left his slice of pumpkin pie and went to the darkroom to develop more pictures from Washington.

There, in the whorish light, it hit him. He was alone. None of his friends was around. He could do anything he wanted.

At a quarter to four, he was on the PATH.

✧

He was walking down Sixth Avenue, just below the Women's House of Detention. In the twilight, the street had the sad, deserted feel of holidays. His hands in his pockets and his collar up against a weak, wet breeze, he stopped occasionally at shop windows to look at things he could not afford.

Approaching the bend in the Avenue at Carmine, he noticed

someone scoot past him, long haired and lightly jacketed. Barry had paused in front of a boutique he didn't remember being on this block when he realized the man had stopped at the next storefront. He felt a vague tingle, and, suddenly, his breathing was shallow. With exaggerated casualness, he stepped back from the Levi's and patterned vests, and, leapfrogging the next set of windows, planted himself in front of the display that followed.

Plumbing supplies.

He stood there, contemplating plungers and showerheads, as the longhair sauntered up next to him.

"Your drain clogged?"

Barry could feel himself blushing. "Ah, no. No."

"Got a light?"

He turned, struck a match. He saw a face not much older than his own, olive skinned with vast, dark eyes and hair shuffling to his shoulders like fine cedar shingles. The man had the droopy posture of New York cool and a sweet, pouting mouth.

They started together down the sidewalk.

"My name's Angelo. What's yours?"

"B . . . Bob," Barry said.

They shook hands. Angelo belched.

"Fuckin' turkey. I hate fuckin' turkey. I spent the whole day in Brooklyn — sisters, uncles, nephews. Drives me nuts. I told them I had to work tomorrow, which I don't. You got a job? Bob?"

Angelo knew he had lied about his name. "Sure, I'm a . . . a photographer. Industrial photographs. Brochures, trade fairs." Barry was amazed at the plausibility of the invention.

"Nice." They had walked almost a block together. "Want to smoke dope?"

Barry stopped. He willed himself not to consider what else the invitation might mean. "Yes," he said distinctly, too loud.

It was a walk-up just off Fourteenth. The cramped room was appallingly hot, the radiator whistling like a teakettle. Angelo began stripping off his clothes before they were through the door.

"Don't get no fuckin' heat for a fuckin' month and then you

can't turn the fuckers off. Here" — he flipped Barry a pair of gym shorts — "you might as well get comfortable."

By that time, Angelo was naked to the waist. Barry, his hands shaking, began to undress. He was so nervous he did not even see Angelo drop his pants and slip on a pair of Fordham trunks.

"You like the Velvet Underground?"

"Sure. Yeah." Barry had never heard of them.

The music started, driving and vaguely sinister. Angelo lit strobe candles. There was a sofa in the room, and pillows, and very little else. Barry sat down, and Angelo tumbled alongside the couch. He produced a Zippo and a pipe and fired up a block of hash, pulling the smoke in greedily. He pressed it to Barry and shot the flame of the lighter deep in the bowl as he leaned into Barry's knee. Barry puffed the pipe, half rigid, but he did not move.

The dope was strong and the music loud. Barry felt the rich, greasy smoke billow through him. His muscles softened, and, after another few tokes, he slid off the couch and onto the floor. Angelo kept passing the pipe. Then, his palm floated up Barry's thigh, as on the stereo a strange, flat voice purred, "I'll be your mirror."

Barry heard the pipe clatter to the floor, but the air now smelled sweet with heat and hash and a dark, Italian funkiness heavy in that closed Thanksgiving room. The orange light of the strobes sputtered. Angelo's hand was in the crotch of Barry's shorts, rubbing in languid circles. As he ran his tongue soft on Barry's neck, Angelo slowly pulled up the leg of Barry's trunks, slipped his fingers inside, and pulled him into the air. He leaned over, put Barry's cock against his lips, and kissed it.

Barry let out a single short cry of either delight or resistance, followed by a breath sharper, deeper, than he had ever drawn before. Through a fog of hash and desire, Barry felt Angelo slipping his shorts down and off and his wet, warm mouth siphoned him toward his throat: thorough, down to the root.

They were on the floor, Angelo's raw hardness rubbing on Barry's belly. Barry knew he needed him, badly. Desperately.

Angelo moved down his body, turned him over.

"Man," Angelo whispered, "I want to fuck you."

"No."

He could not let it happen. He could not let it, and yet he felt the pressing against him, to take him, to make him what he was, what he could not admit, in Rhymers Creek, in New York City . . . No.

"I'm going to fuck you."

Definite. Each word pronounced.

Yes. Please. Barry spreading himself in a dope-fueled fury. "Yes. Please." Aloud now. The oily, sweet touch of spit on that rosebud wanting. "Please."

Then Angelo, pressing. Pressing.

"No. Ow! No. Please. It hurts. It hurts!"

"It'll hurt a little while. But then, it will be wonderful."

Angelo thrust forward.

"Oh, God!" An all-appalling fullness and then Barry moaned, enchanted, horrified to feel Angelo, entire, deep inside him. "Fuck me. Fuck me!"

And Angelo begins to rock. Soft. Soft at first. Then harder.

And Barry cannot be stilled. "Oh, yes. Oh, yes."

A million miles from Rhymers Creek. In New York City. A beautiful Italian man within him.

"Oh, yes. Oh, yes." Crazy. A whole naked void of wanting. "Yes. Oh, yes." Possessed. Desired. Released. "Yes."

Angelo's mouth on his neck. "Oh, man. Yeah, man!"

"Oh, please. Oh, please. Oh, yes."

2

Belva stood in front of the 3-D mirrors at Delaney's, admiring how the back of the dress plunged toward her hips. It was really about the only elegant thing she had seen all day. She twirled a bit, watching what there was of the skirt billow. It was extremely short, but she did have good legs, after all. With the evening wrap, with her hair up, it would make precisely the impression she wanted.

"You don't think it's too risqué?" Belva said to the saleslady. Yvonne, if she remembered right.

"Not at all," Yvonne purred. "For the kind of function you're attending, it should be perfect."

"So, what about you?"

Melva sat tightly on a velvet bench. "It's nice, I guess."

"Nice like an orange or nice like a Buick?" Belva stomped her feet. "Lord, Melva, I should've come with Sally instead."

"It's fine." Her sister shrugged. "Just dandy."

"Perhaps you'd like to discuss it between you," Yvonne said smoothly, then glided away.

Belva smiled after her, then turned back to Melva. "So, what's with you?"

Melva sighed. "Oh, nothing. If you like it, get it."

"No. I won't. I won't," she huffed. "I've had it!" She flounced toward the changing rooms. "Just don't ask me to get off on your fun next time, okay?"

Behind the curtains, she calmed down. She did like the outfit, and she could simply come back tomorrow and buy it. Nobody would snap it up in the meantime. It wasn't what you'd wear to any "function," as Yvonne put it, in Rhymers Creek.

The business with Melva did get her goat, though. Four years at different colleges had made them even more different than before. It wasn't that Siegerford was Berkeley or anything. But, in the last couple of years, at least it felt like part of the twentieth century. Melva's Baptist nuns' camp in Texas was enough to curl Belva's waist-length hair. At Millman, according to Melva, there had not been a single antiwar demonstration. Boys were still restricted to the visiting rooms of the dormitories. Girls were under a midnight curfew. Chapel was mandatory, drinking was on the sly, drugs were nonexistent. They even dressed for dinner.

Every summer, when they were home, it got worse. Melva had

gone out with the same man for three years before they slept together.

"Twice? Twice!" Belva had exploded. "You finally go to bed with someone and the best you can do is two times in a semester!"

"We don't have the privacy you do at Siegerford." Melva adopted a prissiness that implied she found her sister's shock at best impertinent, at worst evidence of some nymphomaniacal obsession.

"You are on the Pill, aren't you?"

Melva had horror all over her face. "Well, of course not. What would Bill think if it looked like I was planning it?"

"You've only been dating since you were sophomores. You'd think it would have entered his mind you might be considering it. Lord, you used something, didn't you?"

Melva stiffened. "Of course. Bill . . . he took care of that."

"A true Baptist gentleman, that Bill," Belva snapped.

She had her jeans back on and was smoothing the evening dress on its hanger. It really would become her, and she was determined to make an impression in Memphis. Belva had figured that her mother would disapprove of this excursion, and Melva was obviously in league with her. She was glad she had had the foresight to wheedle Daddy into agreement before she spread the news.

It began innocuously enough.

"Now, it's only a week. And Randy's counting on me."

"But, honey, couldn't you just go for the party?"

"Mother, I told you. The Ditmars are doing it like they would have if they could have afforded it twenty-five years ago — a rehearsal dinner, the repetition of vows at the church, the reception. And then they're going on a honeymoon."

"So, after Saturday night, they won't be in Memphis?"

Belva realized she had talked too much. "Well, no. But there's the cleanup afterward. I shouldn't bug out when the fun's over, now should I?"

"Why, of course not." Her mother stared at her with baleful skepticism. "Belva, you know I liked Randy from the first time I met him. He's a nice boy, and you think — I repeat, think — that he's going to pop the question. But he is a boy, and all boys want one thing. And you better be awfully careful about giving it to him."

✧

Belva spun out of the dressing room and handed the dress to Yvonne. "I need to think it over a little. But I am tempted."

Yvonne smiled indulgently. "Of course, Miss Beauford."

Melva was looking at the panty hose on sale.

"All right, let's go," Belva snapped.

Melva put on her put-upon face, and they walked to the car.

✧

That night, while Belva was reading an old *Seventeen* she'd found in her closet, Melva came across the hall in her nightgown.

"I'm sorry about today." She thumped down on the bed.

Belva shrugged in her chair, not looking up. "No problem."

"But Mother worries so much . . ."

"Oh, for heaven's sake!" Belva said irritably. "You'd think I was spreading my legs for every truck driver who came down Route 9. I'm probably going to marry Randy."

"Do you really think so?" Melva seemed torn between doubt and excitement.

"Well, of course. One of the reasons I want to go to this silly anniversary thing is because I think it might, just might, put him in a frame of mind to ask me."

That was partially true. They had talked speculatively about what it might be like to go through life together, and several of their friends were already engaged. She did indeed believe his parents' wedding reenacted might convince Randy to go down on bended knee. Still, if all her visit meant was partying and a chance to wear some expensive new clothes, plus four unchaperoned days of Randy, who was gorgeous and fun to be with and appropriately named when it came to sex, she would be perfectly content.

"Well, I hope you're right." Melva sighed. "He is nice, Belva. I really do like him. And he can certainly keep you in style."

"That was catty," Belva interjected.

"You know what I mean." Melva actually sounded wistful. "It's just that, well, you always had a taste for good things, and I think the Ditmars have the kind of money that could really make you happy."

Belva winced. Certainly, she and Melva, Rhett and Tammy had never wanted for anything. Their father was shrewd enough and lucky enough to have made a tidy profit selling out the family business to Redfordshoe of Los Angeles, and to parlay that into a none too taxing living in real estate and investments. But theirs was small-town money, not even one of Mockdon County's larger fortunes. Not a fortune at all. But the Ditmars of Memphis. That was another story.

Belva got up and sat down on the bed next to Melva.

"Look," she said, "I know you mean well and Mother means well, but it is a little silly. You know that Randy and I have been sleeping together for more than two years" — she raised her hand to still Melva's objection — "and Mother would never admit it, but she knows it, too. She thinks that people will talk about this trip, but, Lord, it's not nineteen fifty-five. There's certainly enough going on here to keep everyone gossiping without anybody even wondering where I've gone. Most people don't even realize we're home from school yet."

"I guess you're right," Melva said sadly. "It really is no big deal anymore. You know, sometimes I think what's really bothering me is that you are going to marry Randy."

"What?"

Melva rubbed a palm over the back of one hand. It was a distinctive, nervous gesture she had had since she was a little girl. "It's not Randy especially. I've thought about it ever since you went off to Siegerford. You know how they talk about it, with all those boys' schools around. What did *Playboy* say — 'Free spirits beware, this is the ultimate MRS factory . . . '?"

"How did you know that?"

"We're not totally isolated at Millman." Melva snorted. "Anyway, I was afraid, once you went there, you'd find somebody and marry him, and then we'd be apart and it wouldn't be like it's always been."

Belva felt a twinge, a premature but certain pain of separation. Melva was right. Randy Ditmars would have no place in Rhymers Creek.

"But, Mel," she said softly, "I mean, the same thing could happen to you. You might move off with Bill to Tampa . . ."

"Tallahassee," Melva corrected. "I know. But, even when we were in high school, I'd think about how you'd probably never find the boy for you here, somebody you could really care about. The only time I thought different was when you were dating Bobbo Starwick."

Her stomach clenched, but Belva said nothing. She had put the memory of that box away as soon as she came back from the infirmary, and she had not mentioned it to anyone in Rhymers Creek.

She forced a laugh. "Honey, that was plain old puppy love. Besides," she said harshly, "like you said, no Vietnam Marine would be able to keep me in the style for which I'm intended, now would he?"

❖

That night she slept badly. Snuggled in her childhood bed, despite her best efforts, she could not chase away what Melva had said as, in her mind, the images of Rhymers Creek and her own family and Randy Ditmars and, yes, after long repression, Bobbo Starwick crashed and collided and faded in and out.

She was not a bad girl, she knew that — not some Cindy Nelson down the hall, who Randy and his frat brothers called "See-see

Bang-bang"; not some Mary Muldoon, who'd taken on half the defensive line their senior year in high school. Certainly, though, if her mother knew half of what she had indulged in these last few years, she would have been convinced she had raised a whore. Perhaps that was all sheer hypocrisy. Perhaps, when her mother was young, everything that was taking place now was taking place. It was simply that no one would talk about it. But she could not be certain. Sometimes, Belva felt like some frontier trailblazer, the kind of "new woman" they were talking about in the magazines: not Linda Pearson with her pageboy hair and dumpy sweatshirts and questionable desires, not Roxy Lindberg always hitting the books or the streets with picket sign in hand, but one determined to seek her own pleasures, one who could be a wife and mother without falling into the mindlessness she so often associated with her mother and her contemporaries.

Yet, standing at the border of that brave new world was not all that comfortable, and, at least tonight, she found herself almost envying Melva's quaint relationship with fumbling, Florida Bill — so gawky and shambling beside Randy Ditmars that she had been embarrassed for her twin when both boys had visited simultaneously the previous summer. There was little question that, at Millman, Belva would have been expelled within a semester, but still, the peculiar safety it offered — a staid, patriotic, and devout place where girls were chaste and oh-so-discreet and boys were clean living and true — did strike her as much less burdensome than all the freedom and responsibility her own life the last four years had presented her.

Melva, Belva had no doubt, loved Bill, or, at least, she never questioned that she did, while she herself, before the endearing hunk of her Randy, still found it possible to ask whether the admiration and longing and flat-out lust she felt was anything deeper than the desire she might feel for some sexy car or that dress at Delaney's. It had been so easy to dismiss Bobbo Starwick, and yet, could she truly say her feelings for Randy were more profound?

She imagined Bobbo and Randy side by side — the blond, lithe football player and her square-jawed, hairy tennis star. What was to prevent Randy from being transformed like Bobbo into some furious monster who could not only maim a body but send its parts halfway around the world? She could still not forget that night of the Blue and Gray Ball, when it seemed the blood from that longhair's head had touched some ancient chord in Randy. Might there not be something else that would change him just as wildly? It was merely luck and status and a firm determination to avoid the draft that had kept her boyfriend from Vietnam. There had been the student deferment and, now, a tennis elbow that didn't interfere with his game but that his doctor in Memphis defined as "crippling." If that didn't work, an old fraternity brother of his father's sat on the draft board. Randy Ditmars was destined for a far more significant fate than cannon fodder. There was the family business and — who knew? — perhaps a career in politics, golf tournaments and cruises and Caribbean vacations, a house like a spread in *House Beautiful*, its bedrooms filled with little, even more perfect copies of Randy and . . .

Belva? Belva more than maintained in style. And what would that cost her? What if Randy were not quite the man she thought she knew? What if that casual, college booziness was not simply a frat house aberration but a problem that had plagued his Scotch-Irish house for generations? What if he proved a brutal father? What if he lacked the shrewdness that had made his parents rich, and his lazy ease tumbled into simple redneck sloth?

And she herself? Belva Beauford Ditmars. Den mother? PTA secretary? Chairwoman of the Greater Memphis Muscular Dystrophy Ball? Was that what she wanted: to be an appendage to Randy Ditmars, the faithful wife who stayed at home and raised the kids and made a good impression when his associates came to call? But of course it was. That was what she was supposed to want, what any woman would. Yet, after four years of college, after gradually learning to challenge the wisdom of the Army and the government and the administration at Siegerford, she had to ask if that were enough.

She did not like to think these things, but Melva's recollection of Bobbo Starwick had reminded her just how tenuous our lives could be, how pale our real knowledge of anyone could prove. It pained her to ask these questions at the very moment she dreamt of that one question that would alter her life and set its course, she had to hope, for the rest of her natural days. She might well marry Randy Ditmars, but could she look at that prospect with the absolute anticipation her mother had felt when she wed her father, or even Melva might feel as she contemplated making a home with Bill?

The next morning, she was up almost with the sun and groaned at the circles under her eyes. She had decided to buy that dress, and she was determined to have a fine time in Memphis. She was still filled with hope that Randy might propose. But down inside her, there was that slightest qualm, the sense that the rules of living she had learned — even if no one had truly believed them — no longer applied and that the mystery that men had always represented, instead of growing clearer, seemed now more unfathomable than she could ever have imagined.

3

There in Billy Peters's apartment, Barry popped the cap off another beer. "... The pigs were firing tear gas ..." He flipped his hair and made a broad sweep with his hands. "The Mobo people ..."

In his jeans and workshirt, boots and bandanna, locks past his shoulders, he tipped his bottle with easy assurance. He was different than he had been when he went away. Barry knew they all saw it, even Tully, who, it seemed as he kicked back on the sofa across the room, did not particularly like it.

In Rhymers Creek, he saw small signs of rebellion: sandals,

roach-clip keychains, bird's-foot medallions. But his old friends were cautious. Eddie Hammersmith had talked earlier of being taunted for his hair and then beaten up when he stopped for gas up in Lemon Grove. Tully and Tom Walter had laughed about how, the previous November, they had sat in this very room with Billy and Bill Evans. Each had brought a six-pack, and they got drunker as the sun sank lower, there in front of the television, Tom and Bill cursing and roughhousing and watching for their birthdays in the draft lottery with the kind of high spirits that, Tully said, reminded him of how guys laughed when they were at the bottom of a football pileup.

And Barry thought: Yes, the giggles you get sometimes when you're hurt. Hurt bad.

"But what'll happen next year, do you think?" Karry Piggott had had her eyes on Barry all night, as if he were a rock star, hanging on his stories about marches and meetings.

He cocked his head and smiled, a little drunk. "They're either going to end the war," he said, and then, enunciating every word, "or we'll tear this country down!"

It was so easy to say on campus in New Jersey, in the rallies on Washington Square. But looking at his friends here, did he himself quite believe it? From what they had told him, the last year had been quiet. Tom working construction, Karry still in high school. And Tully, at Constellation Auto Parts, drinking away his Saturday nights, trying to get laid as often as possible, picking up some extra money doing engine work. For them, the War was always there: on television and the radio, in the papers and conversations overheard at work about this boy or that boy in the line of fire, probably more this past spring when the students had been shot at Kent. But Barry sensed he bore exotic tales, that day to day they did not talk about it much. The War, the draft — they were like some dread disease everybody knew was around that might take you or your best friend or your brother, like polio used to do. They were a natural fact like the weather, not to be resisted and challenged, battled, even subdued. Maybe that was what made Barry feel so different. In New York, in other places not Rhymers Creek, they really thought they could change the world.

His own world had changed in ways none of them would ever expect. Even while he rambled on, even while he stirred them with stories of demonstrations and resistance, Barry knew, as he popped another beer, why he was drinking so much. It was not just that it was a party. It was that he had something important to say.

✧

He awoke from dope-laden sleep that Thanksgiving night, Angelo curled beside him, naked in that apartment like a kiln. He got up, dressed, pulled the door shut behind him. For the next three hours, he wandered the streets, sick with a loathing mingled with despair.

It was bad enough to have done what he did. What was unbearable was that he had enjoyed it. He could blame it on the dope, but that would be a lie. Mariana, Pamela: they had tried to save him, but it was no good. He was no better than Elwood Pomeroy, paying high school halfbacks to open their flies. Everybody hated Elwood, and now everyone would hate him: Kip and his friends, the Mobo crowd, his professors, not to mention every last soul in Rhymers Creek.

Barry walked up Broadway: Herald Square, Times Square, Columbus Circle, Sherman Square . . . He continued past St. John the Divine, Columbia, then wandered out to the river: Grant's Tomb and the Riverside Church. The sun came up. He went down into the IRT, waiting for the Number 1 to take him to Wall Street so he could catch the PATH for home.

He got off at Union Square.

The problem was that though his mind told him one thing, his body told him another. Walking through the predawn dusk, his head filled with every ugly word he could imagine — *queer, cocksucker, faggot* — the actual feel of Angelo across his body would well out of some memory not mental but physical and his mind would go blank as a blackboard and he would shudder with electric wanting. He fought the recollections, each time less successfully. He took the train. When he got as far as Chelsea, there was nothing he could do.

It took a while to rouse Angelo, leaning on the buzzer with an Entenmann's coffee cake in hand. When the door opened, Barry smiled. "How about breakfast?"

Angelo, bleary in his Fordham trunks, merely nodded.

Once they were in the apartment, Barry set the sack down, turned, and said, "My name's Barry, not Bob, by the way. And before we eat I'm going to fuck you."

Which he did.

He did not return to New Jersey until Sunday afternoon; left Angelo's apartment only twice for food and cigarettes. For the rest, it was a sweet, drug-laden dream of lusts if even conscious not admitted. Angelo was a tough but patient teacher, alternately touched and annoyed by Barry's naiveté both in bed and out.

"It started when I was thirteen, I guess. I'd take the subway after school and get sucked or jerked off. First, I did it for money, but after a while I figured out I liked it."

"You mean, you, like, sold . . . ?" Barry's voice hung in the heat.

Angelo looked at him, irritated. "Hell, yes. That's how it is. You sell it while you got it, and when you're old, you buy it back."

"Have you had, like, a boyfriend? I mean do guys go steady . . ."

Angelo smirked. ". . . And get married and have kids? Jeez!" He laughed at Barry's pout. "I'm sorry, man. Some queers do. But look. I'm butch, I've got a big dick and I like to get fucked, too. I'm twenty-three. I got lots of time. If all your straight buddies didn't have to give somebody a ring or all that shit to get a girl to put out, do you think they would? That's why straights hate a queer like me. I can go out any night of the week and get laid, maybe even get paid for it. All the sex you want and nobody gets knocked up and says: 'Son of a bitch, you just wanted to fuck me.'"

Barry raised his eyebrows. "So, you just wanted to fuck me?"

Angelo nodded. "Yeah. I wanted to fuck you bad. And I want to fuck you again."

✦

At Billy's that night, Barry was like some soldier with his war stories. Maybe, sometime, that was what Bobbo had dreamed of — recounting those tales of bravery and bloodshed they had all been raised on. But Barry's, of course, were tales of the antiwar. Karry and Rhett and Sandy looked properly appreciative, but Tully still seemed skeptical. Barry knew why. He had felt it on the streets. He had overheard remarks, how he looked like a hippie, a radical, a communist. It was talk that hurt: *His poor parents . . . With his very own brother in Vietnam!*

"On the fourth of May, when we heard about Kent, I thought there'd be a riot . . ."

It excited them. He could see it. The notion of a generation's rising in resistance. He fed on their exhilaration, though the beer made his neck stiff and his head buzz. It was a way of not dealing with what was to come.

"I need to talk to you," Barry had said as he sat in Tully's car on the way to Billy's. "It's important."

"Well, what?"

"I can't tell you right now. It's kind of big deal and you should know about it."

Tully chuckled and pushed the car up over the speed limit. "Shit, you getting married or something?"

"No," Barry said quickly, and then snorted a laugh.

"Trying not to get married?"

"No." It was abrupt this time. "It's something else. Maybe we could go down to the dry lake after and I'll tell you."

"This is heavy shit if we gotta go to the dry lake." Tully laughed, but it was as if he could feel the tension in the car.

"Things shouldn't go too late anyhow. But if I give up some pussy," he added lightly, "you'll be sorry, asshole."

Barry had stared straight ahead, and he didn't say a word.

✧

Angelo probably had just wanted to fuck him. He had a reputation as a cherry picker, Barry learned. It made no difference. Between Thanksgiving and Christmas, New Year's and Valentine's Day, Angelo taught him enough that Barry no longer needed his first mentor.

At first, at school, they did not notice him drawing away. There were the short weeks before vacation, with parties and caroling and papers due, and then the January rush of exams. After the great offensive of November, the Mobo lapsed into quiescence. Barry's absences from the dorm could be explained by the darkroom, the library, studying late, a shoot for his semester project.

The lies were convincing. For Barry, it would not have mattered if they weren't. All his priorities turned topsy-turvy. Ending the war, writing home, taking pictures: all of those receded into insignificance. Giddily, he found that every waking moment of his life — and any dream he could remember — was about sex.

He was insatiable.

He cruised tirelessly, endlessly, always: Macy's men's rooms, Gimbel's basement, standing room at the opera. He prowled Washington Square, Bleecker Street, Christopher Street, Fifty-seventh Street. He scored his way through young Christians and Hebrews in the locker rooms and stairwells of Sloan House, the Ys on Twenty-third, Seventy-second, Ninety-second; locked eyes with likely candidates on the subway, the bus, the Staten Island Ferry. MOMA, the Museum of the City, the Metropolitan; St. Pat's Cathedral, Trinity Church, St.-Mark's-in-the-Bowery — connoisseurs and catechists. East Side, West Side, uptown, downtown: New York, before towers and traffic and grand avenues, became an endless series of men's rooms, men's looks, men's bodies. He fucked and sucked with whites and blacks,

Protestants and Catholics, Jews and gentiles, a Ukrainian priest, an Indian spice merchant, a Greek ensign, and a Japanese flutist. There were stockbrokers, dancers, stevedores, a vice president for development, bartenders and short-order cooks. They were sixteen and fifty-eight and twenty-four and forty-six. Half the time, even before he came, he didn't remember their names. He did not care. All that mattered was that, for two minutes or eight or an hour or five, they made him feel wonderful, unwound just a little that spiral of lust turned tight inside him as the main-spring of a clock fit to burst.

Then he met Edmund.

He was down by Cooper Union, shooting fire escapes for his term project. Two men walked by arguing. He turned to click the shutter before he even registered what they were yelling at each other about.

"It's not just a question of cultural change!" the one man shouted. "You have to see it in terms of class and it's got to func-tion as part of the larger proto-revolutionary situation."

"Fine. Fine!" the other said. "But you can't merely subsume gay liberation under a rubric like that. You know that the Pan-thers and the other politicized elements still don't have a place for us! If we don't organize on our own . . ."

Barry squeezed off a shot, then another. The men were in their twenties. Both had longish hair and one had an NLF flag on his jacket sleeve. The other had a Vandyke and round glasses, which gave him a more than passing resemblance to Trotsky.

They had reached the corner by then. Barry went back to his fire escapes. He remembered Angelo had said that some queers had organized a collective, the "gay" something, which was the word that homosexuals were using more and more when they talked about themselves. Barry had heard about it from a few of the men he had slept with. It all came out of some riot on Christopher Street the previous June.

"You with a newspaper?"

He turned around, and there was Trotsky. "No." Barry studied him. "No. I'm working on a project."

"What kind?"

Barry shrugged. "What's it look like? A photography project."

"Guess it figures," Trotsky said. "Want to have coffee?"

It was a brazen and clumsy pickup, but he could use some recreation. Barry smiled, clicking open his camera bag. "Sure."

It was after midnight when they left. Tully yawned and bitched about having to get up at seven and how he shouldn't have had that last Bud, trying — not very hard, it was true — to get Barry to say they could talk tomorrow. It did not work.

Barry climbed into the passenger seat and slammed the door.

"Sorry about this," he said, "but it's important."

As they drove, Tully put on Creedence and cranked up John Fogerty. Barry stared out the window. He felt a little sick, and he knew it was not the beer.

Bumping down to the lake bed in the used Buick Tully shared with Wellesley, they could see another car parked on the far side.

"Somebody out there getting his." Tully laughed ruefully.

Barry took a deep breath.

They pulled near a grove of brush on what would once have been the southern bank of the lake. Tully cut the engine.

"Want to get out?"

Barry opened his door. Tully went around and popped the trunk.

"I ripped off a six-pack from Billy's." He tossed a can through the air. "So, what's happening, man? What's such a big deal?"

Barry paused, played with the can in his hand. "I've got a doctor's appointment tomorrow. Dr. Brinkman."

"I thought you guys went to Dr. Walsh."

"We do. But Dr. Brinkman's the doctor for the draft board."

Tully looked perplexed. "You got trouble with the draft?"

"Sort of. I'm dropping my 2-S."

Tully let out a deep breath. "You flunk out?"

"No. No. I did okay. But a lot of stuff's happened."

"Well, Jeez, why didn't you wait till we get our numbers? It's only till July."

"I couldn't." Barry raised his voice slightly. Then it got soft again. "I don't know. It was something I had to do."

Tully leaned against the car and folded his arms, setting his beer on the roof. "So, why have you got to see this doctor and all?"

Barry paused, looking at the ground.

"What do you think of me, Tully?" he began. "As a guy? A man?"

It sounded silly. Barry himself hated questions like that, when people asked you to be honest, and even if you were, you still felt they didn't think you were telling the truth.

"Hell, what do I know?" Tully stammered, caught off guard. "You seem just fine to me. You're a nice guy and you're smart and you've been a good friend to me since we were kids and — " He cut himself off, exasperated. "Shit! What I am supposed to say?"

Barry let out a short, shamed laugh. "It's okay." He sighed then. "Back about two months ago, I sent the draft board a letter asking to be reclassified."

"Yeah."

Barry did not say anything.

"So what did you ask for?"

"4-F."

"I don't know, man. You should have asked for 1-Y. They give those out easier." Tully stopped, as if it had suddenly occurred to him that maybe something was seriously wrong — cancer or a bad heart. "I mean, why did you do that? Are you sick or what?"

Barry shook his head. He could feel a small, sad smile on his face. "Not as far as I'm concerned," he said.

"So, what's going on?"

"When I sent that letter, I sent another one, from a doctor in New York. A shrink."

"A shrink?" Tully cocked his head. "What does it say? Like you're crazy?"

Barry reached into his jacket and took out a pack of cigarettes. "Want one?" he offered.

Tully hesitated. Neither of them had smoked all night.

"Yeah," he said. "Yeah, I think I do."

Barry lit them both and passed one to Tully.

"I'm queer, Tully."

Tully's cigarette stopped in midair.

"What?"

"I'm queer."

The second time, when there was no mistaking what had been said, the words might as well have been a fist to the gut. Tully took a mouthful of air. "What do you mean?"

"Just what I said. I'm a queer. I always kind of thought I was, and this year, I found out it was true."

Barry knew what Tully was thinking. He had seen it before: *This does not make sense. You don't have queers for friends. People you know aren't queers. Barry Carraway doesn't look funny and act funny and dress funny. He likes girls. Girls like him.*

"What the fuck are you saying to me!"

"I wanted you to know. People are probably going to know soon, and I didn't want you to hear it from somebody else."

Tully stood squarely in front of him and put both hands on Barry's shoulders. "Look at me," he said. "Look at me, damnit!"

Barry raised his head.

"You are not a homosexual, Carraway. You are not a queer!"

Barry felt it flood over him, clear as the glow of a saint or the glare of wickedness: a weird, serene defiance.

Tully dropped his arms and averted his face. "What the fuck

did they do to you up there? Why the fuck are you telling me this?"

"You need to know," Barry said softly. "When my roommate found out, he freaked. He trashed some of my stuff. He was afraid everybody would think he was gay, too." Barry paused. "People might say the same kind of thing about you . . ."

"Well, it would be a fucking lie!" Tully yelled, his fists balled, throwing himself to the side, as if he might be fouled by mere proximity.

"I know it would," Barry said quietly, "but it's the kind of thing people do."

"Jesus," Tully whispered furiously. "Jesus Christ, Barry! With all the shit we've done together. How could you have . . . ?"

It was an awful replay of April: Kip frantic, rabid: *I always knew. The way you looked at me. And me such a stupid shit I wouldn't think of it. Dropping my goddamn pants in front of you like you were some normal guy instead of some fairy scoping me out, you. . . . You make me sick! You make me so fuckin' sick, you . . .*

"Come on," Tully said gruffly, "I'll take you home."

"Not yet."

Tully, with the door already open, whirled around. "Don't you tell me what to do, you fucking . . . !"

"Fag!" Barry jumped away from the car. "Just get fucked, motherfucker! Get lost! I'll fucking walk home!"

They faced each other, eyes slitted, arms cocked.

It was Tully who looked away first. He took a deep breath. Then another. "I'm sorry," he croaked. "Look, I'm sorry. You're my friend, Barry. I just freaked. Like your roommate, you know?"

Barry stood for a moment, reached in his pocket, lit another cigarette. "I'm sorry," he said. "I mean, I'm sorry it's hard for you. I'm not sorry for being queer."

Even in the darkness, he could see Tully crumple, as if something had been taken out of him — some absolute certainty, some faith in himself and his own feelings.

"So, what's this doctor thing about?"

"They don't believe the letter." Barry was almost amused. "They want me to talk to Dr. Brinkman. My friends in New York told me this would happen."

Tully leaned against the car. Barry felt as if he had beaten him up, somehow wanted to comfort him. But he could not take back what he had said. And he could offer no comfort, because Tully would not understand it was merely meant to soothe him, not seduce him.

"Barry, why are you doing this?"

"Because it's honest."

"Don't get philosophical on me," Tully snapped. "You had a 2-S. Nobody had to know that you were, like, queer. In New York, maybe, but not here." He almost whined. "Why are you doing this to us?"

It took a long time for Barry to reply. "It seems right." He paused, then shook his head. "Sometimes I'm not sure I can explain it . . ."

They looked out over the dry lake. The other car had disappeared.

Tully opened his mouth, hesitated. "Told your folks?"

"Not yet." Barry sighed. "I'll have to. Maybe tomorrow."

"Jeez . . ."

A full minute passed.

Tully pulled his keys out, jangling them idly in his hand. "You want to go now?"

"Sure. We can go now."

They drove back into town in silence. Tully stopped in front of the Carraways' house. Barry sat a moment.

"You had to know, Tully."

"I know I did, Barry," Tully said dully. "I wouldn't want to know it, but I know you had to tell me. I thank you for that." He looked up from the steering wheel. " 'Bye."

"'Bye," Barry said.

He got out and watched the taillights wink away down the gently curving street of a place called home. He knew tonight was merely a rehearsal. It had not gone well.

4

Back in the World.

He folded his arms behind his head.

Big fucking deal.

This was the place he had dreamed of: safe and familiar; his town, his room. After Eggleson died, he had marked off every day on a small desk calendar, each neat x the sign that, this night, he was neither dead nor crazy and so that much closer to Rhymers Creek. But now that he could walk out the door and wander the streets with no fear of satchel charges or bullets or a booby-trapped latrine, all he wanted was to go back to the war.

He had had inklings. Kirkpatrick wrote to him, and Beaubien. There were magazine reports about how vets were not exactly welcome; were liable to go on rampages, shoot people, run them off the road. The World was not a comfortable place.

Too, there had been the letters from home that had made him ill at ease. If he heard one more time how well Lonnie was doing, he had thought he would reup, and his mother sounded like she was already planning Fred's wedding, though it wasn't clear to whom. That was one reason he had stayed in California. Originally, just for a day or two, he stopped to see Canterwell in San Diego. The surrounding countryside was desert, not jungle, but there was something comforting and familiar about it. Perhaps it was all the sailors and Marines; perhaps it was the ocean, that last American landfall and then thousands of miles of blue water until Indochina loomed green and deadly out of the surf.

They drank lots of beer and lay in a pleasant, January sun near Mission Bay, and it seemed not so different from China Beach.

He could talk to Canterwell about old times, and his friend would tell Fred some scrap of Vietnamese history or recollect some funny custom he had seen among the washerwomen or little village boys.

The afternoon he arrived, Canterwell gave Fred his first piece of advice: "Grow a beard." He scratched his own scraggly one. "It grows faster than your hair and nobody'll figure you were in Nam."

That told him that his first set of fears were real.

When he informed the family he thought he would give California a try, the second was confirmed. At least twice a week, letters arrived from Rhymers Creek — hectoring, hurt, accusatory letters — full of outrage that he had not hightailed it immediately for home: *Your little brothers and sister are just so disappointed I can't tell you. . . . They're hiring at Wilson's and I ran into Frank Meachum, who's head of personnel, and I had to tell him you were out fooling around in California. . . . Your father and I are worried sick about all the problems out there. You must not be able to walk the streets.*

Fred hired on as a clerk at a 7-Eleven selling milk and gum and Slushees. It was restful, different and yet not so different from dispensing tons of matériel all over the theater. He often thought about that word: *theater.* He realized more and more that everything that had happened to him in-country must seem for people he waited on like a movie, some long-running series on television. And in only this short time, he was beginning to understand that. He sat in the living room and watched the clips from those places he knew intimately as the dry lake or the Square or Lemon Grove shimmer across the screen like the backdrops for *Combat* or one of those other war serials from his childhood.

That was when he was awake. When he was asleep, though, it was as if it really were a movie and he was the director. He could rewrite scenes, alter the cast, edit things out, change the ending. Deep in his dreams, he was stoned with that Mohawked spade, asking him up front how many multiples of a double vet he was.

He sat with Gómez and talked him out of flying to Saigon, and didn't cheat Kirkpatrick like he always did at poker. One night, Mercer Shaw got greased the first week Fred was on base.

But most of all, Fred saved Ronnie Eggleson's life. They didn't go into town that day; they missed the bus by a mile, and when they got back Michelsen chewed them out just like Eggleson promised; Eggleson came with him to get his wallet back.

There were a few times when Fred would wake up sweaty, with no breath. Those were when he remembered it exactly as it happened.

He lasted two and a half months at the 7-Eleven. Then, one day, he didn't go to work. He listened to *Tommy* until four-thirty in the morning, because for some reason he was afraid to go to sleep, and even then he only managed it by polishing off a fifth of bourbon, which left him like a deaf, dumb, and blind boy next day, which was perhaps exactly what he wanted.

After that, he picked up a couple of other jobs — one illegally on a construction site, another through a city program helping to keep the beach clean. Neither lasted long. He had more and more trouble sleeping, and his drinking got worse.

One day, Canterwell told Fred it was time for him to go.

The minute they saw him, it was as it had always been. Lonnie wasn't there. Lila Mae and Little Joey looked at him as if they weren't entirely sure he belonged in the same family. Across his parents' faces, all there was was disappointment.

He knew what they were expecting, and, oddly, it was what he had expected that far-off day when he had signed up: Fred Bower — straight as a hoe shaft, lean and mean, his face shiny with health, hair cropped, resplendent in a uniform decked with row on row of medals. He was tanned, he knew, but out of shape in his jeans and a short-sleeved shirt. He had kept his hair short so it was easy to dry, but he knew the beard appalled them. Still, it hid the puffiness of his face. That would probably appall them more.

The first night home, with pot roast and sweet corn, reminded him of why he had enlisted in the first place. Lonnie arrived from his summer job, sleek in his suit and tie, mature and established already. Joey and Lila Mae were still kids, though his sister was beginning to show both the gawky womanliness and the moodiness of adolescence. Momma bombarded him with questions: about the war, his friends, California, Canterwell. He answered as best he could, but there was so much he could not tell her — the smaller things like the dope and drunks and screwing, not to mention the greater obscenities of wasting and dying — that he ended up saying almost nothing at all. To fill the silences, she caught him up on various old friends and acquaintances, who, by her telling, seemed to be doing pretty well: in school or getting good jobs or married and with a family on the way, each name and summary like an accusation.

But all that would have been all right if there had been the merest sign from the head of the table that, even if he'd been a pogue, Fred had done something manly and admirable. All the way home, in the hour before dinner, there at the table, Fred waited for a wink, a glance, something that showed his father understood what the vague answers about the war really meant, knew that there were things a man wouldn't want to talk about, not right now, maybe not ever.

"You ever get shot at?" Joey asked. "Like in a battle?"

Fred looked at him and nodded. "Yeah. Kind of. Over there, see, you never quite know where the battles'll be."

"I thought it was almost too bad you got into that logistical stuff," his father said. "You never really got a whiff of combat."

In his nose was the reek of Eggleson's gore, and Fred thought he would gag. He took a mouthful of potatoes and managed something like a chuckle, rueful and coded. "I got close enough a few times to smell more than most people'd care to."

"Well, sure," his father said, "in those guerilla wars, you never can tell. But it was different in France . . ."

Fred watched as Joey's eyes moved up the table to their father. There was only room in this house for one hero, and it wasn't him. Lonnie, across from him, almost smiled.

Fred made it through dinner and the reconquest of Fortress Europe. They went to the living room afterward, and he lit up. He liked a cigarette after he ate. There was a sudden quiet, short but loaded, and then Joey and Lila Mae — nervous as squirrels — went out to play and Lonnie went downstairs and Momma went to do the dishes, though she appeared briefly a couple of minutes later with a can of Glade.

They sat on opposite sides of the room, Fred on the sofa, his father in his easy chair. The silence was heavy as the heat.

"You know, Fred, we really are happy to have you back."

He smiled faintly. "I guess I'm happy to be back. California was okay, but I needed the kind of . . . quiet, I guess, of being home."

"Sure, son." His father sighed. "That's why I headed straight back here after the War. I could've stayed East. A friend of mine's family was bankrolling a business for him in Philadelphia. But I knew I wouldn't be happy anyplace else." He leaned forward. "Now, you. You had a chance to pick up real skills in the service. Me, I was just a standard GI dogface, no hot showers or hot meals. No rotating in and out . . ."

"It was real different, I guess." Fred felt his neck cramping.

"That's for certain. But anyway, son, you learned a few things there in logistics, and they can be real useful to you if you put them to work. Time waits for no man. Your mother and I have been talking, and she says that Arthur Wilson is still looking for people. That's some operation they've got going. I don't know how many chickens they're processing every day, but it's impressive."

Fred stared at the floor.

He had to wonder if there in France his father had held a Ronnie Eggleson, shattered and dying. Surely there had been French boom-boom girls and lectures about the clap and some funny drunken nights and maybe even, as they rammed into Germany, double vets.

"Are you listening, Fred?"

"Oh, yeah. Yeah, Daddy. I'm sorry. It's that bus trip. It really takes it out of you. Maybe we could talk about it tomorrow?"

"Why sure, Fred. Sure." His father touched his arm, clumsily. "I want to make sure you get off on the right foot now that you're back." He dropped his tone. "I'm a little worried about that beard. Where Wilson's is concerned, you know."

Fred bit his lip. "Sure, Daddy. I think I'd better lay down. I'm just not used to home cooking. I can hardly keep my eyes open."

"Hope you didn't pick up a bug on the bus. You never know, traveling with those people. You can get all kinds of funny stuff."

Fred snorted, not sure if it was a laugh or a cry. "That's probably it. Some funny bug from the kind of people you have on the bus." He lurched to his feet. "I'll go kiss Momma good night."

"All right, son. Good night."

"Good night, Daddy."

✧

A week after that, he did go to Wilson's. His mother had made the appointment with Frank Meachum, and it went all right at first. The headquarters was bright and clean, with soft gray carpets and neutral walls. Even in his suit and tie, the very same one he had had in high school (now snug in some places and loose in others), Fred felt secure, even confident, as he filled out the application and then was ushered in to see Frank.

They talked about the last few years, and Frank said nice things about his father and mother and Lonnie. He did not ask about the war, for which Fred was grateful, simply remarking that Rhymers Creek could be proud of men like Fred, and that Wilson's policy was to give those who had made a sacrifice an opportunity once they came home.

"Well," Frank said, "why don't we head into the plant? It's state of the art, and I think you'll be impressed. And this is only the beginning, Fred," he said as he opened the door, "only the beginning of what we're going to accomplish here."

They walked down the air-conditioned hall into a high-ceilinged, corrugated-roofed building where there were forklifts and trucks and vans. At the far end was a heavy door that a uniformed guard pulled open, waving to Frank as they approached.

The instant they were inside, Fred panicked. The temperature was suddenly forty degrees warmer, and the air so thick he couldn't breathe. And there was a smell, still bearable, but barely, of something dead — of blood and shit and rot.

"This is the steam room," Frank was shouting, "where we get the feathers off. Later we sear the carcasses for the pinfeathers."

He could feel his eyes rolling back in his head. He leaned against some towering casing and saw the chickens, blood drooling from their beaks, slung by the feet on hooks suspended from a belt that pounded above them with an awful helicopter noise.

"The slaughter room's over there." Frank gestured to the right. "I'll show you later. Come this way."

Fred gritted his teeth and swallowed the spew in his mouth. He tried to breathe deep. Sweat burst from his forehead. He felt clammy and feverish at once.

"Now, in here" — Frank was yelling — "in here, they've all been plucked, see? So now we gut them!"

There was a line, how many was it? Fifty? Sixty? Men and women, rubber-gloved, in one hand a short-handled knife like a scimitar, the other bright with grease and gore. They plunged the blade into the breasts of the naked carcasses and then plunged the other hand through the slice to tear the guts out all of a piece. Beside each one was a vacuum duct, sucking the bloody, shit-streaked mass into its maw.

"Great process!" Frank screamed over the racket of the belts and the whining aspiration of the ducts. "Though, Lord, we had a hell of a time with the FDA! All they do it bitch about salmonella!"

Fred's heart was racing. It was the smell. He could deal with what he was watching — "These are only chickens. Chickens!" he kept whispering, though then he would hear some unknown voice saying, *"You pogues. You're nothing but chickens. Chickens!"* Even that he could have stood — but he could not abide the stench of gut and blood.

"I'm sorry!" he shouted desperately to Frank, grabbing him too hard by the arm. "I've got to leave! I've got to leave now!"

Frank looked at Fred's hand on his arm, bewildered. "What!"

"Leave!" He pointed desperately at the door marked EXIT.

"Fire escape!" Frank shouted, smiling through the din.

"Leave!" Fred screamed. "Now!"

When they were outside, Fred apologized. "It's this flu," he said. "Picked it up on the bus. These things just hang on, you know?"

Frank nodded, but Fred could see that he simply thought it was strange. And it was, of course, but not in a way he could explain so Frank would understand. They shook hands, and Fred hurried off, unrolling the car window as he left the lot and breathing through his mouth a full ten minutes as he drove. The smell still lurked in his nostrils. He did not want to throw up in his mother's car.

Wilson's did not call him back; neither did Harley's Hardware, or Western Auto. The two weeks since he had last looked for a job had been nothing but evasion. He kept to his room, his besieged little firebase in Rhymers Creek, venturing out in the afternoons to smuggle a little liquor in: half-pints and nips that could be concealed, wishing it were winter so he could wear a deep-pocketed coat without arousing suspicion. He was cagey. He would sneak the empties out each day when he left, so there would be no cache of evidence, no ugly, recriminatory scene. Momma badgered him from time to time but mostly left him

alone, and Daddy now looked at him with the same perplexed in-
difference he had always looked at him with.

Sometimes, he thought of calling up Ricky Graves or Waldo
Henderson, because they might be able to talk to him, or going
back to San Diego and seeing if Canterwell would take him in
again, buying a ticket to Oakland, where Kirkpatrick was living,
or heading for New York, where Glickstein would have some
scam in progress.

But Fred knew it was no good. Rhymers Creek was the place
he was going to serve for the duration. He realized now that he
had hitched his wagon to a falling star, that out of this war there
would be no heroes; no kisses, parades, no slaps on the back and
welcome home parties; no jobs waiting or sympathy either. And
that would make him think of Bobbo Starwick in Quang Tri,
crazy as a june bug and more dangerous than a snake, still out
there somewhere in the bush. He wished, sometimes, that Bobbo
would come home.

And other times, he merely wished that he were with him.

5

In the sun in front of Bannister's, he could feel people's eyes upon
him. He knew they had not heard yet. If they were staring at all,
it was because of his hair, his clothes, the jacket over his shoulder he could not fit in his duffel, making him sweat.

There was no one to see him off. Most people didn't know he
was leaving, and those who did may not have wanted to be seen
with him. It had all worked out pretty much as Edmund had predicted.

"You don't have to do this for me. You've got nothing to
prove."

They were naked under the sheet, Barry's head against his
lover's bony chest. Edmund's goatee tickled his forehead.

"It's not for you. It's for me. It's a political act."

Edmund sniffed a laugh. "Well, which is it?"

"You heard the guy at the meeting the other night. The personal is political, especially when it's about sex."

"Is this about sex?"

Barry sighed. "You know what I mean, Edmund."

He could feel the head nod above him. "I think I do. I'm just afraid you'll get hurt, and you'll hurt people you love."

They were really not boyfriends, they insisted. That would be "bourgeois," and worse, "imitative of discredited heterosexual models." But from March to May, Barry had not slept with anybody else. He was not certain Edmund hadn't, but he didn't think so.

After three months slutting through the smorgasbord of sausage and buns, as Angelo called Manhattan, his own sudden fidelity surprised Barry, and its object all the more. Edmund was almost eight years older, short and a little thin, not at all the type that Barry might have thought would have seduced his heart. Angelo, with his boxy Italian street charm; Errol, the cocksucking Golden Gloves champion: those were the kinds he would have expected himself to go for, cousins of Kip and his lacrosse friends. Of Bobbo. But instead, it was his Trotsky, part-time graphic designer and full-time social radical, one of four cofounders of the Greenwich Activist Youth — GAY — one of the organizations sprung up after the Christopher Street Riot.

After they fucked for the first time, which occurred after they really had had coffee in a café on MacDougal, Edmund loaned Barry *Our Lady of the Flowers*. The dog-eared paperback in his hand, Barry could feel the perplexity cross his face. It was not that he had not screwed with anyone more than once, but no one had ever given him an object, pressed anything concrete into his hand. A book meant something, a book that had been used, read and reread, loved. He consumed it in two days, made a special trip to Manhattan to return it. On the PATH, on the crosstown, he did not cruise.

He got to Edmund's. Gave him the book. They talked. Then they fucked. He stayed for dinner. They talked. They smoked a joint. They went to bed. They talked. Slept. Woke up. Made love. And talked some more.

They did it on Tuesday, on Friday, on Sunday as well. One week, two, three. Edmund loaned Barry more books, took him to meetings, introduced him to friends. Each time they were together, though, they made love at least once, or twice or three times. Seven weeks, eight weeks, nine. By then, Barry wondered if he was falling in love.

✧

"Now, Barry. Level with me. How many times has this happened?"

They were not in the examining room. It was the first time he had been to the doctor's office and not had to take off his clothes or say "ahhh" or show where it hurt. For the letter from New York, he had not gone to an office at all. He'd merely had dinner with Edmund and a psychiatrist friend in Brooklyn.

Dr. Brinkman sighed. "Barry, a lot of boys your age, they . . . ah . . . experiment. They're at camp or something and they, well, they masturbate each other. Or after a party — this happens a lot in fraternities — a boy will be with a friend and they're drunk and they'll both be, ah, excited, and one thing leads to another, and before they know it, they've done something . . ."

The doctor was in the Air National Guard. Barry had seen the plaque among the diplomas in the waiting room. He was in his forties, not bad-looking by Barry's standards, bearish and manly in his crew-cut.

"So, what I'm saying is that, just because you might have found yourself without a proper sexual outlet and so you . . . played around, kind of, with a friend or something like that . . . Well, those things happen." He smiled. "So, really, how many times have you done this?"

Barry furrowed his forehead. "A hundred?" he guessed. "Two hundred?"

"They may not accept the letter," Walter, Edmund's friend, told him. "First, they won't like some New York doctor telling them a hometown boy is queer. Second, the boards don't trust psychiatrists. Third, I'm Jewish, and my last name is Jewish, and boards from your part of the world hate Jews. They'll send you to see somebody there, and it's his job, for a whole series of reasons, to certify you're a straight, red-blooded American male who's either in the middle of homosexual panic or is trying to dodge the draft. If he tells them the first, you take your chances with the lottery. If he tells them the second, they'll do their damnedest to send you to Vietnam, and then you'll probably need a lawyer. If they're not making their quota, they may decide to take you anyway." He took a sip of wine. "Frankly, I don't know why you're doing this."

"Me neither," Edmund agreed.

"Good to see you, Barry," Dr. Brinkman had said when he arrived. "Come on in and have a seat."

"First, he'll try to be your pal," Walter had told him.

"No need to be nervous. I just have to ask a couple questions."

"He'll try to put you at ease, but if he's done this before, or if he's smart, he'll be looking for you to fuck up."

"I know this kind of thing is hard to talk about, but you shouldn't be embarrassed. Anything you say is safe with me."

"He has to report back to the board, so if you've done anything down there where you're from, don't mention it. He probably won't ask you to name names, but if you did, it could be a problem for any friends of yours who haven't made the decision you have."

"You know, this kind of interview isn't all that uncommon."

"He's going to want you to admit to experimentation. The Army can deal with experimentation." Walter smiled. "If my experience ten years ago was any indication, the Army's full of experimentation. Don't lie. From what Edmund tells me you've told him, if you're experimenting, this is the Manhattan Project."

Dr. Brinkman did not like what he heard. His eyes narrowed. He opened his drawer and took out a sheaf of papers.

"Barry, can you tell me what 'rimming' is?" the quotation marks in his voice held the word like clothespins.

He fought the laugh. "Well, it means licking somebody's anus, Doctor, like running your tongue around the rim."

He was being too smart aleck, he knew it.

"You don't want to make him mad," Walter told him. "If you make him mad, he'll make sure you're inducted. They'll take a screaming drag queen if they have to, and they'll arrange to get you killed."

The doctor frowned. "What's" — the clothespins again — "'drag.'"

"Getting dressed up like a girl."

"Would you like to do that?"

He heard Walter's voice: *For them, all homosexuals want to be women. They think every gay man dreams of living in drag. Even if you've never thought of it, make it sound like you have.*

"Sure."

"What's a 'coal hauler'?"

Barry stared at Dr. Brinkman blankly. "A what?"

"A 'coal hauler,'" the doctor repeated with a slow enunciation of a quiz show host.

"Never heard of that one."

"Okay," Dr. Brinkman said neutrally, but his mouth turned up in a tight grin of triumph. "It's a man" — there was real disdain in his voice — "a white man, who enjoys being entered anally by Negroes."

Barry shook his head. "Gee, no black guy ever called me that."

The doctor looked at him with genuine horror. To be queer was awful. To be a queer who went with Negroes was more awful still. To be one who would even imply he would get fucked up the ass by Negroes was, quite obviously, the worst thing in the world.

"I'll be frank," Walter said. *"You've got to disgust him, but not too much. He's already disgusted with homosexuals. If he weren't, he wouldn't be the draft board's doctor. But he's got to pity you, not detest you. If he detests you, he'll send you to Nam."*

"I'd like to examine you, Barry. It's part of the procedure."

Barry stood, and the doctor came around the desk.

"Drop your pants."

The doctor handled him as if he were expecting to find something anomalous, the peter of a five-year-old, a vestigial vagina.

"Turn around."

"They look for something called prolapsus of the rectum, which essentially means your asshole is falling out. They think they can tell how much you're getting fucked by how loose your sphincter is."

"You may feel the need to urinate and defecate when I do this."

"It'll hurt a little while," Barry could hear Angelo whisper, *"but then, it will be wonderful."*

"Doesn't seem abnormal to me," Dr. Brinkman said, wiping his finger with a paper towel.

"What they'll always do," Walter said, *"even the best of them — the ones who maybe really want to get you out — they'll remind you of your family, and your future. It's not as bad as it used to be, and it's getting better since this war is so unpopular. But in a place like where you come from, people may find out why you're 4-F. Somebody will see the records, or people will simply draw their own conclusions. It's not like it was in World War II. But we don't know what will happen down the road. You might screw up your chances for certain jobs or security clearances or things like that. They'll have a record of your being queer. And if somebody like Joe McCarthy comes along, we could all be in deep shit. So, after all the questions and the exam, that'll be the grand finale: 'Think of . . .'"*

". . . what this might do to you, to your family, to your brother who's in the service," Dr. Brinkman said quietly, intensely.

His stomach jumped at the mention of Bobbo. Barry tamped it down.

"A homosexual is condemned to a lonely and unproductive life," the doctor continued. "I know people in New York will tell you different, but they have a much higher incidence of alcoholism, suicide, depression, cancer, bowel disease. It's scientifically proved." He leaned over the desk. "I don't know if you're really queer, son," he said. "For life. Maybe now. I don't know what's happened up there . . ."

Barry took a deep breath he hoped wasn't obvious.

The doctor shook his head sadly, his hands locked together and elbows on the file folder in front of him. "But you can get treatment. Especially back East, there are doctors who have tremendous luck in turning homosexuals into real men. For your sake, for your mom and dad's," he said, "look into it."

Barry nodded. "I'll see what I can find out, Dr. Brinkman."

He did not know what the doctor reported. Even if it were bad, he supposed, in another month he would have a draft number, at best a good one. He could run the interview complete through his mind, imagine telling Edmund about it, and Walter: regaling people with it for years to come. But he knew that he recalled it so he would not recall what had happened last night — the argument in the basement, first with his father, then, his mother. Shouting, tears, the slap. Slamming the door. Spending the night on Billy Peters's floor. And now, sitting on the curb alone, waiting for the bus.

The Trailways turned the corner and growled toward him, the gray exhaust behind it still and heavy in the heat. He was going away. He was going away and he was not coming back.

The bus pulled up and the gears ground and the door hissed.

Then he was inside, in the stale, air-conditioned smell, looking through the green-tinted windows.

He remembered watching a hamlet go up in smoke on the *CBS Evening News with Walter Cronkite* and thinking that the people who lived there, even if they rebuilt the place, would never live where they lived before. They could reconstruct everything so it looked exactly the same, but it would not be.

And Barry realized then he had just Zippoed the places that made him. All he had now was the future.

FRIDAY

✦　✦　✦

1

They were smoking Dunhills, and Belva was coughing. This had to be her fourth, and she felt a bit lightheaded. On top of that, they were laughing a lot, which made her throat rawer. The sex had been good and all the sweeter for having been unexpected this Friday morning. She was glad she had made time for Basil, though it had meant she'd had to double Edith's tip to fit the appointment in early.

"I love the intrigue of your life," he had said when she arrived. "It's like some court memoir or *Les liaisons dangereuses*. Though I don't," he added tartly, "intend to end up like Valmont."

"You won't." She smiled. She had never read the book but had seen the movie. She remembered it well enough to think that, however he might imagine it, he was not Valmont. The lovely boy perhaps . . . "You make too much of it." She let him slip her coat off. "Nobody in Rhymers Creek would have memoirs worth reading."

In their postcoital chat, Basil was finishing a story about his boarding school, where future prime ministers and earls and dukes buggered and beat each other and everyone put it down to fine, adolescent high spirits.

". . . So Bertram now is lord high executioner in the Foreign Office, and the boy he fagged for has to kowtow to him. And I don't think it crosses either of their minds that Bertram might

contemplate the slightest revenge on his brutal deflowerer."
Basil sighed. "England's such a spineless country." He snuffed his
cigarette. "Uh-oh. It's getting toward noon. What time's curfew?"

"I've got a few minutes," she said. "I need to go by the store so
Melva can run her errands. She'll close while I set the kids up for
the evening. Then I meet Wallace and the people from Chicago
for cocktails at Macaffey's by the Lake at five."

"Ah, such an elegant venue." Basil smiled. "At Macaffey's,
you can almost taste the mad sophistication of . . . Denver."

She smirked and slapped his chin playfully. "You are such a
snob, Basil. What do you expect around here, Venice?"

"No." He squinted. "Vicenza? Or one of those grim little
towns in Calabria, with a Romano-Byzantine church half-ruined
by Baroque renovations and blood feuds going back to the Empire
and ending, for the moment, with a rubout by the n'dragheta last
Tuesday."

Belva clucked her tongue. "Not Rhymers Creek. Though
there was the nut last year who chopped up his wife with a machete and dropped her in the pits. And there was my Aunt Carrie, of course."

"She was the one who killed her husband?"

"There was never a trial," Belva said reprovingly. "But that's
what we assume, just like everybody assumed Dewey — her husband — killed the snake charmer who was living with her when
he came back . . ."

"Who?"

"Dewey. He went to jail for killing a friend of his who said
Aunt Carrie was sleeping around. But that was never proved either."

"That he killed his friend?"

"No, no. That he killed the snake charmer."

"When was this, anyway?"

"Oh, forty years ago now."

Basil laughed. "Were they common back then? Snake charm-
ers?"

"He'd been traveling with a carnival. Don't be silly." Belva rolled her eyes. "Anyway, officially, the snake charmer got drunk and wandered off down by the river and drowned. Then Dewey was trying to burn out the trailer where the snakes were and there was a spark and up he went. And then Aunt Carrie left town."

"Never to be heard from again." Basil propped his head in his hand. "That's a nice story. Rococo in the details, mind you, but nice. You wouldn't think a place like this could evoke such grand passions, or murderous ones, anyway."

"You're wrong." Belva kissed him on the forehead. "It's exactly the kind of place you expect it. People don't have enough to do."

"So I was right, you see?" Basil smiled triumphantly. "It can be rather exciting here." Then he knit his brow. "Should I be worried about Wallace coming after me with a machete?"

Belva rubbed her hand softly over his chest and under the covers. "Wallace doesn't own a machete, dear," she purred. "Wallace doesn't own any sharp instruments."

✧

"Your hair's a mess!" Melva screeched as she came into the stockroom. "Couldn't you have worn a shower cap or something?"

Belva wasn't entirely sure the remark was a joke, which made it funnier when they both started to laugh. She passed her hand over her head. Melva was right.

"Help me fix it, honey," she said with some vague irritation. "We don't want Wallace to be embarrassed."

"Embarrassed?" Melva exclaimed, digging in her purse for her brush and motioning Belva to the vanity by the curtain separating the stockroom from the store. "Since when has Wallace's embarrassment been any concern of yours?"

"Don't get nasty." Belva sat down. "Over all the years, I've never flaunted things. It's something I'm proud of. . . . Ouch!"

"Hold still!" Melva snapped. "Why didn't you have Edith give you a wash and rinse if you were going over to Basil's?" She fished her comb out of her purse as well. "Let me get the mister."

She flipped through the curtain.

Belva studied herself in the mirror. Her hair really didn't look that bad, just a bit lopsided. But this evening was important. These were legal people in from Chicago. There was something about mergers or joint ventures in the air, and the deal was so close to done that the men had been prevailed upon to bring their wives.

"It's true you haven't flaunted it" — Melva whipped back through the curtain with the old Fantastic bottle they used to spray the plants — "but you can't convince me, in all the years, he hasn't figured out the score. Even if you've been careful, there's been enough talk."

"It never seems to have reached Wallace." Belva sighed, though she in fact did not believe that either. "He's never said a word."

"Tilt your head up."

As Melva fussed and misted, Belva questioned, as she hadn't in a while, why Wallace had never asked. When it began, she simply assumed he knew nothing; then, that he was merely stupid. When the children were small, he traveled a lot, and she came to think that, while he was out of town, he had his flings or even mistresses. At the plant, later, maybe there had been a long string of secretaries, though, if that were the case, she would have heard about it from Edith, or certainly from Marybelle. Recently, she had come to wonder if he had any libido left at all, or if it had been consumed in his work, in his endless acquirings of properties and poultry for the company, of cars and computers and a solid teak croquet set for them.

Belva had read that men reach their sexual peak when they are eighteen, while in women, it's thirty-four. It had always seemed wildly inefficient to her, though it perhaps explained her and

Basil: both she and he a few years past their primes. Wallace was never exceptional in bed. Handsome, surely, but something else life had taught her was that good looks are no guarantee of good sex. Then again, when she married him, there had been other things on her mind: motherhood and security and her ongoing failure to find a lasting relationship after the one with Randy Ditmars fell apart.

"Let me try a little mousse." Melva opened the drawer of the vanity and produced a canister, her operations accompanied by an ongoing chorus of tsks and moans, as if she were removing splinters. She smoothed some foam through her sister's dampened hair.

Belva wondered now and then if she had ever loved him. Sometimes, she wondered if she had ever really loved anybody. Surely not Randy, nor Dennis McElvay (her first affair), nor any of the other men she'd been to bed with, with the exception of Michael, of course. And, in the end, all he had brought her was heartache. Wallace, in that sense, had given her much more: the respectability of marriage, the children, fine clothes, travel, her own business . . .

"What do you think?"

It wasn't precisely what Edith had created, but it might be even better. She ought to look chic, but not too. These women were from Chicago — away from their hairdressers, their clothes delivered to hotel pressmen from garment bags tossed in and out of airplanes. Her part was to let them take their cosmopolitan vanity home in tact.

She turned her head from side to side. "Beautiful, Melva. Really. You missed your calling."

"Thanks." Her twin snorted. "If business doesn't pick up, I can always get on at Edith's."

Belva shrugged. "Well, it's as good as a dress shop. You can't be accused of stepping out with the customers."

"Are you kidding? In this day and age, I could be stepping out with *anyone*," Melva said nonchalantly, putting her comb and brush away.

Belva was surprised in spite of herself.

2

All that week at work, it had been strange. It did not surprise him really. Ezra had seen it before. It was always the same when somebody lost somebody. It was simply that his own loss had been going on so long, it seemed odd for people to recognize it now.

"I wanted you to know, Mr. Carraway" — Dink Morton grunted, leaning against his bulldozer as they were discussing the contours of the new pit — "how sorry Betsy and I am about your boy."

It touched him: that people had noticed, seen it in the paper or heard it from a friend; that they felt that he should know they knew. They were still anxious to share the sadness that, for him, had festered across all that time.

"You know, Mr. C, we all loved Bobbo," said Nancy Dorris, who had typed in the office for longer than he could remember. "I worshiped him in school. I'm glad we finally got him back."

The return of the remains had been hard. After so much waiting, there was more waiting still for the definitive identification, for all the papers, clearances, till finally the body of their son could come home. It had taken it out of him, brought back all the memories of that awful summer, when — so much younger — he had wondered if he or his wife could go on.

"We're all with you in your grief," Ned Rosen, who had had the office next to his for the last decade, told him with perfunctory sincerity. "It's got to be hard, but at least it puts an end to things." He paused. "I hear your other son's coming, too."

"Yes," Ezra said, and nothing more.

Your other son. He felt the sad trace of a smile on his lips as he drove out of the lot and onto the highway, some small, bitter amusement. The other son. The son who was other. The one who, nonetheless and ineluctably, was Ezra's, flesh of his flesh. People seemed to forget that Bobbo's last name was Starwick, not Carraway, though if he himself never thought much about it, why should they?

The other son: the one who had gone not to war but to hell, or so it had seemed at the time, and surely seemed still in the mind of Rhymers Creek. They remembered Bobbo as an orange and black streak on the football field; a sweaty, blond boy on his teammates' shoulders. They had not read those letters. They had not sat across the table from him in Honolulu, Myrna's hand clutched in theirs, sick with the knowledge that Bobbo was lost, and probably doomed.

The town's image of Barry, conversely, was of the radical hippie who had returned to Rhymers Creek from New York to outrage the draft board and break his parents' hearts. And, even absent, his assault on the good and the Christian continued, as in recent years he gained notoriety as a photographer of naked men, the object of condemnation of preachers and congressmen and political columnists.

And it was Barry who was his son. Not Bobbo. Bobbo was the spitting image of another father, the father who was his — Ezra's — friend and brother-in-arms, his own wife's first husband. To have had Bobbo for as long as they did was to have kept a little piece of Robbie, and now they had little pieces of Bobbo to put in the ground, and then there would be nothing left.

About him, over the years, they could do nothing, but much might have been done about Barry. And it had not been done. He had hurt them. Hurt them furiously, mother and father, some vicious, Old Testament son visited like a plague upon his parents, who in Scripture would have been struck down finally by the Lord Himself.

But no, Ezra thought, not Barry, Barach: Barak — defender of Deborah, victor of Megiddo, whose very Hebrew name meant "lightning." He was bearer, not victim, of the bolt. Or was he the bolt itself: bright and shocking as the burst of a flashbulb? What had possessed him, Ezra thought sometimes, with a stepson, if outlandishly nicknamed, so conventionally christened — Robert — to insist on that name from the Book of Judges? They — he and Myrna — had entertained other possibilities, but it was Barach they chose, for a long dead uncle who had fought in the Civil War, as they chose China for a long dead aunt who had left West Virginia and gone to Boston. And in his way, Ezra supposed, what a battler their Barach had become.

The family had not been pleased when Ezra married. They had once been Presbyterians, but the lukewarm Calvinism of the church as the century waxed drove them even further toward congregations where redemption — for whatever faith and goodness might be offered — was always a chimerical promise. Perhaps that was what drew Ezra to Robbie, and later to Myrna: the doctrines of penance, of good works, of free will. As a compromise after their marriage — for her family, in their way, was as religious and as bigoted as his own — they had begun to attend the Episcopal church, which was where the boys and then China were baptized. There was to the ceremony enough pomp for her and enough sermonizing for him, and they both appreciated the kindness of its God: One who might be gentle rather than just, even avuncular in His way, forgiving of the transgressions of His creatures, who were, after all, merely flesh.

But in that summer of 1970, Ezra once again believed in the brutal and unforgiving Father of his youth, far more terrible than the mortal one launching himself at a terrified fourteen-year-old with a razor strop in hand, One whose powers reached beyond those of eternal brimstone to smite and punish even in this life. In the space of mere weeks, he had lost both the jewels that were his sons, one disappeared, the other in revolt — Bobbo, the very last time he saw him on Waikiki, sneering: *"What do you mean, don't I ever regret it? Did you and my old man regret it when you wasted some Kraut!"* And Barry in the basement: *"What did*

*that mean? What kind of friendship was that! A man you were
so in love with that you . . ."*

Ezra made the turn, and he realized he was shaking. He was
going to see his son, the son who for so long had been merely a
voice on the phone, some words on a page, a picture in the paper.

Out of his mouth came a short, sharp cry. He could not, in
that instant, believe this could have happened. He would not
have allowed it. Myrna would not have allowed it. Across him,
as had not happened for decades, there came a sudden, awful
sense of sin, for sin is finally absence. The absence of good.

He turned into the driveway and parked. His eyes were wet.

In the doorway, he saw Myrna.

And then a car pulled up to the curb.

Barry stood there, the little bell pinging to tell him the door was
still ajar.

His mother was on the threshold. His father in the driveway.
The lawn was brittle brown, dotted here and there with white,
and the shrubs, bare and bent from the remaining ice, were larger
than he remembered. They had taken out a hedge, but the
house — brick and shutters and white trim — was exactly as he
recollected it in New York City: every night that first summer,
then more and more sporadically, until finally it only came to
mind when he dreamt.

His father walked down the icy, pocked cement. He was older,
older, older. His hair was gray and largely gone in front. But the
face was the same, a sincere one, not handsome necessarily.
Barry began to move toward him.

They stopped, both of them, right at the instant they faced
each other. His father put out his hand. Barry took it. And then,
effortfully, like two identical poles of magnets that will not
align, they drew together, hugging clumsily in a one-armed embrace.

"Hello, Pa," he said roughly.

His father's head fell heavy on his shoulder. "Hello, Barry."

They remained like that for only seconds. Even after so long, this was public after all, though even in private, such shows were somewhat suspect. In all his nervousness and joy, Barry still smiled, thinking of the endless embraces, the numberless kisses planted on the cheeks, foreheads, and lips of women and men all over New York for more than two decades. This was another place.

Side by side, not arm in arm, they approached the porch. They mounted the steps, and he stood before his mother, this woman who had not really spoken more than two dozen words successively to him in all that time. She was smaller, and a little bent now. Her face was lined. She put her arms out, and he did the same, and they came together in a nervous embrace as she pecked him on the cheek.

She said only, "Barry."

And he said, "Ma."

Inside, the entry hall and living room had a certain worn coziness. Much was different: the rug, the drapes, the sofa. The end tables were the same, a ruddy cherry, bright with recent refinishing. On the walls were a couple of Impressionist prints, and a landscape that looked as if it might have come from a motel.

His father sat down, and his mother said, "I'll get some tea," and disappeared. Barry perched on the edge of the couch.

There was a long, uncomfortable silence. His father leaned back in his easy chair. "Well, welcome back, Barry. We've missed you."

He relaxed a little. "I've missed you, too."

They eased into conversation then: first about China, who was simple to talk about. His mother returned with a pot and cups and some store-bought cookies.

"Seth and Rachel are both giving her fits right now," she said. "It's funny to see her try to keep her cool."

The words hit his ears oddly. It was not the kind of expression his mother would have used. He did not know these people anymore. They had grown up, too. He realized in some part of his mind separate from that which asked questions and made answers — neutral and amused — that, though his life had changed radically since they had last seen him, theirs had changed as well. They were not the same as they had been when he last confronted them, directly below where they were sitting now, in that furious and final standoff.

"Barry. Barry! That cannot be. It is disgusting . . ."

"It is not disgusting . . ."

"It is disgusting . . . and sick . . . and, and shameful." His father's voice, his whole body, shuddering, scared and appalled. "How could you" — small and soft — "How could you" — almost a whisper — "even begin to admit to something that" — searching for the word that would somehow capture what he felt — "vile."

"The tables do look terrific," Barry agreed. "Did they use one of those polyurethane sealants?"

"Verathane. It makes them so easy to keep," his mother said.

He realized they were not going to take note. Not his father. Not his mother. Not him. They were not going to notice all the years that had passed. They were going to press on, certain that blood was thicker than water, that the pain he had caused them and they, him was something to be borne, something so dark and potent that the very mention of it would blast away all their good intentions, ruin this fragile moment. Then, they might never have another chance.

His mother was there then, weeping, repeating again, "Oh, God. Oh, God. How could you do this? Barry. Oh, God."

And his father, "The draft board! Barry, this will ruin your life. Your whole life blown to hell. If it's true, why did you have to tell anybody? My God! Why did you tell anybody at all!"

"I've been doing better than ever really," he was saying warily. "The publicity, well, in a funny way, turned out to be good. Before, things were pretty much hand to mouth, but now, I've had commissions, portraits, family stuff," he added with a slight smile, "shows here and there. People are angry about how politicized it's become."

They both nodded with a determined interest, all the while wondering, he was sure, what pornography he had been creating, wishing he would talk about anything else.

"I saw a wonderful exhibition last week of photos of West Virginia. Really beautiful stuff. What do you hear from Grafton?"

There was a short pause. His mother sighed.

"We'd hoped Cousin Richard would be coming," his father said. "You all used to play together when you were kids. He's really the only one we were expecting."

Barry realized this was a sore spot, but it was too late now. More than that, he knew that another subject, more painful than his own absence, had been broached.

He looked at the carpet. "Well," he said softly, "I guess not too many of them up there think much about Bobbo anymore."

It hung there, the name, though, Barry reflected, they had to recognize why this had come about, that he had not merely dropped in.

His mother's eyes misted.

"That's true," his father said evenly. "We can't really expect it to mean as much to them as it does to all of us."

None was looking at the others, as if, at last, here in their house — all of theirs — they were feeling his absence. Bobbo had last roamed these rooms in 1967, back from boot camp, just before he shipped out: hair cropped, sweating a boyish masculinity — brash, desperate, for Barry irritating and exciting and frightening at once: a tight end's cockiness heated to the point of danger, football's violence raised unto the lawless realm of murder.

More time had passed since then than Bobbo had been alive.

"Excuse me a sec," Barry said.

He went upstairs. He stood by the railing on the second floor, the bathroom in front of him, but he did not go in. He turned to the left and opened the door.

The boys' room.

They had not changed it to a sewing nook or den. His bed nestled one wall and Bobbo's the other, the matching desks flanking the window. It was neat as a pin — no papers or clothes strewn about, no shoes peeking from beneath the beds. There was a thin patina of dust on the clumsy Zenith stereo in the corner; a newspaper clipping, dry and yellowed, hung from one of the lampshades.

He took a step inside, then another. He wondered if they could hear his footfalls below. He was almost on tiptoe.

On his side of the room, the photographs he had taken in high school — cheerleaders, sunsets, Ambrosia Lane — were hanging where he'd left them. Under the glass of his desk, a group portrait — Tully and Kathy and Karry and Tom Walter — had bleached badly, but those adolescent faces still beamed silly and unself-conscious. All his books were on the bedside shelf — *Demian, Black Like Me, Jacob Riis: Photographer, The Family of Man* — and protruding from the last, the curled petals of a Riki-Tiki-Stiki, its waxed backing cracked, a flower-shaped bumper sticker with MCCARTHY in the center.

He sat on the bed, remembering Bobbo, those last days they had shared this room, Barry just sixteen. Roughhousing just as they always had, Bobbo suddenly threw him to the ground with a force that knocked the wind from him entirely, then leapt upon him, steely as a cat, his knee against his throat.

"I could kill you if I wanted," he said with malicious softness.

And Barry's confusion was complete — utter terror combined with some inexplicable desire, as if, if Bobbo — that perfect brother always finally gentle now turned panther — would not possess him, he could slaughter him and simply end it all.

Barry's head had missed the bedpost by less than an inch.

He looked across the room. Bobbo's side, compared with his, looked opulent in brass and chrome; his bookshelf, his bureau, his walls covered with trophies and plaques: "Most Athletic," "Outstanding Leopard," "Best-Looking Boy, 1966." On his shelves, there was a pristine copy of *The Red Badge of Courage*, along with other equally smooth-spined classics. Under glass on his desk were clippings of those ongoing autumn triumphs, one of the pictures credited to a freshman photographer by the name of Barry Carraway.

He opened the top drawer of Bobbo's dresser. It was not the way he remembered it when, as a teeanger, he had stolen a look in it from time to time. Now, everything was arranged neatly. Their mother had been at work. Barry opened the jewel box — a cheap alligator imitation in black. There were medals, a Purple Heart, which he recognized, along with other stars and ribbons Bobbo must have sent home one by one before he disappeared. He pushed them aside, and beneath there was a darkly tarnished bronze football, attached to a blue ribbon that said, in white letters, AA REGIONAL CHAMPS.

It had been the proudest moment of Bobbo's life — the final seconds, the impossible catch and run, the hysteria in the stands, the page-one story in the *News and Gazetteer*. From the edge of the throng, Barry had watched his brother hoisted aloft and carried around the stadium, everyone screaming himself hoarse, disbelieving of the miracle brought them by this young god of the backfield, unhelmeted now, his own face a study in astonishment. It was at that moment Barry realized just how he adored Bobbo, and how he would never be him, and how, after this senior year, things would never be the same again.

"Barry?"

It was his mother at the base of the stairs.

He eased the drawer shut. "Be right there."

He slipped the medal into his pocket and went downstairs.

They talked for an hour — easy things, trivial things. He asked after his friends, and they told him about the battle to refurbish the Courthouse, about the Beauford twins' dress shop, which sold the wackiest fashions, about the expansion of the chicken works. His father talked about the pits, and retiring. It was two o'clock.

"I better get going," he said, "and, Pa, you better get back to work."

Barry stood, and they stood. They went to the door. He kissed his mother and shook his father's hand, touching his shoulder this time rather than embracing.

Walking to the threshold, he glanced back and smiled, though what his eyes fixed on were not his parents but the door behind them. The door that led to the basement.

As he started the car, he could feel the sting on his cheek from the last time he had left. Eleven-fifteen on a Tuesday night in June, with his jacket and his duffel bag that, before he had gone downstairs, he had placed by the newel post because he suspected he was going to have to go.

"How can you admit this!" His father, furious and stunned at once. "How can you even talk about it!"

His mother on the davenport that had come with them from Grafton, covered with a throw and sagging in the middle, her face in her hands.

"I will not be ashamed!" he said loudly, angrily. "It is true. It is who I am. I will not be ashamed."

"It is wrong!"

"It is not wrong!" Barry's voice so loud it was cracking. "It is not wrong! I will not allow you to say that! You. What am I supposed to make of you! Of you!" The voice rabid now. "You and Robbie Starwick! What did that mean! What kind of friendship was that! A man you were so in love with that you married his wife!"

He did not see her as she flew from the sofa. His eyes were on his father's face, wrathful and tragic. Her palm struck him powerfully, spinning his head away from her and then, for the force, recoiling back toward her.

"Get out!" Screaming at him. "You are unnatural! Get out!"

When he had told it over the years, some people had laughed. It seemed so Shakespearean, Biblical. *Unnatural child.* And he had smiled along with the joke but never meant it. The pain had never gone away. He had stumbled up the stairs, gathered his bags, fled into darkness. Staggering down the empty street, lined with neat and respectable houses, knowing that this was the definitive end of something. As he rushed toward town, on foot though it would take a good forty-five minutes to get to Billy Peters's apartment, he felt some weird mix of triumph and power and loss, some terrible need to laugh and cry at once, something Bobbo might have felt in the moment after a battle was done and he discovered he was still alive.

Barry touched his pocket. The medal was there. He turned the key, released the brake, and set off toward his hotel.

She stood in the doorway and waved. For the first time since she knew that Barry was in town, she breathed a little easier. It had not been quite as hard as she imagined. He had not been extravagant or effeminate. He had not been Elwood Pomeroy, nor Elliot Milliman, the gay biker she had met at Wellesley Coe's wedding. Barry had no tattoos, not even an earring, nor was he pumped up like some professional wrestler. He looked nice: his face unlined, healthy.

That fear, today, had coiled next to her heart: that secretly he was sick. When she had first read back in the eighties of the deaths of young, homosexual men in New York, mixed with the sense that this was somehow God's judgment was the sinking realization that Barry might die. For all her fury, her stubborn insistence on not seeing him or speaking to him, that remained unthinkable: that there would never be a chance to reconcile. That Myrna could not abide, for despite everything she still loved him with that tigerish love that makes women defend murderers and traitors, solely because they are their sons.

She went back into the living room and picked up the teapot, cups, and empty plate. Barry still loved cheap, store-bought sugar cookies, and she wondered if he had noticed she remembered. She carried everything to the kitchen and began to rinse the dishes.

As time had passed, she had sometimes felt she made too much of it. In the years he had been away, the world, even Rhymers Creek, had changed. If people still made jokes and rude remarks, it was not like it was when Barry had first announced to them what he had become. Then, it had been a thing to be hidden: at worst, a choice for sin; at best, a burden imposed by capricious destiny.

Inevitably now, as she looked over her life, as she thought about the strange and terrible shift that had blighted her happiness in the blink of an eye years before, she had to ask what she had done to deserve this. That had been hardest of all: the sense that somehow — with Barry, with Bobbo — she had failed. She had wanted to be the finest mother. She had read all the advice on how to raise your children: make them happy, healthy, normal. In the end, she had felt she achieved what she wished only with China, that somehow, with the boys, she had gone wrong.

And it had been her failure. That was what those books and articles told her. Not Ezra's. Not Bobbo's or Barry's. At least, with her boy who was dead, she could say that history had taken a hand, that the man she met in Hawaii had been twisted by the horror that was the War. Ezra had assured her: she could not understand what the experience of killing could do to people, that the demon in reflector glasses in Honolulu was the product not of their error but of what he had witnessed and what he had done.

But with Barry, it was different. She had been overprotective, or not protective enough. She had been too strict, or allowed him too much freedom. Her love for him had been too smothering, so he did not want any other women; her love for him had been too cold, and so he looked to men for comfort. She knew the theories — the magazine versions of them anyway — and they all accused her. She was to blame. Ann Landers told her so. And Dr. Spock. And all the endless columnists across the years. So, when Barry had faced them — defiant and boastful — in the basement that night, what was she supposed to feel but fury and betrayal and guilt?

And what made it all the harder was what he had said, for was there to it some terrible kernel of truth? Her marriage to Ezra, she sometimes thought, was some sort of strange incest, like having married if not her brother then her brother-in-law. As such, there would be some inevitable and perverse retribution.

Too, as Barry, in youthful and furious voice, mouthed the question of what Ezra and Robbie had felt for each other, she had asked it herself the very instant she slapped him. It was not as if it had not occurred to her, that somehow in her Ezra saw his love unrequited and unrequitable for that golden man who was Robbie, and that she married her lost and straying husband's best friend because the two of them were united in desire and mourning. Along with her horror at what Barry announced was the horror of what he asserted.

It was not true. In an odd and terrible way, that accident on the way to El Centro had been a blessing, as if, in God's eye, Robbie — so much a man born to be twenty or twenty-five, but never thirty-one or forty or sixty — had fulfilled the destiny that had been given him: to bring together a girl from Long Beach and a boy from West Virginia. It was her marriage to Ezra that was fated; that relationship the one certain to endure, as it had despite the loss of Bobbo, of Barry. Most others could never have withstood such rents in the fabric of their lives.

She was standing by the kitchen window, the dishes all in the drainer. There was the steady patter of the ice melting — drip, drip, drip — from the eaves. Like the tick of a clock.

Her hand went to her mouth.

It had been so long since she had seen Barry, their son. Theirs. Not hers. How could they have let so many years pass?

It was getting on toward three. She should call China to let her know how things had gone. But it was hard to move, thinking how they were, after all that time, a family again, though that reunion, in the end, had been purchased at a terrible price.

3

She lay in the dark. Wallace was snoring. That was not unusual. Sex before sleep was something Belva had stopped expecting long, long ago. What was unusual was that the television was not on. She was not there, nightcap in hand, with David Letterman or a detective series with some star from the 'fifties looking gray and breathless. She was absolutely still in her darkened bedroom, and wide awake, and not at all unhappy about it.

She was recollecting.

"That pretty much describes what I've been doing," Barry had said over coffee that afternoon. "Recollecting. Re-collecting. Picking up things I threw down years ago and having a look again. They're a lot different when you're twenty years older."

She had not expected to see him until the next day at the funeral. She had left Letting Loose with the best intentions, striking out for the post office to complain about the Christmas mailing — arriving a full two weeks late so the store was full of merchandise she had never been convinced they could move anyway.

She had a scarf tied under her chin, which made her look like an extra from one of the refugee scenes in *Dr. Zhivago*. Outside, it was treacherous, with massive icicles crashing down from the eaves and tree boughs, puddles in the sunshine and slippery patches in the shade. Wednesday's and Thursday's snow had resolved into muddy slush, and she wished as she crossed to the Square that she had galoshes. Low clouds tumbled across the sun in the stiff breeze, so the play of light and shadow was capricious and rapid, like time-lapse photography. That was the very image she had in her mind as she mounted the curb and squinted across the Square, where she saw a figure on one of the benches rolling film out of a camera.

She hesitated. Approaching him might seem forward, or morbidly curious. She had not known him very well. He was merely Bobbo's little brother. He might think she was speaking to him because of the scandal, for some gossip to share after he had left town.

At that point, he looked up, and there was no way she could do anything but wave. He waved back, and she walked to where he sat.

"Hello, Barry," she said. She could see him searching her face for clues from decades before, and for a name that fit them.

"Belva Beauford. Or Melva?"

She was pleased he had thought of her first. "Belva," she said. She put out her hand. "Long time, no see."

He laughed, and shifted on the bench. "That's for sure," he said as he pressed her hand. "How've you been?"

He did not suggest she sit, merely made room for her so she could if she wanted. She did. She liked him immediately. "Not bad. Better than I deserve probably."

He twisted his mouth into a look of easy disbelief. "I saw your store the other night. It reminded me of New York."

"Coming from you, I know that's a compliment," Belva said, "though a lot of people here wouldn't mean it that way." She realized that sounded wrong, given who he was, where he was from, what people were saying about him. But he seemed nonplussed. "But it's you who made a name for himself. I think it's terrific."

"Well, I suspect that's not something a lot of people here would say either."

"I won't lie to you about that one." She smiled. "But, you know, I've actually seen your work. It was years ago at a gallery in Soho. Some kind of benefit, I think."

"Oh, really?" There was a certain indulgence to it.

"Yes," she said, rising to the challenge. "It was a series. A blond man. There were other photographers in the show. One guy into tattoos, but it was your stuff I liked best."

"'Eighty-three maybe? The AIDS benefit at the Mesta Gallery?"
"Maybe. The woman who ran it was Lydia something."
"Sure enough." He nodded. "How did you end up there?"
"We were on a buying trip, Melva and me," she said quickly. "Some friends went by the show. We were on our way to dinner."
"I can imagine you there. But how did Melva deal with it? The two of you were always so different."

She was pleased that he would grant her that sophistication, but the conversation was taking a turn she felt she could not control.

"She wasn't with me that day. She was sick." She could see he was not convinced. "Those pictures of yours were really wonderful," she continued awkwardly, "though I guess it's only now you're getting your due." As the words came out of her mouth, she realized how they might be read. "I mean, with the controversy. . . . I remember a couple years back some fellow on the news talking about what a genius you were."

"Oh, I don't know, Belva." He looked down at the camera in his lap. "I'll tell you something. I've always thought I was a damn good photographer, but that's about it. I never made much of a living, until now. If it hadn't been for a couple of real geniuses and some congressmen looking to get reelected, nothing would have changed." He grinned. "I owe those bastards a lot."

She began to laugh when there was a sudden gust of wind. She grabbed at her scarf as it lifted off her head.

"Oh, I've got to get out of this," she said.
"Want to have coffee?"

The offer surprised her but intrigued her, too. She really should go to the post office as she had promised.

"Sure. I've got a minute."

On the way into the Tea Shoppe at the Old Courthouse, Belva would later admit to herself it gave her a bit of a thrill to be seen walking in beside Barry Carraway. Marybelle would have a field day.

"So you're Masterson now, is that right?" he said as they sat down. "My mother mentioned it," he replied to her unanswered question, "so I know he came here with Wilson's from someplace else. But you always liked guys from out of town. When I left, you were seeing somebody in Memphis. Randy? Dumars, something like that?"

"Ditmars. I can't believe you can bring all that back."

He shrugged. "I've been recalling a lot these last few days. It's amazing how much you've got stored away that it just takes a little toggle to set loose again."

She could feel a touch of disappointment on her face.

"But I probably could have flipped that switch anyway," he added smoothly. "I always liked you best of Bobbo's girlfriends."

The waitress came. Belva took tea and a sticky bun. Barry, only coffee.

"I mean that, by the way." He settled back in his chair. "I really did like you the best. Though I have to admit, I always wondered if Bobbo could have kept up with you."

She raised her eyebrows.

"You were a lot more sophisticated than he was," Barry said. "Even I could see it, and I was pretty much a hick myself. Back then, when he was still in high school, he was pretty innocent."

"Not as innocent as you think," she said, a little gruffly.

"Not that way, Belva." Their order came. She knew he knew they had slept together. "You had a lot better handle on the world. If he'd stayed with you, maybe he would have learned something. As it was, he went off to school, and then to Vietnam, and, well . . ."

She did not reply. She let the tea soothe her throat, which was still rough from the Dunhills. He sipped his coffee.

"Did Bobbo . . . ," Barry began, "Did Bobbo send you something? There toward the end?"

Her cup stopped in midair.

"The end?"

"There in those last six months or so before he disappeared."

She felt a shiver. In Rhymers Creek, she had never told anyone. And now, years after the fact, somebody had known all along. She was wary, but curious, too. "Yes."

Barry smiled sadly. "I'm sorry. I'm prying. It's just that he never forgot you. He'd mention you sometimes. You were about the only person from Rhymers Creek he ever wrote much about, except for family. I got this weird letter — most of his letters were weird, but this one was weirder — and he was furious. You hadn't written in a long time, and he went off about women. Then, sometime later on, there was this P.S. He said something about how he'd gotten back at you."

"Why do you think he sent me something?"

"Because later, he sent something to me."

"It was an ear," she found herself saying. "A human ear. It was the most disgusting thing I ever saw. For a minute, I didn't even realize what it was. But the smell. If I think about it, I can still smell it." She shuddered. "They put me in the infirmary. One of the girls on the hall threw it in the incinerator." She shook her head to try to rid herself of the memory. She did not look at him. "What did he send you?"

There was a pause. "It was after I was back in New York. Even after he disappeared, stuff would show up. He must have given letters to people to mail. I'd moved, too, so maybe it was just delays in forwarding them. Ghost letters, I called them. One day in October, this one came. I opened it up and a picture fell out."

He stopped. She realized suddenly this was very hard for him.

"At first . . . at first, I couldn't tell what it was. It was fuzzy. They'd had the camera too close and the focus was bad. I finally figured out it was a face, a Vietnamese, and there was something in his mouth. Something bloody. I knew then." Barry took a breath. "I shook the envelope and there was a note. It said, 'This is what I do to cocksuckers.'"

Belva groaned. She did not mean to. But as the photograph flickered across her mind, she could not help herself.

He shook his head. "For years and years, I didn't tell anybody. And then, when I could, nobody could react to it. None of my friends in New York knew Bobbo. It didn't mean anything to them that he'd do something like that. And here, who could I mention it to?" He snuffed a sad laugh. "It's not something you tell your folks. But I figured I could tell you. I'm sorry. It was selfish."

She looked at him with new eyes. He might be Barry Carraway, notorious photographer, but he still was Bobbo Starwick's little brother after all. And the two of them, she and Barry, had shared that boy turned soldier, shared most terribly what he had become.

"I never told anyone here either," she said. "I was afraid it might get back to your family, and they had enough grief as it was. Besides, I didn't want to think of it."

They were silent for a moment.

"The problem," Barry said slowly, "was I could never figure how someone who was so wonderful could turn into someone so terrible. After that picture came — not right away, but not that long after — I'd think sometimes that it was a good thing he was MIA. That he would never be the same after what he'd been through."

"He was the sweetest boy I ever knew," Belva said, almost dreamy. "I mean that. The most special. Gentle. And thoughtful. Sexy. But a boy. Not a man. I never knew him as a man. I don't think he did either. That's what soldiering does. It doesn't make men out of boys. It lets men be boys for longer than anybody should be. And men who don't grow up aren't Peter Pan. They're Captain Hook."

Barry smiled. "I've known enough of those," he said.

She did not know why it occurred to her to say it. "So, you've been in love?"

He rolled his glass back and forth in his hands. She could see his surprise. But surely, sometime, Bobbo must have told him she would say the most outrageous things.

"Oh, yes," he said. "You, too?"

She shook her head. "You're too quick for me, Barry." They both laughed. "But not that many. There's my husband . . ." She let it linger. There was no point in lying. His family had probably heard rumors. "And others here and there. Even in New York."

"It's a good place for love."

Their voices fell to a low, conspiratorial tone. She wondered why he needed to talk about this but then decided it was obvious, that there was no one else here in Rhymers Creek he could speak to about his real life. And she, both a bit sophisticated and a bit scandalous, would be his logical choice, so that at least one person in his hometown would know something more about him than what appeared in the newspapers.

"Was there one who was the most special?"

"Oh, yes. Jacy. He was the one in the pictures."

She took an appreciative breath. "He was pretty special."

He smiled.

"But it didn't work out?"

"No," Barry said with a soft wistfulness. "It didn't work out."

She did not pursue it. She was feeling comfortable, and warm, and surely the story Barry had to tell was sad: the man was lost, and probably dead. "That's the other thing about New York. A lot of things don't work out."

He raised his eyebrows, and she told him about Michael.

"We saw each other off and on for years. I went with him to your show. You were right. Melva wouldn't have stayed a minute."

The two names — Jacy and Michael — floated above them, and she was glad he did not ask her what had happened.

She talked then about Leisel and Ross and being astonished she was a mother, and he told her about what it was like to be back, about re-collecting, and another word she'd never thought much about.

"It's been hard," he said, "all this remembering. It takes me back to a lecture I heard in college, back when Bobbo was alive. It was about *Hamlet*, and the professor talked about Hamlet 're-membering' his father. Re-membering, making him whole again. And somehow, after all those years, I'm trying to take those pieces of Bobbo that are over at the funeral home, and, at least in my head, re-member him, put him back together so I can bury him and not regret it."

Belva thought for a moment she might cry, her own memories mixing with Barry's, about the boy they both lost so long ago.

She glanced at her watch. It was four-thirty. She would have to give up the post office and catch hell from Melva, but she didn't mind. There would barely be time to get home and then to Macaffey's.

She signaled the waitress and tried to pay, though he wouldn't let her. As she left, he kissed her on the cheek.

"I'm glad we talked, Barry," she said.

"Me, too." He smiled. "See you in church."

So now, she was in bed, awake in the darkness. Recalling. Recollecting. Putting it all together, piece by piece, the last twenty years and more, since she had been in another double bed, with Bobbo Starwick sprawled above her, deep within her. It was strange how everything ran together, so you could not really tell when things happened, when you became what you were, when you accepted the world would not be precisely what you once imagined.

And that was why it was so important, she thought there, next to Wallace snoring, to recollect it all and try to make sense of it. It had been so long since the challenge had even presented itself that she should have been scared. But she wasn't.

It was time to take stock.

Time to bring back other times.

It was time to remember.

PLEASURE VICTIMS

❖   ❖   ❖

1

"There's a special on the Four Roses, Fred," Gilly Gilmore said as he turned to the television. "Might want to stock up."

In silver studs across the back of his denim vest, it said: NIX ON NIXON. On the black-and-white portable on the counter, some white-haired congressman said Nixon's conduct was inexcusable.

Fred decided to pass on the Four Roses. "This'll do it, Gilly," he said, hefting the twelve-pack of Miller beside the register.

A voice came from behind him. "Cheetos or Fritos? Make up your mind."

"But I can't make up my mind."

Fred glanced over his shoulder. It was Tully Coe and Chris Eldon by the snacks display. They both giggled. They had the red-eyed, smiley slouch of good dope.

"I know." Tully sighed theatrically. "If you only had a brain." They giggled again.

Fred pulled his money out. "Come on, Gilly."

"Okay, okay." Gilly sidled to the counter but kept his head turned. "Jeez, they're really gonna nail his ass!"

"Yeah, I guess." Fred nodded wearily, watching Gilly make change from a ten with just three quick glances away from the TV.

He stepped into the stifling July and slung the beer into the back of the truck. Through the window of The Watering Hole, he could see Tully and Chris at the counter, and Gilly, still transfixed by the impeachment hearings. Fred was tired of the whole business with Nixon. When it had started two years before, the only thing that surprised him was that other people seemed surprised. After his tour of duty, the notion that anyone would believe a single word out of a politician's mouth was as unthinkable as a snowy day in Saigon. For a long time, he ignored it. He had not been alone in that. At Pep Boys, most people — employees and customers — simply wanted it to go away. But in the last few weeks, it was all anyone talked about. When Momma — after having praised the president through thick and thin — said last time he saw her she thought Nixon was a crook, Fred knew he was as good as gone.

He got in the truck and turned the key. The radio came on. The engine sputtered. He touched the accelerator to give it some gas.

Nothing.

He tried again. The truck turned over but didn't engage. He pumped the pedal and turned the key.

Nothing.

He sat there. Stevie Wonder was singing "Superstition."

He smacked the dashboard. "Goddamnit!"

"Got a problem, Fred?"

Tully and Chris were standing in the lot with their lazy smiles and hair to their shoulders. They wore matching T-shirts that said in the blocky black letters of novelty booths at the County Fair: I DON'T THINK WE'RE IN KANSAS ANYMORE, TOTO.

"Looks like it."

Tully, carrying a bag already damp from his own sweat and that of whatever was inside, passed it to Chris. "Could be your carburetor. Want me to dick with it?"

Fred hesitated. Did he really want some stoned kid messing with his truck? He did not know Tully that well. He and Chris had been three years behind Fred in school; he hadn't been much inclined to give them the time of day back then, and certainly not in the years since. He presumed the feeling was mutual. Still, despite his job in the Pep Boys stockroom, beyond how to pump gas and check the air in the tires and water in the battery and oil in the crankcase, his acquaintance with engines was pretty limited.

"Well," he said slowly, "if you think you can figure it out."

Tully reached in his pocket and pulled out a Swiss Army knife. He popped the hood open, so Fred couldn't see what was happening. Chris stood — patient — staring dumbly into space, the brown paper bag slowly turning darker and darker in his arms.

It occurred to Fred it must be real good grass.

"Try it now," he heard Tully shout.

He cranked it again, but all they heard was the whine of the starter motor. Tully stepped back and slammed the hood.

"Sorry, man, that's not it, looks like."

"Thanks, anyhow." Fred got out of the cab, fishing in his pocket for a dime. "I guess I'll have the damn thing towed to I.J.'s."

"Shit, Fred, don't do that. I.J. Bannister'll charge your left nut just to look at it."

Fred shrugged. "Don't have much choice, do I?"

"Well" — Tully raised his stoney eyes to Chris, who smiled — "you still got that tow chain in the back, don't you?"

"I think so." Chris handed the disintegrating bag to Tully and turned toward his own truck there in the lot. On the back of his T-shirt, in the same black lettering, it said: BORN TO RAISE HELL.

He felt strange at the steering wheel — the cab unnaturally silent, lashed to the back of Chris Eldon's ancient Dodge pickup — and just a little afraid of what he had gotten himself into. "Gimme fifty bucks up front and I'll fix it for you," Tully had said confidently, "plus parts, but you've got to pay me retail at Constellation for those. Nothing from Pep Boys." Fred was tempted to forget it and call Bannister's Garage and Esso, but Tully was winning and knew about cars and it happened Fred had finally cashed his check that afternoon, so he had money in his pocket. And, in the end, it touched him that Tully had even offered.

No one had offered much since he came back home. As the war he had fought became ever less popular and more futile, Fred's isolation grew greater and greater, day to day, year to year. Any Vietnam vet had been too dumb to stay in school, too stupid to avoid the draft, too bloodthirsty to give peace a chance. When he had gotten on at Pep Boys, Roger Hawthorne had made it clear it was charity, something he might not have done but for a cousin who had been on a boat in the Mekong Delta and, once back, could not find a job to save his soul.

With a regular paycheck coming in, Fred had managed to rent an apartment — a dim room with a hot plate. But at least it got him away from Momma and Daddy, from their aggrieved bewilderment at his drinking and his silence and his dreams. To stay in the house where he grew up offered little but a constant reminder of the vast disappointment he had turned out to be. Now, he was saving to buy a trailer that — whether he set it down in a park or hitched it to his truck and took to the open road — would provide him the quiet and tenuous peace that seemed his destiny.

They made the turn into Mockdon Glen. Fred had heard at some point that Chris and Tully had rented a place with Billy Peters and Eddie Hammersmith. Winding through the subdivision, the first one built in Rhymers Creek back in the fifties, it was not hard to figure which of the low-slung ranch houses was theirs. As they turned another corner, Tully could hear the Doobie Brothers, and then he saw Billy and Eddie on an old yellow sofa in the shade of the garage door, lounging in the late sunset. Braking in front of the house, Fred could see they had on T-shirts, too. He knew without looking what they said.

Their faces registered surprise at the truck in tow, and more when Fred got out. He stood by the fender, unsure what to do.

"Hey, Fred," Tully said, "want a beer?"

With cans of Bud open on the cement, the five of them un-hitched the chain and pushed Fred's truck up the driveway.

"Did you listen to the news?" Eddie said, puffing against the fender. "They voted another article of impeachment."

Chris rolled his eyes. "Jeez, you ought to go down and hang out with Gilly. I thought we were never going to get out of there."

Tully picked up his own beer, and Fred's. "Say, man, you change the plugs on this baby sometime?" he asked as he handed it to him.

It sounded almost like an accusation. "Not in a while, I guess," Fred mumbled.

Tully shrugged. "It's not your battery. Could be the plugs are fouled. Or the fuel line, maybe. We'll figure it out, though."

"Right." Chris walked over and slapped Fred on the shoulder. "Ol' Oz the Great and Powerful here'll get it running good as new."

✧

It was dark. The yellow light from the garage pooled on the asphalt, while, over the engine well, the white glare of the trouble lamp cast harsh shadows on the greasy innards of Fred's truck. Tully clicked the socket off his wrench and sighed.

"Plugs are okay," he said, reaching a dirty hand down and snatching the last slice of the pizza they had ordered, now an hour cold. "Has she been running rough? Funny noises?"

Fred tried to think of any peculiar clanks or bangs, but the truck, bought used a year after he got back from Vietnam, had so many wheezes and snorts, whines and groans, that some odd new one would probably not have even drawn his attention.

"I'll check the fuel lines tomorrow. You want to crash here?"

"Huh?"

Tully slammed the hood. "Doesn't look like anybody's getting any nooky tonight, so you can have the couch in the living room." He began to loop the trouble lamp cord around his arm.

"That's the only thing about this place. It ought to have more bedrooms."

Tully moved toward the house, but Fred held back. He was unhappy that it had not been the plugs, that Tully had not yet diagnosed what the problem was. But far more than that, he was stunned he had been invited to spend the night. He had not slept anywhere but his own bed since he came back from Canterwell's in 1970.

"Well, gee. I mean, I don't want to be any trouble."

"Shit, people crash here all the time. Come on in."

In the living room, Chris and Billy were sprawled on the floor. One entire wall was taken up with speakers, a turntable, and tape deck. The other three sported two Woodstock posters, one of Led Zeppelin, and a garish Indian bedspread. There was a sofa and an armchair. That was all the furniture. Between Chris and Billy was another pizza box, a bag of Cheetos, and a bong.

"Hey, it's the goddamn Wiz himself," Billy croaked.

"Yeah, and who ate all the goddamn Cheetos!"

"The Munchkins had the munchies," Eddie said as he came in from the kitchen. "Heads up."

He lobbed a beer at Chris, then one at Billy. Neither caught them. He handed cans to Fred and Tully and opened the last for himself. Billy's and Chris's spewed foam as they popped the tops.

"Jesus," Tully moaned as he slipped down on the sofa. "I don't know about you two."

"Fuck you," Chris said. "Go away and come back tomorrow."

Fred eased himself into the chair. He felt strangely accelerated. It had been so long since he had done this — since the War, since San Diego: hanging out drinking beer with the guys.

Tully sighed. "Just fire up the bong, okay? Jesus, we got company."

Billy rolled into a sit and surveyed Fred critically, as critically as he could in his condition. "Yeah. I guess we do. What star did you fall from, Fred?"

Chris reached over and punched Billy in the arm. "Lay off, ass-hole. He brings you good news, or haven't you heard? You're going to get that thirty bucks Coe owes you."

Tully threw a cushion in Chris's direction. "You fucker!"

Chris put his hands up in protest. "Hey, hey. Be cool, before somebody drops a house on you."

Eddie was loading the bong. Fred leaned forward in the chair. "What is all this *Wizard of Oz* shit?"

"Now you did it," Tully moaned.

Chris popped to his feet, staggered, then wove toward the stereo. "Ol' Tin Man here" — he gestured vaguely toward Eddie — "had this album when he was a kid, an' he brought it over about three weeks ago, an' now we listen to it all the time." He slipped a record from its sleeve and set it on the turntable. "Turns out every chick in the world goes apeshit over it. They all want to be Dorothy." He chuckled. "An' so we say . . ."

Each of them, even Tully in a desultory way, put his hand on his crotch and chorused: "Baby, let me take you to Oz!"

Suddenly, the room was filled with the "Wooo-Oooo" of a so-prano chorus — a bad imitation of a windstorm — and Chris and Billy collapsed in helpless giggles.

Eddie passed the bong to Fred. "Take a hit."

He pulled down a deep drag. He had not smoked dope in a long time. Liquor was his drug: Old Crow or Canadian Club or beer. He held the smoke, savoring the itch in his throat and the weedy taste the marijuana left in the back of his mouth all the way to his nose.

"Don't Bogart that bong, my friend," Chris said as he took it from his hands.

Fred didn't last long. He vaguely remembered hearing, *"I am Oz, the great and powerful,"* and maybe even *"But it will soon be over now."* These melded, though, with dopey recollections from long ago. They were pleasant dreams — stoney moments at the whorehouse or the barracks or on the beach with Canterwell, with Kirkpatrick, with Eggleson. At some point, he found himself on the sofa, with Tully throwing a blanket over him, saying, "We'll check those fuel lines tomorrow." And then he was asleep.

✧

It was not the fuel lines, or the fuel pump. Not the ignition coil or the distributor. Wednesday, Thursday, Friday: all through the week, each evening after work, Tully followed one lead, then another. All to no avail.

"Could be water in the gas, but I hate to pull the tank. And I got this gut sense that's not it either."

For Fred, it was exhilarting, disorienting. After years by himself, of solitary drinking and television and dinners from a can eaten alone, he found himself night to night in Mockdon Glen, holding the light as Creedence or the Stones or the house's present favorite — "Goodbye Yellow Brick Road" — wafted out the windows and Tully tinkered and diddled, cooed and then cursed at the engine of Fred's 1967 Ford pickup. Billy and Chris and Eddie would drift out, ferrying beers or, after dark, a doobie to keep the labor lubricated, making conversation, occasionally a suggestion. Friends of theirs — Tom Walter, Jimmy Martin — wandered by, and girls would arrive, peeking in the engine and grimacing at the oil and grime before continuing into the house. Then, suddenly — "Wooo-Oooo!" — the twister across Kansas would blast through the speakers and Tully would look up, wink, and say: "Baby, let me take you to Oz."

In four days, Fred crashed there three times. On Friday evening, as Tully leaned so far into the engine his feet were off the ground, Karry Piggott parked her car at the curb and headed across the lawn.

"Tully Coe," she shouted as she walked by, "that's still the cutest little butt in Rhymers Creek."

She was to the front door by the time he popped back to the ground and flipped her off.

"God, she's such a bitch," Tully snapped.

Fred said nothing but could feel the surprise on his face.

Tully shrugged. "She's balling Chris right now is all."

"Were the two of you, like, getting it on before?"

"Naw." Tully took a pack of Marlboros from his pocket. "We messed around in high school. But she's such a prick tease." He shook the pack toward Fred, who pulled out a cigarette. "You got a girlfriend, Fred?"

"Nope," he said.

Tully blew smoke out his nose. "Yeah. Play the field, man." He took another drag. "Me? Me, I don't know. I guess it would be cool to settle down, find the right chick and have a couple of kids. But shit. There's time, don't you think?"

Fred concentrated on his cigarette. "Yeah. I mean, everybody wants that sometime. But what's the hurry?"

"You said it, man." Tully set the butt in the crease of the drain spout. "Come here. I've got a fan belt in the garage. We might as well replace yours while we're at it."

Tully had Wednesday off, so Fred took a sick day. He had caught a ride into town with Tom Walter the night before so he could shave and look for the owner's manual, which he was afraid was long gone. He was not even sure there had been one with the truck when he bought it. Tully was fast running out of ideas. Fred did not want to have spent fifty dollars needlessly; at the same time he knew he could not bring himself to ask Tully for his money back. Beyond that, though, he wanted there to be some other option, some new possibility, that would allow him to continue going to Mockdon Glen, to pass the time on the driveway and shoot the breeze and share a beer and listen to *The Wizard of Oz* with a sweet, easy buzz.

That morning, he hitched a couple of short rides but made most of the trip walking. By the time he arrived, it was close to noon, and Tully was already beneath the hood, passing the beam of a flashlight slowly across every inch of the encrusted engine. Fred leaned over the fender. They did not even speak.

Five minutes passed. Tully moved back to the hinge of the hood, shining the light obliquely, deep into the well, his head flush against the fender. He slid slowly forward. He was almost to the headlight when he stopped.

"Goddamn," he said softly.

He lunged down, wedging his arm behind the fan. He ran a finger over a small, gritty box at the base of the block.

"That's it. That's it!" he shouted. "Gimme a rag. Quick!"

Fred scooped an oily scrap off the driveway. Tully forced it to where his hand had been and stroked it back and forth.

"It's the goddamn timing chain, I'll bet my ass. Look!" He pulled his arm back and shined the light deep inside. Fred leaned beside him. "See, there! That crack. The housing's cracked. The chain's slipped off the cam or something. That's gotta be it."

Fred wasn't sure what Tully was talking about, but for the first time in five days of work, there actually seemed a chance he would get his truck back. What was strange was the ambivalence he felt.

"So, how do we fix it?"

Tully grunted. "We'll have to take the whole front end off. And once we do that, we gotta see what kind of shape the chain's in. The sprockets are probably fucked up, which means we'll have to replace those and the chain, too." He shook his head. "I won't lie to you, Fred. I promised my folks I'd go over for my brother's birthday tomorrow. This'll take another week, for sure."

Fred smiled. "No problem. I just hate to bum off you guys all the time."

"Shit, Fred," Tully said. "It's no sweat. I hope . . ."

The screen door slammed. Eddie ran out in nothing but a pair of boxers.

"Did you hear? Did you fucking hear!"

"What?"

"The tapes!"

"What tapes?"

"Nixon's tapes. The Supreme Court says he's got to give them up. They'll crucify him."

They stood silent for a moment. Tully turned the flashlight in his hand and pointed the tube at Eddie. "Pow!" he said softly. "Goddamn smoking gun."

It was complicated, as Tully had predicted. Simply breaking bolts held by rust and grit and years of immobility took forever, demanding not just time but puffing and sweat and incantations, loving or obscene or sometimes both. The grille came off. The radiator. Fred's truck gaped like a junkyard derelict on Tully's driveway. Neighbors would shake their heads, disgusted, as they drove down the street, but neither Tully nor any of the others seemed to notice. Each afternoon after work, Tully — or Eddie or Chris or Billy — would pick Fred up and bring him to Mockdon Glen to hold the light, test his own strength against the frozen bolts, wipe the greasy engine clean.

Through it all — at Tully's, Pep Boys, on the radio and television, at The Watering Hole and the market — there was the constant buzz of impending and momentous change. The king was on his deathbed, though, for Fred, it seemed more like the agony of a dog hit on the highway, rolling breathless and mute on the shoulder, unable even to howl for the grisly damage done to gut and lung and liver. The couple of nights he spent at the apartment, pacing back and forth with a beer or a plate of pork and beans in front of the eleven o'clock news, he watched the solemn delegations stepping out of black limousines — faces fraught, worried, angry — and disappearing into the confines of that house where, so Fred imagined, someone else was pacing, drinking, lonesome. But, instead of the promise the next day of a friendly wave and a "howdy, Fred," there was only the eventual certainty of more pacing, drinking, loneliness, until some final and humiliating darkness.

The housing, when finally revealed, was ruined, a jagged crack running silver and pristine across the aged, ruddy metal. Tully probed and pried and hacked with screwdrivers and hammer and chisel to tear the top off, Fred spelling him now and then in the August sunset, streaked with grime that was itself streaked with lighter lines of gray where rivulets of sweat had washed the dirt away.

"This is it," Tully said proudly, with the box opened like a coffee can. "Chain's climbed right up over the cam sprocket, see? We're almost home, Fred."

He saw the fouled chain, the nicked and mangled sprocket, and felt something like a lump in his throat. He would finally have his truck back. He would be able to go where and when he liked. But, really, where would that be but here? This damage could be fixed, made good as new again. But there were other things — people, countries, lives — that perhaps could not so easily be dismantled, toyed with, reassembled.

"There must be twenty screws on that thing. It's going to take all tomorrow afternoon to get those off. Let's get a beer." Tully clapped his hand on Fred's shoulder and kept it there as he guided him toward the house.

As they stood by the refrigerator, Chris walked in.

"Taking a break?"

Tully wheeled around with a look of triumph. "No, we're having a party." He opened the door and flipped a can of beer to Chris. "Don't you forget it, asshole. I *am* Oz, the Great and Powerful!"

✧

Even with the solution, progress was slow. Both sprockets should be replaced, Tully decided, and the chain itself was useless. They lost a day when they couldn't borrow a gear puller, and, much to Tully's disgust, they had to buy a new chain from Mockdon Ford, which, merely by luck, had one in stock. By Thursday, though, the timing mechanism was in place, and it was merely a question of putting everything back together before the job was done.

Every day, as they worked, Eddie updated them hour to hour on the news. Each new sign of the crumbling presidency filled him with a childish glee, which Fred found both amusing and peculiar, something that would only be expressed by someone who had never really lost anything or anyone important.

"Goldwater says he should get his ass out of the White House now!" Eddie crowed, then raced back inside to make phone calls.

Tully leaned into the engine well. "What do you make of all this shit, Fred?"

"Nixon?" He proceeded cautiously. "He's an asshole. But they're all assholes."

"Hand me that crescent wrench by my foot." Tully wiggled his fingers. "Yeah. I get to thinking about it sometimes. Stupid prick had a war to get out of, and he runs around pulling stupid stunts like Watergate. You and Waldo and people like that have to go and get your butts shot at, and Ray Garcia and David Mackey and Bobbo Starwick get blown away, while old Nixon tries to figure out how he's going to win the goddamn election." He stood up then. "It sucks."

Fred felt a rush of nerves. "Sure does."

"I look at what it's done, Fred. The war, I mean. All the guys who were killed and the guys like you who went over there and even guys like Barry Carraway who got all whipped up about it, and, I don't know, maybe that's why he went queer on us." He sighed. "Or somebody like that goddamn Pincher Bowdin. Everybody got burned by it. You worse than a lot of people, probably. I just hope with Nixon gone that'll be the end of it and we can all get on with things."

Fred nodded, grateful there had been no questions, but struck, too, that, in Tully there was some little sympathy for him, for what he had seen, for what he had lost. *We*, he had said. All of us.

Thursday afternoon, Tully picked him up from Pep Boys. They rolled down the familiar route, not speaking much. Theirs was a comfortable, easy silence, the kind of men who have worked together. Occasionally, Tully would hum along to the radio, tapping the steering wheel with his South Mockdon High School ring.

Approaching the house, they heard music. The driveway was full, and four cars were parked in front. As they pulled up, Eddie ran out, the Doors booming loud from the open windows.

"No work tonight, guys!" he shouted. "It's party time."

"What's up?"

"Tricky Dick's on the tube at eight." He beamed. "It's like Morrison says: The End."

Inside, it was impossible to talk. The music rattled the walls, and faces on the television mutely mimed the drama and elation of what was to come. The bong passed between Billy Peters and some neighborhood kid Fred had noticed cruising by in a Pontiac coupe a couple times while they were working. On the sofa, Tom Walter and Jimmy Martin were already stoned past redemption. A trash can full of ice sat outside the sliding glass door, brimming with beer, and Karry Piggot and Chris were dancing on the patio. There were some other girls Fred knew by their faces but not by name.

"Hey, Fred." Eddie punched his shoulder. "Get your shirt off."

Fred looked at him, perplexed, and followed Eddie toward the back of the house.

"I had to go up to Henderson today, so I went by the head shop." Eddie reached over his unmade bed. "They only had one left."

He handed him a bag. Fred opened it. Inside was a T-shirt, an extra large. He read the front, then the back, and laughed aloud.

Three hours later, at least twelve more people had arrived. Fred had lost count. They were all crowded into the living room. He was wedged on the sofa, wearing his new shirt, stoned with a Bud in his hand. Everyone was silent, and Fred was concentrating very hard, trying to catch every word from the television, afraid he wouldn't remember. This was history, after all.

Sitting there, among people who in a matter of days he had come to care about, he suspected it wouldn't last. Friendships among men rarely do. How long had it been since he had written Canterwell? And he had little doubt that Kirkpatrick and Glickstein and Beaubien were all gradually falling out of touch. In a month or a year or five, all this would be a pleasant memory. The household would break up. There would be fights, or someone would get a new job, or get married.

But, after so long, it was nice to have shared, even briefly, the comradeship he had figured he had left behind when Canterwell saw him off on the Greyhound in San Diego. And for a while, maybe only days, he could enjoy the pleasure of friends, labor shared, and, tonight, some hope that things were changing, that after a youth that had somehow scarred them all one way or another, the times might now allow for peace and pardon. That the sixties had ended. That the seventies could finally begin.

"God bless you," Nixon said. "May God's grace be with you in all the days ahead."

A cheer went up from all of them, and strings of happy curses.

Unexpectedly, it was Tully who began to sing. One line. But by the second, Eddie had picked it up, and by the third, Chris, Billy: "Ding-Dong, The Witch Is Dead."

By the second verse, the entire room had joined in.

And Fred was singing louder than anyone.

2

"Yours is not a relationship." Bowen rumbled darkly to the strains of Gounod. "It is opera."

The door's slam echoed through the apartment, along with the shatter of glass from the woodcut jarred off the wall and the sound of Jacy's footsteps pounding down the hallway. Barry took a breath, started to speak, then thought better of it. Nothing he could say would excuse Jacy, at least in Bowen's estimation.

"I hardly see why you persist in this." Bowen jingled the bell on the table next to him. "I used to worry about your getting hurt emotionally, but now I wonder if your friend isn't physically abusive as well!"

Barry smiled in spite of himself. Abuse, if that's what it was, was very much a two-way street. Kit, tonight's houseboy, hustled into the room dressed in nothing but a pair of white bikini shorts.

Bowen's expression, up to now a furious scowl, softened. "Kit, will you deal with this, please?"

"Yes, sir." He skittered out in search of a broom and dustpan.

He was older than most of Bowen's boys, close to thirty, and he had more body hair than Bowen usually liked. Otherwise, Kit was like the others Barry had seen here: blond, fragile, scantily clad.

Bowen sighed and went to the sideboard. "Sherry?"

Barry nodded. Kit was already busily sweeping up the broken glass. There were times Barry found the entire scene in this apartment so blatantly lifted from one of the pornographic magazines he took pictures for he had to pinch himself to be sure it was real.

Bowen had extravagant taste in language and clothes, wide though recondite culture, and a foppish wit. A Dartmouth degree, a not inconsiderable trust fund, and an inherited apartment on Riverside Drive provided the necessary backdrop for a life Edmund had described once as a fairy's fairy tale. It was Edmund who, years before, had introduced Barry to Bowen, and they had been friends ever since.

He was ten or so years older, but seemed more. Unlike so many gay men Barry knew, Bowen had embraced middle age with what at first seemed peculiar ardor. Only gradually did Barry realize why. Not extraordinarily handsome or blessed with a body that might be disciplined into gladiatorial steeliness, Bowen, at thirty-five, saw his age not as the death of a golden youth but the opportunity to bring to bear his charm, his wealth, his wit to dazzle boys — twentyish, usually new to New York — searching for a man older but not too old, that melding of mentor and master and daddy who would mold them and make them wise, cherish their ephemeral loveliness, induct them into the mysteries of making a life when that loveliness had faded, providing them with a taste for comfort and culture that they would bless or curse him for, depending on where their destinies led.

"I'm quite serious." Bowen handed Barry his drink. "I can't tell you how to live your life, but Jacy has always felt like trouble."

Barry shrugged. "I promised we'd go dancing."

"Dear boy" — Bowen harumphed — "no one was preventing him from going dancing. An hour of conversation was no impediment to his dancing. At least," he added with more than slight malice, "with you."

Barry knew what he meant. He would not see Jacy again this evening. He would not see him till at least midafternoon, and there was no telling how many men he would have been with in the meantime.

"Bowen" — Barry sighed — "it's understood we trick out."

Bowen smirked. "An odd locution. But it's my impression that Jacy's tricking consumes a great deal of his time. Less a hobby than an occupation, and an odd one for one's boyfriend to be pursuing."

"You just don't understand, Bowen . . ." Barry shook his head, wondering whether he himself did, after all.

He fell in love at The Mine Shaft.

He did not go there all that often then. Sadomasochism, he had learned at — not across — Edmund's knee, was politically suspect, an acting out of all masculinity's repressive clichés. Long after that first love had drifted into an easy friendship, Barry held that view, telling himself so even as his eyes followed more and more longingly the ever more numerous leather boys who roamed the Village night.

After the breakup with Edmund, he had tried a few other relationships, but, as the seventies ripened, he became a free agent, as in the first days of his sexual blossoming, sleeping happily but casually with men he met in bars or on the street or sating his desire with a trip to the baths. In those years, Barry worked as a bartender, a clerk in a camera store, a librarian, a waiter, and a stock boy. Through all those noncareers, he took pictures. His interest in urban landscape gave way to portraiture, in part because so many of the men he knew in those heady days — young and beautiful and defiantly out of the closet, as they had learned to say — had a strong streak of vanity, arising perhaps from the realization that their greatest attributes were indelibly stamped with an expiration date. Some of the photographs he took were for the portfolios of the aspiring actors and models and dancers who lurked inside almost every one-night stand he brought to his bed. Others wanted dreamy portraits or campy shots to show to friends. Many of the pictures he took were nudes, a not inconsiderable number obscene, responses to the ads in the burgeoning underground papers that promised romance or, more likely, quick and specific sex of one kind or another.

It was through one of those requests, from a trick named Paul, that Barry became a professional. The morning after a long night of poppers and reefer and screwing, Paul noticed the camera and the darkroom rigged up in the closet. Barry shot a half dozen black-and-whites of him: a good bed partner, somewhere in his forties, solid with the slightest paunch, like the neighborhood mechanic. He was surprised at the call next day to see if he had developed the pictures.

"You know," Paul said, leafing through the photographs after a quick fuck, "these are damn good. You ever work in color?"

"Mostly black and white so I can do my own developing."

"I don't really need these," he said, handing the pictures back. "But I wanted to get a notion if you knew what you were doing. I work for *Roughneck*, you know."

Barry laughed. "Come on."

"Got an issue?"

He went to the closet and rummaged through the pile of skin magazines, the accumulation most men have sequestered for those nights when things do not go precisely according to plan, when they are too drunk, bored, lovesick to venture out in search of easy sex. "Here."

Paul opened it to the masthead: "Photo Editor: Paul Palmer."

Barry shook his head. "Well, whattaya know."

Barry did not quit the day job. The work for *Roughneck* was erratic and did not pay all that well. Still, it gave him entrance into worlds he might not otherwise have known. His pictures were popular with the staff of the magazine, with its public, and, too, with the models, some of whom went home with him for a private session, a few of them out of and then in bed. After the bright, glossy shots in chaps, in knee-high boots and jockstraps, Barry would bring them to his apartment, strip them naked, and through his lens remake these large-muscled, sometimes tattooed men into vulnerable, even winsome figures. He was as surprised as anyone when their gruffness vanished, as they meekly did what they were told, making suggestions with a kind of boyish deference. Before him — often if not always — precisely that roughneckness that had won them the opportunity to pose for the magazine in the first place fell away and they became sweet, childlike.

For his own shoots, he did not pay them. They signed releases, got a set of prints. After a year, many came to his first, small showing in an upstairs gallery on Hudson Street, proud and abashed at once that they had been transfigured; were, thanks to Barry Carraway, no longer mere flesh nor, in New York or Dayton or San Jose, just *Roughneck*'s pecker-tracked mementos of impossible loves, but there, in tones of black and white, each an object of veneration not merely erotic but aesthetic: not a piece of meat but a piece of art.

It was through them that Barry gradually passed beyond Edmund's admonitions and began to experiment, hesitantly, with realms he had thought beyond the pale. It was not much — brief games with rope, the wax of a burning candle — but it finally took him to The Mine Shaft, only to see the first few times, then slowly, slowly, to take part. He fucked someone, sucked a cock. He accepted a cat-o'-nine-tails and brought it down across the back of a man shackled to a post. On that Thursday night, having smoked a roach on the roof, he wandered downstairs. There, in the dim glow of the red lamps, he could hear the sounds of sex: groans and sighs and sharp intakes of breath.

It was then he first saw Jacy.

He was braced against the wall, legs slightly apart, jeans clumped at his ankles. The pandy bat swished through the lurid darkness, and time after time there was a tremendous sound and he shivered and gasped, tossing his head and stamping like a horse that would not be broken. Another welt would bloom bright as a fuchsia across the furred marble of his ass. Barry watched, transfixed, the blond, bearded gorgeousness subdued but unyielding: a wild thing whinnying and bucking, the outlaw captured but defiant.

Barry stood awash with polymorphous lust: to soothe and hurt, taste sweat and feel the warm lave of the tongue that tasted his own, to suck and thrust, control and surrender. He held himself, his eyes unblinking, until the end, when the leather-gloved hand dropped the paddle away. Barry stepped forward and ran his palm across the flaming skin; brushed his cheek against the stranger's cheek, crossed by the trail of a single tear, and said: "I want to make you come."

This was what Barry knew by the time they reached the second-floor walk-up a half block east of Tompkins Square: he was speeding; he was stoned; he had had too much to drink. His name was Jacy.

Stumbling up the stairs, all Barry felt as he had not felt it ever was that he wanted that body — the hairy-chested, pink-bottomed massiveness of it — and the two of them rolled through the door and out of their clothes and into the bed and into each other before either seemed to know what had happened. Barry pulled those fiery cheeks apart and dove between them as he felt himself consumed by the wet warmth of Jacy's throat. Their positions reversed, and then they were outside of time, all squirming, slobbering desire, the snake that eats its tail and whose end is its beginning.

"Oh, Jesus. Fuck me. Fuck me!" Jacy moaned.

Barry, with a strength that surprised him, flipped the other man over and lifted a foot to each shoulder, staring into the violent blue of those eyes, the round, thick-bearded face. Jacy raised himself high off the mattress, shivering, as Barry dribbled some spit on himself and rammed forward, knowing it would hurt, wanting it to hurt, knowing Jacy wanted it to hurt.

"Ahh. Yes. Yes! Like that!" Jacy's breath was ragged, his voice a tight whine. "Oh, yeesss . . . !"

It was quick and brutal, and even as he came, Barry knew it was not over. Jacy had a glazed, wild look. He pulled Barry to him as he lay flat, and Barry felt his hardness there. He reached back to grease himself with spit and then — slowly, slowly, inch to inch — pegged himself upon the heart-crowned shaft that poked beneath him.

It went on and on, as if they were boys only recently aware of what their dicks could do. Barry found himself tingling with a kind of sexual amazement — each kiss ecstatic, each clutch electric, each explosion mere prelude to the next.

It was only as the sun was rising that lust and chemicals failed them. Rolled in one sweating, stinking self, astonished at their own desire, with one last, bruising kiss, they plunged suddenly into sleep, as if striking Earth after a pinwheeling, unanticipated plummet from the moon.

✧

"You don't understand him, Bowen," Barry said again for lack of anything better.

His friend settled across from him. "I won't argue with you. He's not someone I particularly care to understand. He's lovely to look at, if a little coarse. But with all the men to choose from and so many handily available, that's hardly a recommendation."

"*Jugée*," boomed Méphistophélès.

"It's more than that," Barry began. "He's sweet, Bowen. Really. He . . . he touches me . . . Not that way!" He frowned at Bowen's smirk. "Our lives have been very different. It's easy for me to love him."

"*Sauvé*," piped the sopranos.

"Ah, love?" Bowen leaned on his palm. "Worse than I thought. Barry, my innocent friend. What have you gotten yourself into?"

"Don't be avuncular."

"I certainly will, if it suits me," Bowen snapped. He picked up his sherry and turned the glass idly before his eyes. "But tell me then. What is it that touches you? What's so different about him? Different than you or me or Kit here?"

"I don't know how to explain, exactly . . . ," Barry began.

He did not know the answers. Jacy was endlessly winning, the protean lover with an imagination that knew no frontier. He was thoughtful, silly, incapable of shame. For Barry, of course, there was more: not merely that physical semblance but those other facets that he, tentatively, had explored that first morning.

"Did you play football? Sometime?"

And Jacy told him of his career as tackle on the Mt. St. Etienne Eagles. The passing glories of his senior year. The messing around with the first-string guard who got a scholarship to U of V.

And at the diner on Avenue A: "Were you in the service?"

There came the descriptions of boot camp and base life. The close call with Vietnam.

"So you didn't go?"

"Nope. Got hit by a car on the way to chow a week before we shipped out. Ruptured spleen, fucked up my shoulder. With the therapy, it laid me up six months." He smiled. "By that time, the word was 'deescalation.' The CO said he guessed I was supposed to be a soldier in some other war. Ended up in California."

"How was that?"

"Oh, real interesting." Jacy's eyes twinkled as he took a sip of coffee. "My sergeant was into bondage."

Barry shook his head. "What kind of work do you do?"

"I'm a carpenter."

"Didn't you have to go to work today?"

A sweet half smile. "I did. But I didn't, did I?"

And they went to the apartment instead.

He was, indeed, a carpenter, but not in the union, part-timing here and there. Jacy lived hand-to-mouth, working when he could or when it suited him, pulling money together to pay the rent and the groceries, to party and play. His wants were simple, and logically so, as with time Barry heard the occasional tales of a hardscrabble Vermont boyhood resonant with hurtful remembrance. Eight brothers and sisters. The father who drank and worked in the battery plant. The mother who wept and withdrew in the isolated town with a strange college on a hill on the outskirts, filled with rich kids.

"All these snots with trust funds. I hated them, until I started to mess around. There were a lot of queers there. Students and some of the teachers, too. They were the only ones who came into town much. Cruising. It was safer to get it on with them than hang out waiting for a trucker in front of the Methodist church."

That, he had told Barry before: sneaking out and sitting on a stoop on Main Street, waiting for a rig to pass by, slow, flash the lights. That was where Jacy learned to suck cock. That was where two of his brothers caught him one night and beat him up.

"I hated every goddamn minute of it," Jacy said with funny pride in the hot, loud summer as they lolled at West and Christopher. "Split town the minute I graduated: young, dumb, full of come."

Barry frowned. "It sounds hard."

Jacy shrugged. "I'm here now, ain't I? You want another beer?"

❖

Bowen was at the stereo.

"I couldn't believe I came upon it. Anything by Riegger is almost impossible to find." He dropped the tonearm, then brought the decanter from the sideboard and set it between them. He settled back and brought his fingers together thoughtfully. "You must admit, Barry, it seems strange. Here's the man you say you love — perpetually unfaithful, uneducated, from circumstances far different from yours. It's not the best foundation for one of those meaningful relationships, wouldn't you agree?"

Bowen was irritating. And correct, of course. The months with Jacy had been difficult, far more so than those with Edmund or any of those who had followed. Barry thought, when they moved into the railroad flat on Forty-ninth, that cohabiting would somehow tame the wildness in Jacy that was both exhausting and exhilarating. The results had been mixed.

Barry sighed. "You take the good with the bad, Bowen. He drinks too much, he does too many drugs, he tricks out too often . . ."

"A model citizen," Bowen purred.

"But he's good to me. He's good for me. There's something" — he groped for a word that would not make Bowen smile — "something passionate about him, about us, that makes it all worthwhile."

Bowen grinned. "And I suppose the sex is marvelous."

Barry turned on him defiantly. "Yes, it is. It is marvelous."

❖

At first, when they were together, it was merely a little rough. Some biting here and there, the minimum of lubricants, some old wrestling holds. But Barry was curious, and Jacy was anxious, and that anxiousness made Barry eager to please him so as not to lose him. After a few weeks, as they lay in each other's arms, Barry finally brought it up: the scene from that first night.

"But didn't it hurt?"

Jacy laughed softly. "Sure it did. It's supposed to hurt."

"And that . . . that turns you on?"

"It turns anybody on, if they try it."

Barry shrugged nervously. "I mean, it seems kind of weird."

"Ha!" Jacy barked. "Come on, Barry. People think it's weird to take it up the ass."

"I guess."

"What do you mean, you guess? How long's it been since you've seen your folks? Six, seven years? Jeez." Jacy sat up. "I mean, when you think about it, doesn't it break your heart? All those guys who go to their graves asshole virgins? And it's the same with S&M. Sure stuff hurts . . ." Barry could feel Jacy getting hard next to him. "But you go with it. And it changes. What felt bad starts to feel good . . ." Jacy's voice got dreamy. "It's endorphins. That's what I heard. These chemicals in your brain. Like dope. They kick in, and you get real turned on, and your eyes roll back and you can go on and on till you get overloaded. Your nerves start to short out and you kick and shake and it's like" — he took a deep, pleasured breath — "it's like a come that won't end."

Barry lay beside him, tense. He was scared, confused. But he knew, too, more than anything in the world, that he wanted to please that naked man next to him in bed. He got up. He went to the chair and pulled his belt through the loops on his pants.

He doubled it over and handed it to Jacy.

"So. Show me," he said.

✧

"It staggers me, sometimes," Bowen said, "how important sex has become to almost everyone I know."

Barry was feeling put-upon. "Not everybody has the means you do, Bowen. That's why there are all those stupid laws about who gets to fuck who. It's a way to control people, people who can't afford good linen and fine wine and great stereos." He was sounding like Edmund, like his old Greenwich Activist Youth days. "If everybody had your money and your education and your houseboys, maybe sex wouldn't be so important!"

Bowen paused for a moment. "Now, don't be mean about Kit," he said a bit plaintively. "All right. Sex isn't insignificant. But still, I'm not sure you want to base your life on it."

"For God's sake, Bowen. So we have great sex, Jacy and me . . ."

"Jacy and half of Manhattan," Bowen corrected.

"Jacy and me and half of Manhattan, if you have to know!"

That was not entirely true. Barry did trick out now and then, though it was frankly a bit halfhearted, and they occasionally did a three- or foursome, which Jacy especially liked. They would cruise the bars together, or Jacy would simply appear with somebody in tow.

"I think that's important in a relationship. Sex. And I've learned a lot about it since I've been with him. And there is more to it than that."

"Do tell."

✧

Bowen would not understand; Bowen with his well-organized life, the security of his finances, an address book full of young men — nineteen, twenty-three — willing to play the houseboy for a night or the weekend. It was Jacy's very spontaneity, the innocent darkness of his desires, that made him so appealing. When Barry was with him, he felt the dizzying confusion of teetering on the edge of chaos. Even Jacy's endless lustings — the tricking that did not stop after he had introduced Barry to the pleasures of the strap and tit clamps and ball stretchers — shone with a primal energy, as if Jacy had to provide just a little taste of heaven to anyone who came along.

But, too, there was the way his face set in the early morning.

Once or twice a week, Barry would awaken at dawn. For a minute or two, before he drifted into sleep again, he possessed preternatural sensitivity there in the easy rose at the edge of night and morning, and he would turn his eyes to his carpenter's still and sleeping form.

The first night he had seemed a subjugated giant: larger, better. But, over time, Jacy lost the virtue of sheer size, only for it to be replaced by something different, sweet and generous. Barry would look upon him like Pope Gregory upon the Angle, Jacy's hair a nimbus around his head, his square chest rising and falling, slow, metronomic, his mouth curved in a soft and satisfied smile.

Barry had seen similar smiles. On Edmund's face — serious, thoughtful Edmund. On Kip's, snoring away his bruises. And Bobbo's.

With their time together, he had accepted that Jacy was not that brother who was the best in the world. Still, though, there was the sense that he was what Barry might have ultimately wanted his big brother to be: all the teasing and roughhousing and tenderness that did not stop, that was not frozen by the cold fear of passion but burst forth in proud desire that would consummate itself, time after time, until exhaustion brought it to a merely momentary pause.

That Jacy provided, along with the comfort of a shared life, the exchanged details of the day, even when those details were of yet another adventure with another man. Bread broken together, friends, walking the streets, Jacy's arm around him as they listened to Lou Reed or Edith Piaf, the sense that life was better when two pairs of eyes, two pairs of lips, two bodies saw it, tasted it, lived it.

✧

"Piaf," Bowen said. "Now that I wouldn't have expected."

"I was surprised, I guess," Barry agreed, "the first time he put her on. He knew the words to the 'Hymn to Love.' In French."

"Ah, the noble savage."

"Oh, shut up. He knew all about it. About Marcel Cerdan. It's that kind of thing. And he's" — Barry knew it would sound silly when he said it — "he's, you know, like, kind of artistic, too."

"He's also affecting the way you talk," Bowen said grumpily. "But an artist. And what, prey tell, does this art consist of?"

"Well, he," Barry stammered, "he builds models."

There was a long pause.

"Models?" Bowen said softly. "Models! Plastic models?"

"Yes."

"O sensibility," Bowen burbled, covering his mouth.

"Fuck you!" Barry snapped.

✧

His anger was not entirely fair. He would not have thought of it as art had he not watched Jacy, seen the care and diligence, the patience, the standards that made him throw away more of the models than he kept. Barry was struck by the delicacy with which he moved his hands — large and callused — and found himself, with both shame and wonder, excited by it, for Jacy, usually more than a bit clumsy, showed such precision only one other place.

Some of his work — the F-11s and the *Great Eastern* and the wooden replica of the *Spruce Goose* — were good enough to display in the window of the shop he patronized in the East Twenties. Occasionally, Barry would go there with him and listen as Jacy chatted easily with old men, boys, other aficionados like himself about glues, tweezers, paints and decals, name brands, off-brands, foreign makes, shows.

"It was the one thing," Jacy confided to him once in the dark, when they were stoned, sleepy from love, "the one thing my dad and me did together. We'd drive all the way to Albany and go to this shop near the D & H station. My brothers thought it was stupid. But when my dad built models, he stayed sober." He sighed. "Maybe he taught me about models so I wouldn't turn into him."

Barry held him then, not as his lover but as a father might, gently, chastely, his big, blond boy who cruised the streets with an endless appetite for love. It was then it occurred to Barry how Jacy's models were art as his own pictures were art: the means by which we keep the world at bay or give it sense, order it or allow it to ravish us with word or image or scattered pieces of plastic.

When Barry mentioned it, it made no sense to Jacy. Art was paintings, sculptures, and, by definition, dull. He thought it was funny that Barry's photographs would be considered artistic.

"People buy them because they're naked guys," he told him when they were at a new group show on Prince Street. "You think these queers don't kick back and wank off in front of them? Get real."

Barry shrugged insincerely. "As long as I get paid."

He was getting paid, not just by *Roughneck*, not just for the portfolio shots he still did sporadically. In the galleries, they had begun to take note. There had been a small but kindly notice in *The Village Voice*. Barry spent more and more time with his camera, and, combining one love with the other, in Jacy found his perfect subject.

Of Jacy, he took endless pictures — clothed and nude. There was Jacy with a dildo, Jacy with a razor strop; Jacy with an iris, Jacy with a kitten. Jacy sitting, Jacy reclining, Jacy with his fists planted on his hips; his face toward the floor and hands clasped behind his back. Developing the last, Barry realized they looked like the portraits of Mishima: St. Sebastian awaiting the arrows.

Perhaps that was not true. Perhaps the photographs were merely silly, devoid of myth, sanctity, obsession; Barry's vision distorted by his love. Their relationship, as Bowen insisted, defied sense: Barry, with his porn assignments and artistic pretensions, his college education and radical past; Jacy, with pickup jobs and plastic models, his refusal to think of much of anything without considering how it would feel in bed. Yet, toward each other, they had an absolute loyalty, something beyond friendship and, surely, beyond mere fidelity, something deeper, sounder, some commitment that implied, unspoken, they would die for each other. It was, Barry imagined, an emotion only two men who had fucked could achieve. Having superseded the shame their desires should have caused them, surpassed the limits that bodies are intended to respect, Barry and Jacy entered a realm where their wants and dreams and selves could merge and meld and they became one man of a range vaster than any single soul could ever embrace.

✧

Bowen gestured toward the bottle.

"I better not, or I'll never make it home," Barry said.

"Not in a hurry anyway, are we?" Bowen leaned forward and filled his glass again. "Well, next time you bring Jacy by, I'll be more judicious in my choice of music. Perhaps some Lotte Lenya."

Barry had to smile. "Maybe that would do it."

"I don't know, Barry," Bowen said. "It really is all none of my business. You met Jacy. You fell in love with Jacy. That sort of thing very rarely makes sense. I suppose I do worry that you'll get your heart or something else broken. Or, with all that he plays around, he'll give you syphilis or, what's the new one, herpes?"

"Bowen . . . ," Barry whined.

"All right. All right." He raised his hand placatingly. "The two of you are part of a world I don't understand. You must remember, Barry, for a man of our kind who is my age, this" — he gestured around him — "is all any of us could have wished for. We had no illusions about love. Or we assumed they were illusions. You were right before. I have all this privilege — beautiful objects and a lovely home and good friends. And I have Kit for tonight, and perhaps for other nights. I'm too set in my ways to shimmy the night away, as Jacy would put it, or cruise Christopher Street, or sign up at one of those gyms where, so I hear, a good part of the exercising takes place in the steam room. And sometimes I am glad of that. It all seems so tremendously effortful." He looked away, then added softly, "Though I am also envious."

"Envious?"

"Of course. It must be wonderful, in its way, to be young and homosexual right now. My God, even ten years ago, you had to worry about the police and the Mob and your name in the paper. Now, you are all down there like fine, sleek panthers, prowling whole neighborhoods, dancing at the chicest of clubs — chic precisely because you go there. And fucking . . ."

The word surprised Barry.

"Fucking joyously." Bowen smiled beatifically. "You boys, you and Jacy, you have made sex into a religion, which is often dangerous though never wrong, despite what the priests say, or so I have always believed." He gestured to the wall. "See that crucifixion?"

Barry had noticed it many times, a cheap reproduction of a Dalí. It had always struck him as out of place amid Bowen's opulence.

"It was the first print I ever bought. I was twelve years old. It's *The Christ of St. John of the Cross.*" He smiled. "For a long time, I wondered why I should have so liked it. A surrealist painter. An ecstatic saint. But a Christ? Much later, though, I understood. See the way the figure seems to lurch out of the canvas? You are looking down on the head of Jesus, just as you might look down on another kind of head, thrusting toward you." He laughed out loud. "Dalí understood about religion and desire. Not surprising for a Catalan. Still really Albigensians, most of them. Or Adamites. Did I tell you what I read about Bosch?"

Barry shook his head. God knew where Bowen was headed, spinning with sherry and sex and art. "No. No, I don't think you did."

"There's a theory now about *The Garden of Earthly Delights.* There's always been a question as to why the largest of the panels should be committed to earthly pleasures. It's been suggested that that great, central panel is not of this world but of the next. That Bosch was painting an Adamite vision of the paradise."

"Who were . . . ?"

"An obscure ancient sect. Revived in the Middle Ages by people who called themselves the Brethren and Sisters of the Free Spirit. Went around naked. Made love: anytime, anywhere, with anyone. Ate, drank, were merry, totally committed to recapturing Eden. Sometimes I think that's what's happening down on your part of the island with all your Roman pleasures. Part of me says it is all so decadent, and another says it is all so innocent." Bowen paused, raised his glass, studied the sherry with a look of frank concern. "I honestly don't know, Barry," he said quietly, seriously. "Which is it? Are you Caligulans or Adamites?"

❖

He walked home that night, the route not all that different from the one he had walked fleeing Angelo's, except this time in the opposite direction. He knew Jacy, by now, was down dancing his heart out, snorting poppers beneath the strobe lights, his shirt off as he swung it in some complicated fan dance, glistening with sweat and sex.

Barry thought about Bowen, about Dalí and Bosch, about Jacy. It was hard to know what this all could mean, Adamites and arguments and being in love. About all he could be sure of was that, in these last months, he had felt his world expanding as he had not since those heady days with Angelo when he discovered sex, the ones with Edmund when he discovered love. Now, in Jacy, what he created and who he desired converged in the single point that was the two of them together. His whole awareness of pleasure had expanded beyond any bounds he might have conceived, his body ever more anxious for extremity, each extremity opening yet another secret kingdom of sensation and desire. Only two weeks before, Jacy had taken him farther than he ever believed he could go.

He had done it to Jacy, appalled and excited and curious, too, for the ecstatic look in his lover's eyes when finally, finally, he was deep inside. They both knew, sometime, that it was Barry who would be on the bottom. That morning, all Jacy had said as he kissed Barry good-bye, was "I want to do you tonight, fucker." He kissed him again, tenderly. "Okay?"

Barry knew what he meant. He shivered, and nodded. He spent the day preparing.

Jacy did not get back until about five. Barry was almost angry there stiff in his gym shorts.

"Sorry, baby," Jacy said soothingly. "I had to stop on the way for a couple of things." He reached in his shirt pocket and pulled out two joints and a tab. He pressed the mescaline against Barry's lips; Barry opened his mouth and swallowed. "Why don't you light up for me?"

As he handed the reefer to him, Barry noticed Jacy's nails: clipped short, filed smooth against the roughness of his fingers.

"I got a manicure," Jacy said shyly. "Expensive as shit." He lit the joint in Barry's mouth, then kissed him on the neck. "I want it to be right for you, you know?"

That evening, Jacy did not smoke or drink, and their love-making was lazy and slow. Barry, easy now thanks to the drugs, surrendered himself utterly, like he had learned to do when he was on the bottom, but perhaps, this night, even more completely, as he felt Jacy's lips over him, his arms around him, and his fingers, probing — gentle and tentative — inside him. He had no notion of time, which, in any case, he could only have measured in the moans and sighs of his desiring.

One finger, then two, then three. Softly. Softly. Quivering like some delicate creature from the sea. Opening him up. Jacy leaned into him.

"That's it, baby stud," Jacy whispered. "Take it up there. Relax. Daddy's looking out for you. Baby's looking out for you."

Barry groaned.

Jacy pawed across the mattress and pressed a bottle of poppers into Barry's hand. Barry inhaled the sharp, sweat smell and knew a fourth finger was there within him now, that half of Jacy's palm had disappeared into his body, fluttering sleepily like the fin of a fish. Wave after wave of a terrified pleasure washed over him as he breathed deep and steady like a diver.

"I'm going to make the goose head now, baby," Jacy said softly. "It's time now, baby."

That was what he called it, how he had described it that very first time when he was the one with his legs in the air. *Now, just like when you were a kid and made shadows on the wall. Tuck your thumb underneath your fingers. . . ."*

It was happening: Jacy's hand in a cone, the widest part now pushing, constant, insistent against his resistance.

"Take a hit of poppers, baby."

Barry snorted deep from the bottle. The fumes rushed in him, and his will rushed out. He was falling, falling, and Jacy pushed hard.

One sharp protest resolved into a lowing moan as Barry felt his lover's fist inside him and he spasmed around Jacy's wrist.

"It's there, baby. It's where you want it, baby."

For a minute, it was as if he would split in half. Neither moved, as Barry calmed, and his body — curious, tentative — gradually felt and accepted the hugeness inside him. The nerves there slipped from outrage to surprise to some pleasure of fullness they had never known before. He felt lightheaded — faint and dizzy and wonderful.

A soft sound — content and animal — came from his throat.

"I love you, Jacy," he crooned. "I love you."

Jacy sighed, and pushed his fist a little deeper. Barry answered with a pant, ecstatic and astonished.

Jacy flexed his arm softly. "I love you, too, baby. I love you, too." Then a smile — half sweet, half mischievous — stole across his face.

"My hand is up your asshole," he whispered, "and I'm reaching for your heart."

3

It was not an apartment, Belva thought, that would be featured in *Metropolitan Home:* four rooms, really three and a half, no view, and a rent guaranteed to cause heartburn. And yet, the ceilings were high, and stark, white walls gave it the clean, hard feel of freedom. Most of all, it was in New York.

"Damn this liner!" Belva heard from the bathroom.

"No hurry, Roxy. We should be fashionably late, right?"

Belva was not especially anxious to go to this evening's dinner party, though Roxy had assured her she would find the host both interesting and interested enough to make her whole trip worthwhile. She was simply relieved to have ten days away from home, to wander the stores on Fifth and on Madison, to escape the obligations of Ross and Wallace. New York City, even in this steamy August, was someplace she could briefly let loose.

She was barely over thirty, and, yet, the contrast of her world with that of her old Siegerford roommate was vast as the half continent dividing where they lived. Roxy still thought of herself as young, talked in terms of potentials: of moving up the ladder at Altman's; of marrying (or not) her present boyfriend, Roger; of abandoning one career to start another. She hadn't yet gone to law school but had made a good life and recently begun courses toward her MBA.

"It'll be a whole new ball game when we get that wimp Carter out of office," she had remarked at lunch. "Then I'll make some decisions."

Comparatively, Belva felt domestic and dull. Except in private, where she could regale Roxy with the tales of her various trysts, what did she have to talk about? Decorating, and Wallace's job; Ross learning to crawl and say his first words; Melva's domesticity, Rhett's ever-changing careers, and Tammy's ever-changing husbands, her most recent ex- one of Rhymers Creek's few junkies, whom she had escaped only by moving to Dallas.

"Okay, let's go." Roxanne swirled out of the bathroom, face aglow, severe and stylish in eggplant and creme.

Belva stood up, her outfit one that Roxy had picked out in a beige Belva had learned was now called taupe. "You look terrific."

"So do you." Her friend smiled. "You'll knock Michael dead."

They had last seen each other almost ten years before, the day of Belva and Randy's wedding at the Siegerford Chapel. They planned the ceremony for Christmas, and it might have all gone without a hitch but for the war. Throughout the reception, there was an almost palpable tension between old and young, a generational divide signed by the length of their hair and the cloth of their clothes, afflicting even those who had no particular stake in ending the war or winning it. There had been a nasty argument between Mr. Ditmars and Wentworth Corn, Randy's economics professor and dope connection, about Kent State, to the point that Belva had taken to the ladies' room with Melva and had a good cry, because the celebration seemed ruined by events half a year gone in a little town hundreds of miles away, home to a college nobody had really heard of before.

She had later thought it was a sign of things to come. Looking back, Belva could see her marriage had been doomed from the first. Precisely those things that made Randy such a wonderful boyfriend — the wild streak, the unexpected and sometimes sloppy sentimentality, the horseplay with men and flirting with women — made him an execrable husband. It was not three weeks after they had settled into the vast neocolonial Mrs. Ditmars had picked out for them and Mr. Ditmars had paid for that Belva realized her mistake.

It was a Saturday. She had spent the entire previous week unpacking boxes and was not really in the mood for the Greater Memphis Music and Cultural Affairs Council tea. After three hours of white-gloved matrons with shellacked hair and family diamonds ostensibly saved from marauding Yankees, Belva finally escaped into the sweltering afternoon and buzzed back to her new house in the respectable Mercury assigned to her by the family. In all the years since, she still remembered how she felt on that drive: exhausted and put-upon and absolutely weak with desire to make love to Randy as soon as she walked through the door.

That had not happened. There was no one in the house. She was upstairs undressing before she heard noises coming from the pool. She threw on one of Randy's T-shirts and a pair of shorts.

Randy was there with Leon and Bo, two old high school friends, and a girl Belva had never seen — a lusciously figured blond with dark roots and the barest of swimsuits. She straddled the diving board as Randy and Bo nipped at her dangling legs. Leon was farther up the board, jumping, so the girl bounced up and down and finally tumbled, giggling, into the water. At pool's edge, Belva could see Randy through the turquoise water, his face against the girl's bikini, right between her legs, blowing bubbles.

He surfaced, snorting and clapping like a seal. "More fish! More fish!" he chortled. It took a full minute for him to realize she was there. "Belva, honey," he shouted, shading his eyes. "What the hell are you doing back so soon?"

She had a queasy feeling that that would be a refrain she would grow used to. "Teatime's over, sweetheart," she said evenly, slipping into the water. "Time to relax with the boys."

By fall, she had taken a lover — Dennis McElvay, a lawyer with ambitions to move on to Nashville and then to Washington. It was convenient, since he, too, had recently married into Memphis society. Both wanted something discreet with no strings or obligations.

Randy did not know he was a cuckold until the very end, after not one but three had shared Belva's bed. In the ugliness of the divorce, he asked her if the baby that had not come to term was his, and she told him, with a cruelty that surprised her, that she frankly did not know and did not care.

She went back to Rhymers Creek. Her marriage had lasted barely two years, and, despite all the wealth and supposed prestige, it had been hell. Randy Ditmars was one of the most appealing men she had ever laid eyes on — tall and solid and hairy and hung. He would have been a perfect diversion on weekday afternoons, like his tennis partner — her third affair — Ron Killingham had proved. But he was not a man to be married to. She had penned a letter to the "Alumnae Notes" of the *Siegersford Siren* announcing the divorce. Various classmates sent condolences, full of veiled suggestions that she had not been able to make a man like Randy happy and barely concealed glee that he, his money, and his family name were again on the market.

The exception was Roxy's letter:

> He was a shit, Belva. You were far too smart for him. I
> know it's not the thing you're supposed to say, but you de-
> serve better than some Memphis Sigma stud boy like Randy
> Ditmars.

They were caught in traffic.

"So, who is this guy again?" Belva asked.

"Michael?" Roxy turned to her. "Michael. Drop dead gorgeous. Rich and on his way to being richer. Great place in Soho. A nose for real estate. He's a swinger but selective, Belva. Like you."

She hated the way Roxy read her. When, late in 1974, Belva had announced she was marrying Wallace Masterson, everyone thought it was wonderful: a senior vice president at Wilson Poultry Industries, the state's fastest growing company; a handsome, smart, ambitious man.

Only Roxy had questioned her:

The way you talk about him makes me think you don't love him really, that he's just a good, secure investment. Maybe I'm wrong. I hope so. Of course, I wish you guys the best.

That was it precisely. Wallace was a good provider. He had built her the house of her dreams, and — more so, in any case, than the husbands of her friends — was a dedicated father, one who enjoyed his son uncomplainingly, when he was home anyway. He would take Ross off her hands to give her a bit of a break and hinted broadly he would not mind having another child, a girl this time, perhaps.

But despite the fact that he was a man above complaint, Belva was dissatisfied: woefully, desperately, bleakly dissatisfied. Ross — a good child, whole and healthy and cheerful — represented an unending chore for her, and homemaking bored her beyond measure. Wallace — though kind, even courtly to her — seemed to view her finally as if she were merely another object he had acquired on his way to the top, an accoutrement of success no less important but rather less interesting than his Z car and the catamaran docked at the Willowood Reservoir. She had, with Melva, vaguely discussed the notion of opening a business, something tony; an accessories store or a dress shop. Her sister had been enthusiastic but not too, happy enough with Mitch Collins, her stolid and good-hearted husband already going to fat. Belva realized the energy for the undertaking, if it were to happen at all, would have to come from her.

And that energy might fortunately be some of what more and more consumed her. It was humiliating to admit how much her life revolved around desire — sexual desire, pure and simple. In that department, too, Wallace had proved a disappointment, an uninspired bedmate who dealt with lovemaking as if it were a twice weekly extension of his morning exercises: five minutes of foreplay, two minutes of his tongue, penetration in the missionary position, pump until slightly winded, ejaculate, sleep. The routine left her so unsatisfied that most all her waking thoughts, and dreams as well, revolved around screwing. She fantasized about boys she saw riding bikes, men at the gas station, her husband's friends and her friends' husbands. This struck her as an ugly and masculine trait, unpleasantly reminiscent of Randy Ditmars, the hormone-drunk frat boy who couldn't keep his dick in his pants.

Yet each time she initiated some new liaison, she experienced an odd mix of excitement and terror. The first, for the possibility that this man would prove the one who would transport her to the surpassing ecstasy she had known the first few times she made love. The fear, of course, was that he would do exactly that, and she would be forced to choose between the comfort and responsibilities that devolved upon a married woman not just in Rhymers Creek but almost anywhere and the chance to experience the kind of passionate intensity the sixties had somehow led her to anticipate, a romantic fullness that didn't merely have to do with what went on in bed but infused one's entire life, the glow of two people in absolute sync.

Sometimes, imagining what a life like that would be, she remembered her first days with Randy, how they could barely keep their hands off each other. Even more rarely, she recalled the first time she had felt wonder at the act of love, back in a time that was not so long ago and yet seemed a world she had read about or imagined rather than lived, one where she had bedded down with a blond boy on an autumn afternoon in her parents' room and finally understood what all the fuss was about.

"Are you stoned or something?" Roxy said offhandedly.

"Huh? No, no. I was thinking about Bobbo Starwick. Remember?"

Roxy thought for a second. "Him? That crazy guy in Vietnam?"

Belva nodded. "He wasn't always crazy," she said defensively. "Back when I knew him, he wasn't crazy at all."

"He sure turned out that way. Did he ever come back?"

"Never. He's one of the MIAs."

They had made it to Tribeca.

"It's off to the left here somewhere," Roxy said to the cabbie. "Just as well, Belva. That guy was bad news."

"No kidding," she said, although not quite sure she meant it.

Spanidou was different than she expected. Belva had imagined a paneled, white-linen type of place, or checkered tablecloths with candles in retsina bottles. But instead, there on St. John's Alley, they walked into a track-lit, horseshoe-barred fantasy of faux marble and onyx, rich with the smell of grilled lamb, garlic, dill and vinegar. She liked the place as soon as they were inside.

"There they are," Roxy whispered.

Around a table hard by the bar, she saw them, and — from Roxy's description — Belva had no trouble guessing who was who. Roger, Roxy's beau, was the boy-faced blond, all New England prep school, Yalie bright. Loren and Trace, the bisexuals from Soho via LA, were the ones in identical haircuts, paint-stained jeans, and trust-funded languor, looking pleasantly dull, as if they were on Quaaludes. And Michael. Michael was the one in the perfect suit, fitted to the point it took the breath right out of her.

He was so beautiful it almost made her sad. His skin was fair and his hair the color of a tarnished penny. Every so often, as he smiled with a boyish dazzle through the story he told Trace and Loren, one of his hands would suddenly stab the air as if signaling the effort it cost him to maintain that cool exterior.

"All you'll want to do is get in his pants, which my sources tell me is well worth it," Roxy had said as they were getting ready. "He's made for you. Everything Randy Ditmars should have been."

Belva was unsure about the sangfroid Roxy attributed to her. Now, though, all she could hope was that Michael was experiencing the same heart-stopping recognition she was at the first glance between two people God obviously intended to go to bed with each other.

"Charmed," she said as they shook hands.

He smiled. "Nice," he said softly.

And what, she thought, was she to make of that: nice to see you; nice body; nice evening, isn't it? He might prove a challenge, but Belva was ready for that, ready to show she had been through the wars that the decade had offered; not some naive little girl from a lost town somewhere between South and Midwest but a woman who knew what she wanted and how to go about getting it as well.

"Cocktail?" he asked.

"Manhattan," she answered.

"It's a lovely place," she said easily when they ordered ouzo afterward, Loren and Trace long since gone. It was Roxy and Roger. Belva and Michael. "How did you know about it?"

"Keep my finger on the pulse," he said a bit puffily. "You keep your eyes out, ears open, read the papers. That's how you get ahead."

He had grown more expansive as the evening wore on, through the dolmas, potent cheeses and a sour salad, a shellfish casserole the name of which Belva did not even try to pronounce. The owner — Andy, for Andromache — stopped by the table, where she and Michael spoke briefly in French before switching to English. Over dinner, the conversation had turned pleasantly around movies, MOMA, gossip about celebrities. Nothing personal. Nothing serious. Michael conducted the evening flawlessly, as clever in drawing out the reticent as in curbing the long-winded. About himself, he talked hardly at all.

Listening to him now, however, as his comments emerged in staccato bursts, Belva knew he was utterly self-centered. All anything finally meant was what it meant to Michael: Would it make money? Was it worth being seen there? Would it make a difference to him? All that had gone on over the meal was an exercise for him, a chance to acquire information or demonstrate his charm.

She felt the power of that single-mindedness. All Roxy had told her about him over the last few days came back: a modest, Catholic boyhood, his father working an assembly line making light bulbs — no, something for cars — before moving on to a minor supervisory position. There was a mother, surely sweet but steely, who bore three girls and one boy. For him, there had been infinite love and infinite ambition in one of those grimy industrial towns that was not Detroit. Michael had thrived: gone to the City after the college his parents never had, obsessed with justifying all their small sacrifices over the years.

As Roxy eyed Roger with barely concealed lust, Belva felt warm and relaxed. Michael turned to her now, his expression soft and satisfied, a little drowsy, his chin propped in his hand. His knee brushed hers.

"So," he said, "how is it you're visiting Roxy?"

She might have told him she was bored with life. She could have talked of Ross, of Wallace's pressures to have another child, of how Sam Sueter — who had the biggest cock she had ever seen — had now found religion after they had slept together occasionally for two years.

But Belva was no fool.

"My sister and I have a business," she lied with easy conviction, "a clothing store. I'm on a buying trip."

"Nice," he said. "Roxy's a good connection. What's it called?"

Belva looked at him blankly. "What?"

"Your store. What's it called?"

It required absolutely no effort. She smiled. "Letting Loose."

Within fifteen minutes, Roxy dragged Roger away, and Michael dribbled the last drops of ouzo into Belva's glass.

"Roxy says you're a man of many talents."

"Oh?" He was flattered, suddenly both lascivious and shy.
"Banking. The market. Real estate. Which is it?"
He raised his eyebrows. She was sure, by now, he had been expecting a come-on; at least a more overt one.
"Real estate," he said after a pause. "Right now, anyway. I bought another building. Last Tuesday."
"Really?" Belva touched his arm. "Can I see it?"
She had gauged him carefully. He was handsome, smart, and rich. No doubt he could seduce a different woman every night if he chose. She assumed he chose to often.
Consequently, she was determined to be different. Not that she would not go to bed with him tonight, but only after she had made a sufficient impression. A long-distance affair might be very convenient, especially given such an attractive destination. And quite by accident, Michael had forced her into a decision. She was opening a dress shop with Melva; it was called Letting Loose; it would feature all the latest from New York and California. Of course, to keep current, someone would have to make frequent trips to the Coasts to see what was in and what was out.
He excused himself. She saw him speak to Andy, and pay in cash. He disappeared briefly into the men's room, then emerged.
He held out his hand. "Let's go."
They took a cab to the Village, where she did her best to mask her disappointment. It was an old row house, the windows and doorways bricked with cinder blocks. He had his arm around her.
"It doesn't look like much," he said. "But the structure's sound, and we don't have to gut it. The junkies took care of that. In two years, I'll be selling apartments for two hundred thousand a pop. People will pay anything to live in the Village, especially fags. We'll start renovating as soon as the papers are through. It'll be under way next time you're in town, I promise."
Belva liked the sound of that, and the feel of his body as she leaned into him before the dirty facade and the scarred cornices. "Certainly, it's got possibilities," she purred.

She felt his muscles flex against her back. "Glad you approve."

She approved very much of the rest of the evening. They walked to Soho, down the teeming avenue still thronged though it was close to one o'clock. There were street mimes and three-card-monte men, couples hand in hand — men and women, men and men, women and women — and the constant stream of yellow cabs hurtling by, together with the dull thunder of the subway hurtling below.

The loft was white, with a flourishing ficus and blue-and-cream dhurries across a blindingly bright floor of natural oak. Persian rugs hung on the walls, and the furniture was massive and masculine. It was spotless in a way she had never imagined the home of a man could be. A spiral stairway led to the bedroom, and on three sides there were arcade windows that she suspected, in daytime, admitted more sun than most people in the city saw in a month.

Michael settled her on the sofa and put some soft piano jazz on the stereo before dimming the lights as he went to the kitchen, emerging a moment later with two goblets and a bottle in hand.

"An in-house white I keep cold," he said apologetically, twirling a California label past her. "Nothing special, I'm afraid."

"We've had enough special tonight." She smiled back. "Wine anyway."

From then on, he moved with absolute confidence. He sat close to her from the first; pointed out, casually, some of the loft's finer elements — the original brass fixtures, a small rug hanging over the dining table that the fey salesman assured him had been a gift from the Aga Khan to Rita Hayworth. He asked about her trip, the store (which demanded some imagination), the twin she'd mentioned.

"And is she beautiful like you are?"

Then he simply kissed her, and she kissed back.

He led her upstairs with an easy formality, taking her hand to guide her up the loops of the staircase. In the sleeping loft, the structural wall was bare brick, the lighting indirect. The king-size bed was set in a platform a couple of feet wide on each side.

He sat her down on the bench around the bed, knelt before her, and drew off her shoes. He leaned forward and kissed her calves, nipped her ankles. Then he brought her to her feet, and, between soft pecks and caresses, unzipped her dress and gently pulled it off her.

"Here," she said. "Let me help you now."

At first, she thought it made him nervous but decided, as she softly opened buttons, buckles, zippers, that it was merely his body talking. He shuddered and sighed beneath her fingers, his own petting her hair as she felt the taut smoothness of his loins. He allowed her to undress him completely, languidly, before he pulled her to him, whipped her underwear away, and lifted her gently over the platform and onto the mattress.

It was that patience, she knew even the first night, that would make him memorable. Locked together, with him instantly hard against her, they nonetheless only kissed for a very long time. He stroked her breasts tenderly, as if his desire were greater than that of a man with a woman he had met only hours before, as if he wanted to know that body and what pleased it. He was gentle, too, as he guided her mouth toward his crotch, allowing her to play at her own pace, until she was able to give him more plea-sure, and get more herself, than she had ever had there with any of her other lovers. Then he turned on his back, moved her softly above him, and let her slide onto him. She rode him easily, teas-ingly, so they both might enjoy it, until she was comfortable there astride. Only then did he grasp her, roll them over, and thrust deep inside her.

Lying together in the darkness, her head on his chest, she told him sincerely: "Michael, that's the best I've had in a long time."

He chuckled. "We aim to please."

"I'm not kidding," she insisted, mildly annoyed. He squeezed her sweetly, and she relented. "You really are a man of many talents."

"Let me show you another one."

He guided her hand between his legs. He was hard again.

They next were together toward the end of September, after, in a whirlwind, Belva convinced her sister to open the store, wheedled money from Wallace and Mitch, found a location on the Square that looked inauspicious but, taking a leaf from Michael's book, she saw as full of promise. Downtown Rhymers Creek, a sad shadow of itself, would be coming back, and Letting Loose was going to be a part of it.

Melva was initially resistant, but after sufficient bullying her reticence moved through the stages Belva had come to expect: hand-wringing, ambivalence, an occasional backslide into opposition, and final, docile acceptance. Wallace and Mitch were more amused than anything else at their wives' business ambitions and willing — at least for the present — to bankroll what Belva knew they both saw as a peculiarly female eccentricity that would pass within a year or two.

The only person who did not seem enamored with or amused by her idea, or who could not be cowed or cajoled into accepting it, was her mother. Things finally came to a head one Thursday in July. There had been yet another problem with the plumbing, and Belva, due to pick up Ross at her parents' at two, did not get there until almost four-thirty, raging about the cost overrun and how Alton Midley was ripping her off, she was sure of it, because she was a woman.

Her mother let her screech for a full ten minutes, pouring coffee for them, glancing occasionally out the window at Ross playing in the yard. Only when Belva had exhausted herself did she strike.

"You're right, I imagine," she began. "He probably is cheating you because you're a woman."

Belva was surprised at her acquiescence.

"It's a man's world still, after all. It always will be."

Faintly, Belva could hear a rising wind.

"That's what your grandmother said, and she was pretty wise."

Warning flags were being run up flagpoles.

"That's the kind of thing people like your Aunt Carrie . . ."

Sirens. Whistles. Bells.

". . . never understood."

"Mother," Belva whined.

It was like the weird quiet before a tornado.

"Do you see that little boy out there? What's that boy going to do, not to mention Jamie and any other babies that might come along, with their mothers off to work every morning, working late in the evening, bringing work home every night?" Her mother's tone suddenly shot up an octave and trebled in volume. "My God! What has possessed you? Have you and your sister taken even a moment to consider the children!"

The storm blew in full force.

"All day! Every day! Business, business, business! And the store isn't even open yet! What *are* you going to do about Ross? Have you thought about that? Have you? Have you?"

Belva had. Melva had raised the question as well. But there was some decent day care now in Rhymers Creek — she had checked — and where other care was concerned . . .

"Well, we thought," Belva said coolly, "you might help us out."

Her mother looked triumphant. "Well, you can think again!"

There was a long silence. Belva knew her mother imagined she had taken not only the trick but the game, the rubber, perhaps the whole tournament. It almost pained her. But she was on a crusade now. She needed what she wanted. She thought of Letting Loose, and of Michael, not merely the sound of his voice on those sneaked phone calls, how pleasant it would be to see him again, the wonder he was in bed. No, it was his confidence, that self-conviction.

If she had to be ruthless, she would be.

"Well, we'd considered you might not want to," she said slowly. "You certainly put in your time with all of us." Belva took a sip of coffee. "We mentioned something to Rhett about it. He could help us out if he's between jobs." She could see her mother knew what was coming. She pressed on. "And, of course, I've written Tammy."

Her mother was ashen. "You would not do that."

"Things aren't going all that well in Dallas. Tammy misses her friends. She'd be someone Melva and I could trust."

"I forbid you to do that. It was hard enough to get her away from" — she could not bring herself to utter his name — "that monster she married. I will not let you do that to your sister."

Belva looked at her coldly. "You don't seem to understand. We are opening this business. If we need Rhett's help, we'll get it. If we need Tammy's help, we'll get it. I will hire a total stranger to sit Ross if I have to. It's as simple as that."

"What has happened to you?" Her mother sat down, her face aggrieved, bewildered.

"I've made up my mind, Mother," Belva said quietly, intensely. "The seventies are over. Everything's going to change. It's going to be a whole new ball game."

Belva did not blink. She knew she had won.

As fall came, it was time to consider what stock to carry, and Belva flew to New York, to Roxy's apartment and Michael's bed.

"Can you come in November?" he asked her.

"I'm not sure," she said as they played footsie under a table at the St. Moritz. "Thanksgiving and everything."

"No, at the beginning of the month. For election night."

"Election night?" she repeated skeptically.

"Sure. It'll be terrific. Party after party. With this Iran thing, Reagan's got it sewed up. Everybody can't wait to celebrate. Come on" — he pouted before her hesitation — "I want to show you off."

That pleased her, even as she wondered if this type of event swarmed with paparazzi. The vague danger pleased her even more.

"I can work on it."

To arrange for appointments in early November had not been difficult, and her insistence — to her husband, to Melva — that these sort of schedulings were unavoidable came easily off her tongue. Instead of staying with Roxy — who had become rather chilly, as if her own plotting had worked too well — Belva took a room at the Carlyle.

That Tuesday night, walking into the ballroom at the St. Regis, Belva had an uncomfortable sense of déjà vu. Everyone seemed older, much older, and for an instant she was transported back to that stifling afternoon in Memphis. There was a quartet playing music she connected with her parents, perhaps her grandparents, competing with blaring televisions scattered throughout the room, tuned variously to CBS, ABC, NBC. Over everything smiled a huge portrait of Ronald Reagan, his hair the cancerous orange of barbecue potato chips.

"Well?" Michael took her arm, guiding her into the crowd.

"They all look a little" she paused — "up in years."

"Fair enough" — he smiled — "but there's enough money in this room to buy that state you come from three times over." He waved suddenly. "Edgar!"

A balding man about Michael's age approached. "Where have you been?" he said with quiet urgency. "Madison's here. And Kiley."

Michael raised his eyebrows. "Great." Suddenly, he seemed to remember she was there. "Oh, Edgar. This is Belva, Belva Masterson. Belva, Edgar Krueger."

He took her hand absently and smiled, then introduced the woman he was with, Marissa. She was very exotic, a bit like Bianca Jagger. It was apparent she spoke very little English.

A waiter flashed by. Michael snatched two flutes of champagne. "Starting the celebration early, it looks like," he said. "Would you mind sitting a few minutes? I need to talk to Edgar."

Glass in hand, Belva settled into a chair. Marissa smiled mysteriously, as if about to launch into some small talk in a pidgin Belva was sure she would not understand. Then, just as mysteriously, she gathered her evening bag and disappeared into the crowd.

Alone, Belva was irritated at Michael's inattention, but when she found him amid the sea of evening dress, her annoyance faded. Unless she counted dinner at Spanidou, she had never really seen him work a crowd. He moved easily from person to person, smiling, obviously saying the right thing. When he paused, she recognized the look on his face, one of absolute concentration, as if whatever was being said was the most interesting, most clever, most exciting thing he had ever heard, from the mouth of the most interesting, clever, exciting person he had ever met. It amused her, and made her a tad uneasy. It was that very charm he used on her.

"Pardon me. Would you mind . . . ?"

She turned around to face a white-haired man, elegant and very vaguely familiar. He was gesturing at two chairs across the table.

"No. No, they're not taken. Please," she said. She sought Michael again but had lost him behind two large women dressed in red.

". . . eminently silly man. Attractive in a boyish way. But mature? My, no. And as an actor, well, the less said, the better."

She shifted in her seat. The old man was talking to a very young one, punkish and uncomfortable in a rented dinner jacket, perhaps somebody's son dragged to an occasion his parents assured him would be historic. His face was full of skeptical glee.

"What about his wife?"

"A shrike." The old man smiled at his companion's perplexity. "A bitch, if you prefer. Absolutely ruthless. And she, too" — he sighed sadly — "utterly without talent."

The boy laughed out loud. "So, how come you're here?"

"Well, I did know them once, before I left Hollywood, though we really didn't travel in the same circles. They were both . . . a bit dull. But I was coming to New York, and Gwendolyn insisted I stay with her, and she had an invitation and has been quite his supporter. So, here I am." His eyes wandered to a couple standing nearby. "Will you excuse me, dear boy? I'll be back soon."

He lurched up and set off with a dapper stateliness.

"Who is that?" Belva asked in a confidential tone.

"Some old movie star." The boy shrugged. "Stephen something? Lives in Italy, I guess."

That was why the face was familiar, though she could not place him. She tried to imagine him, decades younger in black and white.

The boy sniffed an admiring giggle. "He's got balls for a fossil, though, you know."

The music stopped. The televisions were turned up, the volume so distorted Belva could make out nothing. The cheering started.

"What's happening? What's happening?" she demanded, but the boy was gone from beside her. She stood and looked for Michael, plunging into the throng. In their tuxedos, all the men looked exactly the same. Then, without her being aware of where he came from, Michael was beside her, along with Edgar and Marissa.

"NBC has called it for Reagan." He kissed her deeply on the mouth. "Sweetheart, this is so goddamn great."

"I can't believe it," Edgar enthused. "This is going to be the most terrific decade in history!"

Behind her, almost in her ear, she heard amid the din a soft chuckle. When she turned, the old movie star was close enough to touch. He smiled indulgently, cynically at her.

"Ah, yes," he said in a stage whisper, "the Vandals have entered Rome."

SATURDAY

✧　✧　✧

1

In the quietest part of the night, Myrna lay awake and knew she would not sleep again until the long next day was over. She listened to the wheeze of Ezra's breathing, the muffled tick of the wall clock in the hall. Since midnight, she had dozed fitfully, every so often starting awake to see it across the room, darker than the rest of the darkness.

After the first time, when it frightened her, she knew what it was. Her dress. Her mourning dress on the hanger on the door. She had bought it three days before, though she had known she would need it for months. Getting it sooner struck her as needless, even obscene. She was in no hurry to outfit herself for Bobbo's funeral.

Soon it would be over: all the years of waiting and hoping more and more futilely for something other than what she knew was inevitable. Indeed, that inevitable had haunted her even before the stifling August afternoon when they got the news. She had felt it surely when Bobbo reenlisted; it had shrieked in her head in Hawaii; it had flitted through her consciousness even with those first peculiar letters from the field. In the weeks that followed the announcement of his vanishing, she realized she had anticipated something very like that longer than she cared to admit.

Very like, but different, for what she had expected was the news he was dead. Death, in its searing absoluteness, would have meant far less of a martyrdom for her, as hope, over the years, worked on her loss as not balm but salt.

She sighed, sat up in bed. The last weeks had been hard, and the hardest part of all was that more than twenty years had been erased as if by a spell. All the pain of what had been the most painful time she had ever lived came back. The very incidents she would never have chosen to think of she found herself forced to talk about, hear about, review in her mind again and again. One would have thought, since that summer long ago, she had done nothing but wait, locked away like a grieving widow in a dime-store gothic. And that was not true at all. She had absorbed the loss — the losses, for there was Barry, too, to think of — and she had gone on. She had a husband. She had a daughter. She had herself to think of, and felt no shame about it. She might have dwelt on Bobbo's possible fates; she might have anguished over Barry's revelation and rebellion. It would have made her strange, and finally crazy, and she knew it.

It was not easy, those first years especially, as people asked — not meanly really — if there had been any news of one son and — meanly, perhaps — if there had been news of the other. At the market, on the street, chatting with the neighbors, she would occasionally feel the pity in someone's word or gesture. It was like ice run down her spine. There was no emotion she detested so viscerally.

So, Myrna had gone to work. It was China, the summer after her graduation, who spotted the ad for the opening of Seamstress City.

"You should apply for a job there, Mom."

"Don't be silly. I haven't sewed seriously in years."

"Mom," China said. "I'm going off to school. You need a job. One you'll keep. Try it," she wheedled. "I dare you."

For the first four months, Myrna sold yard goods, the sewing machines the purview of men. That offended her senses of both propriety and justice: the first, because none of these men were

tailors, and so, as far as she was concerned, had no business dealing with needle and thread; the second, because they earned
commissions beyond the marginal salaries they all were paid.
When one of the salesmen quit to move on to the home appli-
ance department at Penney's, she marshaled her courage and
went to see Mr. Maltby.

"Now, Myrna," the manager said when she made her proposal. "The research shows customers trust men more with me-
chanical things."

It unnerved her to question him. It went against more than
forty years of deferring to authority. But she pressed on: "Let me
try. Things are slow anyway. If it hasn't worked out by Christmas, I'll go back to yard goods and you can hire someone new."

Mr. Maltby agreed, largely, he told her later, because he
thought he would save some money by being short-staffed in the
autumn. The very first night, she went home with the instruc-
tional manual for the most expensive machine and read it cover
to cover. She took notes. On Saturday, she had Ezra walk her
through the mechanics of her Singer until she understood — at
least generally — how it functioned. Lunch hour after lunch
hour, she sat at one of the display machines and ran it through its
repertoire: regular stitch, backstitch, zigzag, buttonhole.

Lawrence and Peter, the other salesmen, teased her, while Mr.
Maltby questioned whether she ought to use the store's merchandise.

"What better publicity could you have?" she finally snapped.
"Besides, I have to know how these things work."

By that time, he was intimidated by her energy. Ten days after
starting, she made her first sale. From then on, it was easy. Customers seemed confident a woman would know about sewing,
particularly one who spoke easily about rpms and easy mainte-
nance. She was especially good with men who came looking for
a machine with all the bells and whistles, despite wives who
barely sewed a lick. She steered them toward less elaborate mod-

els that, she suggested gently, could be traded up later. This, too, went against Seamstress City policy, but Mr. Maltby noted customers asked specifically when Myrna was scheduled, because they wanted to deal with her.

When she left, they gave her a sewing machine, a wristwatch set with diamond chips, and a letter of commendation from company headquarters. She might have stayed on, but she had grandchildren to be enjoyed and could justify a rest. She had proved herself, if there was proving to do, but more than that, work had taken her mind off her tragedies, given her, small though it might seem, a life after that one as a mother had gone so horribly wrong.

It was not that she forgot Bobbo and Barry. They were with her every day: the memory of one, occasional news of the other. She even heard his voice now and then, in those rare instances when he called his father and she answered the phone. She could not bring herself to speak with him, much less see him, though after the first couple of years she would write him, regularly, as if to affirm some connection, as if making a promise — both to him and to herself — that someday, for reasons she did not yet understand, things would change.

The old wound of his difference faded with time, only to be reopened with the ugliness over his pictures as the decade turned. Again she felt eyes of accusation, of pity, even of contempt with regard to that boy now a man she had not seen in twenty years.

"Heavens," Matty Renberg had said, "did you see the new *US*?"

She had, with an article about that preacher in Mississippi, brandishing a picture of Barry's, one in which, with a magnifying glass, you could see naked men doing something they shouldn't be.

"It's no particular concern of mine," she said stiffly. "In New York, they seem to think it's fine. Barry's sent reviews."

"Well, things are different there, I guess," Matty said, though Myrna could see the judgment, smug and easy, in her face.

His new fame made her angry, but so did the reaction to it. If what he photographed — to her mind anyway — was ugly, so, too — maybe more so — was the self-righteous shock of people like Matty or that senator on *Nightline*, who did not have to look if they chose not to.

After a while, the controversy calmed.

Then the news came about Bobbo.

And suddenly, Myrna thought there in the dark, it felt like August 1970 all over again. If only that were true, and Bobbo's body had come back then, and Barry — however he or she or Ezra or the town felt — had returned because, finally, he loved his brother more than he loved his pride. How different things might have been.

The alarm was set for seven. She could wake Ezra now, but since he had found sleep, she could not bring herself to call him early. At least one of them would be rested for the ordeal yet to come. It would be hard. But at least it would be over.

And so she could look at that dress — that black ghost across the room — with something more than sadness. For she knew that when she took it off tonight, all she had endured — for better or for worse for one-third of her life — would at last be at an end.

⟡

They came for him before dawn.

From behind the trees, Barry watched the hearse pull up to the loading dock. The driver sounded the horn, then got out as Marco DiGiovanni opened the mortuary's heavy steel doors.

"Jeez. Colder than a witch's tit." Marco puffed.

"There's some gloves in the car," the driver said. "All set?"

"Yeah, open her up." Marco disappeared inside, then emerged again behind the gurney with the stark metal coffin on it.

"Need a hand?"

"Naw," Marco said, "not much to weigh this sucker down." He maneuvered the gurney to the open tailgate and pushed the

casket easily inside. "I'll be damned before I take on another funeral like this one. Yesterday we had the whole sixth-grade class
from Demmers Acres. The Vietnamese can ship us ten thousand
bodies and I don't want a thing to do with a one of them."

When he saw the taillights disappear around the corner, Barry
stepped from where he had hid. He wondered if they had spotted
him, but what would it matter? He had every right to be there,
even if, until now, he could not stand to see the coffin.

Each day, he had told himself he should go. Each night, he
would swear, next morning, he would be at the funeral home.
But it did not happen. Part of it was the compelling strangeness
of returning to Rhymers Creek. The dreamscape of his youth —
so foreign and familiar — filled him simultaneously with wonder and sadness; with visions of a potential life obliterated in an
act of rash and youthful conscience. Today, he would have probably kept that 2-S, ridden out the war, and Rhymers Creek would
have been a place he would have come back to again and again.
But he was nineteen then; he could not know the war would
grow gradually less threatening year to year; he could not imagine that, for his and his parents' stubbornness, he would not for
more than twenty years see the place where he had surrendered
his boyhood.

With time, he had grown comfortable with his decision. He
had learned, growing older, that life is full of the unforeseen.
Questions, in a way, do not bear asking, for things occur as they
do. Good fortune is its own reward. No emotion is so barren as
regret.

He slid down the bank by the loading dock as the sun crested
the horizon. It was still very cold, but most of the ice from the
storm was gone. They had predicted partially sunny skies, with
temperatures in the forties. Not a bad day for a winter's funeral.

He walked down the ramp and stood where they had loaded
Bobbo's coffin into the hearse. It had been only this morning, after a night of restless sleep, that he knew he had to go, so his first

glimpse of that box would not be in the church. He had to steel himself, afraid the final evidence of loss might send him into the kind of hysteria a man — especially a homosexual one — is not permitted. He had realized in these few days he had still kept a tiny hope alive, perhaps for the chance such hope offered to one day confront that man, his brother, whose last word to him was "Cocksucker."

Barry had let himself imagine what a confrontation might have been like: fury and disillusion and fear erupting in angry words and maybe even a fistfight — one, he had thought ruefully, he was certain to lose — but concluding finally in some vague truce. And over time, such a truce might have taken root and flourished. There would have been visits each to each, some of the old understanding and safety and love that ought to be natural to brothers.

That little flame of hope had gone out now. There would be no reconciliation with Bobbo, though Bobbo, of course, in the confirmation of his dying, had finally allowed for the reconciliation of the rest of them. Barry reached in his pocket and touched the cheap bronze medal he had stolen — talisman of his brother's triumph. He did not know what he would do with it, one more sliver of Bobbo. Perhaps he would simply take it back with him to New York, set it among the books and tapes and snapshots, the antique lamp and a silver letter opener: those mementos of others who were gone.

His apartment in these last years seemed less and less a place to live, more and more a shrine, his private solitude broken only very occasionally by some cautious driftings together, then casual driftings apart. Bowen had remarked not long before that Barry's theme of the last decade had been "Don't Get Around Much Anymore," which placed him among the frightened chaste, or mostly so, rather than those for whom an ongoing gamble with death seemed preferable to an ongoing tamping of lust.

The sun was full above the trees. Barry slumped against the cement of the loading dock, everything shimmering in the soft gold of a winter's dawn. He closed his eyes.

He had become a familiar, in the last decade, of the rituals of mourning: Catholic, Protestant, Jewish, and Moslem, sacred and secular. He lived, after all, in the capital of pestilence, epicenter of plague. Year to year, week to week, day to day, he had gone from funeral to wake, memorial service to mass of remembrance. Now, a thousand miles from New York, it was death that had brought him home.

It should, he thought, become easier with time, like the injured limb that numbs itself against the pain. But it had not happened, so each act of recollection was a little piece picked from inside him and cast away. Each tear, each prayer, each stifled sob was, these days, mere harbinger of the one next week, next month. There beside a mortuary in the cold, clear morning of his childhood world, all Barry could see, leading back into the night, was the long, long procession of his dead.

A crowd Belva had expected, but nothing quite like this. Amid the oaks dotting the lawn, Trinity's mossy spire rose above them in the crisp January noon — so many people, and such a mix. Faces glimpsed yesterday on the Square appeared right next to others Belva had not gazed upon for more than an instant since high school graduation. All those girls with two names now three: Wendy Loomis McGuire and Sally Peltz Matthis and Penny Shyer Simpson, children hanging on their arms or there beside them, nearly as old as Belva had been when she counted their mothers as friends, acquaintances, rivals in love. And the boys: Tays Lawton, who had done quite well for a fatherless boy selling insurance in Marysville, Willie Belmon from the family newspaper, even Sammy Gould, who, until three days before, she had not thought about in years.

These she had expected, people returning as if to a reunion, bidding farewell to one of their own cut down so long ago. They had a place here, as did those neighbors of the Carraways — Renbergs and Eldons and Coes. But there were others — Martins, O'Keefes, Valenzuelas, and McMichaels — who had come last year, in 'eighty-four or 'seventy-eight, who had no tie to Bobbo Starwick but were attending all the same, mourning the loss of a boy they never knew.

Belva turned and walked to stand beside one of the oaks. Of course they had come. Part of it was social, which annoyed her even if she recognized the reasoning involved. This was as much an event as it was a funeral, given the hoopla on television and features in the paper. The newcomer and not-so-new could show solidarity with the town as it had been decades before, demonstrate proper respect for whatever heritage Rhymers Creek could boast.

More than that, though, it was the attempt to connect to some other time, some time when, for better or worse, things seemed so much clearer, when lines were drawn, when people were for or agin. If, in these last couple of days, Belva had recalled the horror of those years, she had also remembered the commitment, the righteousness and passion of those drug-taking, free-loving young of once-upon-a-time. Now, despite aerobics and jogging and the endless self-denial of cigarettes and alcohol and fat, here before Trinity they were showing the inevitable gray hairs and bushy eyebrows and hips and bellies spreading, and Belva understood how they could not *not* be here, something which had far less to do with Bobbo Starwick than with a youth that they had lost so long ago, the one that seemed just yesterday and had now receded into some vague past as unreal as that of those landmark events her parents had remembered. *Where were you when the Japs bombed Pearl Harbor? When Roosevelt died? When* Sputnik *was launched?* Where were you when you heard about Jack Kennedy? Bobby Kennedy? Martin Luther King? What did you do when they shot the students at Kent and Jackson State: Were you in Rhymers Creek? Were you in Vietnam?

Today, it had been Ross. She was at the vanity, and when she glimpsed him in the mirror, she almost jumped. When he was small, he would seek her out when she was there in her private space with her rouge and eyebrow pencils. It was perverse — she, always in a hurry, and he, always in distress. She thought sometimes he husbanded his crises so that he could spring them on her when she was least prepared to soothe his feelings or offer him advice.

But that had stopped years before. Now, in her slip, seeing him — gangly, leaning on the doorjamb — made her uncomfortable.

"What do you need?" she said a bit brusquely, rubbing some foundation across her cheeks.

"Nothing, I guess." He paused. "This is a big deal, isn't it?"

"The funeral?" She was searching for the blush bought the previous week. "Well, yes. We all thought a lot of Bobbo."

"How old was he?"

"What?"

Ross shifted. "When he was killed. How old was he?"

"Twenty." She said quietly. "Twenty-two, I guess it was."

He shook his head. "Jeez," he whispered.

She felt a little quiver. She wanted to explain to him, her son, what it had been like. How she had held Bobbo that November afternoon, a teenager like Ross, and he had talked about going to war. When the crisis flared in Arabia, she had felt a similar shudder, as if that response were somehow printed on her bones, for she inevitably wondered, "How long? How long?" Would that war drag on and on, consuming Ross as she assured herself it would all be over long before they might call him up? But hadn't Bobbo's mother said the same thing once, back as Bobbo passed from sophomore to junior to senior to college freshman: *"Don't you worry. . . . It's no problem. . . . You'll be fine."*

"How are you, Belva?"

She looked up, startled. It was Marilyn Coe.

"Oh, fine," she said, pushing Ross out of her head. "I mean, as fine as you can be at something like this."

"You knew him, didn't you? Bobbo?"

"Oh, yes," Belva said. "Yes. We dated for a while."

"Tully was talking about him and his family last night. He moans about all the fuss over it, but he keeps telling me stories."

"He and Barry were best friends then, I think," Belva said, "before all that trouble with the draft came up."

Marilyn shook her head. "It's amazing, isn't it, what Neanderthals we were. And to think Barry's never been home in all these years. Did he say much yesterday about it?"

"Not much." Belva smiled to herself. The gossip mills were obviously turning. "We talked about old times, and some about his pictures. Remember all the controversy a couple years back? I don't know that things have changed that much sometimes." She snuffed a laugh, thinking of Marybelle, then scanned the crowd and found Tully. He was standing with his brother, Wellesley, and Lila Mae, who looked exhausted.

"Has Lila Mae been sick?"

Marilyn followed her gaze. "Oh, it's Fred. I guess he went on a binge again and didn't go to work. Lila Mae and Wellesley had to go and take him to detox. She frets so about him, and I really don't know if there's anything anybody can do."

"You know," Belva said softly, "twenty years ago he was the lucky one. It's terrible to say so, but when you look at the way his life's gone, you have to wonder if sometimes he doesn't envy Bobbo."

Marilyn sighed. "It is terrible. It's true, too."

"Poor Wallace must have found a parking spot." Belva saw him waving from the steps of the church. "I'd better get on in. Are you all going to the house after?"

Marilyn nodded. "See you there."

2

We gather together to ask the Lord's blessing;
he chastens and hastens his will to make known . . .

"Did he have a favorite hymn?" Father Dennis had asked her,
and this was the one she chose. It had simply come to her: the gap-
toothed grin on Bobbo's face as he sang it with the others in the
third-grade Thanksgiving pageant. Later, it occurred to her that,
back then, he had probably liked "Onward, Christian Soldiers"
even better, but if she had remembered that in the parish office,
she would not have been able to bring herself to mention it.

The wicked oppressing now cease from distressing:
Sing praises to his name; he forgets not his own.

Oh, she thought, but he had forgotten, or perhaps it was merely
that she and Ezra, Bobbo and Barry and China, were never his
own to begin with. Faith, long ago, had come easily for her, and
she had maintained it one way or another over these decades of
hurt and loss. Since November, though, it had ebbed away, drain-
ing out of her like blood from a wound, small but deep, till there
was nothing left.

I am the resurrection and the life, saith the Lord: he that believeth in me, though he were dead, yet shall he live: and
whosoever liveth and believeth in me, shall never die."

The words came from the back of the church. Father Dennis and
Father Wilcox — their old priest, long retired — were coofficiat-
ing. The latter had been pleased when Myrna had insisted on the
old Prayer Book, on the service Bobbo would have known. The

body had been placed in the sanctuary before the service, given the crowd expected. The choice was a wise one. When Myrna glanced back after the organ prelude, there were people lined against the screen between nave and narthex, and up the side aisles as well.

> We brought nothing into this world, and it is certain we can carry nothing out. . . .

Bobbo was taking nothing out, except the generalized good wishes of a lot of people who did not remember him very well. Over the last few days, Myrna had realized how vague he had become even to those who had watched him grow. Matty had gone on about his beautiful green eyes, though they were blue as the Pacific Myrna could see from the hospital window where he was born. Dickie Cheever, a name she barely recognized, had called from Miami, mentioning the fun he and Bobbo had had in physics class, though Bobbo had never taken physics.

Sometimes she thought that even Ezra, China, now Barry as well, did not recall him vividly, absolutely, down to the last scar and gesture the way she did. Perhaps that was a mother's blessing and curse, to know her child — to hope to know him, anyway — as well as her own self. In all the years Bobbo had been gone, Myrna could close her eyes and see him exactly as he had been the day he left for the War, the day they moved to Rhymers Creek, the day he started school, the day he uttered his first word. She did not think she had played favorites, but he was, in the end, her firstborn, the one who showed her and all the world she could make a child, and so was special for that, her amulet and ally.

She looked toward the altar, the coffin before it, in it all that was left of her Bobbo. There in the choir stall, next to the tenors, were the pallbearers from Fort Sillings, with their short hair and dress blues, not unlike, once, the boy they were helping to bury.

The days of our age are threescore years and ten;
and though men be so strong that they come to fourscore years,
yet is their strength then but labor and sorrow;
so soon passeth it away, and we are gone.

Soon enough, she thought, she would be gone, she and Ezra both, the promised seventy years up. And hers would be a life bracketed by coffins, the coffins of her Roberts: Robbie and Bobbo. The entire middle of her life, from when she was young to when she was old, was shadowed first by the loss of the one, whose child had gradually replaced him in her heart until he, too, vanished, and for the next twenty years and more, despite all her efforts, he had still been her constant ghostly companion.

How unfair it was, Myrna thought, to her and to Ezra, to be ever haunted by men named Starwick.

So teach us to number our days,
that we may apply our hearts unto wisdom.

Numbered days, Ezra thought. With a number so small, how could Bobbo's heart ever have grown wise?

He held Myrna's hand gently and thought of Robbie, whose own life had been snuffed out, give or take a year or two, at the same age as his son's. And Robbie, though he had been many things, had never been wise either.

Bobbo was Robbie's, after all, though in his whole life the boy had called only one man Pa. And that made him a unique charge to Ezra: the living memorial to the best friend he had ever had, whose life he had saved and who had saved his, the orphaned boy who looked to him for succor and hope and the lessons of manhood.

He had done his best. On the first day, when they settled that baby in the crib he borrowed from his cousin, he had sworn to himself, to Robbie, and to God that, though other children might come, Bobbo was his son, and he would cherish him as his own.

He had fulfilled that pledge. It was he who, bone tired from work, tossed the football and baseball in the front yard in the last of the waning day, attended the Cub Scout dinners and went with Myrna to PTA. He helped with multiplication tables and geometry take-homes, and guided Bobbo, fifteen and a half, through the intricacies of the stick shift. Through it all, he took off his belt only as a last resort, too aware, from his own boyhood, that pain and fear are no cures for error. He tried always, with Bobbo, with Barry, with China, to treat them equally while making each special, to find in each something different to praise.

> Thou foolish one, that which thou sowest is not quickened, except it die . . .

Now he was dead. Now they knew he was dead. Ezra could hear Bobbo's voice the night he came back from school in the middle of the spring term. He arrived when it was already dark, when the dinner dishes had been cleared away and his brother and sister were upstairs with their homework. He had gotten a ride from a friend headed to the capital for a wedding. Bobbo kissed his mother hello and then came to the living room and sat on the sofa and, after a few vague pleasantries, told his father he wanted to talk to him alone.

They went to the basement, and Bobbo — tall and muscled and proud — sat on the very edge of the divan with his fingers bunched in his lap like a child and said he had failed, he was flunking out, across his face a kind of shame Ezra had not seen in years.

And then, awaiting no reply, Bobbo told his father he had signed up for the Marines.

He could not tell him what to do. His boy was a man and had made a decision. Yet, far more than the news of bad grades or money wasted, it was the notion of Bobbo in uniform that staggered Ezra. His own education after high school had been in night courses that allowed him to earn his engineering degree. He could not judge what his son had done or not done there on a college campus.

But Ezra had been to war, and the idea of Bobbo following in his fathers' footsteps, of taking the risks and facing the mayhem they had both known so many years before, was almost too much to bear. He was angry that Bobbo had not come to him. He was hurt that so monumental a step had been taken without his counsel. But, most of all, he was frightened, for he knew what battle could do.

And it had done it. Changed him. Changed him so that Bobbo had come back to them sullied. Ezra often thought the most terrible part of their terrible loss was that he and Myrna had last seen their boy there in Hawaii. It would have been better if they had never laid eyes on him then: monstrous and murderous. Ezra carried that final image of his kind and honest son made demon with him ever after, together with the age-old terror that those sins committed in battle would blot out all the goodness from before and leave Bobbo finally bereft before his Maker and condemned unto the pit. Perhaps, if they had not met him in Honolulu, even how they felt about Barry over the years might have been different — their second son also metamorphosed into someone they did not know.

The lessons were done from St. Paul and St. John. Everyone stood to sing, as Myrna had requested, the Agnus Dei. It was hardly a hymn at all, more an ancient, keening plea:

O Lamb of God, that taketh away the sins of the world,
have mercy upon us.

Have mercy, Ezra thought, on Bobbo, this boy lost so long ago, who surely did the unspeakable in the unspeakable horror that is war.

O Lamb of God, that taketh away the sins of the world,
have mercy upon us.

Take away whatever sin he might have committed, for having tried — spurred by his own wounded pride and his fear of disappointing those who loved him — to make amends by riding into battle, without the vaguest notion, really, of what he was embracing.

> O Lamb of God, that taketh away the sins of the world,
> grant us thy peace.

Peace, Ezra thought, that was all finally one could wish for one's children. All else had no meaning if the shadow of war might fall and blight whatever happiness and hope they might enjoy.

Father Dennis said, "Let us pray," and Ezra knelt with the others on the bench before them. The words of comfort were coming from the priest's mouth, but Ezra heard instead phrases not from the New Testament but from the Old, not promises of redemption and glory but the howl of an old man before the loss of a child far more difficult and rebellious than Bobbo Starwick but his child all the same, his offer rendered up, hopeless and too late, one that every father might tender before a loss so grievous:

> *O my son Absalom, my son, my son Absalom! would God*
> *I had died for thee, O Absalom, my son, my son!*

The sun was out and the breeze had died. There on the gentle slope of the hill, looking down on Rhymers Creek and the river beyond, it was almost pleasant, Barry thought, as pleasant as you could expect in January, as pleasant as any burial day could be. On the drive leading up from the gates, the last cars were still arriving, as the mourners slowly assembled by the awning over the grave.

> *I am distressed for thee, my brother Jonathan: very pleas-*
> *ant hast thou been unto me: thy love to me was wonderful,*

passing the love of women. How are the mighty fallen, and
the weapons of war perished!

The verses played like a loop of tape in his head. He would not have known, ten years ago, that he even remembered them from a brief period of religious fervor just before the move from Grafton, as if like spells such passages might be invoked at moments when he felt the need of power or comfort. Second Samuel had come back to him again and again over the last decade.

So many brothers gone.

The soldiers had settled the coffin upon the grave. ("See how the mighty are fallen. . . ," he wanted to say to them, strong and proud in their uniforms, just as Bobbo had been.) They lifted the flag and folded it precisely, eyes locked each to each until it was nothing but a small, neat delta. ("And the weapons of war perished . . ." Bobbo himself — soldier of flesh and bone — the final, vital weapon destroyed.) One took it and held it next to the family — the four of them who were left — who stood silent. Father Wilcox, white haired and stooped, stepped forward, the prayer book open in his hand.

> Man, that is born of a woman, hath but a short time to live, and is full of misery. He cometh up, and is cut down, like a flower . . .

So much death, so soon: from Barry's childhood when those heroes had been blasted away one by one, then the battles, then the plague. And now, after so many years, it was Bobbo in the grave. This was his first brother.

> Unto Almighty God we commend the soul of our brother Robert . . .

Bobbo! Barry thought, Bobbo.

And then the litany of other names poured from his heart: Philip, Hugo, Lew, Conrad, Brad, Albert . . .

Earth to earth . . .

Ron, Freddie, Fernando, Oscar, Bill, José, Gus . . .

Ashes to ashes . . .

Rick, Payson, Connoly, Al, Art, Kit, Billy, Rex . . .

Dust to dust . . .

Jacy.

First the trowel was in his mother's hand, and there was a soft pattering sound. Then his father's, and the same sound again. Then China. And now, against his own palm, Barry felt the cold shaft of the handle, and his hand was shaking — gently, gently — and there was the dull, quiet noise of dirt on metal. The cold ground stood open and scarred, the ragged grass clutching the lip of the grave. Barry stared at it so as not to look at the coffin, his lips making the words though he could not even hear his own voice.

> Our Father, who art in heaven,
> hallowed be thy Name . . .

It was ending now. All the waiting. All the guessing. Bobbo Starwick's last instant on earth. A bugler played taps. There were three rifle shots. The soldier passed the flag to his mother. Barry touched the medal in his pocket. Father Wilcox's prayers were a low thrum.

> "Come, ye blessed of my Father, inherit the kingdom prepared for you from the foundation of the world." Grant this, O Father, for the sake of the same thy Son Jesus Christ, our only Mediator and Advocate . . .

"Good-bye, Bobbo," Barry whispered.

It was done.

3

He heard the bells toll. First there was one, then another and another, as if, all over Rhymers Creek, all the churches had set their spires pealing. Slowly. Slowly. Each a different pitch, overlapping gradually, until all the air was sundered with the low moan of metal. Even through the sealed windows of the ward, the glass seemed to quiver and then let pass the sound he knew meant that Bobbo Starwick had been carried to his rest.

He would have tried to look outside, but if he did, they might catch him and restrain him again. It was not until this morning that Fred even realized they had him bound to the bed with soft cloth bands. All the previous day, he had drifted up from forgetfulness and exhaustion, briefly realized he did not know where he was or how he got there, and then tumbled again into oblivion.

Just as the sun was rising, he had awakened and remained awake. There were four beds in the room. None of the others was occupied. He lay there, trying to remember what had happened. He moved his limbs, for an instant scared he was paralyzed, then scared still when he realized he was tied up. Had he gone berserk? Killed someone?

Not long after, an orderly came in, twenty or so, looking tired in the pale winter light.

"Hey!" Fred said, and the boy started. "What's the idea with this straitjacket?"

"Those are posies," he said, defensively. "They were afraid you might hurt yourself."

Fred proceeded cautiously. "Now, why would I want to hurt myself? Get these things off me."

"Sorry, I'm not authorized." His name tag read MAX. "The nurse'll be around in a few minutes. You can ask her."

Fred paused. His question embarrassed him. "What day is it?"

"Saturday." The boy bent down beside the bed.

"What're you doing down there?"

"Checking the Foley bag. You've got a catheter."

"Jesus." Fred groaned, sick with humiliation and suddenly feeling the strangeness of the tube inside him.

"There'll be a doctor coming around this morning," Max said. "If you can convince him you're continent, he'll let us take it out."

Alone, Fred tried to bring back the last three days. He had gone to the funeral parlor to see Bobbo Starwick's coffin, and then he had gone home, and then all hell broke loose. All his old buddies had shown up, like had not happened in years and years, and finally the place was full of caskets and body bags and Ronnie Eggleson was there all torn up on the dining table and Bobbo was on top of a mountain of dead shouting, "I Corps. I Corps."

That was the last he could remember. He had no idea how long he had been here. He knew he was at Mockdon General, first because he had been here over the years — in the emergency room or on this, the detox hall. Beyond that, MGH was stamped in faded blue letters on the hem of the pillowcase.

As time passed, he picked up more information on how he happened to be where he was. The nurse named Lorraine who came to take his temperature and his pulse told him his chart showed he was admitted Thursday evening. She also took the posies off of him.

"I don't expect you'll be going anyplace with that bag on."

About an hour later, Max, who brought breakfast to him, told him he had heard he'd been signed in by his sister.

Lila Mae, with Wellesley. Fred shook his head. It shamed him, though at least it had not been Momma or Lonnie. It would be bad enough to have to face his little sister and his brother-in-law, hear what a complete wreck he was when they found him, and endure, finally, a well-meaning and righteous lecture about his drinking — even if he deserved it. But far better them than his mother or brother.

The resident on rounds could not have been more than twenty-five. Fred found that it bothered him more and more that people he had to rely on — doctors and the police and the district managers at Pep Boys — were younger than he was.

"The orderly tells me you can get this hose out of my pisser."

The doctor was checking the chart. He glanced up. "Huh? Oh, I guess I could, if you think you can walk now."

"Sure. Sure, and I should take a shower."

"Yeah. You should," the doctor said with some distaste. "The nurse'll do it. But remember," he said from the threshold, "you're not going anywhere."

It embarrassed him when she exposed him to cut the stopper, and he almost threw up when she pulled the tube out. When she left, though at first he was unsteady, he made it to the bathroom and sponged himself off with a washrag. He glanced in the mirror.

He looked awful.

Bathing took all his strength, and, back in bed, he dozed until he heard the bells ringing, and then he knew exactly what was happening. He had planned to be there. He had a right to be there, and an obligation. People would notice he had not come, and he would regret what he had done for years and years.

Fred bounced his head softly, rhythmically against the head-board.

"Oh, shit," he whispered. "Oh-shit-Oh-shit-Oh-shit . . ."

✧

Coffee cup in hand, Belva stood a little apart, trying to remember what this living room had been like when she had last seen it. Back when she and Bobbo dated, she had only been in the Carraways' house a few times: for dinner, on the way to a dance. There might have been other occasions, but she could not distinguish them, moments long past bleeding together into two or three.

Wallace was across the room, deep in conversation with Wyatt Pruitt from Wilson's. He had proved oddly attentive all day,

as if he assumed the funeral would be hard for her. Marilyn Coe
was on the sofa with her mother-in-law, and Barry had passed
through a minute before and smiled at her. Most everyone else
was in the dining room or out on the sunporch, where they had
set up the coffee urns and put out cookies and pound cake. Belva
shook her head. She found these receptions vaguely creepy, an
ugly intrusion on the bereaved.

Through the window, she saw Melva and Mitch coming up
the walk. Her sister moved with a determination that boded no
good, striding in front of her husband, her face set. Belva turned
toward Wallace, but Pruitt was obviously deeply into chickens,
and there was no pulling her husband away from the description
of what was doubtless a surefire, money-saving procedure when
it came to slaughtering poultry.

Melva erupted through the door and made a beeline for Belva.

"I went by the store and picked up the billings on that last order from Hotchkiss, remember?"

She was digging through her purse, all intense, businesslike
energy. Her voice was so loud Marilyn and Dora Coe stopped
talking and looked in their direction. Belva smiled at them
weakly.

"Oh, I must have left them on the seat of the car. Come on."

"Can't this wait?" Belva whined, looking for a place to set her
cup.

"No, it can't," her sister said brusquely. "It'll take two seconds, and you really should have a look at them."

Melva took her arm and steered her quickstep across the living room as Mitch stepped up to Wallace and Pruitt, set, Belva
thought, to add his banker's two cents' worth regarding chicken
innards. They were down the steps in a flash and headed across
the front yard.

"Do we have to run?"

"Yes. We do," Melva hissed over her shoulder. "Hurry up."

The car was halfway down the block. By the time they got
there, Belva was breathless and chilled to the bone.

"For Lord's sake, Melva!" she exploded. "What's so goddamn important about the Hotchkiss orders?"

Her twin fished for the keys and then popped the lock.

"It's not the orders," Melva said tightly. "I went by the store on the way over, and I found a note for you tucked under the back door." She swept a small stack of papers off the front seat. "From Basil. He says he has to talk to you. It's urgent. He doesn't say why. It's in the envelope with the invoices." She pressed the bundle into Belva's hand. "Have a look."

Belva pulled the note out. It was on college stationery, and the content was more or less what Melva had described.

It made Belva uneasy. One of Basil's charms was his discretion. For him to even pass by Letting Loose, much less to leave a note, meant something momentous had happened.

"Well, I can't very well go see him today," she said, "though I guess I could sneak over to the store . . ."

"Belva, you will not use Letting Loose to conduct your affairs."

Belva turned — suddenly furious — on her twin. "How I conduct my affairs is my business. God knows over the years I haven't been fucking on the stockroom floor! Don't you dare lecture me!"

"I didn't mean it that way." Melva looked away, embarrassed. "It's just not a good idea to have him leaving things there. You know Marybelle and Heck come in at all hours. If she sees him around, the fat's in the fire."

"That's true." Belva sighed. "Well, I'll try to call him after this is over. I should be able to get away tomorrow."

"What do you think it is?"

Belva shook her head. "I don't know. It's not like him." She snuffed a laugh. "At least I know he's not pregnant."

"Belva, I swear!"

Back inside, she went to the sunporch with her sister and said her good-byes to Bobbo's parents, to China, and to Barry.

"It's been good to see you," he said as they shook hands. "I'm glad we talked."

"I am, too." She smiled. "I'll get your address from your folks. Next time I'm in New York, we'll have lunch."

She got her coat and signaled Wallace, still chatting in the living room. He nodded but kept talking. Standing in the archway, it was eerie, for she suddenly remembered being there before, on that exact spot, back from powdering her nose. Bobbo was talking to his father. She had signaled then as well, but he had not ignored her.

She did not care to be ignored. In her purse now, glowing with menace, there was a note from another man who paid her the attention she was due. She felt angry, and sad, and afraid. And if Wallace noticed at all, what was she to say to him? *You see, dear, I slept with Bobbo Starwick when I was no more than a girl, and it was wonderful, and I cannot stand to see that he is dead. And another man, one I am sleeping with right now, and it is wonderful, wants to see me, and I am afraid it's news that I cannot stand to hear.*

She would not do that, of course. Wallace would come soon, they would get in the car, and they would drive home. He would again be solicitous of her, impressed with the crowd, properly respectful of the Carraways. He would talk about Vietnam. It was all predictable: how he would act, what he would say — those, and that feeling she had inside now: just a small itch of emptiness there beside her heart.

✧

Slowly, everyone was leaving. Myrna sat down, suddenly tired, as Dora Coe pulled the plug on the coffee and began to circulate among the groups that remained, gently shooing them out. She thought how lucky she was, having a friend like that, one who was there, as they said friends should be, in your hour of need.

Despite her exhaustion, she felt peaceful. In the moment the coffin began its descent, something came unmoored. It was as if she could hear a wrenching sound down inside her as Bobbo was buried and the whole, long drama in her life came to an end. Some bundle of love and hurt seemed to fall from her and through the air, following that box into the grave of her firstborn son, and she was left with sadness, relief, and her memories.

Bobbo had scorched her life. She did not blame him. It was not his fault that war had taken him and remade him and then swallowed him up. But his vanishing had tormented her like a sore that would not heal. Until today. Today, it was as if that wound had been touched by some final flame of grief and now might close, leaving behind the pale scar of all the years of waiting.

Mechanically, she shook hands and accepted the quick busses of affection and sympathy from Renbergs and Belmons and Bobbo's old football friend, Tays, and then, for a moment, the porch was empty as Dora showed people to the door. Myrna looked around. The walls needed painting, something brighter perhaps, something different from the pale green they had been all these years.

She heard footsteps in the dining room, a man's steps. They were too fast for Ezra's. Doug and China had already left. Before he even came into view, she had guessed it was Barry.

He stood there, one hand on the doorjamb, as if surprised not that she was there but that they were alone.

"Mrs. Coe says she'll be right back, Ma," he said finally, tentatively. "She had to go over to her house for a minute."

She looked at her boy in his black suit: the one from New York, the one who was famous, the one who had come home alive. All day, in those distracted moments when the sheer effort of grieving was too much, her eyes would fall on him and she would start in surprise and wonder, all the stronger for her sadness, that he was here at all.

"Are you doing all right?" He asked kindly.

She nodded slowly. "Oh, yes. Yes. I suppose. I'm glad this is all finished." She paused. "I think it was very beautiful . . ."

Her words hung there for an instant.

"It was, Ma. It was."

Again, there was the silence.

"You must be tired. I should get along and let you rest." He did not move. "I'll come by tomorrow."

Without even thinking, she reached toward him. "Sit with me a minute, Barry."

She simply found the words coming out of her mouth. He hesitated, then crossed the room and took the chair next to hers.

The last time they sat beside each other had been at the dinner table the night Barry left. He was very quiet then, she recalled, more distant even than he had been in the days before, that long-haired radical who had descended upon them from New York, full of Marx and momentous news.

"We all loved him very much, didn't we?" She was looking at the floor, not at Barry. She was fighting hard to control herself. "I think, sometimes, it was a little too much. Not that that was his fault," she added quickly, "but he made himself so easy to love."

Barry leaned forward, his voice low. "Of course he did, Ma."

She had so much to say to him. And she suspected for him the same was true. She knew, though, that words would never be enough. They could not express her sorrow or his. All Barry had done so long ago, really, was reveal who he was, willing to gamble his entire future and even their love to be himself. In these last days, she had come to see it as an act as brave, in its own way, as his brother's soldiering. If it was not shadowed when he told them by the threat of death, it bore no promise of praise and pride.

"I don't know what I'd've done," she said, "if you hadn't come."

He smiled softly. "I could never have done that. Not just for Bobbo. For all of us." He paused. "I always used to tell people Bobbo was the best big brother anybody ever had. Thinking about it the last couple of days, I don't know if that's true, especially because of what happened to him after he left us. But he *was* my brother. When all is said and done, that's all that's important."

She glanced away. "There is something I need to tell you," she began. A strange, confused faintness settled on her. She took a deep breath. "It's that . . . That summer, the summer you left, I was so hurt, hurt beyond words." She wondered if she could say it, if she should say it, but it was too late to turn back. "I was angry about everything you had said and done, and so I wrote — " She choked on the word. She caught her breath. "I wrote your brother and told him what had happened."

Barry flinched as if struck. Myrna saw anger flare for an instant in his eyes. His head sank toward his chest, but then he caught himself, and raised his face to hers.

"I've thought since" — her voice quavered — "that . . . that maybe if he had not known, maybe things would have been different."

There was a long quiet. They could hear Dora on the front porch, talking to someone. Barry looked straight at her.

"Ma," he said softly. "Ma, Bobbo would've had to have known sometime. And if he found out from you, that was better than finding out from anyone else, don't you think? And it wouldn't have changed anything. Not about me. Not about him. Not what happened."

She nodded, sadly.

Then he leaned toward her and kissed her on the cheek. Their hands touched, and, as if from some buried place where love had long lain dormant, a shoot pressed forth out of memory and into the light.

And they smiled.

THANATEROS

✧   ✧   ✧

1

Fred wondered, when it was over, how close it came to never happening at all.

At the family reunion that afternoon, Cousin Edgar had been offering Lonnie pointers on how to control the grease flares singeing the hamburgers. In the heat, both were drinking beer at a rate Fred knew would have them slurring before dinner was done. He himself was not entirely sober, sitting Indian fashion on the grass with Eddie Petrowsky, who had tied the knot with Lila Mae two years before.

"Fred! Get married!" He heard Lonnie hoot. "Ha. He hasn't got laid since Vietnam. Ol' Dateless Fred, that's what we call him!"

Fred looked over his shoulder. Cousin Edgar glanced in his direction with the sick smile of a man caught with his pants down.

Lonnie was still snickering at his own joke, repeating every few seconds: "Dateless Fred. Yep. Ha! Dateless Fred."

Fred patted Eddie's shoulder. "'Cuse me a minute," he said. He walked in a wide arc, so that he came at his brother from behind.

"Lonnie," he said quietly, and got no response. "Lonnie."

Lonnie turned to him, spatula in hand, "Yeah? Yeah, what?"

"Lonnie, why don't you shut the fuck up?"

Around them, suddenly, everybody was silent, and Cousin Edgar said, "Now, boys . . ."

They were expecting him to slug his brother. That was what they still thought of Fred — the crazy vet, drunk and dangerous. Twelve years after his return, it remained everybody's favorite cliché.

He stood there a moment and could see Lonnie flinch.

"Sure, Fred," his brother said. "Sure, no problem." His voice came easy, sibilant, as if soothing a dog or a whining child.

Fred walked back to where Eddie was sitting.

"Catch you soon," he said. "Give my momma a kiss for me."

An hour later, Fred was doing boilermakers and talking to Tommy Lee Henderson, who had quarterbacked the South Mockdon Leopards the year Lila Mae graduated. Tommy Lee had bought The Dynamo from Jack O'Leary some time back. He had put on the Bee Gees and the Weathergirls, installed a mirror ball and strobe lights, and pretty much single-handedly introduced Mockdon County to butyl nitrate.

"I swear, getting rid of the cover was the best thing we ever did. Look at this place. There are people out there from Marysville, damn it. Hours! They drive hours to come here!"

Fred nodded and threw down his shot. He caught one of the waitresses and ordered another drink, surveying the crowd, his mind wandering as Tommy Lee went on about what an operator he was.

Lonnie was almost right, that was the bitch of it. In all the time he had been back, Fred hadn't been with a woman more than two or three dozen times. Half of those, he had paid for. That didn't embarrass him. He had gotten used to sex as a business transaction during the War, though none of the service he had gotten stateside came anywhere near what even the busiest boom-boom girl offered for the price of a pack of cigarettes. He picked up girls now and then, here in the roadhouses, once a blond hitchhiking up near Lemon Grove. Those times had been nicer, but his drinking scared women without exception, and it was usually worse when they found out he was a vet.

"Fred Bower. How are you?" he heard distantly.

He turned, and there was his drink, and above it, in the shiny, spangled blouse the waitresses wore, was Mary Muldoon.

It took him an instant to put a name with the face, but once he did, he had to smile. It wasn't a kind one. Old Prick Pit Mary.

He had not seen her in years. She had moved away, and he figured long ago he would never lay eyes on her again. People with reputations like that stayed away, unless they got rich like Elwood Pomeroy and showed up now and then to rub people's faces in it.

"Howdy, Mary," he shouted over the music. "How ya been?"

"Not bad," she said. "Good to see you." Somebody three tables over signaled madly at her. "I'll catch you later."

"What's she doing here?" he shouted at Tommy Lee.

He shrugged. "Been back a month or so, I guess," he yelled. "She's a good waitress. Always ready for overtime. Besides, I thought I should do her a good turn for all the old Leopards, even though I was too young to get a piece when she was in her prime."

Fred leered, even though he didn't feel it particularly. He had not lost his virginity with Mary Muldoon exactly. Mindy Rydell had taken care of that his junior year in the back of a Ford Galaxie. But it was the time with Mary Muldoon that Fred found made an impression when he was in Nam, as others confessed or made up things about what had happened after the big game or at the frat house or out behind the plant. Canterwell, who never took part in those discussions, remarked once he thought it was weird, that all the guys seemed proudest of screwing a girl after half their friends had gone before and the other half were waiting in line: "Shit, if they got so hot watching each other do it, they could've saved the trouble and fucked each other."

Fred had thought that was a shocking notion, though over time — although he had bragged to his buddies about Prick Pit Mary more drunken nights than he could remember — the incident made less and less sense. He had even been a little embarrassed when it happened, when he was pulled out of the consolation party at Dickie Cheever's house after the only game they lost all season — the very first, to St. Cyprian's in Henderson.

Dickie's parents were gone, and a few girls had come along to drink beer and get everybody's mind off the 14–13 score. The backfield was too upset to even show. Fred was so preoccupied with the failure to block either extra point he really did not notice when all the girls but Mary left, and Dickie took her upstairs.

He had his eyes closed and was bobbing his head to "I Get Around" when Dickie clapped him on the back of the neck and whispered urgently, "Hey, buttfuck, come on! It's your turn!"

He let himself be led to the second floor, teammates smiling after him. In the hallway, he could see Jimmy Martin and Chip Finnerty looking in one of the doorways. Dickie pushed him forward, propelling him past the two spying tackles and into the bedroom.

Before his eyes had adjusted to the dark, he knew what was going on. Directly in front of him, there was loud moaning, and gradually Taylor Lawton's broad, brown-haired butt came into focus, humping furiously up and down as he panted toward release.

"Do it, Tays." Chip giggled half under his breath. "Go for it!"

It excited him, though he wasn't entirely sure who was under Taylor. Any trace of a girl was lost beneath the sheer massiveness of the left guard. Tays let out a wild sound, then collapsed as if he'd been shot.

"Come on, Taylor. Time's a wastin'," Dickie hissed.

He got up without a word, and Fred could see the naked girl on the mattress. Even then, he couldn't tell who it was.

"Do it, man. There's still three more after you. Get going!"

Dickie gave him a shove, and Fred stumbled against the foot of the bed. He got his pants open and began to hike them down. As he crawled onto the sheets, he realized it was Mary Muldoon.

He felt a surge of disgust. It made him nervous to be there with his pants around his ankles in front of his friends. It bothered him that he didn't know who all had been with Mary before him, and — vaguely but surely — he wondered why she was doing this.

Mary had her eyes closed, and she looked very tired. He rolled over on top of her. She looked him in the face.

"Hi, Fred," she said softly.

"So do it, cocksucker!" It was Dickie's voice. Fred felt all their eyes on him, and felt ridiculous.

"Hi, Mary," he said, though it sounded so silly he almost had to grit his teeth. It was like they were across the table from each other in the cafeteria.

He was hard enough to get inside, which was all that mattered. He tried to kiss her, but though she let him for a moment, then she turned away.

"Hit 'em again. Hit 'em again. Harder. Harder!"

All three of the boys had joined in the cheer by the end, their stifled laughter ringing in his head. Fred closed his eyes, tried to stop his ears. It was like jerking off in front of them. He concentrated. He imagined he was someplace else. He thought of the poster of Raquel Welch in her animal-skin bikini in *One Million Years B.C.*

After he came, he yanked himself out of Mary almost immediately.

She was underneath him, breathless. He could smell beer.

"Thanks," he whispered and gave her a peck on the cheek.

"Sure, Fred," she said softly.

He rose up, and there was Dickie Cheever, Larry Coleman beside him with his zipper open.

It hadn't taken long for word to spread. After practice on Monday, the locker room was awash with details, of which Dickie's were most graphic, since he had watched them all do it, every one.

"Tays was snorting like a bull" — he laughed — "and Bower . . . old Bower tries to make nice with her, huh, Fred? All kissyface!"

Fred snapped his towel in the direction of Dickie's crotch. "Fuck you. You didn't last long enough to even get a look at her."

He didn't know that was true, but from the expression in Dickie's eyes, it probably was.

"Jeez, Bower. Who wants to take his time with a prick pit like that? Hey, that's it. Ol' Prick Pit Mary. Prick Pit Muldoon!"

The name stuck for the rest of the year. He never used it, and, the infrequent times he found himself with her in the halls or at a party, Fred tried to be nice. She never made any sign she held what had happened against him, but she made him uncomfortable, her simple presence a reminder of something he knew in his heart was wrong.

✧

"So, stranger. Freshen you up?"

He turned and there was Mary. He smiled, this time sincerely. Perhaps it was that, fifteen years later, he had a reputation, too, different but no less damning.

"Not yet, Mary," he said, pulling out the chair Tommy Lee had left to take a phone call. "Have a seat."

"I can't yet. I don't have a break for another fifteen minutes." She set her tray on the table. "So, where have you been keeping yourself? I haven't seen you here before."

"Don't come around very often. You been working here long?"

"Only about three weeks," she said, "but a lot of the regulars are locals. I've seen a fair number of people from the old days."

She said it without rancor. Still, he changed the subject.

"Where were you all this time? When I got back from Nam, you were long gone."

"LA," she said. "Phoenix. Las Vegas for a year. Oakland. Never stayed one place long. Knocked around all over the West."

"I was in San Diego for a while."

"Yeah?" She was cautious. "I was down there for a few months. . . . Oh, hold it. I'll be back. You want another one?"

"Okay. Why not?"

For the next three hours, she kept him in boilermakers. Even after the club closed, and Tommy Lee's bouncers cleared it out, he was still there, Mary across from him as the barkeeps swept up. Tommy Lee bade them farewell with a broad wink Fred didn't like.

They were both friendly but wary. He knew she had not forgotten what he had done and was not sure how far to trust him, and he assumed she had heard all about how he was a drunk and a vet and a general no-count. Besides, it had been so long since he had confided anything in anybody he had grown taciturn. The few people he associated with either already knew about his past or didn't care.

At some point, he blacked out. It took him by surprise. One moment he was by the truck telling Mary about his job at Pep Boys, and the next he was in his narrow bed, with sunshine filtering bright through the thin curtains of the window above his head. He lay there for a moment, then yawned and staggered up in his underwear. He was about to swing into the bathroom when he stopped.

Mary was asleep in the living room lounger.

He grunted in surprise, and she looked up. "Morning, Fred."

For a moment, he stood there stupidly. Then he was embarrassed. He had no bathrobe and hadn't noticed where he'd thrown his pants.

"Well, ah, hi." He backed toward the bedroom. "Ah, hold on." He yanked a pair of jeans out of the closet. "Didn't realize you stayed," he yelled toward the door.

When he came out again, she was smiling. "Well, unless you wanted me to take the truck, there wasn't much else to do. And from the state you were in last night, I figured you'd wake up this morning with no wheels and have the State Police out after me."

He grinned sheepishly. "That bad, huh?"

"Hell, Fred," she said, stretching and then standing up, "doesn't faze me. I grew up with it, remember?"

That was true. Renso Muldoon had been Rhymers Creek's most notorious and public drunk for years, and Mary's two brothers — Wyatt and Duncan — had followed in their father's footsteps.

"I'll make us some coffee," he said.

"No, I'll do it." She pulled the can of Maxwell House from the cabinet, then rinsed the percolator that was in the sink.

Fred watched her nervously. He had lived alone so long that anyone in his kitchen made him fidgety, as if she would turn on him and criticize, or say nothing but still make judgments.

Mary opened the refrigerator. "How long you had these?" She held up an egg from behind the door.

"Three weeks?" he suggested. "Maybe a little longer."

"Well, we'll chance it," she said, stretching out her shirttail and loading it with eggs. "Scrambled or fried?"

"Scrambled, I guess," he said, and sat down.

Mary worked quickly, mumbling to herself now and then. He turned on the radio, drumming a finger idly to Dolly Parton, not really listening as he tried to recall how Mary had gotten here last night and how he had gotten here last night and what had gone on.

"Gee," he said, "I should've let you have the bed."

She poured the eggs into the hot grease with a dull whoosh. "You tried to, Fred. Even when you're out of it, you're a gentleman." She chuckled. "You needed that bed a hell of a lot more than I did. Besides, I don't mind sleeping sitting up. I used to do it a lot at the Greyhound. Safest place to catch a good rest." She stirred the eggs with a fork. "Always somebody around, and, during the day, everybody figures you're just between buses."

"Did I . . . ," Fred began. He did not want to ask the question really, but he was curious. "Like, did we . . . ?"

"I didn't take advantage of you, if that's what you mean."

He sniffed a nervous laugh as she smirked at him, indulgent, then served the eggs. They tasted good, especially since he himself always tended to overcook them, and she had used a lot and given him an extra-large portion. The smell of the coffee filled the room, and she got up and poured them each a cup. It was only when they were on their second, after they had hardly spoken, that Mary said suddenly: "Who's Ronnie Eggleson?"

Fred froze.

His cup shook, and he set it down. "Why?"

She blew into her coffee. "You talked about him, last night. I know you don't remember. It was right before you passed out, when I put you to bed." She paused. "You started to cry."

Fred stared at the table and said nothing.

"I wasn't going to ask this morning," she said after a long while, "but I thought maybe you'd want to know."

"He was a buddy of mine." Fred shrugged. "Bought the farm."

"That's what I figured. He must have been a good friend."

She rose and started to clear the plates, but he stopped her and took them to the sink himself. He stood there rinsing them, embarrassed at having revealed what he had, relieved she had not pressed it, curious to know precisely what he had said.

He turned the water off. "Usually it doesn't get that bad. It's been a long time. I mean, I usually don't . . ."

"You were fine, Fred. Now," she added quickly, "you gotta take me to get my car. I've got fifty things to do before work tonight."

She drove a '68 Javelin, white with a gray stripe down the side. "A hundred and twenty thousand miles," she announced proudly when he asked. "Got me back here safe and sound and only burns a quart of oil every three hundred miles." She stroked the fender. "Well broken in and still a fair amount of power," she said softly. "Just about the perfect car for me."

They stood there in the heat, and there was a long silence.

"Would you like to go to the movies sometime?" Fred said.

◇

They dated. Fred had not dated anybody since he was in high school, and, even then, he had not been much for steady girlfriends. Mostly he hung around with the boys, and actually going out — getting dressed up and spending money on dinner or a show and worrying about what he was going to talk about with one girl all alone for three or four hours at a time — simply made him sweaty.

But, past thirty, with Mary Muldoon, it wasn't so hard at all.

They would go to the movies, have hamburgers or a drink, and he would drive her home. They would sit in his truck and talk, sometimes about the news, on occasion — and only very carefully — about the old days. Mostly it was about the club or Pep Boys. Those nights, when they were done, she would give him a buss on the cheek, and that would be it. Nothing more. He understood. They were learning to trust each other, because he had really not trusted anybody in a long, long time. And he figured she hadn't either.

As he saw Mary more often, there was talk. Tommy Lee would leer at him when he came by The Dynamo to pick her up. At Lewie Demmers's card parties, remarks were made here and there, snipes about "loose" women and sloppy seconds.

Mary knew. One night in the club parking lot, at 2:00 A.M., she said, "Are you getting trouble? I mean, about going out with me?"

"What are you talking about?"

She sighed lightly. "Look, Fred. I'm no angel. I figured, after being away so long, people would have forgotten all about what happened back when we were in school," she said wistfully. "But they don't. And, hell, while I was away, my life wasn't much different. But it's not like I'm running for Queen of the May. I thought it could be hard on you, though, with your family and all . . ."

He laughed out loud.

"What's so funny!" she barked.

"Shit, Mary. What do you think people think of me? Old drunk Fred Bower. Old Dateless Fred. That's what my own brother calls me. A lot of people probably think I'm queer or something." He shook his head. "They talk. I tell them to fuck themselves. I like you. We have fun. I give two hoots in hell what anybody says about us."

It was a strange declaration of love, but that was what it sounded like to him as he put his arm around her and kissed her softly, their beery breaths mingling. His other hand moved down her flank, and suddenly they were making out like two teenagers in the dark parking lot, her fingers on his hair and his tongue deep in her mouth. He ground slowly against her, and she did not resist but returned his pressing, and he felt himself hard against his jeans.

"Mary," he whispered, "I want you to come home with me tonight."

He remembered later how nervous he was. It had been so long since he had made love. It occurred to him as she unzipped his pants that maybe he had never really made love at all. He had fucked, in Rhymers Creek, in Nam. It was not that he was self-ish. Even with whores, he had tried to make it good. But as he felt Mary's fingers slide inside his fly, and moaned as she touched him through his shorts, he knew he wanted to do this right.

"I may be kinda rusty," he murmured as his own hand moved under her blouse and along her back.

She kissed his neck and popped the buttons on his shirt. He felt her tongue on his chest. "It's like a stick shift," she said with easy wisdom. "If you know how to do it, it comes back fast."

He brought her face to his and licked her lips, her cheeks, her eyes. They both let out small, soft exhalations of wanting. He traced her backbone with his fingers, moved them around to her sides, gripping her, feeling the ampleness there. His palm rubbed lazily over her hip and across her ass as she nuzzled his shoulder.

"Take me to bed," she said dreamily. "Take me to bed now."

He released her, grabbed her hand. As soon as they were in the bedroom, he had her blouse open, and his hands sought first the softness, then the hard, round tips of her breasts, stroking them in tight circles as he felt his pants drop to his ankles.

"Hold on." He thumped back on the bed and drew off his boots. This time. This time with Mary Muldoon, he was not going to be some barebutt, high school stud with his pants down. She watched him undress in the dark, and it made him both abashed and excited. Then she swept her blouse off and pulled off her slacks. They stood for an instant naked before each other.

Then he reached for her, and she, for him.

He entered her with a sweet, tense urgency, after he had kissed her there, and she had taken him in her mouth and wetted his stiff desire. After the initial thrust, he let himself linger a bit in the steamy warmth, listening to her soft cries as he moved. Her nails hissed dryly, delicately across his shoulders, down his back. The memory of the last time he had been with her slowly slid away, and he let his mind go blank as he rocked in and out, her breath, her words, her happy moans all one, as he somehow knew all his noises of desire and delight were to her ears that same sort of chorus of want and promised release.

He held back. This time, as he had sworn, it would be good for her. He needed to come almost as soon as he was inside her, but he would not let himself. There were atonements to be made, and, too, for him as a man now, the pleasure of the journey itself seemed a reward, not merely a necessary inconvenience on the way to climax.

"Oh, Fred, Fred!" she whispered urgently. "Oh, yes. Yes. Now."

He could feel it happen: the beautiful tension of her whole body as she grabbed for him, wanted him. He swept up her, time after time, the sleek softness of her insides slick as ice, hot, as suddenly he clenched from his neck to his ankles and his toes splayed and he was pumping his own warmth into her again, and again, and again.

After it was over that night, they talked, as they did ever after when they made love. And it was in that dreamtalk that they learned most about each other. Once, he asked if there had been someone in California, someone special, and there had.

"Reese," she said, "Reese Benton. From Huntington Beach. He was a surfer. I was down for the day. We hooked up in a nightclub, the Golden Bear, and he took me home. About a week later, I moved in."

"Did you marry him?"

Mary shook her head. "We talked about it. But we didn't." She sighed. "And that was a good thing, because I think I always knew it wouldn't last. Things like that never do, for me. I just get hurt."

"So did you talk to him?"

"No. One night, when he was out, I just packed up."

"You leave a note?"

"Not even." She shrugged. "No point in it, Fred. When something's over, it's over. I never believed in good-byes."

Afterward, he found out that was true. But then, in the dark, sated quiet he came to cherish, there was no shadow of parting. He finally even felt safe enough there to talk a little about the War.

"It wasn't bad for me like it was for a lot of guys," he said. "But it was bad enough."

She snuggled closer. "When I was in San Diego, I met a lot of guys who'd been there. It didn't make much difference if they'd been in combat, or flying, or on a ship. It was bad for all of them."

He drew back a little. "What did you do in San Diego, Mary?"

She didn't pull away in the slightest. "Probably what you think, Fred. Probably what you think."

It made him feel not angry but tender, and he kissed her head, and he told her about Canterwell, and Kirkpatrick, and Gómez. About Bobbo Starwick at Quang Tri. And about Ronnie Eggleson, because he thought, having heard the name, maybe she had a right to know. He could not tell her every detail, but he told her more than he had ever told anyone.

When he was done, his eyes were wet.

"Awful shit happens, Fred," she whispered. "Even when people aren't in wars, awful shit can happen."

That stabbed his heart, because of what he had done to her so long before, like some marauding grunt headed to be a double vet.

"I never told you I was sorry, Mary. In all this time, I — "

She touched her finger to his lips. "I'm glad to hear it. And I thank you for it, honey. You were too good even then to let yourself do something like that." She sighed. "I remember you wanted to kiss me. You were the only one. And you said thank you . . ." Then her voice hardened. "The one I blamed was Dickie. He was the one who wanted it. I don't think he could have gotten it up without the rest of you watching." She stopped, and he could feel her anger evaporate in sadness. "But who knows? Back then, Fred, I didn't think enough of myself to even let it faze me."

"But how come . . . ?"

"Fred," Mary said, with that soft tone of confession matching confession, the echo of his own when he talked about the War, "I was thirteen years old when I lost my cherry. And it was Duncan who took it. My own brother. And then he did it a lot of times after that, and Wyatt did too, now and then. So finally, I figured that's what boys are like. Which isn't too far wrong. They're just taught that way. To take things. That's what everybody tells them to do. That's why you did what you did. Even if you tried to be nice . . ."

Her voice hung in the darkness, and he held her closer to him, wondering how she could even stand his touch. It was true that had he balked, or squealed and gotten them all in trouble, he would have been an outcast, and what happened to Mary would have happened anyway. But at least he now would not feel that he had once — unwittingly, ironically — been party to the hurting of the one woman he had ever loved.

It was not a long time they had, and perhaps they both knew its ending was foreordained. But in the days they were together — Prick Pit Mary and Dateless Fred — they were given a kind of sweetness they understood is rare in any lives. They did not move in together, but she kept clothes at the trailer and he at her apartment, and they joked about having a city place and a country place. They danced at the club on her nights off and went to matinees. He taught her to fish, and she took him to swap meets, where she liked to look for souvenir spoons for the collection she had started in California.

"I've got a whole box," she said. "First, I'd only buy them when I went someplace. But now, I pick up any one I can find."

At her apartment later that afternoon, he saw them, a hundred or more, wrapped individually in tissue in a carton in the closet — small, delicate mementos of towns and states and countries she had seen or hadn't: San Juan Capistrano and San Luis Obispo, Minnesota and Connecticut, Ireland and Venezuela. He held one in his big palm, trying to form an estimate of its size. He was already thinking of a plan.

Fall was coming by then, the nights brisk and breezy. Christmas was not so far away, and though he had plenty of money to buy something expensive and silly, he wanted his present for Mary to be special, something he had thought about, something that was his.

The next week, he went to Linderman's Lumber and Home Supply in Mockdon and looked through the selection of hardwoods: maple and birch, mahogany and teak. He decided on the last, its rich darkness seductive and heavy in his hand. Then he went by Lonnie's, where he hadn't been in months, and borrowed a drill and a set of bits. His neighbor, Arnold Spather, loaned him a crosscut saw and a coping saw. Along with some steel wool and sandpaper, some doweling and lemon oil for the final, glowing touch, that was all he needed.

In October, they drove all the way to Henderson one Tuesday night for an indoor tractor pull — "About the silliest goddamn thing I ever saw," Mary said, and Fred had to agree — and took in at least one movie and often two every week as the weather grew colder. The feature didn't much matter. It was enough to be in the dark together, thighs touching and hands held, capturing some sort of romance they both knew they had missed earlier in their lives. Perhaps, in those moments, Fred sensed the slightest tension in Mary, some vague unease at their gradually drawing closer, but he was so happy that whatever blindness he suffered was not so much selfish as an expression of his love.

At home, at night, he would work on the project: drilling the holes all in a row, each equidistant from the last, then gently, with the coping saw, opening the channel to allow the shaft of the spoon to pass so its larger head might rest on the shelf and the bowl hang free below. The rack grew larger and larger, as he scrapped his original plan for one that would hold the hundred spoons she owned and instead designed one for two hundred, so there would be room for those she accumulated as time went by. He was not a skilled carpenter, and he bought more teak as he spoiled one piece or another. He threw away the first two shelves he had made, which now looked clumsy and coarse. The unit gradually came together, and he was especially proud of the fine bores he made to take the pegs, which with just a few drops of glue should hold the horizontals to the uprights for years and years to come.

With the kind of arrogance, he would later think, that only men have, he thought a lot of how they might get married, especially on those nights he was working on the rack. It was not so much the ceremony he imagined but the experience of a shared space: of watching television with his head in Mary's lap, walking together through the grocery store, waking at night, any night, to find the full, warm mass of her beside him. He did not bring it up with Mary, but he talked about it once to Eddie Petrowsky. It was early November; he had run into Eddie after work and they shared a quart of Bud behind Pep Boys, collars pulled up against the wind.

"So you think the two of you might really tie the knot, Fred?" Eddie said, and Fred noted then no skepticism in the voice.

"Well," he said expansively, "you just can't tell. She's a wild one still. But I can see it, I really can."

"I hope you're right, Fred. I really do. It would be great for the both of you."

Fred always respected Eddie afterward: all the time Eddie and Lila Mae were married and even after they were divorced. As far as he could determine, his brother-in-law never said anything to Lila Mae about their conversation beside a Dumpster full of busted pallets and motor oil crates, for, from her, a word was never spoken about that dream he once had.

✧

The Friday he staggered up to the apartment, a couple fingers still left in the bottle of Wild Turkey, he was wondering why she had not called in two days. He did not have to knock. The curtains were open, and the living room empty. The door was unlocked, and beside the front closet was a Campbell's soup box with his things inside.

He made no scene. He went back to his truck, drove home, and opened a fresh bottle. He took a claw hammer and the half-finished spoon rack, and battered and ripped it to pieces right there in the trailer. Then he went back to bed, took from the closet one of the blouses Mary wore to work, and held it. Just held it.

The only comfort he could find, the one explanation that made any sense, came from one dreamtalk that again and again would pass through his mind over the years when he thought of her.

They were lying in bed. They were almost asleep. They were warm in each other's arms, and he whispered: "Mary. Mary. I just want this to go on forever."

And she cuddled even tighter to him, and stroked her hand across his chin, and he heard her say softly: "Nothing this good lasts forever, Fred Bower. Nothing this good ever lasted forever in the history of time."

2

"Billy's dead."

He had bought a black suit.

"I'm sorry, Rex. I am."

"Ah, the fashion statement of the eighties," Bowen had said at Gus's memorial service. *"Doesn't everybody have one now? Next to the ball gown or the chaps? Always, the simple black suit."*

"It's all right." The catch in the voice. "It was . . . time."

Barry did not doubt that was true. "Is there something I can do? Do you want me to call the paper?"

It was a wretched idea, but it was all he could think of.

"No. No. Billy's brother did that. Parrish. From Vicksburg."

It would be, then, a discreet obituary. "Cancer." "Pneumonia." "A long illness . . ." Odd conditions for a man of twenty-eight. How good they had become at reading the encrypted announcements. Survived by parents, sisters, nephews, "many friends." But not Rex. The expletive deleted: *Rex Nash, lover, spouse.*

"If you need me, call."

"I will." Then the exhausted, lonely sigh Barry had come to know. The one he had sighed himself. "Thanks."

Mendelsohn — Felix the Kitten — stirred from the window-sill where he sprawled luxuriously in the midwinter sun. Barry cradled him in his arm and rubbed his belly, listening to the purr, looking into the slitted, ecstatic eyes, his fingers warm in the short, soft fur.

So much like a man.

He teared up.

It was getting dark.

✧

When it began, they did not believe it.

He was with Jacy then. Still living with Jacy, though it had been long since they thought of themselves as a couple. Monogamy was hard for anyone in New York. Hard for men and women. Harder still for men and men. Difficult for Barry. Impossible for Jacy.

They did not have sex at all. In a peculiar way, that made them unique, each to the other, for they might sleep with almost anybody else. They talked together, ate together, drank together, even went dancing. But their bedrooms were inviolable.

It was not that Barry willed it. He loved Jacy still, believed Jacy loved him. But he realized that he could not hold him, that Jacy could not settle into a quiet and comfortable life when all New York waited just beyond the door to worship him or be adored. And if Barry could not have him, if he could not possess him solely, he knew he would be poisoned by a jealousy uncontrolled. So they were roommates now, old friends and onetime lovers.

The night it came home, Barry did not get in until 4:00 A.M. After the day's shoot, he had run into a longtime fuck buddy at Trilogy, only too happy to share an evening of naked good times. When he arrived, Jacy was on the sofa in nothing but a T-shirt, the air sweet with a joint, a single light burning in the corner.

Barry stopped. Even though they were no longer lovers, even though a hundred times he himself had been the one there on the couch, it still embarrassed him when Jacy caught him coming in at some odd hour. He had no sense Jacy felt any similar qualms.

Jacy looked up, his eyes a little red. "Howdy." He scratched his chest slowly. "Hot time?"

"Yeah. Very nice," Barry said noncommittally. "Want a beer?"

"No. No thanks."

When Barry came back from the kitchen, Jacy had not moved. "You go out?"

"Yeah."

"Any action?" Barry always knew the answer.

"I saw Kit," Jacy said quietly. "Remember him?"

"Bowen's Kit?"

"Yeah."

Kit had last houseboyed at Bowen's a couple of years before. He had simply stopped coming, replaced by other boys in white bikinis.

"His lover's dead."

Barry set down his bottle. "Oh."

There had been rumors. Then stories in *The Native*. The *Times* had even run one or two. Barry had done his best not to believe them. "Gay cancer," they called it. Now they were calling it GRID.

Jacy shifted but did not look up. "His brains came out his ears, Kit said." He coughed. "He was pretty drunk. He was crying."

"Sure." Barry sighed. "I don't know. This is getting scary."

In the last two months, he had felt it circling. Somebody on a shoot would whisper something about a model, one of those beautiful boys he had photographed for *Roughneck*, in the hospital. Night sweats. Diarrhea. Meningitis. Cancer. Or weird diseases: something from pigeons, something from sheep. It might be a friend of a friend. Somebody's ex. When he and Jacy were still lovers, there was a group they had seen once at The Saint:

sleek, coke-snorting stallions who summered together at Fire Island.

They were famous now. Half of them were dead.

Jacy had not moved. "He got one thing, and another thing . . ." His voice drifted away. "And then his brains came out his ears."

Barry straightened up. "Baby," he said, coming slowly across the room. "Baby. It's late and you're stoned. I think it's time to go to bed." He touched Jacy's shoulder.

"Leggo!" Jacy yanked away. "Don't you get it?" he yelled, then whispered. "It's over. It's all over."

"What?"

"Everything!" Jacy put his head in his hands. "Everything's over. Everybody's going to die."

Barry caught his breath, then shook his head. "Hey. Hey, come on. It's not that bad. I mean, there's something going on, sure. And maybe we ought to settle down." He gritted his teeth. That was what they had tried before. What had not worked. "Cut back on fucking around a little. But it's not the end of the world."

He laid his hand on Jacy's neck.

"Barry." Jacy's words were so soft he could barely hear them. "Barry. On my thigh. I've got these two purple spots . . ."

The express screeched through the Eighty-first Street station, and Barry stood up. He could have called Bowen about Billy, but he needed to get out. Right at sunset, clouds had rolled in from the west. There was a light dust of snow on Broadway as he jaywalked.

He let himself into the building with the key Bowen had given him. Even as he got off the elevator, Barry could hear the bass thump coming from the end of the hall. He knocked once. Twice.

"Well, hel-lo, handsome!"

Across the threshold was a shrunken, nut brown man, somewhere in his early thirties but with the skin of a seventy-year-old, dressed in a bright orange caftan. He was wearing false eyelashes, fuchsia lip gloss, and had two perfect moons of rouge on his cheeks. Barry recognized him: Maravilla, a Newyorican transvestite who, years back, had been the toast of some of the darker leather bars along the Hudson.

"Hi," Barry shouted over "Material Girl." "Is Bowen here?"

"The Mother of Us All? You'll have to ask Ethan. He's in the living room, I think. You know your way?"

In the parlor, there were half a dozen men. Three were emaciated. One merely stared blankly at the chandelier. Another, lying on the couch, covered with an afghan, was playing checkers with Bowen's newest boy, Ethan: doe-eyed, with his shirt open to the navel to display his shaved chest.

Seeing Barry, he popped to his feet. "I'll take your coat, sir," he said with an unaffected humility. "Bowen's in the library."

It had begun when Kit had fallen ill, and been evicted, and had nowhere to go. Bowen had taken him in, nursed him, buried him. Along the way, others had shown up — friends or ex-boys or somebody's neighbor — and Bowen's apartment had gradually changed from the echoing redoubt of a very private homosexual to a shelter cum hospice for the helpless sick who had nowhere to turn.

Barry tapped on the door and opened it. Bowen was at his desk, papers piled high, his eyes closed and a pair of earphones on his head. The library, always a bit chockablock, was fuller than ever with occasional tables and objets d'art moved from the bedrooms to make space. Even the old Dalí reproduction, always so out of place in the parlor, now leaned unceremoniously against some books on a high shelf. Out the window, refracted in the street-light, the snow swirled in a sparkling eddy.

"Bowen," Barry said softly. "Bowen."

His friend looked up, then smiled. "Oh, sorry." He pulled off the earphones. Barry could hear the rumble of a male chorus. Bowen leaned out of his chair and bussed him on the cheek. "Sit down."

"Tired of Madonna?"

Bowen shrugged. "It's a new recording of Shostakovich's Thirteenth. Wonderful, really, but . . ." He cocked his head toward a disorderly stack of tapes behind him. "I keep this kind of thing back here. *Kindertotenlieder,* the requiems. . . . Not appropriate for the children, you know. Snow's picked up, I see," he said, glancing out the window. "What brings you out on a night like this?"

"I'd been cooped up all day with nobody but Mendelsohn . . ."

"Ah, yes. Beautiful hair. That cute goatee. A nice Jewish boy and so talented." Bowen smirked. "But you must mean your cat."

"And I hadn't seen you in a while and . . ."

"Odd you didn't call." Bowen spun slowly in his chair, around and around. "You always call. It's a long way up from Chelsea."

Barry sighed. There was little point in lying. "Billy died."

Bowen stopped spinning. He looked at the desk. "Which Billy?" he said softly.

"Billy Parker. The blond from Mississippi. Rex Nash's lover."

"Oh, yes. Yes, him." Bowen paused a moment, folded his hands. "It's that there are so many Billys to keep track of, Barry. And so many could have died."

That was not how it was with Jacy. Jacy grew sick in secret. There was terrible loneliness to it: the despair of the pariah, the weird misfortune of the freak. And, too, all around, there was smugness, judgment, fear. *Trashy* was a word Barry would hear on a job or in the bars after work, especially the more sedate ones on the East Side or the ones in the Village that catered to an older crowd: "A bunch of trashy leather queens get sick. Who cares?" That, and the seeds from pulpits in Lynchburg or Baton Rouge or St. Patrick's Cathedral broadcast over the air waves and spewing out the television, which then — among not just marauding breeders from the boroughs but straight friends, gay friends —

took root and sprouted in speculation: "Maybe it is God, after all . . ."

And so the fear.

"We won't tell anyone," Barry said. "There's no need to tell."

And Jacy agreed to the silence.

Aside from those spots no bigger than two thumbprints, Jacy looked fine, felt fine. He worked and stayed in shape and built models, drank and danced. But that could not last, and the two years — and that was what it finally was, two years — of his dying were an endless sequence of good-byes.

The first, and what seemed then the worst, was to sex that was spontaneous and unpredictable, anonymous and urgent.

"He says I shouldn't screw anymore," Jacy said after his first visit to the doctor.

"Why not? You can't catch cancer."

He shrugged. "They think it might be contagious. I told him to shove it." Jacy's laugh caught in his throat in a sob.

Barry put his arm around him, a gesture endlessly repeated in the coming months: comforting, fraternal, futile.

"He asked me if I loved men enough to kill them."

So, from the first, there were those things that ought to be done and those things that ought not to be done, for there was no health in one of them. Strangely, in those first months — as Jacy's illness spread, slowly, very slowly, blooming sudden and unexpected in some new location like a sly and noxious weed — their days were peculiarly like the first ones, when it was merely Barry who was needed to sate Jacy's wants, Jacy to sate Barry's. They invested in more plastic and leather and rubber, playing the fantastical games of two boys in grown-up bodies with needs unknown to children. But always, always cautious. Ever wary, as they began to be with everything.

Washing dishes, Jacy accidentally broke a glass.

Barry grabbed a paper towel and lunged. "God, you clumsy shit."

"Get back!" Jacy shouted, yanking his arm away and sending a spatter of red across the refrigerator. "Get back! Don't touch me!"

The two of them stood frozen across the kitchen. Jacy raised his arm and stared as blood drooled in a lazy spiral down his arm.

"I am poison," he whispered. "Poison."

Barry sometimes thought it might have been easier with drugs, if the both of them had spent those days in a fog of altered consciousness. But, again, Jacy could have no drugs but those the doctors — for gradually there were more and more — began to prescribe. Poppers went first — the acrid, appley smell that Jacy loved — and uppers, which made him insatiable. Then marijuana, which made him sleepy and sexy. Cigarettes — that postcoital totem of serenity after all the guns were fired and both shooters still miraculously alive — were next, and alcohol: no whiskey, no rum, no sherry sweet upon his lips for Barry to kiss away. The wine that fueled his wanting, the beer that made him swear like a trucker and beg to be fucked, these gave place to juices and waters and teas.

Red meat was replaced by broccoli. There was citrus and nuts and tofu. Dancing, where Jacy had sparkled in sweaty, nitrate-fueled abandon, turned first to the baleful seriousness of jogging and aerobics, though in the end those evaporated too in listless inactivity. More spots appeared. They were still hidden by his clothes, and to the world Jacy looked all right. But he was tired. On certain days, to dress, to bathe, to eat demanded all the strength he could muster.

Those times Jacy felt better, which at first were usual and then frequent and then fewer and fewer, they would go out. The city took on a sweet, autumnal cast. Barry could see, as they watched the cruising on Christopher or walked by St. Bartholomew's, Jacy breathe the details, as if, fixed in his heart, he could in days to come savor the image and sound and feel of each place he had ever loved.

On occasion, there were slips. He left one day to take one of his models — the *Constellation*, the last he would ever make — to the East Side. Two hours passed. Barry went to the market. Four hours. Six. Barry was on the phone to all their friends. Eight hours. Morton from across the hall came over. Frieda from downstairs. They called the police. The hospitals. Bowen arrived in a cab.

At ten-thirty, Jacy walked through the door, grandly drunk, ruddy and affable.

"Hey, it's a party." He beamed, even as Barry stormed: "Jesus Christ! Where have you been? Oh, Jesus!"

Morton slipped out and came back with a Quaalude. They mashed it up in the kitchen and mixed it in a glass of beer. Twenty minutes later they slipped Jacy into bed.

He slept till three the next afternoon. Barry waited, torn between despair and fury. When Jacy awoke, all Barry did was stare.

"I didn't fuck him." Jacy groaned, not moving, hardly opening his eyes. "He wanted me to, but I wouldn't." There was a long silence. He sighed. "But the drinks felt so good. And the cruising. For a while, things were just like they used to be."

Barry worked as much as he could. The medicines were expensive, the doctors' visits, constant as the hospital loomed inevitably, repetitively, time after time after time before the end.

He met Bowen for lunch one day, a quick one in midtown near Grand Central Station. By then, Kit was back on Riverside Drive, sick and alone. Bowen was talking about a new *Madama Butterfly* and a promised re-release of Callas's *Tristan:* "You'd never expect it. So remarkably good with Wagner . . ."

Barry forked his pasta listlessly.

"You're not listening."

"Sorry," Barry said. "It's . . . I was thinking about the shoot."

"You're working too much," Bowen observed blandly. "Do you ever do your own pictures anymore?"

"Not much. I've done some printing, played with some of the old negatives. I've been invited for a group show over in Brooklyn." He rubbed his temples. "I just have to try to keep ahead. The thing with Jacy, it costs so much to — " He stopped. "But you know that."

Bowen nodded. "Yes. Yes, I do." He folded his napkin slowly. "Do you want to go?"

Outside, Bowen took his arm. "It's still early. Let's walk."

They went to Bryant Park, mingling with the junkies and the lunchtime crowd. The sky was a pure, almost unnatural blue, and though there was a chill in the air, everyone seemed possessed of a determined sense of spring. They sat on a retaining wall.

"Kit's in the hospital," Bowen said.

"Oh, God, Bowen. What's it — "

"Pneumonia. He'll pull through." Bowen paused. "This time."

They sat unspeaking. Four children raced by, shrieking, playing tag. The smell of hot dogs wafted over the shrubbery behind them.

"Barry," Bowen said quietly, "there will come a day when Jacy will be in the hospital. I do not want you to worry then."

Barry looked at him quizzically.

"You are proud. And he is proud." He scratched his ear and looked at a middle distance. "I have a great deal of money. I want Jacy to have the best, as I want Kit to have the best."

Barry opened his mouth.

"You will not refuse me this." Bowen's voice was low, almost a threat, his mouth a thin line. "I forbid you to forbid me."

"Roland's mind is going. He just stares into space. Three weeks ago, you wouldn't have believed he was sick at all. And then, like that" Bowen snapped his fingers. "There's no predicting with this disease. Why his brain and not cancer? Why Kaposi's, not lymphoma or pneumocystis? My God" he snorted — "what ghastly Latinate pidgin have we learned to speak these days?"

Their vocabularies, it was true, leafed with words as complex and exotic as the illnesses they described.

"Has Maravilla taken up residence?"

Bowen smiled. "Adds a bit of dash, doesn't she? And 'she,' I should add, is what he prefers to be called. But no" — he stretched — "no, she's a friend of Roland's. She's ill, too; has been for some time." He shrugged. "Drag queens, I suppose, know something about survival. And she's certainly an appropriate addition." Bowen smiled. "It's incredible sometimes. I walk into my own living room and feel like I'm browsing through the hagiography of saints."

Barry raised his glass to his lips. The sherry made him warm, and he surrendered to the slight, soft relaxation of his drink and the room a tad too close, the lull of Bowen's voice and the delicate music, Satie now. If he closed his eyes, relied only on his tongue and his ears, it might be years before. Carter was president, Gloria Gaynor was popular, people worried — if they worried at all — about crabs and the clap. He had dropped by after dinner, before a night on the town — dancing and barhopping and maybe the baths or a spontaneous party with six or eight or a dozen men suddenly naked and high and groping in dimmed lights to the slam, slam, slam of a disco beat, laughing and moaning and ready for love.

"I remember once" — Barry leaned forward in his chair — "Kit was the houseboy that night. I came with Jacy, remember? He was mad because he wanted to go dancing at some club, and he went slamming out of here and knocked a picture off the wall."

"Oh, yes." Bowen smiled at the reminiscence, resting his chin in his hand. "Yes. He could be a difficult one, couldn't he?"

"That night you talked about some heretics you were interested in. Something about Bosch."

Bowen tipped some more sherry in his glass. "Oh, the Adamites."

"Caligulans or Adamites? That was the question you asked. You thought we were all Adamites."

"That's right." They were silent a moment. "Which would still be my answer, if that's what you're asking."

Barry nodded. "I guess it would be mine, too," he said softly, turning his glass in his hand, "but I have to wonder sometimes."

"We all wonder, Barry. Those of us who bother to wonder. But the sad fact is that the model we have for this sort of thing tells us" — he gestured toward the reproduction of *The Christ of St. John of the Cross* — "that if you teach people how to love, you also have to teach them how to die."

In what, it turned out, were the final months, Jacy began to lose weight — suddenly, rapidly — and the spots turned to welts that snaked down his torso and over his arms and legs.

Barry was in a constant panic — desperate to be with Jacy, desperate to be away; working for the money that was essential but, just as needfully, dealing with a world in which things might be important or trivial, pressing or merely promising, rather than dulled to equal insignificance by the horror looming larger right beyond tomorrow.

On a shoot, for four hours or eight, Barry could put aside all the shapes of what was and what was to come and focus purely, completely, on the image framed in his viewfinder. He directed postures, regulated light, controlled and captured everything on film. Even in the midst of such respites, however, inevitably and always, the razored point of what was happening would slash through his calm: Jacy could be suffering, could be dying, could be dead. The hours spent away from him were irrecoverable, and the hours he had left to him were few.

There is no time. There is no time. There is no time.

They still, now and again, made a kind of love. Once afterward, as they lay there, sperm opalescent on their bellies, Jacy said softly: "If I ask you, will you kill me?"

Barry threw himself off the bed. "Jesus, how do I know!" He leaned against the window frame and took a deep breath. "If you couldn't stand it anymore, maybe. If you were . . . were . . . I don't know."

It was early evening, autumn. There was the faintest trace of twilight still in the apartment. They were both naked.

"Promise me you'll think about it," Jacy said softly. "It's not the pain I'm afraid of. Maybe I should be. It seems funny, though, after getting so much pleasure from pain." He snuffed a laugh. "But I'm tired of being tired. And now I'll be ugly, and I don't think I can stand to be ugly." He stroked his throat, where a new spot had appeared. "My face will be next. And I could go crazy, like Kit did . . ." His voice trailed away. "Think of it like the movies, or like the war." He propped himself up on his arm. "Your brother, I bet he had a deal like that with a buddy. That they'd kill each other before something awful happened."

"I don't know, Jacy," Barry repeated, his voice rough.

"I bet he did." It was an insistent whisper. "I bet he did."

Barry thought of Bobbo more than he had in years. It was not just because he knew that, at first, it had been the actual physical resemblance that had drawn him to Jacy, not merely because, just a bit more than a decade after Bobbo had vanished, he was facing another loss: more intimate, more terrible. It was the specter of the madness and suffering and gruesome end of a man he adored even more than his brother. And this time, it would not be his own ugly imaginings before the sudden void where Bobbo should have been but something he would witness, something his mind could not merely shut off, something not to be assuaged or set aside by a walk or a drink or a phone call to a friend, but something he would see and hear, as if he were a prisoner in one of those South American countries where, day to day in hidden prisons, people, rather than being tortured, had to watch those they loved — lovers, mothers, sons and daughters — slowly torn to pieces before their very eyes.

✧

"He's still with you, isn't he?" Bowen said softly.

"Jacy?" Barry lit a cigarette. "Of course he's still with me," he said, gray wisps seeping from his nostrils. "Not as much as before. Then it was every day, every hour. But still . . . I dream about him, or I'll jerk off thinking about something we did. I'll hear a song or come across one of the pictures of him or look up and, for a second, see him standing there or walking toward me . . ." He stuttered suddenly, and took another long puff. "Sometimes I get so angry at him. Mad at him for leaving me. Mad at him for getting sick. Mad at him for all the fucking around." He sighed. "But I don't stay mad for long, and he comes back to me as beautiful as the night that I met him."

Bowen did not move, leaning back in his desk chair, hands folded across his stomach, eyes focused on the dim ceiling high above. "It happens to me, too. Mostly with Kit still, though there have been so many others since. But Kit was my special one. Even today, with Ethan — and he is sweet and good and I do love him very much — I was taking a nap, and I felt someone crawl into bed. I was half asleep, and I stroked my fingers across that smooth little bottom, and I thought it was Kit there beside me." He cleared his throat. "Don't you ever tell Ethan. He'd be crushed."

Barry smiled. "Your secret's safe with me."

It was Ravel now on the tape. Barry finished his cigarette. Across the desk, Bowen rubbed his eyes. The flesh on his face sagged. He looked as if he might simply fall in upon himself, like some figure made of dust.

Very, very low, Barry heard Bowen's voice. "They're going to regret this, you know."

Barry straightened up. In Bowen's tone there was a bitterness he was not used to, one real, not affected.

"What?"

Bowen snapped against the back of his chair and made a wide arc with his arm, strange, almost drunken. "They'll regret it. The ones who haven't lost their Jacys or their Kits." He stood up, jarring some papers onto the floor, and swung toward the window. His words came out in a steady, angry rat-tat-tat. "All day I was on the phone. Raising money. Trying to raise money. Groton alumni. Dartmouth alumni. People from museum boards, music society boards. All of them with money, great, shiny scads of money!" He barked a laugh, and then his voice came out a high, strangled wheeze. "And not one of them would pledge a cent. Even the queers! Not a goddamn nickel." He shook his head somberly. "And they're going to regret it. Next year or in five years or ten. When their darling boy — their rugby player, their honor student — or their darling girl — their cheerleader or debutante — curls up like an ember and flickers out at Sloan-Kettering. And I can't wait for that day," he said breathlessly. "I cannot wait for it!"

His hand went to his lips. It had never occurred to Barry that what was hard for everyone was even harder for Bowen, insulated, raised on noblesse oblige, incapable himself of real unkindness. The money and position he had always enjoyed could only save or salve the passing of so many, and, after hour upon hour of disappointment, he was realizing just how loathsome hatred could be. It was a lesson Barry had learned in Rhymers Creek, one Jacy had learned from his brothers' fists. Across America, it was being learned every day.

"Forgive me." Bowen sighed. "It was difficult."

"You did what you could." Barry pushed back his chair and propped his feet on the edge of the desk. "And you're right, Bowen," he said, with a gloating, acid passion he himself did not expect. "They will regret it."

The end began in the February dark at 3:41 in the morning.

They had put both beds in the same room. There had been no

crisis really, but, since Christmas, Jacy's weakness had grown more and more profound. There were new rashes, shortness of breath, and the splotches now swirled hideously over his face, swelled his nose, half-sealed one eye, as if he had been beaten in some brutal interrogation. He moved painfully, haltingly. His gums bled. His joints ached. Decades of aging had been telescoped into months.

Barry awoke to a strange whinnying.

"Jacy," he murmured, and then, even though he could not see, he could hear the covers thrashing across the dark. "Jacy!"

He bounded off the mattress and tore the blankets away. His lover flopped like a beached fish, the hiss, hiss, hiss of air that would not penetrate his lungs wheezing through his lips in shuddering gasps. Barry lunged for the lamp and in the light saw Jacy's face strained tight, eyes wet with tears and an expression of terror like that a man must have in the split second he sees the lobbed grenade as it arcs toward the earth where he stands.

Barry dashed to the phone, then swirled into the bedroom again, trying to calm the sweaty, shuddering body.

"Shhh! Shhh! Be still. Don't panic. Don't panic!" He grabbed Jacy's struggling arms. "Be still! Be still! Now breathe! Breathe!" There was that weak, stopped sound again. "Breathe!" Barry pleaded.

Then he breathed, pulled air as deep as he could into himself. He pinched Jacy's nose, and locked his mouth over his, and blew, blew hard: once, twice, again, over and over, breathing for both of them. Breathing so Jacy might breathe. So Jacy might not die. Again and again like a kiss, lip to lip, until he heard the banging on the door and Morton yelling, "Barry! Barry!"

Then the attendants were there with the gurney and a respirator and he was in the back of the ambulance holding Jacy's hand, in St. Vincent's with Morton and Freida, who had followed in a cab, then in a spring-sprung, vinyl chair in the dead, white light of the waiting room.

Bowen woke him, come to relieve the neighbors so they could go to work. It was 8:15.

"He's all right," Bowen said quietly.

Barry looked woozily around him, trying to remember where he was and what Bowen could possibly be doing there. Then it came back.

"Oh, Jesus, Bowen." Barry started to cry. "Oh, Jesus."

Jacy did not leave the hospital. It was as if, that night, something strained and torqued and stretched had finally broken. Amid the institutional green and the smell of medicines and the midnight squeak of rubber soles on old linoleum, despite pills and shots and machines, the entire empire of his body rebelled. One by one, the provinces that made him whole surrendered. Barry sat as doctors came and went, a harried general staff who improvised moment to moment as front after front collapsed.

Briefly, for hours, for an entire day, there would be a truce. Jacy would open his eyes, surfacing from a stupor of drugs and pain. Barry would lean against the bed, talking sometimes, more often silent, his hand in Jacy's hand or stroking softly over his forehead.

They had given him a morphine drip. There would be no healing but the end. His strength was gone; his weakness, absolute. Mostly he slept. When he spoke, it was brief and often nonsensical. He sang snatches of songs: "I'm an old cowhand . . ." "It's raining men, hallelujah!" He talked about Vermont, about football. Once, in a dream, he laughed. "Oh, yeah. Oh, yeah. Do it. Do it!"

On the fifth of March, Barry arrived at the hospital after four hours' sleep. Jacy was awake. Barry slipped beside him.

"Gimme a kiss," Jacy whispered.

Barry took a deep breath. He felt his throat tighten, and the tears that threatened. He tamped them down, leaned over, and put his lips to Jacy's. The sour breath of a body already lost squeezed his stomach.

Barry swallowed, and they kissed.

Jacy smiled, almost mischievous. "You know, I fucked a thousand," he said in a voice hardly a voice at all, "but I only made love to you."

Barry bit his lip.

"I'll be quiet now."

Soon, Jacy's eyes closed. The morning passed. A nurse came in. Barry was still on the bed.

"Don't wake him," he said simply.

She hesitated, looked down on the sleeping form, then went away.

The day faded slowly. The light of sunset was very red, then everything resolved itself, first in soft gray, then into darkness. Barry's mind drifted, so that sometimes he was not sure if he himself were asleep or awake.

He was aware, suddenly, of the glow of the streetlights through the windows. His hand was in Jacy's hand. He looked at Jacy's face, serene, and heard the faint sound of his breath.

Then there was nothing.

He waited.

He counted one minute. Two.

A third.

He reached over and pulled the cord for the nurse.

"It's close to the anniversary, isn't it?"

Bowen was back at his desk. Their glasses were refilled.

"In three weeks."

"I wonder if José will have a novena said for him again?"

José had been a friend of Jacy's since before Barry knew him, a Cuban tailor, a devout Catholic with a taste for bondage.

"I imagine," Barry said. "He's been diagnosed, too, you know."

"No. I didn't." Bowen fingered his glass. "Amazing, isn't it? It's as if there's a war going on and nobody knows, as if this might be happening in Dahomey or Paraguay."

Barry killed his sherry in a gulp. "I should be going, Bowen."
Bowen nodded. 'I'm sorry about Billy. And about my temper."
"It's my temper, too, pretty much," Barry said.

They walked past the quiet parlor. Roland was still staring at the chandelier. Ethan popped up and retrieved Barry's overcoat.

"Do you remember," Bowen said at the door, "that snow as we came out of the church? So rare for March."

The memorial service had ended, and everyone had left, all but Bowen. Barry had retrieved the canister of Jacy's ashes. The tape of some of Jacy's favorite music was finishing for the second time, the reedy sadness of Edith Piaf before the loss of Marcel Cerdan winding its way incongruously around the Gothic fili-gree of the chapel, the voice almost triumphant — despite a love illegitimate, despite a love cut short — before the simple fact of love at all.

They walked outside, the canister unceremoniously gripped under Barry's arm, and it was snowing. A tiny flurry that sent flakes dust-deviling down the street, making people stop and look, despite their discomfort struck by the beauty of it, just as, Barry thought, they might once have been arrested by the beauty of Jacy passing as they walked.

"Certain you don't want me to come tonight?" Bowen had said.

"No. It's probably illegal. And I should do it alone."

At four-thirty the following morning, Barry had stood on Christopher Street, a little beyond the entrance to the PATH. A bitter wind howled up from the Hudson, but that was all the bet-ter. There was no one around.

He opened the nylon gym bag — Jacy's, as it happened — and pulled the canister out. He heard Jacy's voice on New Year's Eve, a forbidden glass of champagne in his hand. He had gone to sleep at eight o'clock, but Barry waked him just before midnight.

"This is probably going to be the last one," he had said, "so I've got a resolution. But you're the one who's going to have to do it." He smiled. "What I want is . . ."

Barry unscrewed the top of the canister and lifted it carefully away. The wind seemed hungry, whipping around him, already lapping at the contents, which rose in thin, gray puffs. He held the cylinder high, at arm's length, and began to twirl, slowly at first, then faster and faster, around and around and around. The ashes tumbled, sprayed into the air, sucked up by the wind, whirling and scurrying and spiraling up and down the street, skittering over the curbs and exploding into the streetlights, mingling in the filth and cement and very air there in New York City, in the heart of the Village, on the street of the dreams of a million men where Jacy — the man he loved, who had loved him — could finally belong to them all.

3

In the laundry, loading the dryer after getting the delicates started in the washer, Belva decided that having it all had turned out to be a great deal of work. She was everything a modern woman was supposed to be. From a convenient lie on tipsy night in New York, she had built a business that paid its own bills and gave Rhymers Creek a venue for fashions not to be found for 200 miles around. She had kept her figure — her fanny firm and her breasts still tight — and she cunningly chased away the gray that encroached on her temples. And with all that, even her parents agreed, she had been a good mother. Ross and Leisel did not want for anything. She helped them with their homework, conferenced with their teachers, patched their scratched knees and wounded egos. If she were out of town when one hit some major milestone, Wallace was there to backstop, and when she returned, she always arranged for something special: a present picked up on the road or a trip to McDonald's or the yogurt bar.

She had been a good wife, too: unorthodox, true, but Wallace never complained. He was fed, the house was clean, she shone at dinners and receptions. She stoked his ego. She fussed over him in a way that would have done her mother proud, the way a man expected.

And, through it all, she had followed her own desires. A parade of men had fulfilled those wantings that Wallace was unwilling or unable to address. She had tried to be discreet, though surely, sometime, her car had been spotted someplace unexpected, or, in a roadhouse, a drunken boast had been made that could not be called back. With the caution that, perhaps, comes with growing older, she had lately confined her affairs to the road.

She was anxious to see Michael. She had called from the store a couple times over the last month but had spoken only to his answering machine. As always, she wondered if, finally, he had found the woman who had stolen his heart. Over the eight years of their affair, he had had many girlfriends, which she not only expected but welcomed. She had no desire to have him panting across a thousand miles and more while she went about her business in Rhymers Creek.

The washer sloshed next to her. Belva leaned against it, letting the vibrations buzz through her, a naughty smile on her lips.

It was funny how good it still was with him, good enough that she suspected it was not merely that he was handsome and skillful. Others she found sexy or exotic or intriguing. But Michael was the only one — at least, the only one since she'd married Wallace — for whom she had ever felt something like love. On his arm at the theater or at Le Cirque, dancing and merely being seen at The Palladium, Michael was to her the fulfillment of a whole world of might-have-beens. When she was in New York, she felt his energy and ruthlessness course into her, and for those days she was someone other than the dress shop owner from Rhymers Creek, mother of two, good Wilson's Chicken wife.

The pace of his life had never slowed. Belva had no notion what he was worth these days, nor a much firmer notion of what he did. He was still in real estate — buying buildings, renovating buildings, selling one to buy another. But, along with the brick and mortar in Soho, Noho, Tribeca, his energy was sucked up by stocks in New York, stocks in London, stocks in Tokyo; options, points, bond ratings.

Occasionally, still, they would visit some new property. Standing claustrophobic in yet another dreary, whitewashed warren for the young and hopeful on the Lower East Side, Belva would think how he had shown her the original brasswork in that loft years before, his almost feminine appreciation of it.

Michael had no time for such things now. Over the decade, she had watched him change as he moved from Soho to the East Eighties, from a downtown gym to the Athletic Club, from business class to first class. Even with her, he had turned abrupt, and a mean streak he had always had — one Belva had assumed he would lose as he grew older, richer, surer of himself — instead grew wider and deeper.

Even his associates were not safe. At a party at the Waldorf, where they ran into a famous bond trader and his wife, she mentioned she was surprised at how domestic they seemed.

"He's bought himself a Ferrari." Michael laughed cruelly. "Thinks he's some big swinging dick, but he's still nothing but a greasy little Jew from Queens."

She stiffened. It was not that she was unused to that kind of talk. In Rhymers Creek, the casual slur was still not out of the ordinary. But here, among people who talked of millions of dollars in a way that took her breath away, it made her almost angry, though whether for its essence or merely its crass inelegance, she wasn't sure.

His recent inattention miffed her. He had gone west in late August, and she had hardly spoken to him since. Even when calls were inconvenient, there was usually a postcard, an unexpected present in the mail. The few times she had caught him after his return to New York, he had seemed distracted, harried, though she supposed, in the wildly fluctuating world he moved in, she ought not be surprised.

The washer kicked into spin. The machine hummed against her. Her complaints about him vanished in a warm whirring deep inside her. She felt Michael's breath on her neck, her ear, and her hands at his waist, across the twin hard muscles of his behind. She breathed quick and shallow, her eyes narrowing to slits. His lips . . .

"Mommy!" The back door slammed.

"Damn." Belva yanked herself away from the washer and stiffened against the shudders rocking through her. "In he — " She caught her breath. "In the laundry, honey."

Leisel appeared in the doorway.

Belva took one look and squatted down. "What is it, honey?"

Her little girl rushed into her arms, the tears blotting on Belva's blouse. "Kathy says I'm fat!"

Belva held her daughter close — "Oh, honey. Honey" — rolling her eyes toward heaven. What kind of a world have we made where to be chubby is a sin? "You're fine. You're exactly the way a little girl should be."

"But Kathy says if you're fat, you can't be pretty."

"Well, people say silly things sometimes." Belva cradled Leisel's head against hers. "You're a pretty girl and you'll be a pretty young lady, and don't let anybody tell you different."

"Kathy says I should go on a diet," her daughter wailed.

Damn Vera Martin, Belva thought, with her Pritikin and Weight Watchers. What in hell were they all doing to their daughters?

"Don't be silly," she soothed. "Now go to the den, and I'll be there in a second. Then we'll get some construction paper and make that mobile you liked."

Leisel stepped away. "Okay," she said, still tearful, and headed back through the kitchen.

The spin cycle was almost done. Belva leaned against the washer again, innocently. The mood had passed. She watched her little girl skirt the refrigerator with her eyes averted. Belva sometimes wondered what the country was coming to, even Rhymers Creek. Five-year-olds obsessed with their bodies.

She sighed. With an actor for president, what could you expect?

✧

The October air was fresh and cool. Across the Square, the trees had mostly lost their leaves, but there was still a certain softness to the day, not yet the bleak, sad edge of winter. Belva stood in the midmorning light, her Louis Vuitton bags beside her, less than convinced that Arlene Peters could be trusted to keep the store afloat the five days she and Melva would be away.

"You off again?" It was Marybelle with her sack of doughnut holes, leaning out the door of The Phone Store.

"For a little while," Belva shouted, craning her neck to see if she could spot her sister. "We have to go to New York."

"New York? Say, did you hear . . . ?"

"Oh, here's Melva now!" She could see her sister's beige Lincoln steaming majestically down the street. Melva eased the car to the curb, which she scraped as she took her eyes from the road to diddle the various knobs and buttons she had never quite learned the use of. Before she came to a halt, the trunk lid was heaving skyward and the passenger window was coming down and Belva could hear every one of the door locks unlatch with pops like cracked knuckles.

"Hi, Marybelle!" Melva shouted cheerfully as Belva heaved her bags into the trunk. "What's new?"

Marybelle wandered out and poked her head in the car, her panoramic backside blocking any entry. Belva tapped her arm.

"Sorry, we've got to get going."

"Have a good trip!" Marybelle yelled as Melva put the car into gear. "Don't let any of them stockbrokers smush you!"

Belva waved, then settled back in the seat. "Good Lord, that woman drives me crazy. What do you suppose she meant by that?"

Melva looked at her quizzically. "Haven't you heard? It's been on the radio all morning. The stock market's in free fall."

✧

From that point on, the trip was dolorous. On the local leg, there was a constant buzzing of rumor and hearsay and speculation, while the bars in the terminal in Chicago were full of smartly dressed men and women, all with briefcases, drinks, and, Belva thought, the look of roadkill on their faces. The New York connection was even worse. There was some quiet but unmistakable blubbering here and there, along with a number of conversations that were entirely too loud. The cabin crew dashed madly up and down the aisles serving doubles, which were thrown down with abandon with one hand as the other leapt like a guided missile for the attendant button. Even more disquieting, Belva decided, were those people who sat, apparently unmoved, shell-shocked or, perhaps, planning some desperate, possibly suicidal strategy to be launched the instant a phone was available.

As soon as the plane touched down, passengers jumped to their feet, clawing at the luggage racks. The stewardess appealed for calm, and the pilot came over the PA system, to Belva sounding for all the world like a junior high school principal and having about as much effect. She and Melva, along with an elderly woman, three punk rock types, and a mother and child, waited till the cabin cleared before they headed for the jetway.

The terminal was bedlam. They were jostled and spun and shoved by people who looked to be — in another life perhaps — highly paid professionals.

"Two hundred?" shouted one man to an elegantly suited woman he dragged through the crowd. "It's three hundred and still dropping."

"Oh, fuck! Oh! Fuck!" His companion yelled as she broke into a run, now pulling him behind her.

"Do you want to call Michael?" Melva shouted over the din.

Belva did not bother to answer. She cocked her head toward

the bank of phones nearby, with people half a dozen deep, change or plastic cards clenched in their hands and mayhem in their eyes.

He will have made it through, she thought. He will have landed on his feet. She had been repeating this in the back of her mind ever since Melva had told her what had happened there in front of Letting Loose, through the reports they caught on the radio and then all the frantic energy in both their planes and all the airports. Michael had surely seen it coming. Michael would be sitting pretty. Tonight, they would laugh about it over a late supper.

At the cabstand, however, as she glanced at the somber, worried faces waiting to ride into the city, she was not so sure.

As soon as she tipped the bellboy at the Plaza, she sat on the bed and punched in Michael's office number. Busy. The house. Busy. The private line to the bedroom. Busy.

Melva puttered around the room, unpacking for the both of them, arranging their toiletries in the bathroom, setting their calendar — each appointment neatly penned in her flowing, feminine hand — on the desk. She changed her clothes, fussed with her hair, retouched her makeup, settled their shoes on the closet floor.

All the while, jumping from one number to the other to the other, Belva was calling. "Shit!"

"Belva," Melva said softly from the closet, "why don't you try later? He's probably not really up to talking to you right now."

"I can't believe this!"

"Well, he must be at home, mustn't he? Even his private line" — Melva said it with some distaste — "is busy."

"You're right. I'll take a cab over."

She started up from the bed, but Melva swung around the doorjamb and blocked her way. "Belva! Listen to me. This is not a time for you to show up on Michael's doorstep."

"What do you mean?" Belva snapped. "Get out of the way!"
"No." Melva folded her arms. "You know I'm no great fan of Michael's, but" — she raised one finger warningly — "I do know that the last thing he needs right now is for you to come barging in. Either he's lost a lot of money or he's making a lot of money. And you've said yourself that you think he'd rather make a deal than fu —— " she caught herself, "go to bed with you."

Belva stood there. What Melva said made sense.

"Let's go downstairs. We'll have a drink. You can try to get hold of him then. And if you still can't get through, you can try after dinner. This isn't a time to mess with him."

The words had an odd, sisterly sincerity to them. It was true she could be of absolutely no help to him and perhaps, as Melva said, rather than being in a panic he was making a fortune.

"All right," she said. "Let's get dressed and go. I know. I'll call Edgar. Maybe he can join us. He'll know what's going on."

He was surprised to hear her voice. "Why, Belva. I didn't know you were due."

"My sister and I just got in. I've been trying to reach Michael, but no luck."

"Under the circumstances," he said dryly, "I'm not surprised."

"That's pretty much what we thought. Anyway, Melva and I are at the Plaza. Would you like to stop over for a drink?"

He paused. It made Belva uncomfortable. She could also feel him fishing for excuses. "Ah, sure. Sure, I think I can do that. Say half an hour? No, make that forty-five minutes."

"That's fine. We'll be in the Oak Bar."

Every time she saw Edgar, he had less hair. That was all that changed. Otherwise, he looked exactly like he did when they met that night in November of 1979: Brooks Brothers suit, horn-rimmed glasses, a discreet but expensive tie — the uniform of lawyers who handled million-dollar litigations and drew up billion-dollar contracts.

Belva introduced her sister, and, for a few minutes, they made small talk, catching one another up on Rhymers Creek and Manhattan, on Edgar's stint as a counsel for the Department of Commerce.

"But you?" He took a sip of his Scotch and water. "How long's it been since you were in New York?"

"When was the last time, Melva? May? No, it was April."

Melva, pouty at being excluded, merely nodded.

"Have you talked much to Michael since?"

The question was innocuous, but there was something in his tone she did not like. Nothing accusatory. More curious, concerned.

"Well, no. I've hardly been able to reach him the last couple months. I left a message yesterday, telling him I was coming." Belva raised her eyebrows. "Is there something wrong?"

"Oh, no. No," Edgar said, too quickly, she thought. "But he's been working hard and playing hard and I wonder if he shouldn't slow down. None of us is twenty-nine anymore." He killed his drink. "I should be getting along. How long are you in town?"

"Only four days. Here, I'll walk you out." Her sister looked at Belva, annoyed, as if she were afraid she might be mistaken for a lonely woman in search of adventure. "I'll be a minute, Melva. I'm going to try Michael again."

They walked into the lobby. Edgar seemed anxious to be gone.

"Edgar," Belva said with quiet insistence. "What's going on?"

He slipped on his overcoat. "What do you mean?"

"Something's up. If it's got to do with me, I'd like to know."

"No. It's not that." Edgar looked uneasy. "He's not getting married, if that's what you're worried about."

She was sure he could see her relief, which irritated her. "Then exactly what's the problem?"

They were to the doors by then. They stepped outside, and Edgar moved toward the cabstand.

"It's nothing really, it's . . . " His face lit up when a taxi pulled to the curb, though he was immediately jostled aside by a man who had dashed across the street.

She grabbed Edgar's arm. "Is it the market?"

"Well, that's probably made everything worse. Look" — he leaned against one of the light standards — "you know as well as I do that Michael's always driven in the fast lane. It's just started catching up with him in the last few months." He looked at her meaningfully.

She returned his gaze, blank. "What? What is it?"

He seemed almost peeved at her. He gazed out over the avenue. "It's the nose candy, okay."

"What are you talking about?"

"Don't play dumb with me, Belva," he snapped. "We both know there's been a potential for a problem as long as we've known him."

On Fifth Avenue in the chilly October night, for the first time, she felt the cold. She wrapped her arms around herself and breathed deep. "I don't have the vaguest notion what you're talking about."

His face softened, slipped from annoyance to genuine surprise. "Maybe you're more sheltered than I gave you credit for." He touched her arm. "Belva, Michael's been doing coke as long as I can remember. It gave him an edge, he always said. And I guess, for a long time, it did. I'm sorry, Belva. I thought you knew."

The awareness sank in slowly. She stumbled, grabbing Edgar's shoulder, feeling nothing except ineffably stupid. "And now?"

Edgar shrugged. "He was in LA a couple times this summer. He got involved in some goofy movie scheme. I don't know what happened, but after he came back, he was out of control. He really had been able to do a toot when he needed it — when he had a deal cooking or had to be up for a night on the town. But now, he's been snorting every day. It's bad enough his friends are talking . . ."

Belva could tell he felt her stiffen.

"Not gossiping. We've been talking about how maybe he ought to" — he paused uncomfortably — "get treatment or something . . ."

She raised her hand to stop him.

"I'm sorry," he said. He looked at her guiltily, as if she might blame him for the bad news or not having told her before.

"No, it's all right," she said. All she wanted was for him to be gone. "Really. I have to get back to Melva. Do call us." She was already backing away. "Bye-bye."

She swept through the doors, the lobby, into the Oak Bar. Melva looked up morosely from behind a second glass of Chablis.

"I got Michael," she said abruptly, gathering up her purse.

"Belva. Belva," Melva called after her. "At least go up for your coat. Belva."

She was back on the street, in a cab east, then north, before she ever caught her breath. *"It's the nose candy, okay."* They had done coke now and then, before the clubs, before sex, after a party in Tribeca they had left at dawn to ride the Staten Island Ferry. The occasional toot . . . *"the nose candy."* But now she wondered. Those nights he was on the phone until all hours, calling all over the world, to those places the markets were open? The times she would come on to him when he was bone tired and he would slip away for a minute to get brandies or a bottle of wine, returning bright and ready for action — was he snuffly then? A shade shiny in the eyes? *". . . nose candy."* Even at Spanidou, the first time they met, after he paid Andy and continued on to the men's room, was it the call of nature or marching powder that drew him behind the locked door?

It was as if, after so long, Belva had discovered Michael had a clubfoot or a glass eye, something obvious to everyone that had eluded her entirely. "More sheltered," that's what Edgar had said. And was that what they had been saying, year after year when she appeared on his arm: *That girl from the boondocks, doesn't even know he's a snow bunny!* Belva had imagined the things people might think of her — that she was a gold digger, a slut, an adulteress. But now, it occurred to her they might merely have found her silly.

By the time she reached his door, her anger made her almost faint. She rapped hard, barking her knuckles on the wood, and leaned again and again into the bell. It was a full minute before the light came on in the entry hall. She could see a shadow pass across the eyepiece of the peephole, and then the door swung open.

"Belva! What the hell!"

His shirt was open. He looked tired, tense. But he was smiling, and, just for an instant, that was enough.

She fell over the threshold into his arms. "Oh, Michael . . ."

He held her close, chuckled softly. "Well, come in," he said. "I'm sorry I haven't called. I got your messages, but things have been crazy since the end of September, and then this shit to-day . . ."

He was closing the door, and she was gradually regaining her composure. She did not know quite what she had imagined she would find: Michael sick, strung out, crazy? The relief that had flooded over her the minute she saw he was all right momentarily stanched her rage. But she felt it again now, smoldering.

"How have you made out?"

"So far?" he said, showing her into the parlor. "So far, I've taken a bath. But this isn't 'twenty-nine. If things go like I think, I'll do okay." He sighed and slid the doors to the foyer closed behind him. "Want a drink?"

"Sure," she said evenly.

She curled onto the sofa and, as always, took in the room: baroque, elegant, rich in a way rooms in Rhymers Creek never were and never could be. What to do? She did not want to involve Edgar, who had told her something he had assumed she was long aware of. Yet she could not keep silent — for worry, and for pride, too. Perhaps it would be better to bring it up tomorrow. But, somehow, she felt if she did not confront him now about it, she never would.

He gave her a bourbon and stood before her, Perrier in hand.

"I won't stay, Michael," she said. "I know it's a bad time to interrupt." Slowly, she thought, go at it slowly. "But I wanted to come by tonight. I've been worried — "

He interrupted her with a laugh. "That I'd jump out a window?"

"No, it wasn't the crash." She took a sip of her drink and glanced up at him. His eyes were red, but then he had probably lived and died a hundred times today as the market fell and fell some more. "The last couple of months, since you got back from LA," she added, "it's been so hard to get hold of you, I wondered . . ."

She let the words linger. He had a slight, pleased smile on his lips. She knew what he was thinking and felt her anger flare.

"No," he said quietly. "Like always, there's nobody very special, except for you."

She wanted to melt, put it behind her, be his in New York as she was accustomed, for three days or a week. But she wouldn't.

"No, it wasn't that. I was afraid that maybe . . . you know, well . . ." What was she supposed to say: nose candy, toot? "That the, the cocaine might have . . ."

The word. She had heard herself utter it. Nothing accusatory. Not even surprised.

Michael's eyes narrowed. He took a long, deliberate sip of water. "I don't know what you mean, Belva," he said lightly.

She held her glass in both hands. She could let the whole thing go. She took a long breath. "I think you do, Michael."

His jaw tightened. "No, baby," he said a little more firmly, "I haven't got a clue."

She set her glass on the table and bit off each word: "I think you do."

He turned from her suddenly. "Who've you been talking to?"

"No one," she lied, smoothly if insistently. "It just occurred to me. Knowing you used. I started to put two and two together."

"Look," he snapped, "there's nothing to add up, okay? I'm not hooked, if that's what you're driving at."

"Aren't you?"

"No!"

From his absoluteness, she knew others must have mentioned it. Maybe Edgar had said things he hadn't been willing to repeat. The report of Michael's single word shuddered through the parlor, so the silence that followed seemed even deeper than it should have.

"Michael," she began, "I know it's not the time. But I want you to know that — "

"I think you should go, Belva."

His back was to her. She could see the strain in his shoulders beneath his shirt. Later, she would wonder if he really meant to do it. But by then it was too late.

She walked behind him. She was still angry: hurt he had not called her, hurt he had ignored her, hurt he had a problem that she had not imagined and that he would keep from her. She was more than a mistress, she told herself. She was determined to save him.

"Michael, be honest with yourself. If it's treatment . . ."

"Please, Belva! You . . ." He swung violently to face her.

The back of his hand hit her full in the face.

She stumbled, and her cheek burned. She touched her nose, and when she brought her palm away, there was blood.

"Belva!"

She steadied herself and felt tears in her eyes. She strode to the sofa and grabbed her purse. She flung the sliding doors aside. The phones were jangling upstairs, in the back hall. She threw open the front door, not looking back for fear that, if she laid eyes on him, she would forgive him. She half-tripped down the stairs.

The phones were still ringing.

As soon as she was to the sidewalk, Belva began to run, unsteady in her high heels until she slipped them off — never really stopping — and carried them in her free hand.

"Belva! Belva!"

He had hit her! She was trying to help him, and he hit her. He had not returned her calls or thought to call her and had gotten himself hooked on coke and refused to talk about it and he hit her.

There were no footfalls behind her. She kept running. The faint echo of the telephones vanished.

She slowed down, winded, bloody. The pain in her cheek had not gone away. She touched it, gingerly, then massaged it. Nothing seemed broken. Her nose was still flowing. She dug for a tissue in her purse and held it across her face as she tipped her head back.

Glancing down the street, she saw no light pooling from an open door into the night. He had gone back inside. Even now, he was probably on the phone.

He had hit her. And then he had not even followed her.

A low growl came out of her throat, all her anger burrowing up from her gut and ready to explode into a roar. In her whole life, only Randy Ditmars had struck her, the night she walked out. And if that was what she did at twenty-four with a man she had married, she was damned if she would go back to one who'd never even bothered to ask if she would think of him as a husband.

As soon as that word crossed her mind, she panicked, for if her nose had already clotted, she knew she would have a bruise below her eye. A bruise that would last, that would have to be explained. And what would she say to Wallace? To Melva?

She looked up the block. A car or two had passed, no more than that. In the distance, she could hear the avenue. She reached in her billfold and pulled out a ten-dollar bill, which she stuck under the strap of her bra. She slipped up to the wrought-iron fence of the brownstone before her, opened her purse, and flung it into the boxwoods next to the house, cosmetics and her wallet and pencils and business cards clattering out as it flew. Then she began to run.

Rounding the corner, she screamed. "Help! Help! My purse!"

As she told the story later — the part that was true — she would always remark on how New York's reputation was unfair;

how two nice men had come immediately to her aid, flagged down a patrol car; how the policemen were polite if unoptimistic as they took her report about the young black man of medium height in a stocking cap (the one she had seen a thousand times on *Kojak* and *T. J. Hooker*) who grabbed her bag and, when she resisted, slugged her in the face and ran away.

They offered her a ride to her hotel, but she declined, and they seemed a bit suspicious when she drew the money from her blouse.

"I may be just a country girl," she said, "but my momma always taught me to be prepared."

And they laughed.

From the look in her eyes, it was obvious that Melva did not believe her. She knew that there had been no mugger but Michael, that the purse discovered and waiting for them at the precinct house the next morning had been thrown with calculation over that wrought-iron fence. But Melva said nothing. Nothing when Belva told the desk to hold all calls. Nothing when Belva insisted they move from the Plaza to the Penta — so much cheaper and more convenient.

As the moment faded, Belva herself would wonder what might have happened if she had not talked to Edgar that night, if she had not gone to Michael's, if she had left when he said go. She never called him, and he never called her. It made her question whether he had ever really loved her at all.

Perhaps it was time for it to end. Eight years was long for an affair: her daughter had been born, her business had been founded and prospered, a president had been elected and re-elected and was about to leave office triumphant.

But still, if ever she doubted how she had felt about Michael, Belva recalled the flight back from New York — the buying done for Letting Loose, the nation's economy on the mend — when she realized that she would never see him again.

She got up from her seat and walked to the lavatory. She went inside, locked the door, and ran her finger over the brown stain now turning to yellow across her cheek. Oddly, in that moment, she thought of Bobbo Starwick, of that ear that he had sent her, of his transformation from angel to demon. She would never have believed that Michael, so many years later, would strike out at her like some war-crazed soldier, expunging in an instant all she thought that she knew of him.

She sat down and cradled her head in her hands. And there, for the next half hour, despite the occasional knocks on the door, she cried.

SUNDAY

✦ ✦ ✦

1

Sunday evening, Jamie came over, and the boys settled in front of the television with Cokes — unspiked, Belva had checked. Leisel had had toast for dinner and was asleep though it wasn't even six. *Vogue* open on her lap, Belva watched Wallace with Friday's *Wall Street Journal* across the living room. He had, she knew, already scanned it at least twice, but on Sundays he liked to settle back with a week's worth of the paper and linger over the listings, taking note of stocks up and down, those they owned and those they didn't offering equal pleasure or disillusion.

It seemed extraordinary today that she had chosen him. Not merely him, of course, but the world he was part of, not the other that had offered itself after all the years — a place not Rhymers Creek where she might begin anew.

Returning from the funeral, they had discovered that Ross had been in the beer again and that Leisel, arrived from the Martins' next door, had a fever of 102. It was merely the flu, rampaging, Belva discovered after various phone calls to other mothers, through Demmers Acres Elementary. This had meant a long evening dealing with unending whining and upchucking. Pale and waiflike among her stuffed animals, shivering with chills one minute and covered in sweat the next, Leisel was the portrait of misery, while Ross, whether for real or in a fit of fraternal couvade, was not feeling too well himself. Belva had visions of herself and Wallace as well laid low by the middle of the week.

Though it violated her usual procedures, when Wallace went out Sunday morning to take in a fresh supply of Tylenol and Dramamine, she sneaked a call to Basil from the kitchen.

"I'd almost decided you'd opted for suttee," he said with edgy sarcasm. "Casting yourself on old flames, et cetera."

"Oh, Basil," she whined and then explained the delay. "But I did get your note." She paused. "So, what's the news?"

"I'll only tell you personally."

"Come on." She sighed in exasperation. "Break it to me now."

"Only in person," he said tartly. "Can you come by today?"

She paused. "I'll try. Maybe this afternoon. I don't know exactly when."

"That's all right," he said. "I'm trapped here all day with *Daisy Miller* papers. See you later, pet. 'Bye."

As she went to get her coat a few minutes before three, she found Ross lolling on the den sofa, still in his pajamas with his Walkman on and a *Sports Illustrated* open on his lap.

"Do you need anything?" she said from across the room.

He was oblivious.

She moved closer, into his peripheral vision. "Do you need anything?"

He lifted an earphone.

"I've got to go to the store for a couple hours."

"How about the new *Penthouse?*" He smirked.

She smirked back. "Not today, mister. You need to save your strength."

He adopted a phony pout. She reached over and tousled his hair. He did feel warm. "Ask your father later," she whispered.

She left Wallace at Leisel's beside, reading *The Poky Little Puppy* aloud. It was one of their daughter's favorites. He merely nodded and made an A-OK sign when she told him she was off to Letting Loose to see if she could figure out the Hotchkiss orders.

In an icy mist, she set out for Basil's. The thaw was over, and, along the route, everything looked soaked and droopy in the renewed chill. The gloom matched Belva's mood. She tried to steel herself.

He had a new job, that was obvious. That was the only explanation for this kind of display. On the one hand, she should be happy. It did seem a tremendous waste of skill and talent that Basil, who could discourse at the drop of a hat on writers and theories she had never even heard of, should be teaching composition and Introduction to Literature I and II at Mockdon County Community College. Still, it meant he would be leaving — leaving her behind, going on with his life while she remained in Rhymers Creek: growing older and losing her figure and watching an unmistakable wattle form beneath her chin.

He greeted her in the robe she had given him for Christmas. Her heart clenched at the sound it made when she rubbed his chest and dropped her hands to his behind when they embraced — the *shzzsh* of satin across the coarse hair of his body.

"Ah, the Nightingale of the bedridden and flu afflicted," he said as he put his arm around her and bussed her on the mouth. "Ought to be careful, I suppose, or you'll have to come nurse me through my puling and puking." He took her around the waist and led her to the bedroom. On the nightstand was a bottle of champagne, two flutes, and a burning candle. "I was invoking St. Rita, patroness of lost causes." He swung the two of them onto the mattress and planted a kiss on her throat. "She apparently heard my prayers."

"Don't be silly," Belva said irritably. "The kids are sick."

"Ah, yes" — he nodded — "the kids."

"So." Belva stood up and pulled off her coat, draping it over the desk chair. Then she settled onto the bed again. "I think it's time you told me your news."

He smiled shyly and pulled a folded sheet off the nightstand.

There was the crest on the letterhead, the formal salutation, the opening sentence she expected: "We are pleased to inform you that . . ."

"Chicago?" she said. To her surprise, despite all her preparation, something like a sob formed in her chest. She swallowed, blinked. "Congratulations, Basil," she managed bravely. "I know how much you've wanted this."

She kissed him.

He smiled wider. "It's a good position. And quite a good school really, not first rank but a respectable university. Interesting students. Fine library. And it's in a real city, with restaurants and museums and an opera." He reached across her, took up the bottle, and gently poured the champagne. He sat straight, handed her a glass, and grasped his own. "To us in Chicago."

She had raised her flute already and did not really register what he said until the lips of their glasses met with a soft clink. "What?"

"I'm going to Chicago. I want you to come with me."

Belva sat with the flute in both hands, a flush passing over her. "Basil," she began, "Basil, I couldn't do that."

"Of course you could," he said simply. "It's what you've been looking to do for years, and here's your chance."

She smiled sadly and set her glass on the nightstand. "It's sweet of you, Basil. But I can't very well walk out . . ."

"Your son will be off to college in a couple of years," he said abruptly. "We can take Leisel with us. I'm leaving this wretched place behind, and so are you. Chicago is where you can be yourself. It's what you've always wanted."

She was touched, there was no question. This lithe, strong Englishman — so young, at his life's real beginning — who wanted to take her with him into his new world. For only an instant, the shimmering possibility left her speechless.

Then she said, "Basil . . ."

"I know what's coming." He bounced up off the bed. "When you're my age," he pinched his voice to falsetto, "I'll be sixty. You won't even want to look at me." He leaned toward her. "But that's not true. I love you, Belva. I love you very much. And I want you with me."

It flickered across her mind: what it would be like to be the professor's wife in Chicago — Marshall Field's, North Michigan Avenue, the Art Institute; Basil, with his graduate students: adoring young things, busty and leggy, hanging on his every word and imagining hanging on something else. And how could he resist, as over the years she grew grayer and droopier? But it was more than that.

"Basil," she began again, "you must understand . . ."

"I don't want to understand!" he yelled.

"Sit down," Belva said quietly, patting the mattress. "Sit."

Petulantly, he dropped down beside her.

She put her hand on the back of his head and stroked his hair gently. "Basil, part of me wants to say yes. There's nothing in the world that would make me happier than to pack my bags and kick the dust of this burg off my shoes and spend the rest of my life with you in Chicago or Oxford or Oshkosh or wherever you wanted to go. If I were your age, I would. But I'm not — "

"I don't care," he interrupted.

"Shhh. Shhh," she cooed soothingly. "I'm not, Basil. I have a house and a marriage — maybe not the best one, maybe not the most normal one, but a marriage all the same — and children and a business. It may not be the life I would have made, given a second chance. But it's the one I've got. And, much as I love you, and I do, I simply cannot leave it behind."

He huddled, sullen, next to her, looking at the floor for a long minute. Then, he took his flute and threw it against the wall, where it shattered in a singing shower of glass and champagne.

"I knew you would do this," he muttered. "I knew it!"

"I imagine you did." She sighed. "There comes a time, Basil, when your world is simply too complicated to set it aside. It's not even particularly that I'm so much older. I could leave Wallace, and we could negotiate about the kids, and I could even give up Letting Loose, though God knows Melva could never keep it going. But even then, without meaning to, I'd drag you into my world, a world that's very different from the one you live in, and one you shouldn't have to deal with till you're my age."

"Oh, come on, Belva, we're both adults!"

"Of course we are. But that means different things for each of us, and rocketing you forward to what it's like to be in your forties doesn't seem fair to me, just like it doesn't seem entirely possible to rocket me back to my twenties. Oh, Basil" — she felt her voice thin — "it's going to be so hard to let you go."

She hadn't expected the tears, but they came anyway. He held himself away from her for a moment or two, obstreperously unconcerned. But then his arm snaked across her shoulder.

"Now, now," he said a bit gruffly. He drew her to him and sighed. "I knew it would be like this. I knew you would say no and that, in the end, your reasons would be unassailable, at least from your perspective. But I thought it was worth a shot." He touched her chin and pulled her face gently toward him. "When I came to Rhymers Creek, the last thing I expected was that I would fall in love. And the last thing I want is to leave with a broken heart. But I suppose you'd say that that simply brings me one step closer to whatever place in life you're at."

Belva raised her head. He kissed her lightly, and she kissed back. His fingers found the zipper on her dress.

"Shall we do it anyway?" he said with a kind resignation. "For auld lang syne?"

"Not only once," she said, smiling. "there are months and months yet, and we have to pretend that they'll just go on and on."

That was where they left it, as if that letter had not come at all. The remaining time would not be easy. Basil was special, and losing him would leave a tender spot the next affair would not entirely assuage. Letting go would hurt enough that, right now, Belva did not even want to conceive it.

And so, she thought, why not Chicago? And the answer, its emblem anyway, was across the room behind *The Wall Street Journal*. Wallace. Kind, dull, long-suffering Wallace. The handsome, middle-aged, blond executive she still was not really sure she knew. The man she could count on for *The Poky Little Puppy* for Leisel and *Penthouse* for Ross. The man she would not leave to be a professor's wife in the Second City.

There were those other reasons, of course. Belva had no desire to put the children through the pain of separations, movings, stepparents and vague cousins and grandparents sprung out of nowhere. And Letting Loose, almost like another child — she could hardly consign it to the tender mercies of her well-intentioned but none-too-able twin. And this room, and this house; this neighborhood in this little part of the world that was Rhymers Creek: she could not lightly leave any of it behind, along with the comfort that she knew, that she took for granted, that would not be hers in an expensive city on a professor's earnings.

But, with all that, still there was Wallace, the man she had married the second time around. Over the years, not really consciously, as she went from affair to affair, as she traveled, built a business, worked to be a good parent and a good if unconventional wife, she had tried and tried to parse out what kept them together. His reasons, she had concluded, were unknowable to her, now and perhaps forever. But here in the last week, with all the remembering Bobbo Starwick's funeral and all that went with it had encouraged in her, she had come to realize what it was he offered her, what she did not know if any other man she had ever met would grant. He did not, it was true, love her the way she might have wished: jealously, passionately, utterly. But because of that, because he knew he alone was somehow not enough, he gave her her freedom, the freedom to pursue what she wished, do what she liked, and, yes, to slip into other men's beds for those occasional moments of blinding desire he could not provide her. A man who could — a Basil perhaps — was also one who would require a fealty she was not sure she could give; would demand in exchange for his passion the liberty she had come, with the years, to cherish. And she had understood instantly this afternoon that this was a possession she would not surrender, even to someone she knew she loved.

She might wish that Wallace would drop the newspaper, sweep to her side, take her hand, and guide her to bed, locking the door against the children's intrusions, making wild-eyed love to her all night. But Wallace would not, and that was the price — not a small one, but one not unpayable either — for the life she had made her own.

She smelled something drifting in from the den. It was sweet, a little prickly, the kind of scent that makes you sneeze. Wallace remained immobile behind the newspaper.

As unobtrusively as possible, she got up and slipped through the doorway into the dimness of the den.

"Ross!" she said in a sharp whisper. "Jamie!"

2

Barry sat unmoving in night's dark embrace.

Below him, Rhymers Creek twinkled through the icy black: there the high school, there the Square, there the tattered strip of lights that led toward the distant glow of Mockdon. In the winter starlight, the slope before him was clean and dead as bone. He bounced his feet idly against the granite.

At China's for breakfast that morning, over lunch with Tully Coe, he knew it was time to leave. It was nothing that was said exactly, merely the gulf of years, the one between his queer and complex life and the linear, suburban ones of those who had remained here. It was as if his world was some planet far away, where trees were blue and night was day and the streets were roamed by anthropophagi.

Barry smiled. In the last, perhaps, there was some germ of truth.

In the afternoon, he had driven to his parents' house. Along the curbs, the county crews were out, doubtless earning double time, cutting up the tree limbs that had brought down wires and cut off power, the ice that had wrought such havoc now vanished into air.

When he arrived, his mother was still at the grocery. His father pushed open the screen, dressed in a ratty sweater that, Barry suspected, he had rescued from the ragbag.

He poured them coffee, then led the way to the basement. Barry had expected a surge of panic, like that of a claustrophobic who thinks an elevator has stopped between floors. But as he descended, he felt no disquiet at all. The den was a room like any other. It had no magic, held no echoes now: *"Vile," "disgusting," "unnatural child."*

"Here, we'll warm things up," Ezra said, flipping the switch on the old radiant heater with its dark mesh grate.

Barry sat on the sofa. "How's Ma doing today?"

"Pretty well, I guess. Better than you might expect." Ezra shrugged. "Last night was rough, but she's done all right."

"She told me," Barry said softly, "she told me yesterday that, back then, she wrote Bobbo" — he paused — "about me."

"She did." Ezra's voice was flat. "I thought it was a bad idea. But she was mad and hurt, and she told him about" — he cast around for the right expression — "that you were gay and about the antiwar stuff in college." He sighed. "After he disappeared, she blamed herself. She thought it had all been too much for him. I told her I didn't believe that. And I don't."

It had occurred to Barry that Bobbo's knowing might have finally pushed him to do something angry and desperate. But he had decided that was vanity, a notion that bequeathed him a role in Bobbo's death both false and self-important, transforming it into a suicidal act that made Bobbo seem not a victim but a fool, and dead, dead, dead nonetheless.

Ezra knelt before the heater and rubbed his hands reflectively as the coils began to glow. "Sometimes, I'd hope that Bobbo was one of the POWs they were always talking about. But I finally realized that was selfish. Could you have wished that on him? All those years in a Hanoi jail or out in the jungle, starved and beaten and scared? And so I had to accept he was dead." He stood up, crossing his arms as if suddenly chilled. "Sometimes I even think it was for the better. The war had done an awful thing to him. I'd seen it do that, back in my war. When somebody's hurt like that, hurt inside, they never get over it. Even if he had gotten out in one piece, the ugliness of all of it would have eaten him alive."

There was a silence then. In the quiet Barry thought how often he had been through this process, imagining that death had come at the right time, just a little past the right time, maybe. In New York, he had mastered all the rationales of loss.

"I don't like to say that," Ezra spoke again, paused. He was searching for words. "Bobbo was a good boy. Everybody loved him, and, like your mother says, he made that very easy to do. But that also made it easy for him not to face things. He was like his father that way."

"Like Robbie?"

"I've thought that many times, that Bobbo was fated like his father was. Robbie was never made to grow up. Maybe Bobbo wasn't either."

"Do you really believe that?" Barry said.

His father glanced at him, surprised. "Of course. Robbie was like a brother to me. But he was a boy, and he always would have been. When he came back from the War, there really wasn't any place for him. It would have been the same for Bobbo. Worse because he was so bitter." He shrugged. "When I found out your mother had written that letter to him, I knew it would do no good. I knew he would not understand."

Barry sighed ruefully. "Of course he wouldn't. Not back then. I should have known that none of you would understand . . ."

Ezra picked up his cup and held it in both hands. "Oh, I understood, Barry. In a way, that wasn't so hard. I didn't even recall when you left. Maybe I'd blotted it out, though it wasn't something I didn't want to remember." His voice had fallen into sweet, soft reverie. "It was in Italy, spring 'forty-four, I think.

We'd been out on patrol. Robbie and me and the rest. We hadn't slept in days, and we'd lost half a dozen men, and twice as many wounded.

"We were on a beach. There were these beautiful dunes and the Mediterranean. The captain decided to let us rest. Most of us just stripped down right there and ran into the water, horsing around — dunking each other and splashing like kids. Hell, we *were* kids." His voice grew even softer. "The others went back to camp, but we stayed. Robbie and me. He was still in the water, and I was waiting for him on the beach. I must have fallen asleep. Then I felt these cold drops on my stomach, and Robbie was squatting beside me, naked. He started to laugh, and I pushed off the sand and grabbed him, and we wrestled around. And suddenly, I was on top of him, holding him down. He looked up at me, and he was smiling, and I looked down at him, and I smiled. Then all his muscles went limp. Just like that. And mine did, too." He stopped. "It was only a few seconds that we were lying there, the two of us. Me on top of him . . .

"Somebody shouted from the other side of the dune, and I jumped off." Ezra cocked his head, curious. "But I wondered then, and I've wondered since, what might have happened." His voice was raspy, sad before an instant fresh in his memory as Barry's face before him. "I loved Robbie Starwick, Barry. Maybe that's why what you said that night cut so deep. It wasn't true, the way you said it. It wasn't fair to your mother. It wasn't fair to me. But I'm not ashamed I loved him. And if something had happened, it would have happened, and that's all. I don't know if that describes what you've felt. But don't think I could never understand."

One brief bolt of rage crashed through him — *How could you? If not then, why not later? How could you not have told me, not have said it, not revealed you understood?* But quick as it flickered, it died. There was no point to recrimination. And besides, Barry knew, it was not the same. Loving a man, even making love to him, was not the same as loving men. But it was the door that allowed for comprehension, the passage through which a man could go and see the world as another sees, even when that other is his son.

"And after?"

"After?"

"Was there ever any other time? Or other man?"

Ezra shook his head. "No," he said. "Robbie was the only one I ever felt that with. And that was the only time I really felt it."

"And Robbie?"

The word had begun to form on Ezra's lips. Seconds passed. "With Robbie," he said finally, "with Robbie, I don't know."

Barry shifted on the sofa. "And Ma . . . Did she . . . ?"

His father's voice came weary. "There are things we know without knowing." He drew a long breath. "Perhaps there was something with Robbie. Perhaps she only sensed it. Perhaps that's why, that night and then all the other nights, she could not quite forgive you for what you said and who you are. Till now."

Barry nodded. He paused a very long time. "Thank you, Pa."

Not long after, they heard his mother's car in the driveway. Barry carried the groceries in, and then, as he hadn't in years, since long before he left, when China was too small to help, he broke the lettuce to make the salad, cut celery and tomatoes with the same sharp knife that had been, when they were young, an emblem of maturity. It was almost as if Bobbo would be coming soon to take the plates out of the cabinet and pull the silver from the drawer to set the table.

Barry glanced toward his mother and caught her staring at him. "Are you okay?"

"Yes. Yes." She busied herself for a moment at the stove, then said, "There's something I want you to tell me, Barry."

He set down the knife.

She was standing with a pot holder in her hand, arrested in midmotion, reticent and yet determined. "It is not my business really. You have made your life, and you have made it well, and if we could never say it before, both your father and I are proud of you. You must know that." She paused. "What happened with Bobbo was very hard. But now that it's all over, I think we always knew we would never get him back. But with you, these last years . . . Even though we didn't talk about it, we were . . ." She took a breath. "Were afraid you might be sick." She swallowed. "You're not going to leave us, too?"

Barry wanted to lie then. But he could not. "I don't know," he said.

The question was in her eyes before she could utter it.

He leaned against the counter. "There was a man I loved. A man I loved more than all the world. His name was Jacy." He let it linger for a moment. "He was one of the first ones to get sick. And he died." He could see, clear as if he were present, his soldier in another war, who never knew this place, these people, this world where Barry came from. "Since then, I've led a careful life, a cautious life, not only with my body but with my heart. But in all that time . . . In all that time, even after I could have known, I have not found out."

"But, Barry, why . . ."

"Maybe it was that if I knew, I'd try to live my life in such a hurry. Or maybe, after seeing Jacy die, I could not face what might happen to me. He wasn't the only one. One after another after another. They've all died. Some of them quietly, but most, most horribly. It must be like what Bobbo went through, watching his friends wiped away. Bobbo was part of it, too, and all of you. Maybe I didn't want to know what would happen to me until he was home again. Till I was home again."

She came slowly across the room, stood before him, took his hand. She hesitated an instant, then looked directly at him. "Will you find out now?"

He looked away. "I think I might."

A chilly breeze rustled the trees behind him. Barry slid off the gray granite monument engraved MCKENZIE and approached the rough, white cross they had placed temporarily. A real marker would come later, after the grave had settled. It had been easy to sneak into the cemetery. The gates were locked, but he had found the breach in the fence — made by some partying teenagers probably — where the chain link was peeled back and he could squeeze through the hole and head for the hills.

He would take the test. He could stand the knowledge now that Bobbo had been laid to rest, now that he had seen his father's face, his mother's, had met his sister's children, had walked again the streets of Rhymers Creek.

By his brother's grave, he remembered his dead then, every one — Children of the American Century: Jacy, chalice of dreams; Bobbo, monstrance of hope. And he considered himself, Barach — victor upon the field where the last, universal battle would be fought — who might soon know he would not survive to the year 2000.

He had often thought in these last days about his father and Bobbo's father, about that world of his parents when they were young, where all, for half a decade, had been consumed in a holocaust: millions dying year to year, old and young, men and women, bullets and gas and starvation and bombs. In his own life, for his own generation, there had been no single, massive extermination. Rather, there had been terrible but somehow limited conflagrations that, first in the guise of Mars snuffed out 60,000 of his brothers and then came back in the shape of Venus to snuff out 200,000 more.

He knelt amid the wilting flowers bright with frost. He reached in his pocket, then took off his glove and began to dig, his fingers aching with the cold at first, but then, not so far below the surface, soothed by the fresh-turned earth the sun had warmed the day before.

He did not dig far. There was no need. He caressed the bronze medal, emblem of Bobbo triumphant, then pressed it into the dirt. With time and the rains, his brother's talisman would settle toward the coffin. It should go with Bobbo to wherever he was destined, or lie patient in the earth beside him. Perhaps someday, hundreds of years hence, some fine, blond boy would find it, some boy sly as the leopard, fleet as the eagle. And as he held that medal in his hand, he might envision, as in a miracle, someone not unlike himself, kneeling on a pine knoll, waiting for manhood.

Barry filled the hole, tamped the earth, stood. Tomorrow he was going home, to his true home after all, that city he had loved since his own manhood had begun. And for having come to Rhymers Creek, for having made his peace with his family, with that brother he had lost; for having spoken Jacy's name in the house of his childhood, he could return, sure in the knowledge of a life made whole, even if it were cut short. From this burial, from the healing he was blest with, all his mournings past and all those mournings yet to come might now be faced with grief but without rancor. He had buried Jacy. He had buried Bobbo. But they lived in his heart, and now, after so long, he might again open that heart and begin anew.

3

"Howdy, Fred."

It was the drugs, Fred told himself, the drugs they had given him.

Tracers arcing across the sky like the arrows of the Apocalypse. He was on that watchtower about to ask that black, scarred warrior if he really were a double vet; he was turning away from the wash of rotors at Graves Registration; he was holding the hand of Ronnie Eggleson and his lungs were filled with burn and blood and shit; he was in that bar with Rogers, and the shrill, mad laugh of Bobbo Starwick was echoing across the room.

Over the last days, he had vomited, endless dry heaves, again and again, but he couldn't stop. And he didn't stop until they jabbed that needle into his arm and he plunged precipitous into a deep, drugged sleep.

So much to cast out. So much he had held so close for all the years.

Fred clenched his fists, pulling himself back, back to Mockdon General Hospital, to his empty room on the detox ward. It was will, sheer will, that drew him back from Vietnam, back from the heat and the green and Ronnie Eggleson's gore. He took a deep breath, as deep as he could, to slow the beating of his heart.

"Howdy, Fred."

He was not alone. He sensed the presence beside him. Fred did not even have to look to know who it was.

"Hello, Bobbo," he whispered.

Fred turned his head slowly on the pillow, woozy and weak. He could see Bobbo in silhouette, squatting by the wall, elbows on his knees. His hair was short, and if he had put on much weight, it was not apparent in the gloom.

"Didn't expect to see you around," he said softly.

Bobbo shrugged. "Curious, I guess. Like to check things out now and then."

The voice had not changed much: deep though not a bass, a little rougher maybe, but that was all.

In the haze of exhaustion and sedatives, it occurred to Fred he ought to ascertain if he himself were asleep or awake, if Bobbo were alive or dead. In the soft starlight that filtered through the window, he looked as substantial as he had that long-ago sunset in Quang Tri. Then again, he looked as real as rain on the mound of corpses in the trailer. But, in the end, what difference did it make?

Fred proceeded cautiously. "They had a nice funeral for you. I was going to go, but I had some trouble."

"Kept them waiting long enough, I guess."

"I guess." He was feeling stronger now, his eyes adjusting to the dark. "We missed you, Bobbo. Everybody, I think." He paused. "Me, especially."

Bobbo laughed.

"I mean it. Over the years, it's seemed things might have been a hell of a lot easier if you'd been around. Back in school, I was jealous of you and all," Fred confided, "and when I saw you in Nam, I thought you'd lost more than the jokers out of your deck. But maybe if you'd come back, a lot would be different."

Bobbo shook his head. "Nothing would have changed, Fred. And I'd have never come back."

Fred did not argue. He had to assume Bobbo would know that, no matter if he were a ghost or the invention of Fred's doped imagination. Or if he were not dead at all? He would know all kinds of things Fred himself could only guess at. He realized he should be scared, but he wasn't. That Bobbo, whatever he was, had chosen to appear to him tonight, a buddy taking care of another who wasn't doing too good — that was an honor, if nothing else.

"What happened to you, Bobbo?" Fred asked quietly.

He could see Bobbo smile. "I died. That's what the paper said."

"Well, yeah." Fred remembered how the backfield treated the linemen, that teasing superiority that made them hateful. But he was not to be put off. "But when I saw you there. In Nam. Something'd happened to you."

"War happened to me, Fred," Bobbo said flatly. "That's all."

That was not an answer that told Fred much. War, in its way, had happened to all of them, even the ones who weren't there. "I know that, Bobbo," he persisted, "but there was something else. There was something that made you crazy."

Bobbo leaned forward and put his fingers against his lips. A long moment passed. Then he began to speak: "It was my fourth month in-country, Fred. We'd passed through this village. Everybody was all over us, asking for candy bars and cigarettes, just like we used to see in the movies.

"About a week later, we swept through again. There was a pilot who'd gone down. He got hung up in the trees. They'd poked his eyes out, and hacked his nose off, and cut off his ears. They cut off his balls, too, shoved a punji stick up his ass all the way to his stomach. They tried to hide him from us. But we found him.

"We didn't know what to do at first. Then we all decided. Nobody said anything. We went up to the village and herded them all down in the hollow by the body. Everybody — men and women, old people and kids. Every one.

"And then we let loose. We emptied everything we had into them, round after round after round. Making them look at that flyboy, making them look at what they had done or what they had let be done — that ball-less flyboy hanging by his parachute.

"And after we spattered them, we bayoneted anybody who looked to be alive, and Gordon, who was my good buddy, Gordon says all of a sudden, 'Heads up, Dickstar,' because that's what they all called me, and he cocked back his arm and threw something. And I caught it. I caught it good as I caught that pass in the Marysville game when we were kids a couple years before.

"And when I looked, it was a baby. There in my hands with his head split open. And I stared a minute. And then I laughed, and I took a skip, and I drop-kicked that baby back to Gordon easy as you please. And from that day on, Fred, nothing made sense." Bobbo sighed tiredly. "And so anything made sense."

It ought to have shocked him. But this night, for a veteran with another veteran, no horror would be too great. Fred appreciated that Bobbo would tell him. And he understood now how Bobbo had lost that Grace that had once sustained him, how a moment like that might make you mad.

"We've had some other wars, you know," he said.

Bobbo only nodded.

"They went a lot better than ours did." Fred shook his head. "They're going to think it's easy now."

"You'll have to tell them different, Fred."

"Shit, I don't — "

"No, Fred." The voice through the dark was no louder, but vehement still. "It's all you can do. You saw enough to know. You found out what it is to be afraid. You've lived long enough to understand it. They've got to learn that there should never be a time when a boy just out of high school thinks he's got to drop-kick a baby. They're coming up to the year two thousand. Somebody's got to tell them to be careful."

Fred sighed. "There're people who aren't even worried. The people from the churches. They say it's going to be the end of the world."

"Our world, Fred? Look around. It's already gone." Bobbo paused. "Fred, the world ends every day. Piece by piece. Person by person. Each one lost one that can't be replaced."

The dizziness hit Fred again. He tumbled back against the pillow. He swallowed, concentrating on what Bobbo had said. It was true. The world he had been raised to expect was long gone, if it had ever been there to begin with. Those who had peopled it had died, or moved away, or he had simply lost track of them. Perhaps, in the end, as Bobbo said, all you could do was live things, see things, tell the tale. Bring what there was of your world to others, so when you were gone, if you were lucky, somebody might save a little piece of it, might make some good choices, avoid some bad ones. It did not seem like much, though then again, it was one small way to give sense to what too often seemed the senselessness of passing time.

"Do you think . . . ," he began, then realized Bobbo was gone.

Effortfully, Fred pulled himself up so his back rested against the headboard, looking around to assure himself he was, indeed, alone. Bobbo had disappeared, silent as he came. Fred drew his hand over his face, took a deep breath. Then another. His chest hurt.

He might be dying. Maybe that was what Bobbo's visitation meant, the extended hand of the angel with a familiar face, sent to draw him out of this world and on to the next. He turned his head toward the window, to the darkness outside. Perhaps now the sky would brighten, the tiny pinpoint of a star growing and growing until a celestial light covered everything and he would drop his gaze to see the fleecy swirl of clouds and hear the sweet refrain of harps. Or, instead, the sky would plunge into some absolute black, the last planet flickering out, and the room around him would erupt in flames and he would find himself in the very pit of hell.

Slowly, his chin dropped. There was no sound. As his eyes closed, Fred knew these dreams might be his last.

But, too, there was the possibility that tonight he had seen a sign, that he had found some small reason to things, that Bobbo Starwick — his hero and his secret enemy, madman and brother-in-arms — had left him with new vision and new purpose.

Perhaps in the very fact of fear was hope. Perhaps in experience's very heart was wisdom. Perhaps, Fred thought, as he drifted into sleep, he would awake next morning as at the sound of a trumpet, in the twinkling of an eye.

And he would be changed.